Full of Grace

Also by Dorothea Benton Frank

Full of Grace

Dorothea Benton Frank

AVON

An Imprint of HarperCollinsPublishers

First Avon A trade paperback printing: July 2008
First Avon Books printing: April 2007
First William Morrow hardcover printing: May 2006

HarperCollins books may be purchased for educational, business, or sales promotional use. For information please write: Special Markets Department, HarperCollins Publishers, 10 East 53rd Street, New York, NY 10022.

Library of Congress Cataloging-in-Publication Data is available.

ISBN 978-0-06-137453-1

13   ID/RRD   10 9 8 7 6

For the fabulous bad boys of Sullivan's Island
my brothers
William Oliver, Theodore Anthony,
and Michael Kent Benton

The weight of love is the heaviest burden
you have learned to carry.
In the silence of the heavens,
it's a dream that wakes you
with the sound of your own voice singing.

—Marjory Heath Wentworth,
   South Carolina poet laureate,
     "The Sound of Your Own Voice Singing"

CONTENTS

x

Contents

PROLOGUE

A Message from Michael

Until I met Grace Russo, I did not know that my Lacoste shirts did not have to be dry-cleaned. In this area alone, she has saved me a very tidy sum. But in matters of serious significance, quite simply, Grace has changed my world. She showed me how to understand and value love, and on a lighter note, to crave all things Italian. But that's not why I love her.

I was a lonely guy, living in a world of lab rats, trying to discover a way to save humanity from any and all illness. I lived on Chinese takeout, pizza to go, loose women, deli roasted chickens, baseball, frustration and beer. Grace popped into my life like a cork exploding from a bottle of champagne. Okay maybe Asti Spumante, but something highly explosive. Oh, she thought she was all kind of chill sophistication, but she was nothing but effervescence. Truth? Just being around her pumped carbonation into my veins, too. This bubbling and rumbling of volcanic eruption began the very first night we met. No one was more surprised than I was, except for Grace. We were avowed nonbubblers and the living embodiments of the immovable object meeting the irresistible force. Two hard-core cynics met their match and two other innocents out there were saved from our callous foibles. It may not sound romantic to you, but no one has ever accused me of being sentimental. Or Grace.

Why am I telling you this? I'm getting my two cents in now because once Grace starts telling you our story, I won't be able to get a word in with a crowbar. Grace is a wonderful gal, but she can be very chatty, especially when she is excited about something. Anyway, here's what I would like for you to keep in the back of your mind as this tale unwinds. I guess you could say I'm a happy slave to science but a curious skeptic all around. For all of my life I have believed wholeheartedly that if I wanted the cosmos explained, it was best to find the explanations myself. I always wanted proof. Irrefutable proof that could be measured and qualified.

Soon enough into my research, I had to throw out the old rulebook because some strange things began to happen. I would run an experiment fifty times in my lab and get the same results. But if I ran the exact experiment in the lab next door, the results changed. Then I heard about these guys in California, physicists in quantum mechanics. They ran a series of experiments using meditation in an attempt to lower the pH of water. Yes, you heard me. Meditation. But here are the facts: Four guys meditated on a canister of water and lowered its pH by one full degree. Just by the way, if your pH was lowered by one degree, you'd be dead. But then something interesting happened. When they performed the exact same experiment in another room, the results changed.

Okay, at first blush I thought they were a bunch of crackpots because I wasn't exactly spellbound by meditation or the pH in water. It was interesting but not mesmerizing. However, what had me nailed were two things. Duplicating the experiment in another space caused a measurable change in results. As I said, I had witnessed and experienced the same phenomena in my own work. And I was fascinated that the intentions of people merely meditating could bring about a chemical change in the water.

What did it mean? Well, it implied that space had memory and you could condition space. And that you could apply human intent and bring about physical change. It had monumental implications. It might just explain a lot of the inexplicable.

You know the old story. A guy walks into a church and begs God for something. No answer. Another ten thousand people do the same thing. Another ten million. God is apparently busy with other matters and does not reply to them either. Here comes someone in need, just there to sweep the floor, too humble and meek to ask for a toothpick much less anything else, and *boom!* His secret prayers are answered. Why? Perhaps because the space was conditioned by the millions of petitions of others. All those pleas of desperation from those believers who had gone before him had left a memory in the space. *Please! Help me! Save me!* But here's what science can't answer. Why *him?*

Why him indeed? You see, before Grace, I never paid much attention to a lot of things. After Grace . . . well, let's just say, none of this could have happened without her. Grace and I are like infinitesimal pieces in the most complicated jigsaw puzzle there is and yet we found each other. Was this an accident? No. I can tell you this with certainty. The world holds more wonder and optimism than ever. Because of Grace, I'd say anything is possible. Seriously. Anything. I really would. And that's why I love her. But I'll let her give you the whole story.

CHAPTER 1

Firecrackers

Everything Michael just told you is true, but you have to understand our lives in its whole context for this story to make any sense. What happened to us was so unexpected that I think it's worth understanding how we came together and why everything could only have happened as it did.

So let me take you back to the beginning and, for the moment, offer this singular thought. There are still a few pockets of the earth that transcend the realities of the modern world. To my complete astonishment, the Lowcountry of South Carolina is one of them. No one who knows the area would argue. Not every square inch of it is spiritually uplifting because it's got its commercial sprawl like all cities. But just minutes south of historic Charleston's ageless glories and the plastic outskirts of suburbia, the neon world of consumerism begins to melt away.

Soon, moving along on Savannah Highway, there is a small rise in the road. Rantowles Creek. The deep blue water is vast, shimmering like fields of sequins, their tiny edges catching flashes of the afternoon light. Every single time I passed over the tiny bridge I would literally gasp with surprise. It was so vibrant with life and naturally beautiful.

For the trillionth or so time, I wondered why I didn't sublet my carriage house in downtown Charleston, move out here and sink roots in this blue and green paradise. But as soon as I asked myself the question, the answer was on the tip of my tongue. The answer was simple. I was still in the game, running with the ball like my hair was on fire. Besides, I was still too urban. I mean, moving to Charleston had been a concession to my family after decades of living in and around New York, working for a luxury travel service that paid very little but took me everywhere I ever wanted to go: Cambodia, Chile, the Galápagos, Patagonia, Istanbul—dream it up, I can arrange it and you will travel like royalty. It was a niche business, but a very nice niche.

Eventually, I moved to the Lowcountry. I had been terrified to leave New York and in other ways just as terrified to stay. My family knew it, too. Truly there wasn't much happening in my personal life except the packing and unpacking of luggage. So as usual, my father decided to take the matter of my future into his own lovable hands. He begged me to just try Charleston for a while, and after the big showdown, I finally caved. Here's how that happened.

He called me one morning and said, "You gonna be home tonight?"

I said, "Yeah? Who wants to know?"

"The FBI. Be home at seven and that's it. Don't ask no more questions."

So without any further hullabaloo, Big Al flew to New York and showed up that night with a sack of Chinese takeout. I opened the door to my apartment on lower Fifth Avenue and there he stood. Delighted to see the man who loved me more than anyone ever had, I threw my arms around his neck and hugged him with all my might. I was a mainlining daddy's girl and not apologetic in the least.

After a feast of hot-and-sour soup, steamed dumplings, Peking duck, pork lo mein, and a lot of chitchat, he stood up and read his fortune cookie aloud.

" 'The Buddha sees Big Al's only daughter in Charleston living happily in a carriage house on Wentworth Street that her wonderful father already bought for an investment and will allow her to live in rent-free but she has to pay the utilities.' Humph! Well, what do you say about that, princess?"

What could I say? Even though I was an adult, I still loved the fact that my dad wanted to spoil me rotten. And that he missed me. The next day I called Eric Bomze, who owned the company I worked for, and who by coincidence had relocated to Charleston after opening another office in Atlanta. He said, Come to Charleston immediately. That was the end of the New York chapter of my life. I called a mover and began to pack.

To my surprise and delight, it turned out that Charleston had everything I thought I needed and more. Like New York, it had neighborhoods and corner stores. It was old but not decrepit. What it didn't have was snow, ice or, to date, terrorists.

It was little things that made me happy—frothy cappuccinos and the *New York Times* at my fingertips. I loved chamber music and theater. Salsa dancing, tennis and biking. Restaurants and shopping. Charleston had that and lots more, and best of all, I could walk to work. And once Michael became my "other," he could be at the Medical University in five minutes. We didn't pay a fortune to park or live on *gridlock alert* during the holiday season. So living downtown was the perfect decision for us.

We couldn't be bothered with a house and a yard. And I hated to admit it, but a suburban house would have destroyed our relationship in about two days. It wasn't about who was going to cut the grass or clean out the garage. No, it was fastidiously manicured neighborhoods with married couples having block parties, backyard barbecues with coordinated paper products, children, dogs and bicycles strewn helter-skelter like randomly placed garden sculpture. That whole scene had the malodorous quality of long-term commitment. The M word. Like cheap chocolate—it looked good, but ultimately it made your teeth hurt. Marriage was not for me. Or Michael.

We didn't want to live among a sliding-scale population of predictable failures. Like stick-figure couples in a PowerPoint presentation, diminishing with each screen until over half of them disappeared by the end. We were together because we wanted to be together, not because we were stuck under the heel of a legal agreement, the guilt of custody and every kind of social convention you can name: country-club memberships, religious affiliations, shared bank accounts—the list of entanglements was endless. We shunned them all. I mean, it was great for some people but not for us. It wasn't who we were.

The only reason I bring this up at all is that I was en route to Hilton Head to visit my entire family for the Fourth of July holidays. I loved them like mad, but every visit to their new home was like the Spanish Inquisition—Italian style. This trip would be no different from all the others. They just couldn't help themselves.

It was a relief to pass the last red traffic signal that would crop up in the next hour or so because even though it was four in the afternoon, the heat was still eating me alive. I could taste salt in the beads of perspiration that tickled my upper lip. Taking a long swig of water from the sweaty lukewarm bottle in my cup holder, I decided it probably hadn't been the best idea to make the trip with the top down. But I loved summer and the rushing warm wind on my face and arms. Being a little on the other side of thirty, I bought into sunscreen and its merits. But any way you sliced it, getting older was a drag.

I inhaled the facts of life deeply and exhaled the reality that you really couldn't have it both ways. Balance was everything. If I wanted to be with Michael, it was best to keep things as they were. And *how things were* was pretty fantastic most days. Besides, I wasn't certain that I really wanted children. Let's be honest here. From the practical side, it would have meant giving up my career because I traveled all the time. Or I would have been forced to change industries and start all over again.

I wasn't willing to gamble the salary cut that might come with an industry switch. And even if the mortgage was covered by my father, I still had bills to pay: groceries, utilities, clothes, cell phone, whatever . . . Besides, I wasn't bohemian enough to have children out of wedlock or brave enough to face the possibility that I might wind up raising them myself. Alone. Me, alone with a kid? And truly, illegitimate children would have put my parents in their grave. For sure.

I envisioned calling Connie and Big Al and telling them they had a new precious bastard grandchild. My father would have cut out his own heart and FedExed it to me. My mother would have swallowed every sleeping pill in CVS, washing them down with Pellegrino—wait! No! Not Pellegrino—she never would have wasted the money on something so frivolous. Tap water. She would've used tap water. And she definitely would have left behind a soggy, smeared epistle, drenched in her tears, apologizing for not teaching me better morals. And Nonna? My grandmother? The queen of Naples, Italy? Don't ask. No. Rock stars acquired children in that unseemly manner, naming them after food groups, not the Russos of Bloomfield, New Jersey, whose great-grandfather played bocce with Mussolini when he visited Naples. And now that my parents were nicely settled in the posh environs of Hilton Head, with nice friends and a membership to two golf clubs, a book club and a bridge club? Nope. Not happening.

"Oh, fine," I said aloud, and changed the radio station.

As I passed each stretch of forest that thumped with the ghostly heartbeats of soldiers long gone to glory, honestly, I could feel my chest constrict. The minute I got there they would start asking questions, implying I was wasting my life, telling me how shallow I was. But in a nice way, of course.

Look, some of the details in my bio might help you understand my case. As you know, I'm Italian Catholic, now a ripened thirty-two and, as you know, God help us, the only daughter and unmarried. If that wasn't enough, Michael, the one true and only love of my entire life, is unfortunately Irish. He insisted his red hair was actually more blond and that his freckled nose was merely sun-kissed, but for my family's money, he

was as Irish as Paddy's pig, even though they had never laid
eyes on him. Worse, as my parents would say, he fell away from
the One True Church. He's basically an agnostic.

I mean, he had never come right out and declared himself
to be an agnostic or an atheist, but I knew Michael inside and
out. He doesn't want to support the Vatican machine and he
thought science would eventually explain everything. He might
be right. He might just be right. Or not.

All I know is this. From the first moment I met Michael Higgins I knew I was going to spend the rest of my life with him.
Okay, I didn't really know that. But I knew there was a high
probability that my sheets were in his future and that I would
work every last trick in my female toolbox to get some kind of
serious relationship going. On sight, it was that intense.

My boss invited me to his annual Labor Day outdoor barbecue, right? I remember that I really didn't want to go because
it was hot in a totally surreal way. Boiling oil. Mosquitoes the
size of small birds. Flying jaws. Hurricanes looming off the
coast. But we're talking Charleston in August, so what else was
new? Think handsome men with golf tans, drinking gin and
tonics, wearing long trousers printed with little whales and
no socks. Women in pink floral sundresses, Lilly or Liberty,
sipping frosted stems of Prosecco, toned arms and bony décol-
leté glistening in their marinade of perfume and glow. All the
while an ancient man in a starched linen jacket refilled drinks
at a makeshift bar in the brick courtyard and his companion
moved in the background in a waltz of service, through the
throng, offering pickled shrimp speared with little toothpicks.
At the other end of the garden, on an oversize grill, skewers of
pork, chicken, onions and pineapple sizzled, filling the air with
glorious, mouthwatering fragrances. They would be served
from the buffet over steamed rice, with salad and rolls. It was
Lowcountry civility and propriety in tandem and completely
irresistible.

Anyway, there was Michael leaning over the banister of the
veranda, surveying the crowd, and I caught his eye. He was

wearing a cream-colored linen jacket over a navy T-shirt with navy lightweight gabardine trousers. By coincidence, so was I. But my navy T-shirt was actually a camisole and my jacket hung from the crook of my finger over my shoulder. I gave him a small smile and a slight nod.

Just to clarify the varying degrees of "small smile and slight nod" and what they meant, this one meant *The drawbridge is lowered. You may approach.* At the far end of the spectrum, there was the jaw-dropper, in which your face was agog and you looked like a total ass with zero odds to recoup your cool. And at the opposite end there's the vacant stare as your eyes slide elsewhere that says *Don't even think about it.* Well seasoned in reading social signals, the smiling and self-assured Michael came down from the porch and made his way to my side.

"Don't I know you from someplace?" he said.

"Good grief. Is that the best you can do?" I said. And I fell like a fool into the endless blue of his eyes.

"Do you want to live together? My apartment is over-air-conditioned," he said with a grin and dimples that were beyond adorable and irresistible. He reached in his pocket and pulled out his keys. "It's freezing there."

"So is my place, and you're pretty optimistic," I said. "Shouldn't we start with something like, I don't know, *dinner*?"

"I don't know. Sure. Hey, do you like baseball?"

"What red-blooded American doesn't?"

"Well, want to come see me play?"

"What's up with you and baseball? You play for the Yankees?"

"No, no. I play for the MUSC team to benefit the terminal patients in the children's wing. My friend Larry works there with critical-care kids. Got me involved."

Well, that stopped me in my lustful tracks. I mean, any man eager to play ball for a good cause in that heat had to be a great guy. I looked at him and said, "Sure. I'd love to."

What ensued over the next few weeks were many baseball games, too many romantic fattening dinners, lots of sweaty hooking-up and me holding out on the deed. Rule one: If you want a man to take you seriously, keep your britches on. Besides, there were so many things about him I didn't know. Like, was he a pathological liar? A philanderer? In huge debt? Did he have a drinking problem? An ex-wife with anger issues? Twenty children? A drug problem?

Did any of these things matter? Not really. No, they didn't really matter at all because for the first time in my life I was dumbstruck, absolutely flattened by the stupefying, powerful all-consuming feelings I had for a member of the opposite sex.

Eventually our bloomers hit the floor and I gave him keys. He put his stuff in storage and moved in. I had never been as happy as I was then, and in my head I was doing the hippie dance of stoned-out love every waking minute. Ah, yes, life was pretty darn near perfection in the domestic arena. Until I talked to my mother or my father or any member of the clan. Little by little my parents wheedled the facts about Michael from me. They were aghast that he was Irish, but the fact that he was doing stem-cell research in a project to repair heart-wall muscle sent them over the moon. He became *the Irish Baby Butcher*.

What happened over the next ten months was this widening of the distance between us and them. They didn't even know him. They had never even met him. Worse, they were always putting me in these awkward positions to choose them over Michael. I was left to manipulate the situation with Michael so that he wouldn't notice that I always capitulated to my parents. But that didn't mean I didn't try to resist or that I didn't resent my folks. And I'd tell you this, my parents were wearing me out.

For example, I'd had no intention of driving to Hilton Head for this holiday until Mom called.

"Big Al is digging up the front walkway again," she whispered. "Did *I* ask for a new walkway with a nonskid surface of some revolutionary composite material?"

"Probably not, but I'm just guessing. Why are you whispering?"

"Because I don't want Nonna to hear me! Did *I* ask for a team of Mexican gentlemen to show up at six this morning and start jackhammering to wake up the entire world? Because if I did ask, I have no recollection . . ."

"What do you want *me* to do, Mom?"

"Talk to him, Grace. He doesn't listen to me! I have my ladies' club coming here next Thursday and . . ."

The front walkway was once again experiencing some unsolicited renovation that I was sure basically left the front yard a mud hole. For the sixth time in three years. I had to agree with my mother; it was a little much.

"How are the members of my bridge club supposed to navigate the planks of wood, wobbling on sinking bricks? Should I bring them in through the garage like cases of paper towels from Sam's Club?"

"You want me to come for the Fourth?"

A deep sigh from the Grand Canyon of my mother's despair followed and I could imagine her curtains billowing and then settling from the g-force of her breath.

"You're always welcome, Grace. And your brother is coming with his family. It would be so nice to have my family all together one more time before I . . . you know . . . die."

You're always welcome, Grace. That was Connie-speak for *You're welcome, not your boyfriend; it's a family weekend; he's not family.*

"You're not even sixty, Ma. Bad news, you're not going anywhere for, um, I don't know, thirty or forty years?"

"You never know, Grace!" Another huge sigh. "It's in God's good hands."

So that's a snapshot of my mother and what she's like. Helpless. All my life it irritated me that my mother could never stand up to her mother or to my father. Good grief! Old Connie had been a loyal and dutiful wife for a million years and had produced three reasonably successful children who were educated and self-supporting with the tiny exception of my mortgage and my stupid brother Nicky. But even Nicky was actually doing okay—at least he had never been in rehab or arrested for anything. Sometimes, and especially with family, it was just best to just, ah well, lower your standards of judgment.

My parents were some duo. Connie and Big Al. Big Al was my dad's well-deserved nickname. A booming voice, emphatic opinions on everything from the cost of gasoline to the amount of garlic in the shrimp scampi, Big Al gave highly quotable commentary that usually came across as, well, slightly naive and, let's spell it out, a little bit gauche. Big Al bellowed the final word, Nonna agreed with every syllable he spoke, and my poor mother cowered, sneaking to her bedroom to call me, looking for an ally or just a few moments to vent to a sympathetic ear.

I reminded myself all the time that Big Al meant well. His brand of politics and his crazy work ethic had kept us way beyond solvent, but he was never going to be the American ambassador to France, if you get my drift. Never mind that the BMW I drove, the house I lived in and the diamond studs in my ears were all spontaneous gifts from Big Al's generous heart. Okay, he still paid the mortgage and held the title, but that was how he held on to me.

On the other hand, that generosity produced another kind of emotional sand trap. You see, he bought Mom one-carat diamond studs for her birthday. That would be one-half carat for each ear—I mean, Al's successful, but he's not Donald Trump, okay? At the same time he bought me diamond studs of the same quality that were one-third of a carat each, because I have an extra hole in my right ear. Mom's face fell when Dad slid the little velvet box toward me at Mom's birthday dinner, and it was obvious that the thrill of the moment had been diluted for her. Same thing happened when Dad bought my convertible. He bought Mom a BMW sedan. She wanted to know if he thought she was too old to drive a convertible. Big Al couldn't understand Mom's edgy resentment, but I am sure some shrink would have had a ball with it. I didn't really blame her for her ambivalence about these double-edged swords of gratuitous gifting. Anyway, there's probably a pill that could help her, but that would be the last thing I would suggest to anybody.

"I'll see you for the Fourth," I said.

You know how you always wish that you came from the perfect family? That they were wealthy, classy and smart, but never pretentious? That they were all good-looking, stylish, funny and never cruel? Well, keep wishing, right? There was no Ralph Lauren ad layout waiting for me to step in on Hilton Head.

It was about six in the evening when I arrived at my parents' home and steam was still rising from the grass. We're talking ridiculous steaming Tennessee Williams–Somerset Maugham kind of heat. I pulled my duffel bag from the trunk and looked at the house. Mom was right. Dad's little construction project looked terrible.

Here's a little more on him: Big Al was supposed to be retired and he relocated the family to Hilton Head for the multitude of golf courses. He loved golf so much you would've thought his father had run the PGA and that he had caddied for Arnold Palmer or somebody. For years he talked nonstop about Hilton Head, the weather, the blue skies and the various challenges of each course, one more fantastic than the next. But to be perfectly honest, in a little over a year he got sick of golf and then there was the problem of Nicky. My little brother, Nicky, is a handsome devil, but he's not exactly Albert Einstein. It took him eight years to graduate from Caldwell College in New Jersey with an associate's degree in communication. Most people would be a doctor after eight years in college. Not my brother. He has a degree in skirt.

Anyway, true to his amazing nature, Big Al opened his second business so that Nicky could have a career and something to inherit someday. In New Jersey, Dad was in the paving business, mostly parking lots. In Hilton Head, he called himself a hard-scaper, which still entailed the pouring of asphalt from time to time. It was actually more gentrified, as they did work with all sorts of new materials that resembled that which they weren't. Cement that looked like bluestone, cement that looked like sandstone, et cetera.

You had to love my father. Everyone did. And I had always been his favorite. Until the advent of Michael. Maybe he couldn't stand the thought of his little girl having a man and a sex life. Maybe he was jealous. Or maybe he was just old-fashioned and didn't approve of his daughter sharing a home with a man without the benefit of marriage. I knew the fact that Michael was Irish didn't help. Anyway, life delivered Big Al and me to a Mexican standoff. It was stupid because everyone was entitled to live their lives the way they wanted to, weren't they? No. The truth is that you could, but there were consequences and the Big Chill from Al's corner was mine. I thought I had compromised by agreeing to live nearby in Charleston. We could see each other often enough and I could still live my life. But the fact of the matter was that I could have been living in Patagonia and if Connie yelped I would've jumped on a plane. The familial choke chain had no respect for distance.

In this case, Mom was right. The front yard was an archaeological dig. If that wasn't bad enough, red, white and blue bunting was draped across the garage doors and a municipal-building-size American flag hung from a flagpole in the front yard. Over the flag of Italy, of course. It was just too much for anyone's definition of normalcy.

The New Jersey plates on my sister-in-law's minivan announced Frank and Regina's arrival with their trio of thugs-in-training. Nicky would be there with his insipid girlfriend, Marianne, the pre-K substitute teacher who never got called in for work and who spoke to my brother in her five-year-old's voice all the time. I braced myself and chose the garage entrance over the muddy bricks and planks. This was going to be some weekend.

I opened the door to the mudroom and entered the kitchen. Fresh pasta hung from the handles of every mop and broom in the house and every ladder-back chair. Nonna's marinara sauce (which she called gravy) simmered in a large cast-iron kettle, and truly the room did smell like a warm and heavenly afternoon on Mulberry Street. I don't know why it irked me that we couldn't serve just hamburgers on the Fourth of July like everyone else. Tomorrow my family would have spaghetti with meatballs and braciole, antipasto, sopressata, mozzarella and tomatoes with basil oil, a half-dozen baguettes dipped in this and that, and *then* we would have hamburgers, hot dogs, corn on the cob and more pasta, macaroni salad. With pickles. Don't forget the pickles. After every last person would moan from the excess of it all, the men would fall asleep on the sofas, the children would make themselves scarce, and the women would clean up so we could do it all over again in a few hours.

The television was blaring, and sure enough, Nonna was positioned in Big Al's La-Z-Boy recliner crocheting at fifty miles an hour. I called out to her, knowing she was fully absorbed in her soap operas and had not heard me come in. She is as deaf as a doornail, but don't say I said so.

"Nonna! It's me! Grace!"

"What? Oh! Maria Graziana! Thank God you're home safe! *Vieni qua!* Help me up!" I gave her a kiss on her cheek and helped her to her feet. "*Oh, Madonna!* My knees are killing me. *Avecchiaia,* old age—that's just how it is. Now let me look at you!" Her milky eyes that streamed water traveled from my head to my toes and she said, "Humph! Too skinny!"

"Oh, Nonna!" I gave her a big hug and I could feel her smiling. "What are you making?"

"What? Oh! Oh, I'm just putting the finishing touches on the cover for the extra roll of toilet paper for the powder room. See? It's the Capitol building!"

"Wow! It's great! Someday you're gonna have to teach me how to do this, you know."

"Well, you'd better hurry up. Madonna!" she said again, and blessed herself. "I could go any minute." We exchanged looks and then smiled at each other, the knowing smile with which we acknowledged each other's white lies.

"Nonna, you've been threatening to die since I can remember. You *and* Mom."

"Humph," she said, handing me her masterpiece. "Go put this where she belongs. I have to check my gravy. Everyone's out by the pool, running around in this heat!"

"Okay."

With her hand in the small of her back, Nonna toddled off in the direction of the kitchen, waddling her generous proportions from side to side as she walked, which I thought was probably brought on by some arthritis. I examined her work. Indeed, it was the Capitol building. No doubt the toilet seat had Paul Revere or something like him crocheted in three-dimensional relief. Mom never complained about the Santa tissue-box covers Nonna made for every Christmas or the lilies she crocheted for Easter. She never complimented her either. But she did have an issue with the toilet-lid covers.

If you put them on the back of the lid, the lid flopped forward. If you put them on the front of the lid, the lid flopped forward. When my mother voiced a squeak of concern over the possibility of one of her grandsons losing his manhood in a slamming accident, Big Al read her the riot act. "Connie! 'Ey! Come on! This is art!"

It wasn't art and we all knew it, but just like parents who enthusiastically hang their children's artwork all over the refrigerator, my mother, with some reluctance, displayed the entirety of Nonna's yarn creations with pride, albeit a worrisome pride.

I put the Capitol building cover over Mom's extra roll, inspected the American flag on the lid and the fireworks on the tissue box, and had a flash that the fireworks would actually have been pretty cool if she had used a yarn with a little shine. Then I asked myself if I was losing my mind and went to my room to change clothes.

Like the rest of the house, my room was moved in its entirety to Hilton Head with a few choice additions from the Vatican gift shop—a holy-water font over the light switch by the door, a large white glow-in-the-dark crucifix over the bed, a small statue of the Holy Family on the bedside table and a statue of my patron saint, Maria Goretti, on the chest of drawers. No doubt there was a scapular pinned to the mattress to thwart dreams of anything not approved by the Church.

I realized that until I got married, and perhaps until I produced a pack of children, Mom was determined that my bedroom would remain exactly as it was because, who knew? I might come home again. Simply put, my life in Charleston wasn't real to them. And frankly Mom's life in Hilton Head wasn't real to her because she desperately missed her friends and her sister in New Jersey.

I ran my hand over the fading flowers of my upholstered headboard and all of a sudden I felt sorry for my mother. In my life I went a million miles an hour trying to get what I wanted and to enjoy every minute of it. Had my mother ever had that chance? Did she have what she wanted?

I threw on a pair of shorts and a T-shirt and went outside to say hello.

"Turn the gravy!" Nonna called out as I passed through the living room.

"Sure thing!" I called back as I sailed into the kitchen.

As I stirred I stared through the sliding-glass doors. There on the terrace was my brother Nicky with his hand cupping Marianne's southern cheek. My mother, Connie, was taking pictures of Frank and Regina's baby, Paulie, belly flopping into the pool. Big Al, arms waving, was talking to Frank and Regina. And although the shank of the day's tanning rays had disappeared, their Lisa, who couldn't be a day over twelve, was lounging like a movie star in her bikini reading *Teen People*. Tony, their oldest at fourteen, was sneaking a cigarette behind the grill.

I slid the heavy door to the left and called out, "Hello, fam! I'm home!"

CHAPTER 2

Grating Parmesan

With the metallic thwack of the sliding door slamming back against its frame, Nicky and Marianne glanced in my direction. Nicky's face lit up and Marianne assumed a wide smile, one almost as disingenuous as that of the first runner-up in a Miss America pageant. Petulant Marianne would have to share Nicky's attention for maybe, I don't know, twenty-two seconds?

"Hey, Gracie!" Nicky said.

"Hey, yourself!" I said, and gave my brother a hug and a noisy rhubarb kiss on his cheek. "Hi, Marianne! How are you?"

"Gooood. Gooood. Nicky, dahlin', let me wipe your sister's sa-lie-vah from your preciousth face . . ." Marianne said, using the napkin around her plastic cup on my brother's cheek.

"So things are good?" I said to my brother, not really having anything to say to him then or ever except *Your girlfriend is a freaking jerk, you egomaniac lunatic,* which I didn't say in the interest of a pleasant evening.

Nicky nodded and kissed Marianne on the forehead. "Never better."

"Well, fine. Good. Better go kiss Big Al and Connie, right?"

"Duh," Nicky said.

"You are one articulate so-and-so, little brother," I said with a giggle, hoping he would take my assessment of his command of the language as a joke, which of course he did. Who would insult the prince?

I wandered over to the pool, kissed my mother, waved at my nephew Paulie in the pool, blew a kiss to my niece, ignored my nephew behind the grill and joined Big Al, Regina and Frank.

"Here's my little girl!" Big Al bellowed, and placed his can of beer on the table, throwing his arms open to hug me and give me the standard family chiropractic adjustment.

"Daddy!" I said, and despite the heat and his sweaty shirt, I hugged him mightily. "How are you?"

"Are you kidding? I'm the richest son of a bitch in the world! Look around you! The only thing I could ask for is—"

"I know, I know," I said. "More grandchildren, right?"

"You got it! Hey! Speaking of which . . . I met a nice guy I'd like to introduce to you. He's from Pennsylvania and is a helluva golfer. He's a little bit older, mind you, but good people, if you know what I'm saying to you . . . ."

"Italian, right?"

"You know it, baby, and—"

"Over fifty? Widowed? Grown children?"

"You're a mind reader! Hey, Frank! Didn't I just finish saying that our Grace was the smartest one? Didn't I?"

"You did, Dad, you sure did," Frank said, and gave me a normal hug.

Then, in the pause of the moment, Big Al searched my face for an answer to the proposed widower. He scowled and said, "No way, am I right?"

"They gotta have hair and teeth, Dad. And besides, you know I'm involved with—"

"That Irish baby butcher?"

"He's not—"

"You're blind, princess. Love is blind. Go get your old man a cold beer, okay?"

"Sure." I turned to Frank and Regina. "He does a little stem-cell research, just so you know."

Frank and Regina were shaking their heads as if to say, *There's just no end to the goading and the guilt, is there?*

I pulled a freezing can of beer from the bar area's refrigerator, put it in a foam rubber coozie—which I figured was a variation on cozy, as in the cozies that covered teapots to keep tea warm—a coozie kept a canned beverage cold. Looking at the cook area, I decided my father might have been a narrow-minded bigot from time to time, but he sure did know how to design and construct an outdoor barbecue. It had every new gadget available. Naturally, its most important feature was the decking.

It appeared to be ancient stone from maybe Greece or Corsica, but of course it was a cool-touch product. It was pitted here and there to give it character and the color varied throughout to give it dimension. The decking began at the doors of the kitchen and, like a lava flow, moved out past the barbecue area and the dining area and ended surrounding the pool in a wide band, allowing ample space for twelve lounge chairs.

When my parents bought this place a few years ago the backyard had been a wasteland. But Big Al had a vision of seeing his family all around him in a double kidney-shaped pool on a hot day like the very one we were enduring. He brought in earth-movers and backhoes. Dump trucks of sand and depleted dirt were hauled away; yards of topsoil and sod were brought in. As if it all happened in the blink of an eye, Al created a verdant paradise, complete with cement statues of half-dressed women of Roman antiquity pouring recycled water from great vessels balanced on their slim shoulders.

I think an argument could have been made that Big Al loved cement as much as he loved women and that cement women were the epitome of it all. If you had taken these voluptuous creatures away, your eyes would have been drawn to the lush landscaping, the rare specimen trees and shrubs from Hawaii and Costa Rica. The border plants that were handpicked from nurseries all around Miami and the Florida Keys. But given the crowd of Pompeians, the extraordinary shrubs went almost unnoticed.

Well, it could have been worse, I thought. Al could've chosen little boys pee-peeing or giant frogs. Or a great row of cement dolphins, leaping in unison, spewing water from their jaws, underlit by a color wheel. The possibilities for worse taste were infinite. But for the statuary and the turbo-Catholic grotto dedicated to the Virgin Mary that lurked around the corner of the house by my grandmother's patio, this was a beautiful place. Really beautiful. Oh, the front-yard walkway situation was a mess, but that would be remedied immediately after the holiday. Over dinner my father promised my mother he would take care of it.

We gathered at the dining table, all eyes focused on the platters loaded with cold antipasto and clams oreganata, and the fresh tomatoes and basil from Nonna's garden. The breadbasket was being passed from plate to plate with small bowls of olive oil for dipping. Dad poured a wonderful Gavi di Gavi in small measures for the adults.

"I've been saving this one for a special occasion," he said, and everyone accepted that pronouncement had a probability that was perhaps partial truth. Maybe he had only been saving it since yesterday when someone from the Piggly Wiggly recommended it to him, but that would have been good enough to save Al from the venial sin of a lie. Spared a decade in the flames of purgatory on a technicality.

Connie poured Orangina soda for the children and everyone couldn't wait to eat. Al blessed the food while Frank's offspring squirmed and snickered at his long-winded thanks for the presence of each person, their health, their long life and their worldly possessions. Nonna shot the kids the evil eye to behave themselves, to which Regina responded with a backup evil eye.

"Buon appetito!" Al said, raising his glass.

The first official meal of the holiday weekend was under way.

"We're eating light tonight," Connie said, "because the barbecue tomorrow is pretty . . . well, it's a lot of food."

Light? The table struggled to remain upright.

After the antipasto was gobbled up and the platters cleared,
Nonna and Mom served steaming bowls of pasta with shrimp
in Nonna's gravy and another baguette was sliced and passed
around. The adults were now on their third bottle of Gavi
di Gavi, and between the sun exposure and the alcohol, our
tongues loosened.

"So where is what's his name this weekend?" Dad asked
me.

"He's visiting his mother," I said.

"Yeah, she's in a nursing home," Nicky said.

The table fell silent at the mention of a nursing home.

Nonna, who could barely contain or swallow the food in her
mouth, threw her arms in the air and cried out, *"Madre Dio!"*

"Thanks a lot, asshole," I whispered to Nicky.

"I'm sure there's a reasonable explanation for her being in a
home," Regina said.

"She has very advanced Alzheimer's," I said. "It's so sad and
very difficult for Michael to see his mother that way."

"Is that all?" Nonna said. "A little Alzheimer's? Next thing
I'll forget where my purse is put and everybody's gonna say that
I've got this Alzheimer's! Spend the rest of my life in a nursing
home? Is that what you want?"

"And she's a severe diabetic, completely blind, and don't ever
say I said this, but she's incontinent. Very incontinent," I said.
"I mean, Michael can't take care of her, right?"

I looked around the table for a little support. Nicky was staring at Al, who was staring at Connie, who was staring at Frank
and Regina.

Marianne, in her continuing campaign for brownie points,
spoke up. "I could *never* put my mother in a nursing home, no
matter *what*."

I considered slapping Marianne's teeth out and just getting it over with. No, something stronger, like a tragic farm accident—Marianne needed a tragic farm accident . . . a swan dive into a threshing machine or something like that.

"That's very easy for you to say, Marianne," Regina said, putting her hand on my arm to hold me in my chair and giving me a supportive squeeze. "I work in a hospital. You wouldn't believe some of the things I see."

I took a deep breath and looked from my mother to my grandmother.

"Like what?" Nonna said. "How bad could it be that your own children turn their backs on you and dump you in some filthy place?"

"Uh, could we table this discussion for another time?" I said. "Because, Nonna, you are as healthy as a horse and you're gonna live to be a thousand years old."

"Humph," she said, obviously unsatisfied with my answer. "*I'm* not the one who has to worry here! I *have* a daughter to take care of me . . ."

"And I would never put you in a nursing home!" Connie said.

"But *her* daughter has a boyfriend who thinks he knows more than the pope himself, and he thinks it's fine to put *his* mother in a nursing home and *she* agrees with him!"

"Please, Ma," Mom said to Nonna. "I worked so hard on this dinner . . ."

"What did *you* do?" Nonna said. "It's *my* gravy, *my* clams, *my* tomatoes that I grew *myself,* my basil . . ."

"Ma . . ."

Big Al wiped his mouth with the dish towel he used instead of a napkin, got up and went to Nonna's side, leaned over and kissed her on the top of her head. "Nobody's going nowhere, okay?" he said. "We're a family! Now how about some fish? Huh? I'm starving here! Give Connie a hand, Marianne. That's a good girl."

I felt my temperature rise. Al had chosen Marianne over

me to help my mother with dinner all because of Michael and his mother living in a nursing home. It seemed that he used every opportunity, no matter how small, to show his displeasure with me. Sure, I got a nice hello, but after that he went for my throat.

Regina couldn't help serve dinner; she had to watch her kids, especially Tony, who might drink all the wine left in the glasses, because, well, that's just how it was. I put my platform-sandaled foot on top of Nicky's and pressed down hard, wishing I were wearing cleats instead.

"Ow!" Nicky hollered.

"Oh! Excuse me! I'm so sorry," I said, and turned to Frank, knowing I was being sarcastic but thinking *what the hell*? "So Frank? Welcome home. Didn't you miss all this?"

Later that night, after the last glass was dried and put away, after the kitchen floor was swept, after Nonna and Connie had gone to take their showers, and after Big Al had smoked Robustos with Nicky and Frank in the backyard and finally turned in for the night, Nicky took Marianne home.

When I felt the heavy silence of the house and was reasonably certain everyone was finished with the day, I crept from my room and bumped into Frank in the kitchen. He was watching CNN on mute and dipping a piece of biscotti in a glass of anisette.

"Oh!" I said. "I didn't know you were in here."

"Yeah, I just finished pumping up the air mattresses and thought I'd check on the outside world . . . you know, make sure it's still there."

"Yeah," I said, inspecting the contents of the refrigerator. "Make sure there's no nuclear war dropping bombs on I-95 and that we're not stuck here for all of eternity, right?" I poured myself a glass of skim milk. "Where's the biscotti?"

"In the cookie jar over there." Frank turned to me, smiled and said, "Sit down, Grace, talk to me for a minute. Then I gotta crash. I'm exhausted."

I reached in the jar and pulled out two pieces of biscotti—

one that was dipped in chocolate and one that was dipped in chocolate and then coconut.

"Well, it's a long drive, especially with three kids. I only had to drive from Charleston. Know what? If I had a cookie jar in my kitchen, it would be crawling with bugs."

"You wouldn't have a cookie jar with actual cookies in it."

His words were beyond the obvious, but the remark stung a little. Did my brother think that I was obsessed with my weight, or that I wasn't interested in baking, or that I was gone so much cookies would be wasted? Even though all three possibilities were fact, I pouted. But Frank was always the one in the family to call a thing what it was and he was right. I looked at my brother, and in the blue light of the kitchen cabinet's underlighting, I saw how strongly he resembled our father, and had the thought that he was a kinder, more educated and definitely more genteel version of Al.

"You're right. You look like the old man, you know."

"There are worse things, I think," he said. "So what's the deal with this guy Michael?"

"We're living together in mortal sin," I said with a little laugh, and dipped my cookie in the milk.

"In the house Al bought? Is he Italian?"

"No, he's Irish. I'm going to hell for all of eternity."

"Okay, you're a fornicating sinner and your eternal soul is smeared with mortal sin like cream cheese on a bagel. Well, at least he's Catholic."

"Not really. He sort of believes in science more than the Church."

"Okay, let's sum this up. You're living with an agnostic Irish guy in a house Big Al paid for and you've got no intention of marrying him either, right? And he does embryonic stem-cell research for a living, which is solidly condemned by the pope? And his mother is in a nursing home! And you want to know why he's not the favorite son?" Frank started to laugh and then added, "You're crazy!"

I laughed with him, got up to bring the cookie jar back to

the kitchen table, and when I sat down again I said, "So he does stem-cell research. Big deal. He's a Rhodes scholar, for God's sake."

"The only Rhodes Big Al cares about are the ones he paved himself, lemme assure you."

"Yeah, well, Michael says that if we can manage to stay alive until 2050, we can live to be five thousand years old and in perfect health."

"Five thousand years? Who wants to live for five thousand years? Would you?"

"I don't know. To tell you the truth, I'm not so sure it will work on people anyway, except that they have some pretty amazing evidence on age reversal with rats."

"It always starts with the poor lab rats, right?"

"Well, Professor, they share like ninety-nine percent of our genetic code or something . . . or maybe it's mice?"

"Immaterial. No, I know that. I mean, think about it. It does proffer some extremely interesting ethical questions, like how would you end life—when you hit your five thousandth birthday?"

"Seriously. Can you imagine what you'd look like in a bathing suit at five thousand?"

"Let's not go there. It's bad enough now," Frank said. He got up and poured himself a glass of water. "So how'd you like old Nonna ripping Connie a new one at dinner? She's getting meaner than hell."

"She's always been mean to Mom, but now she's mean in front of anyone. I think it's a little weird that Dad doesn't ever come to Mom's defense, but I guess he figures Nonna is old and all."

"Who knows? Anyway, I wouldn't get too shook up over their opinions of Michael. Remember Sophocles said, 'The good befriend themselves.' As long as you are happy and satisfied with your relationship, that's all that matters."

"You guys still up?" Regina came around the corner in an

oversize Rutgers jersey and flip-flops. "I'm so tired I could die." Frank got up and pulled out a chair for his wife. She sank into it and put her head on her crossed arms on the table.

"I'm an old woman tonight," she said. "All I see when I close my eyes is interstate."

I smiled and tried to remember if Michael had ever pulled out chairs for me. I wasn't sure, and I decided if I wasn't sure, then it probably wasn't something that really mattered. Still, it was a nice gesture and Regina kissed her husband in thanks. They had an easy tenderness between them that was enviable.

"Want booze or milk?" I said, pushing the biscotti in her direction.

"Do I have to pick? Can't I have both?" Regina said.

"How about Kahlúa and cream?" Frank said.

"There's some that Dad made in the bar," I said. "It's in the Colavita bottle."

"Perfect," Regina said. "With ice please, sweetheart?"

"It's about two hundred proof," I said, "so go easy. You don't want Regina to get brain damage."

"I'm already brain-damaged," she said. "I've got kids."

"You've got great kids," I said. "They're growing like weeds!"

"Growing. Lemme tell you something," Regina said, winding up for the pitch. "I gotta watch Tony like a hawk—if he's not smoking something, he's snitching a drink of something . . ."

"I saw him smoking today behind the grill," I said.

"I'll smack him in the head first thing in the morning," Regina said. "And my Lisa? The good Lord gave her all my estrogen. I'm a thousand degrees and all of a sudden she's got these breasts. And the boys are calling! Mother Mary, pray for us. No, just pray for me!" She blessed herself and looked up to heaven for emphasis. "She's not even thirteen and shaving her legs already."

"Well, Paulie is a sweetheart," I said. "Lisa's normal. Everyone says girls are tough."

"They are. And Paulie's an eating machine! Did you see the fat on his belly?"

"Make him play football," I said.

Regina nodded and said, "If sports were the answer to everything, life would be very simple."

"Life's not so easy, is it? This whole family drives me crazy," I said.

"What do you mean?" Frank said, and put Regina's drink in front of her.

"Oh, come on, Grace," Regina said. *"Salute!"*

"Think about it. I come in today and there's pasta hanging everywhere, Nonna's crocheting like a bat out of hell . . ."

"She talked to Nonno yesterday," Regina said in a whisper. "She told me almost first thing when we got here."

Nonno was Nonna's husband, who had been certified dead and well buried for ten years.

"See what I mean?" I said in a hushed tone.

"What did he say?" Frank said. "Is he coming for her?"

"Shh! Bite your tongue!" Regina said. "She said he was dancing, like he was at a big party—a wedding maybe?"

"A wedding. You watch," I said. "Nicky's gonna marry that twit and then I'll have to look at her every holiday for the rest of my life."

Frank and Regina stared at me and then burst out laughing.

"What? You all don't think she's obnoxious?"

"Not obnoxious . . ." Frank said.

"More like, I don't know . . . all that baby talk is a little . . ." Regina said.

"Ridiculous," I said.

"Well, Grace? There's nothing you can do about your family. They just are as they are."

"I just don't see Michael fitting in here, that's all. And it worries me because I really love this man."

"If Marianne can fit in, so can Michael," Regina said, and then covered her mouth, stealing a glance behind her as though she might have been overheard.

"How do you define fitting in?" Frank said. "Anybody want a glass of wine?"

Regina declined and I said, "Sure, why not? Never mind, I'm drinking milk."

Frank pulled the cork on an unfinished bottle from dinner and poured out two glasses. "If we don't drink it, it will go bad."

"Thanks," I said, smiling at my brother. "Mud in your eye."

"*Salut.* Look, it's late but I'd like to throw in my two cents on this. You're over thirty, Grace. Them's the facts. If you want to have a family and Michael's the man for the job, then it's your decision. Regina and I are gonna love whoever you love as long as he's good to you. You can't live your life trying to please everyone else. Will he fit in? Who fits in?"

"I never worried about fitting in," Regina said. "I mean, maybe a little in the beginning."

"Yeah, because it's easy for you," I said. "You play by all the rules, Regina. You're Italian, you go to church, you have really nice kids that do the normal stupid stuff but they are seriously nice kids . . ."

"Not so hot in school," Frank said.

"Not that terrible, Frank."

"You cook, you keep a nice house . . ."

"Uh! The house is a disaster all the time!" Regina said.

"Whatever! When Connie and Big Al and Nonna look at you and Frank, they are thrilled. Connie and Nonna say novenas of thanksgiving and Big Al spreads his feathers like the NBC peacock. They look at me and think, Oh my God, where did we go wrong?"

"No, they don't, Gracie," Frank said. "You're paranoid."

"Maybe. Maybe not. I don't know what to think. All I know is that every time Michael's name is even breathed, the sharks start to circle like there's blood in the water. They don't know what he's been through."

"What do you mean?"

"Well for one thing, he had a little brother that died when he was just two months old."

"Mother of God!" Regina said. "Let me tell you what that can do to a family!"

"What did he die from?"

"They think it was SIDS. I mean, you can imagine, right? His mother was never the same. And he grew up terrified of little kids."

"So needless to say, he's a little ambivalent about having a family? Am I right?" Frank said.

"You got it! And I don't blame him. He says his mother became very morbid, and when his father died, that was it for her. She started fading away."

"Look," Frank said, "you have to live your life. And think about this: If Big Al, who still suffers from the terrible twos, can adjust to living with his mother-in-law under the same roof for the past ten years, he can get used to anything. And anybody. Kids or no kids. Stem-cell research. Humph. So what? Scientists will always search for answers. That's their purpose."

"He has worked with bone marrow, too," I said.

"Look, I'm a nurse," Regina said, "and I'm a Catholic. I understand the Church's objection—they don't want the medical world to clone life to be used as an organ bank or to create life designed to be destroyed. Who does? But so far, nobody's cloning anybody. Maybe a couple of Korean doctors."

"Who Michael says will probably be exposed for fraud . . ."

"Who knows? I think everyone knows it's an ethical conundrum. It's the biggest ethical conundrum since a woman's right to choose! All that said, if I had a child who was critically ill and their disease could be reversed with stem cells, you'd better believe that I'd be on line for stem cells. I see too many children get sick and die that shouldn't."

Everyone fell silent then. Regina's words summed up the larger part of the issue with a stunning succinctness. No one disagreed and no one applauded. Stem-cell research was a grave concern of Regina's because she was a devout Catholic living in the medical community. As a philosophy professor, Frank had wrestled with the ethics of it. And me? I was in love with a man whose general livelihood already compromised the affection of my parents and grandmother.

"It's late," Frank said.

Regina and Frank hugged me and said good night.

I struggled to find sleep but was consoled that I had something like allies in Frank and Regina. It had been a long time since I had felt at home with my family, and what tormented me into the early hours of morning was the *why* of it. Indeed. Why? Well, I was willing to admit I had changed. I loved Charleston society and the way my friends there lived. I loved my work and traveling like a billionaire. It made me feel like one. And getting away was my specialty. My parents had remained the same, and if anything had become even more provincial. But the real kernel of the problem didn't lie with them and I knew it.

I was afraid that if Michael met them, he would love me less or maybe stop loving me completely.

I wondered what Frank would have said if I had told him that. I knew exactly what he would have said—that it wasn't morally right to enjoy our father's generosity if I was ashamed of him—to stick up my nose while I stuck out my hand. For all my worldliness and sophistication, I had become a hypocrite. That was the despicable truth I saw in myself as the sun cracked the dark on the dawn of the Fourth of July.

CHAPTER 3

Hide-and-Go-Seek

The entire Fourth of July celebration at my parents' house was very bittersweet. While I was always glad, even if it was in a halfhearted way, to be with my family, I had never felt like more of an outsider than I did that weekend. I went for Mom's sake because of the walkway. Messy and inconvenient as it was, it really only represented a few hours' work to put it all back together again. It was hardly the travesty my mother had described. Why, then, had old Connie been so insistent about my presence? Maybe because Frank was there with his family and Mom really did want to see us all together around the table? Yes, I decided, that was probably it. After all, wasn't she the sentimental one who took the only pictures that ever recorded our history?

I felt a twinge of guilt because earlier in the weekend I'd had thoughts that the solo invitation was another attempt to relegate Michael to the sidelines. And Michael, sensitive to my family's positions and accustomed to being slighted by them, had announced his own plans to save face. But after my late-night talk with Frank I realized my parents were acting the only way they knew how to act. Provincial. Inflexible. Judgmental.

I couldn't have the relationship with my parents I wanted as long as Michael was in my life. Dad thought he was satanic, Nonna thought he was a horrible influence, and even though Mom said nothing, I knew what she thought. It was exasperating. The minute I walked into my parents' home, I was made to feel like a child again, pushed into corners and outwitted by everyone. That was one source of my discomfort. And the straight-out refusal of my family to accept my adult life as it was. I knew that at some point I was going to have to discuss it with them. We were going to have to find some peace about this because there were better-than-even odds that Michael was going to be with me long into the foreseeable future.

It was nearly seven o'clock when I reached the city limits of Charleston. I dialed Michael's cell.

"Hey, sweetheart! I'm almost home. Want to meet me somewhere for supper? Where are you?"

"Welcome home! I'm just leaving the hospital. I missed you! How was your trip?"

"Fine. You know. The usual sociology experiment—see how much food you can eat before you explode." I sighed and Michael laughed a little. "Want to meet at Rue de Jean's? I could really go for a bowl of mussels."

"Sure. I'll head over and get us a table. See you in a few."

"Okay. Love you."

"Love you, too."

We clicked off, but with that one statement of *Love you, too,* I slipped right back into my life with Michael. For the larger part of the drive back to Charleston I had worried about where I belonged in the world, and then inside of a one-minute conversation with Michael, I knew.

I only ever saw the world as worth the effort it took to navigate when I was looking at it through his eyes. With him my worldview was complete, or maybe the world had become so complicated that it took two brains to digest the daily struggles. No, I decided, Michael was my perfect partner. He was all that I was not. I had become addicted to the balance his point of view offered for sorting out everything. I loved the way his thoughts were so carefully constructed, and I loved everything else about him, too, especially his professional work, which provided hours of thinking about and talking about the very real future of humanity. And he did so much charitable work that I wondered how he found the time for it all. When he wasn't raising money through baseball, he was gathering donated children's books for hospitalized kids or large-print novels for folks in his mom's nursing home.

I parked on historic John Street and locked my car. Rue de Jean was located right next to Gallery Chuma, which housed the work of Jonathan Green, one of the South's most revered artists, who painted startlingly beautiful images of the Gullah culture. His work was one more instance of the unique gestalt of the Lowcountry's living history. Someday, I thought, I would love to have a small piece of his work.

Looking up and down the street, I thought about how much I enjoyed summer nights, the fading light that lit the streets and streaked the sky with color until almost nine o'clock. To call the summer weather of Charleston sultry was the understatement of the year. There was something about the toasted air and the diffused light that was a drug. I was happily addicted.

With a little reluctance to leave the pretty scene, I went inside the restaurant and spotted Michael at his table.

Rue de Jean was a popular place for its old-world ambience as well as its fare. It was a classic bistro in the Parisian Left Bank style offering the dishes you would expect in such a place—croque monsieur sandwiches, salade niçoise, steak au poivre with pommes frites and, of course, the mussels steamed with garlic and white wine that were on my mind.

The hostess brought me to the table and Michael stood, giving me a polite kiss on both cheeks, barely brushing my skin.

"*Très Frrrranche, mon cher!*" I said, in exaggerated and poor but humorously executed French.

"*Très bien,*" he said as the hostess held my chair and handed me the menu. "You are zee sight for zee poor eyes."

"I think we can drop the French," I said with a giggle. "The foreign-language police have a warrant out for our arrest."

"And the grape police are just around the corner. I'm doing my bit for California's agricultural products. Not France. Gosh, you look wonderful! You've got nice color. Did you go to the beach?"

The waitress appeared and said, "Can I start you off with something to drink?"

"Sure," I said. "I'll just have a glass of whatever he's having." The waitress nodded and left. "The beach? No, no. We just hung out at Big Al's version of Nikki Beach. There were too many moving parts to try and organize a trip to the actual ocean. Besides, Big Al hates the sand."

Smirking, Michael stared at me and said nothing.

"What?" I said, knowing he was about to lob a cherry bomb my way.

"No, it's okay. I was just thinking how funny it is to buy a house at a beach resort when you don't like the beach . . ."

"You know he moved there for the golf," I said.

"Yeah, I know, but still . . ."

"Right, they could've gone to Palm Springs or something . . ."

"Right. And I was thinking how much better I feel just to see you sitting there in front of me."

We went into our lovers' trance of smiles, stares, then sweet leering and thoughts of lying down together at the end of the evening. Our fingers were intertwined and I said, "Oh Lord! Isn't love just about the most wonderful thing in the world?"

"Yes. It's amazing."

The waitress put the glass of wine in front of me and said, "Ahem? Specials, anyone?"

We listened, and after a cursory glance at the menu, we ordered.

"I'll have the mussels with a lot of bread to soak up the sauce," I said.

"And I'll have the roasted chicken with string beans and French fries. And a bottle of the Merryvale."

"Very good," she said, and left.

"A bottle plus two glasses? Are we bingeing?"

"No, just easing the stress."

"The stress of what?" I said, and before I could finish that thought I realized I hadn't asked about his mother. "Oh, God, sorry . . . how's your mom?"

"Considerably worse than the last time I saw her," Michael said, rubbing his temple in a circular motion with two fingers. "She never recognized my voice, not even for one second. She thought I was my father, that it was a Sunday afternoon in the sixties and what did he want for dinner . . . Then she just stops in midsentence and drifts away again. My own mother doesn't know me. Nice, right?"

"Oh, Michael, I'm so sorry. I can't imagine such a thing."

"Yeah, and I can't stand seeing her like this. You know?"

Changing the subject, I said, "Do you have a headache?"

"Yeah, probably pollen . . ."

"Or stress . . ."

"Yeah, maybe. I'm fine. I'll take an antihistamine and it will be fine. Listen, Bomze called."

"When?"

"This afternoon. I tried calling you on your cell, but it didn't go through."

"I hate cell phones. I wonder what . . . Well, I'll call him back when we get home."

Eric Bomze and his elegant third wife, the famous Romanian baroness Adriana Katerina Kovacs, were the designer travel source for successful executives and their families. They were known throughout the industry as Bomze and the Baroness. I was their favorite rising executive in a cast of sixty or so others in assorted offices around the world. They'd nicknamed me La Principessa.

If you wanted to book the rambling eight-bedroom chalet at Suvretta House in St. Moritz that had once belonged to Reza Pahlavi, the former shah of Iran, you called Bomze Platinum Travel. If you wanted to cruise the Mediterranean on the yacht once held by Niarchos or Onassis, you called them. In fact, every CEO, COO and CFO spending their retirement years as *a guest of the state* once had the Bomzes' personal cell-phone numbers on speed dial—before they were confiscated, that is. It was true enough that all the SEC investigations had cut into their business, but not enough to cause substantial alarm to Bomze and the Baroness. They merely raised their fee by six percent to cover the losses and continued on their merry way.

But a phone call from Bomze on a holiday weekend was unusual and I knew something must have happened.

"I'll call him later," I said again.

As we talked and ate and drank, the round and square pegs of our life fell back into their round and square holes and our comfort with each other was easily reestablished. But it was only so easily established because somebody—both of us actually—weren't exactly forthcoming with the facts.

I skirted the details of my weekend at my parents' home like an Olympic dodgeball gold medalist—Nonna's jungle of hanging pasta, her OCD for yarn and communion with her dead husband, the Niagara Falls of Big Al's dees, dems and dozes, the sheer mass of my brother's children and how the noisy choir of their voices and Regina's shrieking reprimands sent me scouring my makeup bag for ten milligrams of something, anything to smooth the edges of my ruffled nerves. Never mind my brother Nicky and his idiotic Marianne and all the rest of it. It was just better left unexplored.

Michael's recounting of the holiday was equally false. He didn't tell me until much later about his mother and how he had found her half-naked and crying. That she had screamed bloody murder at his arrival. He said not one word to me about his mother's violence when he tried to dress her and wash her face. Or that Michael had wept all night in the dark silence of our carriage house wondering what kind of loving God would do such a thing to his beautiful mother, who had never hurt anyone in her entire life.

His mother had been a dignified woman, every inch of her

refined and lovely. When his father was alive he remembered seeing them waltzing to recordings of big-band music in their living room on Murray Boulevard, Dom Pérignon chilling in one of his mother's ancient silver wine buckets—one of many alleged treasures I had never seen, all of them stored away with antiques and other things for Michael to have if and when he needed them to furnish a house.

The lives his parents led had been elegant, privileged, and they were highly sought after among the bastions of Charleston's elite society for every event of the season. But then his father died suddenly in Michael's seventeenth year. Heart attack. Just forty. What a sin, everyone said. The world stopped after the funeral, the flowers and the procession of obligatory visits, and Michael thought his mother would never stop crying.

Michael went off to college at Duke and returned that first Thanksgiving to find his mother withdrawn and distracted, her voice reduced to whispers. By Easter the principal trustee of his father's estate recommended a full medical workup for her. The best diagnosis the neurology team at the Medical University of South Carolina could offer was that she was extremely depressed, and so Laura Higgins became another guinea pig in the emerging medicine of psychotropic drugs. The private nurses, the extensive visits to sanitariums, the experimental medicines didn't matter except that they depleted his father's estate and his mother disappeared into her own world anyway. Every time Michael visited his mother, he was filled with self-loathing that he was unable to stop her deterioration.

But Michael persevered as I did, him doing his duty, me doing mine and neither of us discussing it too much. Discussing our families at any length would have made Michael's mother and my family real and three-dimensional, an extension of our own relationship. There was only miserly space in our world for all the trouble and ill health of Laura Higgins, Al's patriarchy and the unending peculiarities of the entire Russo clan. It was too dangerous.

*   *   *

Later, at home, Michael flipped through the four hundred stations on our television and I called Eric Bomze.

"Bomze? It's me. Is this a good time to talk?"

"Ah! La Principessa! I'm with the Baroness, and as we uncork this very excellent bottle of Pétrus, I have a special favor to ask you. Tell me yes right now!"

"Yes! Of course the answer is yes. What do you need?"

"Well, there's good news and bad. Which do you prefer?"

"Bad first."

"Missy Belton in the Atlanta office was in a terrible automobile accident and broke her leg in fourteen places."

"Oh! God! That's awful! Is she gonna be all right?"

"Of course! She'll be fine after a year or two of physical therapy and hopefully she won't limp for the rest of her life."

"Good Lord! What can I do? Can I send flowers?"

"What? Oh, of course. If you want to. But she's not in a room yet, so I'd wait a few days . . ."

"She couldn't get a room? That's awful! What exactly happened?"

"What happened? An eighteen-wheeler came flying down an exit ramp in the pouring rain and didn't see her little Toyota. Mashed it like a bug. And a Honda and a minivan loaded with gospel singers. She's lucky to be alive. They all are. But apparently it caused a lot of commotion at the ER. Anyway, she was supposed to take a group of execs and their families to Sardinia next week for five days. I need you to take her place."

I swallowed hard. I hated what Bomze was asking of me. I didn't know the clients, I hadn't planned the trip, and suddenly I was supposed to step in and take over? I knew Missy from annual sales meetings and liked her well enough, but I also *knew* her well enough to look into my mind's eye and see an itinerary peppered with black holes of unfinished details.

"Of course I'll go," I said. "But I'll need the entire folder first thing in the morning. Bios on the guests, food allergies—the whole thing, okay?"

"Done, done and done! You're an angel!"

I'm an idiot, I thought, and hung up. I turned to Michael. "Want to run away to Sardinia with me for five days?"

"You know I'd love to, but—"

"Right, I know." I leaned into our refrigerator and pulled out a carton of orange juice. I poured myself a glass. "Results of a test study due and blah, blah, blah?"

"You know it."

I hadn't expected him to come with me. He rarely could. His work was as all-consuming as mine was erratic. Later, I came out of the bathroom from my shower expecting to find Michael waiting in bed. He wasn't there. I went silently down a few of the stairs thinking he had probably fallen asleep reading. But when I saw him I knew immediately that Michael was in trouble. Whether it was a headache or heartbreak over his mother's condition, Michael was sitting at the dining-room table holding his head. His shoulders shook. He was crying. Frightened, I went back upstairs without a word.

CHAPTER 4

Darwinia/Sardinia

At around four in the morning, I was fully alert; but that was how it always was with me. If I went to bed worried about the slightest thing, any noise or movement would wake me and I would never go back to sleep. The devil of it was that I would drag myself through the next day like an old hag.

As quietly as I could, I untangled myself from the sheets and got up. Michael was there sleeping as though everything was right in the world. I knew the peaceful look on his face was a midnight illusion, but I made a conscious effort to tell myself that we were fine. He was fine, I was fine, we were fine—if I kept conjugating our status it would become true.

My first steps on the cool bare floor felt good. Small things could bring such pleasure, especially when stealing time from the deep hours of night. Without leaving the house, I knew what it would feel and look like outdoors. Silent streets lit in soft angles of blue light, air thick with dew, the low hum of the transformers that swept the streets of Charleston with enough light to pass from a car to a porch. You would hear the murmuring of a window-unit air conditioner somewhere in the neighborhood. The changing gears of a few cars would be well off in the distance, background music to the dreams of thousands. The parks would be empty, the skies silent for another hour or so, the sanitation department had yet to begin its rounds, and the only things moving around would be cockroaches, moody cats and a patrolman looking for coffee and a doughnut.

I pulled the sheets and coverlet over Michael's shoulders, and kissing the tips of my fingers, I transferred the kiss to the edges of his hair.

We had thick area rugs, unmatched kilim runners on each side of our queen-size bed. I had brought them home from a trip to Turkey two years ago. Many people preferred the quiet muffle of wall-to-wall broadloom carpeting for their bedrooms—something to match the curtains, something that didn't cause static shock, tasteful but reasonably priced. But I loved the uneven slope of the ancient floors and the patina of the heart pine, lovingly buffed over the decades to a glossy shade of coffee. I never thought of covering them with anything that would detract from their integrity.

The geometric Anatolian motif of the kilims reminded me of Native American rugs. I always marveled to discover that all over the world, similar designs appeared in arts and crafts, no matter how disparate the cultures and how far-flung one might have been from the other. Sand paintings in New Mexico resembled sand paintings in Tibet. And rugs from here were like rugs from there.

Without turning on any lights, I used the bathroom and filled a glass with water, drinking it straight down. My mouth was dry from sleep and the water seemed especially cool and crisp. I refilled my glass and drank again until my thirst was finally quenched. Returning to our bed, I stood over Michael, watching him breathe, looking for any sign of discomfort. He seemed fine and so I quietly slipped between the sheets, concentrating on not disturbing him. But my best sleeping hours were finished for the night and I lay awake for a long time before drifting off into a kind of half-dream, half-waking state.

In the hour or so between waking and drifting through nonsensical dreams and thoughts of the day, my nervous mind ran through the fast-approaching trip to Sardinia. I dreaded learning what Missy had left undone, knowing there would be hundreds of loose ends. Missy ran her business one way and I ran mine another. The good thing was that I had four days to get my arms around the itinerary and I could catch up as the trip unfolded. In addition, because of the level of hotels we patronized, I was sure the concierge would be helpful. Yes, I thought, I will enlist the hotel talent to pull this off.

I turned over to face Michael's back and readjusted my pillows. My thoughts drifted again to him and wondering what in the world could cause him such anxiety. I thought about my fierce love for Michael and then, for some inexplicable reason, my thoughts were of the lines I had nearly drawn in the sand with my father. How Freudian! I pushed both of them away—that is, my father and even Michael.

Sardinia. I would figure that out and it would be fine. I knew I had all the resources at my disposal to make it happen as it should. But my mind drifted back to Michael again. I couldn't bear the idea of Michael so upset over something that he would go off alone to cry. That just wasn't like him. Surely he was frustrated and worried about his mother. I would make a great dinner that night for him and encourage him to tell me what was on his mind. After all, that's what a good partner would do and what the other would want.

With work tucked aside for the moment and with the framework of a plan for Michael—because, practical girl I was, I realized there was nothing to be done anyway at that hour—I began to dissect my weekend with my family. I had really loved my brief visit with Frank and Regina, although I saw that I had virtually ignored my niece and nephews, and why was that? It was always the same at my mother's house—chaos caused by feeding crowds, and always the brunt of the work fell to the adult women. It was all we could do to get from meal to meal, and so the only conversation I had with the younger relatives was around the table, and that was scant at best. Nonna and my father seemed to monopolize all the airtime, and sidebar conversations were looked upon as poor manners.

And Nicky? God in heaven! Nicky and that stupid Marianne of his. I envisioned the wedding and the thirty bridesmaids Marianne would want to have at her side. All dressed in lavender taffeta gowns and matching hats copied from *Gone with the Wind*. There would be a bubble machine and their names monogrammed on every possible item at the reception. Marianne would tear up and her mascara would be blotted by a friend with a lavender linen handkerchief. Everything would be lavender and mint green or pink and she would order so many flowers Big Al would have to pave every parking lot in South Carolina and Georgia to pay for them. They would release doves. The doves would drop poop on Marianne and I would snicker . . .

I did not think I had turned into a snob. Not really. What kind of a girl had I expected Nicky to wind up with anyway? One like Marianne who worked that southern thing to death. But I surely would have loved a little sister with a brain instead of a bobble head. Regina was great but she lived too far away. Even with e-mail and cell phones, we were too busy in our very different lives to pursue anything more than what we had.

I loved my family and my father with everything I had in my heart. Oh, Big Al, Big Al, Big Al. Why can't you be fabulous like Paul Newman? Smart like Al Pacino? I knew it was selfish to wish he was a different kind of man. But I did.

At his best, he could pull off a kind of Robert De Niro— handsome and appealing, warm and welcoming and even marginally elegant in some moments. But if Big Al had one too many beers watching the Golf Channel and an ad for Victoria's Secret went slinking across his giant plasma television, there was no mystery about which part of his anatomy he would grab and yell, "I gotcha secret right here!" Even if the president of the United States were there eating peanuts. What could you say? Big Al was a loose cannon and best served up to the public or maybe someday to Michael in a controlled environment.

As at last the beginnings of daylight appeared and the light in the room began to rise, I realized with the sounds of the alarm clock and the smells of coffee brewing that I had in fact fallen into a dreamless sleep. Michael was already in the shower. I poured two mugs of coffee, and when I returned to the bedroom he was dressing.

"Hey, g'morning," I said. "How are you feeling?"

"Thanks!" he said, taking the coffee. "I'm fine. You?"

"I didn't sleep all that great." I pulled a white linen skirt from the closet and began to rummage around for a top. "Whatever . . . I have so much to do . . . You home for dinner tonight?" I reached down for my low-heeled green pumps and threw them behind me on the bed.

"Yep."

"Good. I'm cooking."

Michael looked at me and smiled. "I'll bring home some wine."

Within the hour, the steamy bathroom had raised the temperature of the house by five degrees, but the dishwasher hummed, the bed was made, the garbage had been put by the curb, and we were off to our respective places of employment. For the moment Michael seemed perfectly fine, and I decided to put his troubles aside for the day.

When I arrived at my office, the phones were ringing off the hook. I thumbed through the waiting stack of messages while Joanie, the receptionist, answered and redirected calls to various people.

"Bomze wants to see you on the double," Joanie said, and answered another line. "Bomze Platinum Travel. How may I direct your call? That line is busy. Would you like his voice mail?"

"Well, it's right after a holiday," I said.

"You can say that again! Bomze Platinum Travel . . ."

I jammed my messages into the side flap of my bag, making my way down the hallway saying "Hello! How was your Fourth?" to a number of coworkers and their assistants, and arrived at Eric Bomze's door. I rapped my knuckles lightly on the frame.

"Come in!" he called out. He was on the phone with the Baroness. "Yes, my angel! Yes, my precious! I'll be there! Don't worry!"

I stood just inside his door, waiting for him to end the conversation.

"_Yes,_ my sweet. _No!_ It's all arranged. She just came in. I'll call you back!" Bomze hung up the phone, took a deep breath and looked up at me. "Being married to royalty can be a royal pain."

"Yeah, right? I'm sure. Okay, so what have we got on Sardinia?"

The morning blew by with phone calls and faxes flooding the wires with details. The guest list for Sardinia was made up of trustees and actual and potential donors from a major university in Atlanta who had a special interest in architecture and archaeology. I liked architecture well enough, but I had zero interest in or knowledge of archaeology. Missy had had the foresight to engage the services of a historian from Emory University who studied and lectured on both topics. Dr. Geraldine Post had just returned from the islands around Greece and said she could make herself available to us in Charleston as soon as her clothes returned from the dry cleaners.

"I'm sure I can be there by Wednesday," she told me.

"That would be wonderful," I said. "I just want to go over everything with you."

"Sure thing. These nice folks are gonna get the weirdest education. Sardinia—home of nuraghi and dolmens."

"Yeah, I was about to bring them up. Are we speaking English here?"

Dr. Post had a good laugh then. "Actually, I'm sure not! Probably some derivative of some Roman language . . . but anyway, between the Phoenicians and the Barbarians . . ."

Dr. Post was quite a character—obviously knowledgeable about the obscure and the ancient. She would add some scholarship laced with good humor to the days just ahead. That was what the crowd always wanted, a good time, a little takeaway value and, in addition, some pampering of the mind, body and spirit.

A real itinerary began to fall into place that included historic tours, shopping, meals and time slots for other indulgences. I began to feel more optimistic and actually impatient to make the trip.

By the time I got home that evening, loaded with groceries to prepare veal Marsala and risotto with fresh asparagus, I was mentally fortified to investigate Michael's anxiety from last night. If I fed him well and we drank some wine together, I felt reasonably sure that he would tell me what was on his mind. It was probably about his mother. If that was my mother—estranged as we might be to each other these days—I would surely cry my eyes out, too.

The heat of the day was broken by six and I decided to serve dinner in the brick courtyard that spilled out from our living room. We loved eating outside; somehow everything tasted better. And I could decorate outside and create an atmosphere that ranged from tropical to elegant. Sometimes, when we were in the mood for Bali, I took our potted palm trees and rolled them up to the table. I would have as many as fifty votive candles lighting the wall (thank you, God, for inventing Pier One) and serve a seafood stew in carved-out loaves of bread. Or I could stretch for eighteenth-century elegance, using every piece of crystal, silver and lace-trimmed linen I owned, which wasn't a lot, but Michael was always good enough to say he got the picture. We loved the fantasy of pretending to be somewhere else or in a different time, and the night always progressed to a walk on the Battery Wall, time spent marveling at the stars, the breezes that floated across the water and, most of all, a moment reflecting on the profundity of Fort Sumter.

Michael would always say something like "Can you believe all these people died for their country, just like that? Crazy!"

I would shake my head and say something like "Only to be

outdone by the crew of the *Hunley*. Those guys were completely nuts!"

It wasn't that we weren't patriotic; like too many of our peers, we couldn't imagine the passions of war. And the H. L. *Hunley* crew that drowned was the third crew to do so. Can you imagine the guy in charge asking for volunteers? *Okay, men, here's the deal. Even though the first and second crew drowned trying to sink the Yankees, we need seven good men to keep the* Hunley *going and a crew captain. Our target is the* Housatonic *and those sumbitches who will burn Charleston to the ground if we don't get 'em first . . .*

For as much as Michael or I would have done to save Charleston—and that was a lot—neither of us could envision offering to die for the cause with the full knowledge that we most assuredly *would* die for the cause. I was a major chicken.

I went outside to check the weather wondering *What would I die for?* Was there anything? Or anyone? No. The president? In theory, perhaps I would, or I could understand that the Secret Service was trained to take the proverbial bullet. I had never entertained one second of ambition to join the Secret Service. Would I die for Michael? Better yet, would he die for me? And what happened when you died anyway? If Nonna was right, the guys from the *Hunley* were all up in heaven having a big party with the martyrs from the Roman Colosseum. But I didn't think that was an actual possibility. Heaven and hell just didn't make any sense to me. It was true enough that my faith had wobbled for years and then gone into hiding. But my theory on the afterlife and the possibility of its existence was like Occam's razor—all things being equal, the simplest answer was usually the correct one. When you died, you died. Except for Nonno? In any case, it had been a long time since I had really thought about it.

I was saving my energy for more urgent things—feeding Michael and finding out what was on his mind.

It was still in the mideighties. Luckily, there was no rainstorm in sight. But it was oppressive. I decided the air would

be most comfortable if it was moving, so I brought a fan outside with a long extension cord and positioned it on the brick
wall.

"Freaking mosquitoes," I said to no one, and slapped my leg,
reducing the population by one and only a hungry one.

Little clay pots of burning citronella would keep the nasty
things at bay. I took a pack of six from the cabinet over the
refrigerator and encircled the table with them. Next I set the
table with red-and-yellow batik linens I had bought ages ago in
Thailand and put a hurricane in the center of the small round
table. How was I going to convince him he was in southern
Italy?

"I'll break up some Parmesan in a little bowl and drizzle it
with olive oil. And music. I'll play that new CD, um, what the
heck is the name of it? Il Divo!"

I continued talking to myself, working out the logistics for
the night. The phone rang, scaring me half to death, and I hurried back inside to answer it.

"Hello?"

"Hey, it's me. Do you mind if I go to the gym for an hour?"

"No problem. I'm building a little theater here for us."

"Dinner outside?"

"Yep."

"What country?"

"Italy. No, wait. Sardinia."

"Ah, so I'm going with you after all. White or red?"

"A good Chianti or a Pinot."

"What are you cooking?"

"It's a surprise, Mr. Wonderful. I'll see you later."

I hung up, leaned against the kitchen wall and said to the
thin air, "God, I sure do love that man."

The smells of sautéing shallots and mushrooms welcomed
Michael home, and sweaty as he was from working out, he
grabbed me and kissed me all over my neck and face.

I jumped and shrieked, "Take a shower! You smell worse
than a skunk."

"No, I don't! I smell good! Come here!"

"Trust me on this," I said. "You absolutely reek."

"Does that mean no predinner nooky?"

"Definitely not! Go!"

Within the hour, we were enjoying the cool of the evening and popping the cork on a second bottle of wine.

"So you hated that, right?"

"Yeah. You little Italian girls should get somebody to teach you how to cook. Seriously."

"Yeah, sure. Well, now that you've taken a break from stuffing your face, tell me, how was your day?"

"The normal. It was a bad day for the mice and a good day for mankind. Do we have any more risotto and veal? A little more sauce?"

"You know it. I can't cook for any less than twelve. The food gene."

I took his plate and refilled it. Michael resumed eating with gusto and was wiping up the sauce with a hunk of Italian bread as he attempted to explain his current work.

"We've got this experiment going on that shoots gold nanoparticles loaded up with reagents that are capable of . . . Grace?"

"Hmm?"

"I see that dull look in your eyes . . ."

"Sorry. Please. The bottom line?"

"It's gonna cut tumor growth in cancers. Which is fascinating. But in about, who knows . . . five years? They'll have little nanobots that they can inject into Joe Blow and they will go directly to the site of old Joe's tumor, obliterate it, and *poof!* No tumor! No cancer! All done in about three or four hours! As opposed to stem cells that the body can reject for all kinds of reasons and that still take forever."

"I'm sorry, but are you not working in stem cells?"

"Yeah, but this is a totally different approach that has everybody buzzing. There's another team of guys working on all these experiments—nanotechnology—could absolutely beat stem cells to Stockholm this year."

I assumed he was referring to the Nobel Prizes.

"Michael? Are you thinking about switching fields?"

"No! No way. But I have to tell you, Grace, this is some awesome, awesome stuff."

"Man. Don't you just . . . I mean, sometimes isn't it completely amazing to be doing this work now? I mean, are we really on the edge of curing about a billion diseases?"

"A billion and one. I'm telling you, baby, it's happening so fast we can hardly keep up with our own progress and the implications of it all. These guys at the Mayo Clinic just finished up a study on spinal-cord nerve regeneration, and it worked. Well, it worked on lab mice anyway. Now the trick is to get to the place where it's safe to do trials on humans."

"And funded."

"Yeah, there is that little caveat. So tell me the truth. Is your old man still raging about my allegiance to stem-cell research?"

"What do you think? It doesn't matter, Michael. He can get up on his hind legs and bark like a fox and it doesn't change the way I feel about you, okay?"

Michael reached across the table, took my hand in his and then covered it with his other hand. A small breeze moved across the courtyard, ruffling the tablecloth and my hair. It was dark as pitch and in the candlelight Michael's face appeared more angular and masculine than in the light of day. There were dark smudges under his eyes. I hadn't noticed them earlier, but I wrote them off to fatigue.

"Well, tell Big Al to tell his priest that stem cells are going to be ancient history before they can get them to work consistently."

I leaned across the table and whispered, "Good. But you're the only man I've ever known who would use this irresistibly romantic moment to launch a discussion about science versus religion. Any other man, after this gorgeous dinner, would be trying to see what color my panties—"

He put his finger to my lips.

"I'll get to your panties, Miss Russo. Listen, especially embryonic stem cells. Go tell Big Al that there's a bunch of guys down in Sydney who figured out that olfactory stem cells do the same job, and get this—the study was funded by the Catholic Archdiocese for a mere hundred thousand."

"Big Al wouldn't know what you're talking about. Olfactory? Isn't that where lots of people put together fuel equipment on an assembly line?"

Michael looked at me with a wide grin and shook his head. That look said, *And you don't either.* This didn't offend me in the slightest. I knew that Michael was a genius and he was going to save the world. Okay, he would be a cog in the wheel that saved the world. But he did have the most splendid mind I had ever known.

Later, Michael was upstairs and I was just finishing up the dreaded dishes—there's nothing like that extra glass of wine to ruin your enthusiasm for cleaning a kitchen—and I heard him turn on the news. We had truly become like an old married couple. We went to work, came home, ate dinner, cleaned up, watched the news and went to sleep. I loved it—each and every day and night was so happily anticipated and I knew it was because of Michael. Michael thrilled me. This was real love—romantic love, physical love, intellectual love, companion love—you could name it anything you wanted to and it was the same thing—still growing stronger and deeper with no resistance from either side.

I heard the toilet flush and thought I had better move myself upstairs if I had hopes for any ooh-la-la that night. Then I heard it flush again and again.

"Michael? Are you okay?"

No answer.

I rushed up the steps and found him on the floor of the bathroom. He had obviously been vomiting.

"Michael! What in God's name . . . ? Do you need a doctor?"

"I am one," he said. "Just help me to bed."

He was weak and unsteady on his feet as I helped him up and walked him to the bed. His arm was around my shoulder and mine was around his waist. I knew he had consumed a fair amount of wine, but no more than I had, and I felt fine. He got under the covers and I pulled them over him.

"What can I get you, baby?"

"Nothing," he said. "I'm a little dizzy. Probably worked out too long . . . something . . . the heat? Who knows?"

I relaxed as I heard him diagnose himself. That was a sign that things weren't too far from normal. I turned off the television, tiptoed to the bathroom to get him a cold cloth and a glass of water to sip, and tiptoed back.

"All my good veal wasted!" I said in a whisper.

The corners of his mouth turned up even though his eyes were closed. "Only a Russo would think about that," he said.

"Only a Higgins wouldn't!"

I decided to sleep on the couch that night, thinking that if he had the whole bed to himself, he would be more comfortable. But I had the worst night's sleep I'd had in years. I got hot and pushed off my quilt. Then the air-conditioning kicked in and I got cold. The quilt was on the floor, and by the time I was resituated, I was half-awake. And when I finally slept, I had the strangest dream.

I was in the car with Michael and we were going over the bridge to Mount Pleasant. The car was going too fast, and when I looked over, Michael was gone. Then the steering wheel was gone. The next thing I knew, the car was falling down to the Cooper River with me in it. I was screaming in the dream and woke up with a jolt, drenched in sweat. What the hell was that all about?

CHAPTER 5

Room with a View

In July, it is often said that the only thing that separates Charleston, South Carolina, from the bottom floor of hell is the flapping
of a flimsy screen door. May I just say that the poetic souls who
say this have yet to visit Sardinia? America understands and em-
braces air-conditioning. Sardinia, Italy, does not. And it was just
as hot and humid.

The very first thing that struck me about Sardinia was its
landscape. As we circled low and around, preparing to land, I
felt like I had been thrown back two thousand years. Huge juts
of granite, smoothed by millennia of salt and wind, lurched
upward from the earth. Some resembled animals and others
looked like objects. The landscape was craggy and arid. I
would not have been at all surprised to see herds of goats or
sheep led by ancient bearded men in long homespun caftans
and turbans navigating the scrub growth and sharp pitch of
the hills. Sardinia was biblical, exactly as you would imagine
the world looked when Abraham walked the earth.

While I waited at the Olbia Airport for my driver, I perspired,
furiously slapped bugs and felt the humidity do its worst on my
hair just as if I were in the Lowcountry. I stood for a long while
in the sticky morning air, my cartons of work-related materi-

als stacked next to my own luggage. If the driver didn't show up soon, the extra day I had planned for myself before the arrival of the group would be wasted. My mood became darker. I crinkled my nose at passing workmen who hadn't bathed with enough vigor and gave pitiless stares to women with wailing children on their hips. I will admit that I recognized I was behaving a bit like a princess. But it had been a long trip and I was overtired and really cranky.

Finally, the hotel car appeared and I was en route to a cool shower, some breakfast and finalizing the details of the trip, which, when done, would result in a massively improved disposition.

The slow beginning at the airport was the opposite of my hotel arrival. The courtyard of the Cala di Volpe was cool and serene. From the minute I stepped foot from the car, I knew my troubles were over. Built by the Aga Khan in the early sixties, the hotel was designed as a playground for the very wealthy or those with a certain celebrity. Every detail was unique, especially the floral arrangements all around the lobby and the large chunks of colored glass built into the walls, the sunken lobby bar, the hand-hewn archways of timber—the amount of thought and design that went into each square inch of the property boggled the mind. But that was Italy in general—the food, the architecture, the wine, the art—the whole Italian style of just about any area of living knew no peer. At least in the opinion of this humble Italian girl.

I took in all these details as the smelling-swell concierge at the reception desk took my passport and exchanged pleasantries with me. This guy had his own subtitle—Signore Hottie. He was tall and olive-complexioned, and his dark eyes were so filled with mischief they could have belonged to the devil himself. Massimo Floris was simultaneously all-business and sex appeal. I had expected he would be enthusiastic in his assistance, but I had not expected Massimo to be so . . . I don't know except to say that he reduced me to lewd thoughts and schoolgirl giggles.

"Signorina Russo! *Che bella! Buon giorno!* A cappuccino? I make it for you with my own hands!"

Just so you know, *che bella* meant he thought I was a babe. As addicted to Michael Higgins as I was, it was all I could do to keep a straight face and a loyal heart. Massimo was a walking aphrodisiac. Then I reminded myself that Italian men think all women are babes, no matter what their age or girth, countenance or manner, status or means. If they have a pulse and breasts, they are worthy of carnal consideration.

"Thank you," I said, snickering internally. "Caffeine is just what I need."

He disappeared for a few minutes, and when he returned he handed me the cup and saucer. Don't you know he had somehow produced a miniature replica of palm-tree fronds in its foam?

"The cappuccino is for free, but for the artwork is twenty euros," he said with a wide grin, revealing perfect teeth.

"In Vegas they comb in a king and queen of hearts," I said, lying off the top of my head.

"*Sì?* This is true? Playing cards or portraits?"

"Neither. It's not true. I was just kidding. Sorry. Dumb joke."

He smiled again. "It's okay. We like jokes at the Cala di Volpe. Now how may I help you prepare for the arrival of your guests, *bella?*"

To hell with them. Let's run away and do something wicked. That's what I was thinking with a laugh every time I looked at his face. Shoot. It wasn't dangerous, it was just flirting, and believe me, Italian men don't know how to talk to women without exuding some very powerful pheromones. They have to be the most virile and dangerous creatures on the planet.

The morning was spent going through the hotel together, touring all the shops and meeting rooms and, most important, making sure that every guest would have a view of the water and that the board president had the nicest suite. (All those beds! What a waste! I'm kidding, all right? I was committed to Michael; I wasn't Mother Teresa of Calcutta, okay?) Then, in descending order of board position, ego, donor history and donor potential, rooms were assigned. But with a high-season basic rack rate of fourteen hundred euros a night, the rooms ranged from glorious to spectacular. The marble bathrooms were stuffed with Acqua di Parma soaps, shampoos and body lotions. And, not to worry, breakfast was included. Like we used to say in New Jersey, *Such a deal.* Honestly, some people might have said the rooms weren't that fantastic, but they all fit the style of the hotel, which was a little rustic, somewhat resort-like and a little spare. Italian Opulent Zen.

Speaking of opulence, just yesterday, at Saks Fifth Avenue in Charleston, I had picked up tons of sunscreen products for men and women that were to be put together in Burberry tote bags and labeled by guest name. In addition, each guest was to receive gourmet chocolates, a nice bottle of champagne, a book about Sardinia and a video that gave an overview of the history of the island to take home. The biggest dogs would have flowers in their rooms and monogrammed bathrobes. This was all included in the cost of the trip. But somehow finding these luxury goodies neatly displayed in their rooms on arrival made them feel they were special and therefore somehow entitled to something extra. After assembling the bags in my room while munching on a panini, I called the bell captain. When he arrived, we loaded up the trolley and took them down to the lobby. Massimo's part was to deliver them to the rooms.

"We're going to take extra care of your guests, Signorina Russo. You don't have to worry about one thing."

"Well, I'm sure you have been through this a thousand times, but since I don't really know this group, I'm a bit nervous."

"Don't worry. You'll get old too quick! Worry makes little lines—"

And with that, I felt someone tap my elbow. It was Dr. Geraldine Post.

"Hi! Grace? I'm Geri Post," she said, and extended her hand for me to shake. "We meet at last!"

"Oh! I'm so glad you're here!" I shook her hand soundly. I would've known her anywhere. She was in her midfifties, short in stature with cropped gray hair. She wore khaki pants and a tucked-in khaki shirt. She had a red baseball hat from the Galápagos Islands and her wire-rim glasses were insured against loss by the strap around her neck, printed with tiny turtles. Neat and tidy. A neat and tidy pixie, built for speed, dressed for action.

"Do you have your room yet?"

"Nope! Just got here."

Massimo looked up and said, "Ah! Dr. Post. Welcome to the Cala di Volpe. My colleague will take your bags to your room, and may I offer you a cool drink of something? Wine? Lemonade?"

She was awfully perky for someone who had just crossed the Atlantic, sleeping in a seat designed to barely hold people with severe eating disorders.

"A Coca-Cola would be great," she said. "We're from Atlanta, you know!"

Massimo looked at her with a tiny question on his face that was almost instantly hidden behind his mask of professionalism. Italians knew that Coca-Cola came from America, but there was no significance in getting more specific. Atlanta? Peoria? Chicago? I mean, did Italy care about anything besides Italy? A cure for cancer would be good, but where Coke came from? The average Italian could not have cared less.

"Come, let's sit on the terrace," I said. "It's beautiful outside."

The glass doors parted automatically and the harbor of La Costa Smeralda—the Emerald Coast—was before us.

Dr. Post stood rooted to her spot, hands on her hips, looking out into the distance. "Whew!" she said. "There must be ten to twenty colors of blue in that water. Beautiful."

"Yeah, it's pretty breathtaking," I said. "Gorgeous blue water, mountains in the distance . . . just like the brochure."

My travel-speak broke the spell and she looked at me, shaking her head. Then she reached into her oversize shoulder bag and pulled out an envelope. "Here's my suggested itinerary for the week. Let me know what you think. ASAP, okay? Sorry I never got to Charleston."

"Oh, that's okay. Actually, it's nice to have this little slice of time to review and I'm sure whatever you have planned is fine."

"Well, first it was my dog-sitter. I especially hate leaving Hambone at the kennel because he gets cage anxiety, you know what I mean?"

"Hambone?"

"Yeah, he's an old bloodhound—got too old to hunt, so I took him from a friend who runs a hunt club up near Clarksville. Anyway, he's a drooler but I love him. Drools on everything. So finally the sitter shows up and she's got a cast on her leg from her toes clear up to Bangor, Maine. So I say to her, This ain't gonna work, sister, and she says she'll be fine. But I'm not so sure, so I hung around for the next two days so my mind could rest. Turns out she gets around just fine and dandy."

Hambone the drooler was in good hands and the world can rest easy now.

"So you just have the one dog?" I said.

"What? Oh, Lord no! I've got Hambone, Alvin and Bessie Mae, my two Scotties, Elvis and Liberace, my two old fat toothless Persians, and Scarface, my parrot."

"You have a parrot? Can he talk?"

"Are you kidding? He never shuts up! Every time I give him a treat he tells me I'm wonderful. I love him."

She went on and on about her pets, the Cokes arrived, I shook the itinerary in the air and she finally stopped yakking. We began to go over it.

"Okay," I said, "tomorrow night at seven-thirty, we have cocktails in the bar by the pool, and dinner is at nine at Da Gianni Pedrinelli."

"And I suspect it's a nice place, this Gianni Pedrinelli joint?"

"Massimo, the concierge who looks like a movie star, says it's the finest fish on the island."

"Then I'll bet it is. And first thing the next morning, we take the group to the Cathedral of Cagliari and have lunch around the piazza. I'll ask Mr. Hollywood for a lunch recommendation."

"Good idea. I'll come, too. Then we can come back to the hotel for a swim and a siesta or what? Golf? You know somebody will show up with clubs, right? Probably half the men. I'll ask Massimo about a golf course. I know there are some guys who travel the world trying to play every golf course there is. My father plays. Personally, I don't get it."

"Me either. Takes too much time and you don't learn a thing. Boy, it sure is hot here, isn't it?"

"Yeah. It's almost one hundred. The U.S. didn't corner the market on heat, right?"

"No. We surely did not. But Sardinia sure is gorgeous. This is work?"

"Right?"

She laughed and shook her head.

That night I had a long bubble bath, and swaddled in the hotel's velvet cut terrycloth bathrobe, I had a small feast delivered from room service. My room was so beautiful that I hated Michael not being there. He would have loved it. We both loved the water and the Mediterranean was so different from the Atlantic around Charleston. It was at least fifteen degrees cooler and clear, like a piece of handblown glass. No sharks—a meaningful selling point for my money. But the water had jellyfish and prickly sea urchins, so you would be well warned to watch where you went. No, Michael would have loved this place and I knew it. I pulled back the sheets and slipped in. Linen. Oh, how I loved linen sheets! There was something so natural about them. Maybe it was my imagination, but I thought they were cooler to sleep in during the summer and somehow warmer in the winter. They were so impractical I would probably never own them, never mind the expense. But for the next few nights, I could wrap myself in gorgeous Italian linen and pretend to be a real *principessa*. It was just one more imagined bonus of my crazy job.

I tried to call Michael. There was no answer at the house and his cell phone didn't answer either. I left messages in both places and told myself he was all right. Surely someone would've called me if something had happened. But who? A neighbor? One of Michael's friends? Maybe something happened to his mother. The thought of Michael dealing with his mother's illness or death alone was so upsetting that I finally took a sleeping pill and washed it down with a dose of vodka from the minibar. This was the major drawback of my job—I might have been sleeping on Italian linen, but I was sleeping alone, incommunicado with the outside world.

The next morning, I was up at six, showered, dressed, fed and in the lobby by eight. Guests began to trickle in. No doubt the Olbia Airport was littered with GIVs and GVs, and rolling racks probably groaned under the tonnage of designer luggage. I was there to greet them with Massimo and Geri at my side.

The board president, Stan White, and his wife, Liza; Harvey and Marilyn Gross; and Dylan Holmes and his meaningful other, Caroline Sutter, were the first to check in. At first glance they all seemed nice enough. Liza White and Marilyn Gross were Stan and Harvey's original wives, but Caroline Sutter was at least thirty years younger than Mr. Holmes. Liza and Marilyn had endured numerous surgical procedures—lifting, tucking, peeling, enhancing and paralyzing—and Caroline Sutter was oblivious. In minutes I realized that Liza and Marilyn were barely speaking to Caroline the Younger, and by that evening the reason was obvious.

We were gathered at the bar by the pool with another dozen of our group. Although it was seven-thirty, the temperature still clung to the midnineties. After a day of sweltering heat, everything, even the bamboo furniture, was warm to the touch, everything except the highball glasses the new arrivals clutched.

Liza and Marilyn, thin as rails, were dressed and accessorized beautifully. Despite years of personal trainers, salon treatments and plastic surgery, their hair showed traces of chemical ravage, their hands were cruelly freckled with liver spots, and their earlobes drooped with age. But they were gorgeous and gracious and wonderful women inside and out. They just weren't in their thirties anymore.

Thirtysomething Caroline, bejeweled in ropes of turquoise to match her eyes, was wearing a fabulous Indian skirt of sheer aqua gauze encrusted with tiny opalescent paillettes. Her silky camisole barely covered the goods, and her rock-hard tanned abdomen was exposed, revealing a rose tattoo on the top of her right hip. Her embroidered espadrilles brought her to nearly six feet in height and her shoulder-length blond hair was layered, swinging and moving every time she tossed her pretty head. Mr. Dylan Holmes couldn't keep his hands off her bare shoulder, bare arm or bare waist. The eyes of Stan and Harvey were riveted to her every move and their ears perked for any cookie she might toss their way. If great looks and being totally chic weren't bad enough, Caroline was the head of pediatric oncology at Emory University Hospital in Atlanta. If she had only been a moron she would have been a lot easier to like. They had all flown from Atlanta together on Dylan's GV, but there was little question that Liza and Marilyn were considering a commercial flight home.

"This part of Italy is so beautiful," Liza said. "Maybe we should stay and go to Corsica for a few days?"

"I think that sounds like a marvelous idea," Marilyn said. "Maybe our tour guide could help us arrange it."

I inwardly bristled at the title "tour guide," but who was I kidding? That's what I was—to them at least. The hired help— not the *principessa*.

"I'd be delighted to," I said. "Just let me know."

Caroline Sutter, M.D., was a constant reminder to women like Liza and Marilyn that if their Jedi husbands so chose, they could be dumped in an instant for a rising superstar. If someone like Caroline Sutter could burn brightly in the company of a fat old coot like Dylan Holmes, then someone like her could also be very satisfied with their balding Stan or paunchy Harvey in his Madras sport coat. All the men were on guard, and after the initial henpecking, icy glances, pinched inner arms and whispered remarks, they finally settled into behaviors that put their long-suffering wives slightly more at ease. After all, their attention to Caroline could cost them a trip to Buccellati. In this crowd, everything had its price.

I turned to see Massimo stepping sprightly down the walkway toward us. He wore a black suit, a white shirt and a black tie. Even in the intense heat, he seemed perfectly at ease, but a lifetime in the climate was probably the reason why.

"Are the buses here?" I said.

"Sì. Whenever your guests are ready . . ."

It was long after nine when the sun finally sank into the sky and we were all gathered, three tables of eight, in Da Gianni Pedrinelli, enjoying the cool breeze. Without any menu or any consultation, we were served a creamy gazpacho garnished with tiny shrimp, followed by spinach ravioli stuffed with Pecorino cheese topped with grilled langoustines and, finally, branzino baked in a thick paste of salt. It was the most delicious meal I had ever enjoyed on Italian soil and I was wishing I could pack up the chef and take him back to the States with me.

I finally began to relax a little, thinking with relief that Massimo had delivered on his promise. And, of course, as soon as I stopped obsessing about the success of the trip, I started obsessing about Michael. He had not called and I had been unable to reach him. I pulled out my cell and checked the messages. No messages. No missed calls. Well, maybe no news was good news, I told myself, and turned my attention back to the dinner and my clients. I went from guest to guest, inquiring about their rooms and asking if I could do anything for them. One guest couldn't get his wireless connection to deliver his e-mail. I said I would have it running smoothly by nine in the morning if he would give me his laptop that night. Another guest said she would love a massage the following afternoon and I said it would not be a problem. A few others had small requests, but overall, they loved their rooms and couldn't wait to have a swim in the gorgeous saltwater pool.

We lingered over gelato and coffee, no one really wanting to end the first night. Perhaps they were too weary from travel or too entranced by the setting. It had been a magical night, to be sure. But finally the men began to stretch and the women left to use the powder rooms, the signal that dinner was over.

"That was absolutely delicious," a guest said.

"I'm so glad you enjoyed it," I said, helping her up the steps of the bus.

Back at the hotel most guests returned to their rooms and a few of the men ambled over to the bar to smoke a cigar and have a whiskey. I went to my room to call Bomze and Michael. Bomze was first. It was just before five o'clock in Charleston.

"Hey! Just wanted to let you know that the group is all here and we are doing fine." I told him about dinner and the plans for the next few days. He was pleased and then became especially animated when he broke the news that he and the Baroness were headed to Moscow with the management of a huge software company and then on to St. Petersburg for a black-tie soiree at the Hermitage. Bomze liked nothing better than a chance to sport a white silk scarf, and heaven knows the Baroness was probably doing tiara inventory. My next assignment, he told me, was to take a group to Napa for a think tank on the food and wine industry.

"Wanna swap trips?" I said, knowing the answer in advance.

"Not a chance, tootsie."

"Well, Napa's better than Poughkeepsie," I said, adding, "You haven't heard from Michael, have you?"

"Michael? Heavens, no. Why would I hear from him? Is something wrong?"

"No, no. Everything's fine. Well, not really . . . I just thought . . . Well, he wasn't feeling great when I left and I've been trying to call him . . . Anyway, if you do . . ."

"Did you e-mail him?"

"No, my BlackBerry's signal isn't that great, so . . . Hey, don't worry about it. I'm sure he's okay."

"Okay, then . . ."

We chatted for a few more minutes and hung up. Bomze didn't sweat my competence and I was surely glad for that. I dialed home again and let the phone ring eight times. Voice mail didn't answer as it was supposed to and I wondered if Michael had received my other messages at all. Just as I was about to hang up he answered.

His voice didn't sound right. Was he sleeping?

"Hey! Loverboy! It's the woman of your dreams! Are you asleep?"

"Hey, sweetheart. Yeah, I just came home and took a nap."

"What's up with that? You sick?"

"No, no. I just keep having these headaches and today I got so nauseated . . . so I came home and decided to lie down for a while, that's all. I've been a little dizzy. But I'm fine. Really."

I knew he wasn't fine. Something wasn't right.

"Listen to me, Dr. Wonderful, lawyers shouldn't represent themselves and doctors shouldn't diagnose themselves. I want you to go see someone, okay? You work in the Medical University of South Carolina, for heaven's sake. There has to be somebody who can take a look at your gorgeous head tomorrow. Promise me, okay?"

"Okay. I'll go in and see who's there. How's the trip?"

We talked for a few minutes and then hung up. Michael did not sound like himself at all. Something was definitely wrong. Was there another woman? No. Michael wouldn't do that. Would he? No. Not in a million years. I just hated it when I couldn't reach him.

I went to my makeup bag and pulled out my sleeping pills. I couldn't afford a night of tossing and turning. It was going to be me, Mr. Smirnoff and the wonders of chemicals that would get me to sleep.

And they worked.

*   *   *

The morning brought cottonmouth, but two cappuccinos and a lot of water cured that. I wandered down to the breakfast buffet tent, and although it was early, you could already sense that the day ahead would bring no relief from the heat. Two couples from our group were at one table. Another couple was having breakfast with Dylan and Caroline. Everyone seemed chipper and anxious to start the day.

"The bus leaves at nine-thirty," I told everyone, and advised them all to bring bottled water and sunscreen.

We were an army of Burberry tote bags as we descended on the little town of Cagliari and its Cathedral of Santa Maria.

"It was built in the year 1200 by the Romans . . ."

Geri Post had begun her lecture and the group followed her like ducklings from side chapel to side chapel. I hung back, preferring to focus on the locals, who were there in the middle of the day, lighting candles and mumbling prayers, pushing along from one decade of the rosary to the next. A young woman kneeling before a statue of the Blessed Virgin caught my eye. She seemed so distraught and sincere, as though the statue would come to life and solve her problems. Wouldn't that be nice, I thought. And then I thought of Michael.

I looked at the statue of Mary and stared at her face with curiosity. I spent more time in churches than a saint, with all the tours I ran. But it had been so long since I had considered them to be anything more than historic buildings. The reality was that they were a brick-and-mortar extension of man's desire to connect with something greater than himself, something good and all-powerful who resided there, waiting for mankind to just ask if he/she/it/they could please take away the pain of the world. And it was then that I knew I was at risk of losing the only man I had ever loved. Don't ask me how I knew. I just did. Danger has its own internal stench.

I looked at the face of the Madonna and began to panic. What was I supposed to do? Pull out a rosary from thin air, shake off the mothballs, wipe off the dust and start to pray? Yeah, sure.

Like every other woman in the world who senses an imminent disaster, was I supposed to suddenly have this spiritual rebirth and connect with God? Forget God. After an absence such as mine, did I think God was waiting around for me just so He could grant me my wish? I had better odds on finding a genie in a bottle. But a woman might understand. A woman who had lost her own child would surely be more sympathetic. Still, with all the devout petitioners out there in the universe, would she even hear my rusty, creaking question? I knew I had a long trip to travel if I wanted access to Mary's heart—if there *was* a heart there or *somewhere* that would hear my plea. Hear my plea and show me the way to salvation? The thought of going to Mary in prayer made me shiver with trepidation. If she was in earshot, why would she listen to me?

All at once I was weak. I began to tremble and I couldn't control it. I had to get out of that church immediately or I was going to be sick.

I stumbled out through the heavy doors into the sunlight of the Piazza Palazzo and sat on a low wall. Despite the searing sun, I had chills and continued to shake. The last thing I remembered was closing my eyes to try to regulate my breathing and gather my composure.

"You okay?" I looked up to see Geri Post and some of our group.

"What? Oh, gosh. I must've passed out."

"We thought you were like dead sitting here like I don't know what."

"I'm fine," I said. "Is everyone here?" I stood up and felt okay then. Whatever bizarre physical reaction I had experienced had passed. "Are we ready for lunch? How did you like the cathedral?"

I chattered on like a magpie, trying to convince myself that everything was normal. After all, the act was half the battle. If you acted in control, people thought you were. If you appeared to have just had a religious experience and then passed out cold on the outside wall of a cathedral, people thought you were a lunatic. I was the lunatic in control. But what the hell had happened to me?

Later that evening, long after dinner, Geri Post and I had drinks on the terrace with some of our group. The late night was cool and clear and the sounds of the Mediterranean waters slapping our dock were almost music. One by one the guests surrendered, claiming jet lag or habit, and by midnight we were alone to review what the next few days would bring.

"After breakfast on Monday, I promised the ladies shopping in Porto Cervo. It's really fabulous, Geri. They have every Italian shop you can think of—well, the high-end stuff anyway."

"I hate shopping."

"I'm not mad about it either. Some of the men are playing golf at Pevero. Hey, here's a tidbit. Would you believe Robert Trent Jones built that course? Remember him? I only know this because my dad is a golf fanatic. Anyway, I met his son, Reese, and his wife, Susan, once. They were on a trip to New Zealand I ran for a museum in New Jersey. Loved them. They were the best. His old man wore knickers, you know."

"No kidding? You mean like flood pants?"

"Yep, argyle and tweed. And listen to this—Pevero? They spend a fortune to build this course and wild boars destroyed the greens. They had to fence it in. How crazy is that?"

"Pretty crazy," Geri said, and by the look on her face I could see that I might as well have been discussing a yo-yo contest. She continued: "So I've got boats arranged for tomorrow afternoon to take a group out to the national park for a swim and a picnic. I hired a mini fleet of old Chris-Crafts that were built in the sixties—relics but beautiful."

"Sounds good."

We chatted for a few more minutes and then out of the blue Geri Post said, "Are you a diabetic?"

"What? No! Why would you think that?"

"Because you looked like you might be. Today. You know. When I found you outside the church. You should be glad some little hooligan didn't run off with your purse."

"No. I'm not diabetic. I just felt sick, that's all, and when I got back outside in the heat I must have just drifted off. Probably jet lag and the heat combined."

"So what's wrong? I can tell when something's wrong. Yesterday, when we met, you were gregarious and outgoing, and this morning you seemed very out of sorts. Want to talk?"

I looked over at Geri and thought it surely would be very unusual for me to reveal all my worries to a colleague. It was something I had never done. It would have been unprofessional, and besides, even if I had decided to, the hour was late.

"Thanks," I said, "I'm okay. I really am."

"Well, if you need an ear . . ." She turned away to speak to the waiter about the bill.

"Thanks."

I needed an ear, just not one that could go back to Atlanta and run her mouth that was connected to an express train. It was very hard to know whom to trust and so far Geri seemed to be a talker. I hadn't been in Charleston long enough to establish any close friendships, and when I ticked off the list of those I had left behind, they were married or had moved, and to be honest, I didn't even know how to start to find a lot of my old girlfriends. Lots of women had cell phones whose numbers weren't listed with information and many of them changed their names when they got married. And anyway, what would I have said to them? That I'd left the country for business and I thought something was wrong with my boyfriend? They would've laughed and said he was probably worn out from carousing with a bunch of MUSC tomcats. They would probably have been right. Or something terrible was happening.

CHAPTER 6

Bad Boys and Bimbos

By ten in the morning the ladies were whizzing all around Porto Cervo, in and out of couture boutiques, and I watched them spend money so fast it seemed like a marathon. There was no negotiating, no calculating the exchange rate and worrying if they could do better in Atlanta, and half the time they didn't even look at the price tags. They just whipped out the black, platinum or gold American Express cards and never missed a beat in their conversations. My hands got sweaty just watching them. I would take their shopping bags, label them and give them to the bus driver while they continued on to the next string of boutiques. For a few moments I wondered what it would be like to have that kind of money to burn and then I decided that even if I did have it, I probably wouldn't spend it like they did.

But it was easy to be caught up in the frenzy of the moment because Porto Cervo was an absolutely charming seaside town. The large stones of the piazza spread out over an area probably two hundred feet by two hundred feet, and as in most of Italy, space was at a premium, every inch of it used wisely. In the middle of the square were several open-air restaurants serving lunch at simple tables with umbrellas. Down the hill, not too far in the distance, was the harbor. Sailboats and yachts of every description, tied up to their moorings, bobbed gently in the waters. When I thought about the afternoon's excursion to the national forest, I couldn't wait. It would feel awfully good to be speeding across the open water. But until then I was content to enjoy the beautiful landscape that sprawled before me and load my charges' packages on the bus.

"Would you ladies like to eat here or return to the hotel?" I said to some of the women standing in the shade. "They have that fabulous buffet . . ."

My cell phone rang with my mother's ring tone. That was unnerving because she knew I was in Italy. Stepping away from the group, I dug through my bag and answered it as quickly as I could.

"Mom?"

"Grace?"

"Is everything okay?"

"No! Nonna had a terrible fall. Grace, she broke her hip! She's in the hospital. When are you coming home?"

"Middle of this week. Oh my God! Is she all right?"

"No. No, she's not. I'm afraid she's going to die, Grace."

Some uncharitable things went through my head like *We're all gonna die sometime, you know.* And *At least you'll have a little peace and quiet.*

"She's not gonna die, Mom. Let me call you when I get back to the hotel, okay?"

"Fine. I just need—"

"I'll call you within the hour." I closed my phone, ending the call. I put my game face back on and returned to the group. "I have made an executive decision. Anyone who wants to stay here for lunch—that's fine. I'll send the bus back in"—I stopped to look at my watch—"one hour and fifteen minutes. That will give you thirty minutes to change for the boat trip, if you are signed up for that."

Everyone nodded and one lady said, "You sure are a little bit bossy, Grace."

"Somebody's gotta be in charge," I said. "It may as well be me."

Everyone snickered. At that moment I decided I disliked this group. I knew these dark feelings were rooted in my fears about Michael and fertilized by my grandmother's fall. Nonetheless, these women were so shallow and not the most intelligent humanity I had ever carted around, with the exception of Caroline Sutter, the oncologist. But even her—I mean, why in the world would she hook up with a disgusting old fart like Dylan Holmes? Money, I decided. HMOs had all but decimated the wealth of the medical community. She needed a walking wallet, and a Gulfstream jet—a Five, thank you, which, depending on how you fitted it out, could have a dozen recliners, enough burled walnut to choke a horse and an ivory leather toilet seat—didn't hurt either.

On the other hand, I reminded myself that these women were not obligated to entertain or impress me. Even though they made me feel like a travel agent. And even called me a tour guide. Well, what could you say? It *was* what I did. I was not their peer, and it irked me every time something would happen to remind me of it. On another day, I might not have minded them at all. I was just gestating dark thoughts because of Michael and my mother's phone call.

I finally got to my room and called my mother back. I could tell she was crying when I heard her voice.

"So tell me what exactly happened, Mom."

"It was all my fault, Grace."

"Oh, come on, Mom!"

"No, I swear on the Bible, it was my fault. I had just washed the kitchen floor and she came in looking for the newspaper and she slipped. The next thing I know she's screaming and yelling . . ."

"So what's new? That doesn't make it your fault."

"Please, Grace! Yes, it does!"

"Sorry."

"Anyway, I called 911 and I told her not to get up. But she tried to get up anyway and fell again. Oh, dear heaven, was she mad at me! I have *never* seen her so angry."

"She's *always* angry with you, Mom."

"Sometimes it seems like it, doesn't it? They took her to the emergency room and I followed her to the hospital and I called your father because I had to call him to fill out all the papers and he came . . . . I'll tell you, Grace, it's too much for me. She had to have an operation. All this is just—"

"How is she now?"

"Sedated—she's sleeping. But even your father, even Daddy is angry with me. He blames me, too."

She began to sob and I felt terrible for being so unsympathetic.

"Oh, Mama, come on now. Don't cry. Don't you know there's nothing worse than listening to your mother cry?"

"I'm sorry, but I just don't know what to do next. If she dies and I have to carry that on my conscience, I think I might just die, too."

Oh, please, I thought. "Did you call Aunt Theresa?"

"No, I don't want to bother her. What can she do?"

"Well, she might want to send flowers, Mom. And God forbid something happens . . ."

"You're right, you're right . . . I'll call her tonight when your father gets home."

"Why are you waiting for Dad to get home?"

"Because he'll want to talk to her about this, too, and I don't want to waste the phone call."

"But, Ma! What if Aunt Theresa wants to get on a plane or something?"

"Grace, you know she can't do that. She doesn't have the time to go running all around the country."

"Would you like me to send her a ticket?"

"No. Don't bother. She probably can't take the time off from work anyway."

"Well, look. Call your sister, and if anything changes call me back right away. Otherwise, I'll call you tomorrow and I'll come see you next Thursday or Friday, okay?"

We hung up and I just sat there on my bed staring at the wall. My poor mother was so desperately insecure. It was frustrating for me and awful for her. I was so "solution-and-next-step-oriented." She was actually taking the blame for my grandmother's accident. She was too unsure of herself to fill out hospital forms. She didn't think her own sister would accept her description of Nonna's fall as accurate, that Aunt Theresa would prefer to get the real story from my father. And my aunt Theresa, who owned and ran a bakery with my uncle Tony back in New Jersey, probably wouldn't take the time from work because they never hired enough people to cover for them if they weren't there. They never went anywhere. Aunt Theresa would send some carnations through FTD and two pounds of the cookies she made with pignoli nuts. Nice. Nonna would go on and on about how wonderful they were, and at the end of the day my mother would be miserable.

My mother could not possibly be a happy woman. I wondered for the second time in a week what there was to be done about it. Looking back quickly over the Fourth of July holiday, I could hardly remember a kind word that my father or my grandmother had had for her. It had to stop. What had she ever done to deserve such a lack of respect and affection? Nothing. I knew that for a fact.

I looked at my watch and realized I had better hurry if I was to take this group out on the boats we had reserved. I was late and I thought to myself that they were probably all waiting on the docks, rolling their eyes, tapping the dial of their diamond-encrusted wristwatches with their acrylic fingernail tips.

Sure enough, they were.

"Hi! Sorry! I had to make a phone call."

Some of the people looked extremely annoyed and I thought, *Oh, screw you. I don't make enough money to take your grief.* You have to understand that although I lived a vicarious existence through my clients, I wasn't in a perfect mood every minute of every day. And these were not long-term relationships; this group would be replaced by another within days. Let's face the facts. Doing what I did made you jaded and I decided the tiniest guilt trip was in order—nothing that could rise to the level of unprofessional. Just a small dart. I jumped on board the first boat and offered one of the older gals a hand to make the little leap.

"My grandmother broke her hip," I said. "I had to talk to my mother, who's understandably hysterical."

"Oh!" she said, no longer irritated. "How dreadful! I'm so sorry!"

Cluck, cluck, cluck. She told another lady, who told another wife, and suddenly the Pucci, Louis and Hooey bitches of the Smeralda Coast were the souls of compassion. And as they put their attitudes of entitlement aside, I thought, *That's more like it, girls,* and began to relax again.

The captain of our boat opened a bottle of champagne and poured out eight plastic glasses.

"Salute!" he said.

In minutes we were tearing up the Mediterranean and the guests were back at work on building their afternoon buzz. The good thing about the ride was that the boat was so noisy I couldn't hear their chatter. They gathered on the stern, lounging on the huge white leather cushions, and I checked out the picnic the hotel had packed for us. There were small sandwiches of ham, salmon and some kind of cheese spread. There was a large bag of pretzels, a small box of cookies, fruit— grapes and apples. The cooler had bottled water and sodas that would surely go untouched. Because there were four bottles of champagne and four bottles of white wine. For six guests, the captain and me. Stunning. What could you say? The chef knew his audience.

This bunch drank wine with lunch, cocktails around the pool, champagne on the boat and vast quantities of wine with dinner. The amount of alcohol they consumed was unbelievable. It was a wonder they didn't drop dead, fall into the sea or pass out in their macaroni. They didn't. Obviously I knew they were on vacation, no one was driving a car anywhere, and they were old enough to do as they pleased, but let me tell you, every group didn't drink like these characters. They were a gang of Judy Garlands and Dean Martins on the express train to liver-transplant hell. But in a first-class cabin, of course.

Later that afternoon, right before the cocktail hour that was so highly anticipated by my group, I ran into Geri Post at the outside bar. She had an open notebook on the table along with Michelin guides and maps.

"You're sunburned," she said with her typical aplomb. "That's gonna hurt like the devil."

"I'll take an aspirin. Move over and I'll buy you a Coke. Hey, two of the guests want to do a 'go-see' at some of the ancient sites," I said. "What does tomorrow morning look like?"

"Sounds like a road trip to me. I was thinking about touring the interior, but that's a whole day's trip. I'll call Massimo the Gorgeous and ask him to line up a couple of jitneys. It's a little bit of a hike, but we could visit the old church in Sassari first. They have a patchwork cathedral from the thirteenth century. It's Spanish and Gothic. Then we could have lunch in the square . . . ."

"And they can drink a case of wine . . ."

Geri giggled at that. "Or two! Then they can sleep it off while we drive over to Nuoro to see the nuraghi and the local color."

"Geri?"

"Yeah?"

"What are nuraghi?"

"Cone-shaped stacked-stone buildings from two thousand years ago. Maybe longer. Built by the Cretans. Hey, by the way, I heard about your grandmother. How's she doing?"

"Well, she's in the hospital, which is the best place for somebody with a broken hip. And I'm sure she's got enough pain medication. My mother's hysterical over the whole thing—

thinks it was her fault. And actually, my grandmother blames her. So does my father. Families, right?"

The strangest look came over Geri's face. "Is your grandmother your mother's mother or your father's mother?"

"Oh, she's my mother's mother. Why?"

"Just seems kind of unnecessary. Oh, I'm sorry. I'm so opinionated. I just hate finger-pointing, that's all. I mean, unless your mother is diabolical or something . . . ."

"No, don't apologize. I'd love a sane adult opinion on this. My mom's a pussycat. Connie Russo wouldn't stomp a bug."

"So she didn't push her down the stairs or anything, right?"

"My mother? When I was little, my mother used to go to her room and cry all afternoon if she spanked my backside for being fresh or something. I didn't cry. I was as defiant as I could be."

"I'll bet you gave your mother lip, all right." Geri smiled and so did I.

"Yeah, I did."

Geri looked me square in the face and spoke with deliberateness. "Then what's the point of making her feel bad? And why is your father taking your grandmother's side? You have to wonder."

"I do wonder. My father has an odd personality sometimes. He's wonderful and all, but I guess he thinks Nonna has no one but them—she lives with them—and he's *the man* and all that. My grandmother? She's just crabby and picky. Always has been. I feel sorry for my mom."

"Well, then, just be sweet to her and as supportive as you can. Everybody needs somebody to stick up for them now and then."

"You are absolutely right, Geri Post. Thanks for the inspiration. I have always just been my mom's daughter and it's time for me to take up her cause."

"Well, congratulations, Grace Russo. You've just jumped another hurdle into womanhood!"

"I'll see you later."

Crossing the lobby, I saw Massimo and he waved me over.

"*Buona sera,* Signore Floris, how was your day?"

"*Ciao! Perfecto!*" he said, and clasped his hands. "I just want to know from the big boss how the trip is going. Are your guests happy? Can we do anything for them? I just booked a return trip for two of the gentlemen. They are coming back in two weeks and bringing their nieces. Isn't that a wonderful idea? I have to say that Americans are so generous . . ."

"Massimo?"

"What a country!"

"Massimo?"

"*Sì?*"

"I've got a hundred euros that says they aren't nieces at all."

Massimo covered his mouth in mock horror and widened his eyes. He whispered across the counter, "*Prego! Bella!* What have I said?" Then he winked at me and we started to laugh.

"People are so stupid," I said. "Don't worry. Our suspicions go to the grave with me."

"You wouldn't believe what I see."

"And you wouldn't believe what I see either."

Later that night after dinner, after drinks, after pleasant good nights and inquiries about my grandmother's health (the story had traveled throughout the group), I found myself alone in my room, unable to sleep.

I had a sudden realization.

Sometimes young women just needed to cry. You needed a good cry, where the tears would run down your shirt or your nightgown and you could wail in private about all your disappointments. And since they might have seemed petty to others, that privacy thing was essential. Maybe it was hormonal. Maybe it was hormonal, with reality thrown in. But I had my reasons.

My mother was miserable on a very deep level and I had never done a thing to address it. What did that say about me? That I was a terrible daughter. I had recently admitted to myself that my father was an embarrassment, but I still took his support. What did that say about me? That I was a terrible daughter. Michael was acting strange and that was completely unnerving, so how secure was I in his love? And I made my living this way. With all these *people*.

I made a brave effort to defend myself as I stood looking out at the dark waters of the Mediterranean and made a few brief calculations about life—brief out of deference to the hour.

One, I had gotten into this business because I loved to travel and maybe there was a part of me that loved running away to have an adventure.

Two, I had never felt like my clients were so frivolous before today, so therefore I must have been suffering a hormone surge or deficit. Or maybe they *were* a bunch of jerks, but I should remain professional and overlook it. After all, they were the source of my ability to support myself.

Three, I loved Michael, and I would never abandon him despite the ravings of my family; his love was the most important thing that had ever happened to me. It was the first time I had really taken the risk of emotional mutilation and I wasn't going to get paranoid just because of a couple of strange phone calls.

Four, Nonna's broken hip was not the fault of my poor mother. Well, if I had anything to do with it, she wasn't going to be *poor mother* anymore.

Five, I found it strange that for the past few days I had developed the habit of invoking God's name when I was shocked or surprised or annoyed. For someone who wasn't sure about a warm, loving and personal God's true existence, why did I keep calling? Was it an old habit, conditioned response, or was I truly searching for something?

CHAPTER 7

Shooting from the Hip

I landed in Charleston at four-thirty on Wednesday. I was dead bone tired. I had been offered a hop on Dylan Holmes's Gulfstream, but I declined. For all the traveling I did, crossing the Atlantic Ocean strapped into something only slightly larger than my sofa still scared the liver out of me. So I sucked it up, flew commercial and obsessed about the two people on my mind—Michael and my mother. My brother Frank might have called me paranoid, but I'd had female guts long enough to know that just because you're paranoid doesn't mean something's *not* out to get you.

The flight from Rome to Atlanta was long enough and then there was the short flight to Charleston. By the time it was all over, I had been flying and waiting around, flying and waiting around, forever. There was something so strange about crossing time zones. I always felt like part of me had been left behind. Jet lag. Although over time I would feel normal again, I didn't feel whole when I unlocked my door. Part of me was still flying. Part of me was still in Sardinia somewhere. If I'd had a fishing rod with a special hook, maybe I could have reeled the rest of me home. That might sound crazy, but I would have bet a couple of dollars that somebody in a lab somewhere was figuring out how to do just that.

Jet lag caused even my initial perception of my surroundings to appear different. The bedroom looked smaller, the living room seemed sterile, the kitchen felt unfamiliar. I knew that by tomorrow the place would feel like mine again, but meanwhile it looked like it could use brighter lightbulbs, a coat of paint and some fresh flowers.

Michael wasn't home. It was late afternoon and I was glad that I had time to unpack, take a shower and figure out dinner. And to call my mother.

Yesterday when we'd spoken, she told me Nonna was driving the nurses crazy. Nonna wailed about the food, the room was too hot, the room was too cold, the neighbors were too noisy— she had survived her surgery and was pissed off in purple plaid and lavender paisley. The physical therapist was seeing her once a day and doing some gentle exercises with her to move her hip. Nonna screamed the whole time. Nice, I thought, very nice. I couldn't wait to see *her!*

Mom was still beside herself. If Nonna needed additional pain meds, Mom needed something for nerves. She answered on the second ring.

"Hi! I'm home!"

"Thanks be to God! Are you coming tomorrow?"

"You know it. I'll be there before lunch. Give me the update."

"Update? Oh, Lord, Grace. She's fighting with the orthopedic surgeon. She's fighting with the physical therapist."

"Not the model patient?"

"Not the model patient."

"Is she giving you a hard time?"

"Are you kidding me? If I was the kind of woman who liked alcohol . . ."

"Got the picture. Hang in there, Connie. Your widdle girl is coming to the rescue tomorrow. What can I bring you?" Oh, no! I had used the Marianne voice!

"Nothing. Just come."

"I was planning to pick up a lot of magazines. Listen to me. I've been doing a lot of thinking. You and I need to have a serious talk."

There was a long silence and then she said, "About what?"

"About your personal happiness and about our mother-daughter relationship."

"We're fine, aren't we?"

"Yeah, but I could be a little more useful. I think we need to figure out why Nonna and Dad are always picking on you, and put a stop to it. I don't like the way she talks to you and—"

"Ah, Grace. Don't worry about it. She's an old lady with a broken hip, and even if I turn one hundred years old and she's one hundred and twenty-five, she'll still add salt to my gravy and tell me what's wrong with everything I do. It's how she is."

"And so what's Dad's excuse?"

"He's not so terrible."

"Okay, we'll talk. I'll see you tomorrow. Love you . . ."

We hung up and I thought, Shoot, she didn't even ask me how my trip was. She *must* be stressing.

I dialed Michael's cell and got his voice mail.

"Hi, sweetheart," I said. "Just wanted to let you know that I got home in one piece. I'm sure you're busy, so gimme a shout when you have a minute and let me know what you want to do about dinner, okay? Love you . . ."

I decided a bowl of pasta was in order for our meal that night and that making the sauce before the exhaustion of the trip set in was probably a good idea. I unpacked, threw my dirty clothes in the wash, made a pile for the dry cleaners and put cold water on my face about five times in the struggle to stay awake.

I chopped and sautéed two large onions and three cloves of sliced garlic, added two large cans of whole tomatoes, which I cut into chunks in the pan, and a handful of fresh basil from the garden, and I let it simmer for an hour, periodically adding a little white wine or a little olive oil. It smelled divine. I filled a large pot of water to boil the noodles and rescued a loaf of frozen garlic bread from the very back of the freezer. All I would have to do was boil water and throw the foil packet of bread in the oven.

I was putting the second load of laundry in the washer when Michael finally called.

"Welcome back," he said. "I missed you."

"Hey! Come home!" I said. "I need a man in a very desperate way."

"ASAP," he said. "Just gotta tie up a few things here. Can I bring anything?"

"Yeah, a bag of radicchio and endive and your gorgeous bod," I said with a smile in my voice. "Oh, and a lemon."

"Sure thing. See you before six and don't give me the business about you being tired. I have expectations, you know."

"Thank God. Hey, how are you feeling?"

"What? Oh, I'm fine. I spoke to this guy who's a neurologist and he said it was most likely seasonal allergies. There's been some nasty sinusitis going around—anyway, no big deal. So he sent me to see this ENT guy and I'm taking an antihistamine. I feel a heck of a lot better."

"Good! Well, I can't wait to see you . . ."

Wait to see him? I was sinking like a stone from the trip and I thought that maybe a nap might be the ticket. On the other hand, I knew that if I closed my eyes, I was gone for the night.

"Cold shower! Coffee!" I said out loud.

The shower helped. I was dressed and stirring the sauce when I heard Michael coming up the walkway. Stay inside and be coy, or run outside like a schoolgirl and tackle him? I opted for the tackle.

"Wow!" he said when I threw my arms around him and one leg over his hip, nearly toppling us into the azaleas and boxwood. "That's what I call a welcome home!"

"I am so glad to see you. You have no idea." He looked so good to me I thought I might faint. I laughed instead.

86   *Dorothea Benton Frank*

"Feed me," he said, and kissed me like he was starving for more than a hot meal.

"Yes, sir!"

I served dinner, we talked a little about my trip and more about my grandmother. I was too tired to relive it all, but I told him I was going down to Hilton Head to check on her the next day.

"You have to go," he said. "And if you don't like the looks of things, we can have her moved up here in a heartbeat. I mean, I'm sure the hospital there is great, with all the geriatric population and all that, but MUSC is state-of-the-art, right?"

"Right," I said. "My grandmother would be thrilled to be under your watchful eye. We could put Big Al and Connie on the sleeper sofa while we're upstairs doing the wild thing, and—"

"Well, give them my best anyway and tell them I made the offer, okay?"

"You know I will. Thanks, baby."

As a result of the time change, morning came early for me. I slipped into the bathroom and, making as little noise as possible, showered and dressed in a pair of jeans and a T-shirt from an old Rod Stewart concert, and with my flip-flops over the hook of my finger, I left Michael a note.

Hi, sweetie. I'm off to see the Wizard and I'll be back before ten tonight. Call me later. Love you!

I stopped at a Krispy Kreme and bought my grandmother a dozen glazed doughnuts because I knew she loved them. And I bought her an armful of tabloids with cover stories on such important happenings as definitive proof of alien babies, Elvis sightings and real photographs of Bigfoot because I knew they were one of her guilty pleasures. Not that any of this would truly please her, because while she was an old battle-ax, she loved her independence. As long as she was confined to a bed and working with a physical therapist, she was going to be insufferable.

It was eight-thirty when I arrived at my parents' house. Dad's car was gone and I was slightly relieved that I wouldn't have to deal with him. I could envision Mom washing up the breakfast dishes and I was right. I came in through the garage and there she was by the sink with CNN blaring in the background. I had tooted my horn to let her know I was there, and a second pot of coffee was already brewing. The house smelled like it always did and in the space of that moment I was a child again. Well, not a child exactly—maybe a teenager.

"Hi, Mom!" I said, and gave her a kiss on the cheek.

"Oh, Grace!" She dried her hands on her apron and hugged me. "I'm so glad you're here! Did you eat, baby?"

"No, but I could sure go for an Eggo or something. What's in the house?" I went digging in the freezer, pulled out a box of frozen waffles and dropped one in the toaster. "Do you have peanut butter?"

"Smooth or chunky?" She pulled out a jar of each variety from the cabinet.

"No one buys groceries like Connie Russo."

I sat at the table and spread a knifeful over the waffle. Mom sat down with two mugs of coffee and sighed. She brushed the nonexistent wrinkles from the tablecloth and sighed again.

"Cream?" she said.

"Sure."

I watched her get up again and go to the refrigerator. She opened the door and, as though in a trance, poured a measure of half-and-half into the little ceramic cow she had used as a creamer since I gave it to her for her birthday when I was about ten. I loved that she was so tenderhearted. That cow and the old potholders and all the things we kids had given her over the years were precious to her. It must have been wonderful to be satisfied so easily, I thought. But then she sat down again and sighed again and I thought I would lose my mind then and there.

"Talk to me, Connie. You're sighing too much. Excessive sighing is a sign of depression. What's going on around here?"

"Oh, well, let's see. Nonna is doing fine. They want to put her in a rehab facility at the end of this week and she won't go. She says it's a nursing home and she'd rather die than go and she says that I am a lazy good-for-nothing daughter to say that I can't take care of her at home. She just doesn't understand that she needs physical therapy and not just someone to make her meals. But your father says that if Nonna doesn't want to go to this rehab facility, then she doesn't have to, that I can take care of her right here."

"Did he really say that?"

"Grace, you have no idea. They think . . . I don't know what they think."

"Mom, this is exactly what I mean about there being some very big issues between you and them. Why, for the love of God, would Dad think it's okay for you to be in charge of Nonna's day-to-day recovery from something major like this? You're not their slave! Just because Dad and Nonna want you to do something, you don't have to go along with them, you know. How about if you just say no?"

"Grace, you know I can't do that."

"This is crazy. Get in the car. Watch how we're gonna figure this out together. You and me, Mom. We're gonna figure this out."

"I can't go now. I have to shower and fix my hair and then I have to wait for the sprinkler man to come . . ."

"Your hair is fine. Get your pocketbook. We can leave the sprinkler man a note."

"Oh, Grace, I don't know . . ."

"I do! Where's a pen and some paper?"

She handed me a notepad and a Bic pen and left the room. I turned off the television and the coffeepot and wrote on the paper.

Hi! Please fix the sprinkler and clean the heads. If you need us you can call us on my cell at 843-555-7788. Thanks a lot!
Connie Russo

"I could use a cell phone," Mom said as we rode toward the hospital. "But Al says it's not necessary. Why spend the money?"

"You'll have one before lunch," I said. "They're a crummy ten dollars a month or something. Dad's wrong. Not having one limits your ability to go where you want to go when you want to go. You have to blow your morning waiting around for a sprinkler man? I don't think that's the best use of your time. Do you?"

"You're right. But I don't want to defy your father, Grace. You know he's got a temper."

"Like a freaking wild animal he's got a temper, but so do I. You can have a phone on my account, okay? Call it a Christmas gift."

"I don't know, honey. I don't want trouble."

"Mom! Stop it! We're gonna organize Nonna's recovery, get you a cell phone and then figure out why you think it's okay for them to treat you like this. Okay? *That's* what we're gonna do."

During the ride to the hospital and as we made our way down the hall toward Nonna's room, I could see my mother wring her hands and wipe perspiration from her forehead. She was completely unnerved at the thought of upsetting Nonna and my father. But how in the world could they expect her to be Nonna's primary caretaker? Nonna weighed almost two hundred pounds and, as you already know, was one cantankerous walrus when she felt like it.

"Stop fretting, Connie. We've got doughnuts."

We pushed the door open and there was my grandmother, half-reclined, pushing the buttons on the television remote like a madwoman. She spotted my mother and started complaining.

"I want to watch *General Hospital,* but I can't get this stupid thing to work! Get me out of here! I want to go home!" But when she spotted me her voice softened and she smiled. "Oh! Maria Graziana! *Bella mia!* You finally came to see your poor old dying grandmother! Did you bring me doughnuts? You good girl! There's nothing to eat in this whole place. Put them right here and come let me look at you."

"Hi, Nonna," I said. "You're looking pretty spry for someone with a cracked hip. How are you feeling?"

"I'm going to miss my story and Julie Barr is going to a big party today. I have to see her dress! You understand, don't you, *bella*? Now fix this for me. *Prego!*"

Even though I never watched the soaps, I knew what she was talking about. Nonna had watched *All My Children* and *General Hospital* since before I was born. I changed the station and Nonna smiled.

"Now give me one of those doughnuts so I can enjoy my story!"

"Okay, okay. Let me get some napkins, Nonna."

"Wash your hands, Graziana. There are germs everywhere, especially in this filthy place."

I stepped into Nonna's little bathroom and I could hear her warming up her rant.

"Your mother wants to put me in the nursing home, Grace! Did you hear me? A nursing home! I knew this would happen! I knew it!"

"Hush, Ma, you know that's not true," I heard my mother say.

"You don't tell me what to do! Where's your respect? I heard you talking to that nurse!"

I hurried out of the bathroom and back to Nonna's side and took her hand, patting the back of it.

"Nonna, I think what we have to do is get your doctor and your physical therapist in here and get the facts, okay? I'll be right back. You just stay cool for a few minutes, okay? Promise?"

Nonna exhaled the rancid breath of someone who had brushed their teeth hours ago and since then had consumed many cups of strong coffee. The caffeine probably wasn't helping her mood either and I would bring that up with the doctor. I went to the nurses' station; there was a zaftig but saintly woman behind the counter who looked up when I approached.

"Francesca Todero's granddaughter, I presume?"

"Yeah, hi. I'm Grace Russo. Um, listen, is there some way that we could get my grandmother's doctor and physical therapist together in one room to talk about my grandmother's rehab?"

"I think our padded room is booked, but I can see about the visitors' lounge for y'all. How's that? I'll be glad to make the phone calls for you. She's a real spitfire, isn't she?"

"Is she giving you a hard time?"

"Not me, honey. I'm the nurse that hands out the pain meds. She's a sweet little lamb when she sees me coming. And when she goes to rehab—and she *will* go—I'll look out for her there, too. I'm over there on my days off. Two kids in college!"

"Got it! Thanks."

The nurse, whose name tag read *N. Divine, RN,* gave the half chuckle of one in charge and I smiled and shook my head, knowing exactly what she meant. When you had something Nonna wanted, she was the living embodiment of heaven's sweetest, most radiant angel, with gossamer wings and the scent of paradise all around her. When you aggravated her and she didn't want what you were selling—in this case, a short stint of rehab in a dreaded nursing home—she would curse you in Italian and gesture so wildly that you knew your grandchildren would be born with disfiguring warts and uneven limbs. Trolls. Your grandchildren would be trolls. You were well advised to weigh your odds and gauge your battle strategy to minimize your own wounds and those of your progeny. An argument with her was not one to be taken up on a whim. I made my case to Nurse Divine and it was short and sweet.

"Do you have a moment?"

"Sure."

"Well, here's the story . . . ."

I told her about Nonna's phobia regarding nursing homes . . . .

"She thinks they're like Roach Motels—the roaches check in but they never check out?"

"I remember that ad," she said.

I told her about Nonna's fear of abandonment and that nursing homes just weren't the old-world Italian way of doing things, that your grandmother stayed in the hospital until she was well. Nursing homes were the biggest *disgrazia* that could happen to an Italian because it meant you had nobody who loved you, and what did it say to live a whole life and have nobody who loved you? That there was something terrible going on, that's what.

Nurse Divine understood perfectly.

"And your little skinny mother is supposed to bathe her and dress her and perform her physical therapy? And your little skinny mother is supposed to judge how well she's coming along? I don't think so."

"You got it. My father and my grandmother would wear my mother out and never suffer a moment's guilt about it. It's a daughter's duty to take care of her mother even if she's not qualified and even if it's not a realistic situation."

The divine Nurse Divine shook her head. "I hate that attitude, but it happens every day, Grace. However, don't you worry. I'll do my best, okay?"

"Good. Thanks. I mean it."

"Glad to help. Now, did I see a box of Krispy Kremes in your hands?"

"I'll be right back."

If all it took was a couple of doughnuts to get my mother off the nursemaid/private-slave hook—no, the giant *flying gaff* my father had her hanging from—then Nurse Divine would be drowning in glaze, sprinkles and cream filling. I made a mental note to tell Mom to buy a box of a dozen bribes for every day Nonna remained in this place.

When I returned with two glazed beauties on a napkin, Nurse Divine was on the phone. "Hold on," she said, and smiled from ear to ear when she saw what I had for her. She whispered, "I'm on the phone with her caseworker."

We gave each other the okay signal and I went back to Nonna's room.

Nonna wasn't going to be completely happy about it, but she wasn't going to terrorize my mother. She was going to a nursing home just for rehabilitation, not forever.

CHAPTER 8

When It Rains It Pours

The sprinkler company had come, done their work, left a detailed bill in the mailbox and gone on to their next job. Mom was a little bit amazed that she hadn't had to sit there and hold a vigil until they showed up and then stand over them to ensure that they did the job right.

"If they didn't really, really clean the sprinkler heads, Al will throw a fit," she said in a worried voice.

"Well, then, let's go have a look and see," I said.

It was noon and we had come home for a bite of lunch and planned to go back to see Nonna around two.

"I'll get us a glass of tea," she said.

We walked around the yard inspecting the work, and overall the crew had done a fine job, only missing one or two sprinkler heads that we simply cleaned ourselves with the toothpicks Mom produced from her pocket. I had to admire her advance tactical thinking—she wasn't going to take any more grief than was absolutely necessary. There had been a broken pipe in one zone, but that was all fixed, too. She evened out the dirt around it with her hands and spread the ground cover here and there to disguise the fact that a little surgery had been performed in the area of Big Al's blue myrtle.

"You worry too much, Mom," I said. "Let's go make some tomato sandwiches."

We were sitting at the kitchen table eating and I was fooling around with her new cell phone.

"Ma, look. Here's the ring tone for Dad." I pressed a button and it played "That's Amore." "And here's mine." It played the same song I had for her when she called me: "Over the Rainbow." "So every time you hear this coming out of your purse, you'll know it's me. And if it plays Italian music, you'll know it's Dad. It's simple, really."

"And all I have to do is recharge it on this gizmo?" She held up the long wire.

"Yeah, but you gotta *remember* to recharge it, so let's find a place where you can leave it. Where do you put your purse when you come in the house?"

"In my bedroom, on my dresser."

I found a plug behind her dresser and plugged it in, anchoring the plug around the bottom of a statue of Our Lady of Guadalupe.

"That's sacrilegious," Connie said.

"Oh, it is not," I said, and smiled. "For all the statues you have in this house, at least let one of them do a little something to help you out."

My mother gasped and then she looked sheepish.

"What?" I said.

"Nonna would never approve," she said, and attempted to hide the wire.

"Can I ask you a question without you thinking that I'm being fresh?"

"Sure."

"How old do you have to be before you can stop living your life trying to please your mother?"

"I guess it depends on who the mother is."

"Good answer, but in this case, you *do* realize that you will *never* please Nonna, don't you?"

"It's the price I pay for being the one she lives with, I guess. Familiarity breeds contempt."

"That's pretty lame, don't you think? I mean, you take care of her, and that gives her the right to pick at you all the time? Mom, we have to talk about this. I thought the Fourth of July was completely out of control."

"What are you talking about?"

"Mom, Nonna and Dad act like they own you for the pleasure of kicking you around. I mean, maybe you're just so used to it you don't notice it anymore, but everyone else does."

"Oh, honey, I don't care . . ."

"Even Frank and Regina had a few words to say about how Dad and Nonna acted toward you."

"What do you mean?"

"Look, let's start with this whole thing about Nonna's hip. You wash the floor every Monday and Thursday night after supper since I can remember, right?"

"Well, sometimes there's a special novena on the first Thursday of the month. I go down to St. Francis—"

"Okay, okay. But *usually* the world can set its watch by when Connie Russo's kitchen floor is wet, correct?"

"Except now I have this Swiffer—"

"Yeah, I got one, too. So it's actually less wet, right?"

"Yeah, maybe. So?"

"So she *knew* the floor would be damp or wet! How is that *your* fault?"

"She says I should've told her to watch where she was walking. I mean, she's probably right. I heard her coming and I didn't say anything."

I could hardly believe my ears. It was so completely ridiculous.

"You know what? I think it is incredibly frustrating to be you, Mom. Because you can't win. If the floor is wet and you do warn her, Nonna could say she didn't hear you because she's deaf. We all know she's capable of throwing blame your way for any and everything. If she had slipped in the bathroom, she might have said you put the wrong bath mat down and it wasn't flat enough or something—it had a wrinkle. She's got you reduced to something like a punching bag. She sits in Dad's chair, barks orders to you and you hop."

"Oh, come on. Listen, Grace, the worst thing is for an old person to feel like a burden. She's my mother, you know? I mean, I want her to feel like this is her house, and yes, I know she's a little overbearing. And I know that she's very critical of me. But you have to understand, Grace, she comes from another world, where the mother is the queen of the family and her word is law. And I honestly think she just wants me to be the best wife and mother that I can be."

"Sorry, Connie. I'm not buying that." I searched my mother's face and got the same placid look she always had—her shield. "There's something else between you two and I don't know what it is, but it's not good. It's almost like she doesn't trust you to choose which tomato to pick from the garden."

My mother became tense and I could tell from her voice and from the position of her shoulders that she was going to tell me the least amount possible to get through this conversation. "Oh, it's not so bad. Really. It's not."

"Mom, can I ask you something else?" Not that I thought she had the slightest intention of giving me a truthful answer or that she would share a confidence with me.

"Of course."

"Are you and Daddy happy? I mean, are you in love with each other?"

At the moment it seemed like the most outrageous question anyone had ever asked her. Without warning, there came forth the greatest sigh of all Connie Russo's sighs, which no doubt whooshed the butterflies on the west coast of Africa all the way to Beijing. We looked at each other for a moment and then we laughed, each of us for a litany of our own reasons.

"He's impossible," I said, realizing that whether she and my father were in love or not was a matter of no consequence.

"Of course I love him, Grace!"

"He means well," I said, knowing that they loved each other in a way that was enough for them. Needless to say, it was a love that never would have been enough for me.

"He's a devil, you know."

"Mom? Are you about to reveal something I don't know?"

"Listen, you tell this and I'll never tell you another thing."

"Pinkies to the sky, Ma. Spill it."

"Okay. You know that gentlemen's club over near the border of South Carolina and Georgia? Oh, I guess it was early last December. I was on the way to Savannah for a holiday house-and-garden tour and I saw his truck and two other trucks of his in the parking lot."

"You've gotta be kidding me."

"Nope. It was payday."

"Wait a minute. Are you telling me that my holier-than-thou father, Big Al, takes the guys to a titty bar on payday?"

"Watch your mouth! But yep. Isn't that nasty?"

"Oh, great! Yeah, it's nasty, but it's also pretty juvenile! What are they doing . . . looking at a bunch of crackhead losers pole-dancing in their skanky thongs? It reminds me of when Nicky was little and he used to watch reruns of *I Dream of Jeannie*! You had to peel him off the television."

"Right?"

"The perfect woman with a gorgeous body who calls you 'master' and never disagrees with you about anything. And when you get tired of her you can stick her back in a bottle."

"Oh, well. Look, your father was good to marry me and all these years we've had a good life. He's nice to my mother and I never had to work . . . . what more could I want?"

I looked at my watch. It was almost two.

"I don't know." *A lot*, I thought, *you could've wanted and probably had a lot more*. Like some respect for starters. But there was no point in bringing that up then. "We had better get going. I told the head nurse we wanted to talk to Nonna's doctors and her physical therapist or whoever she could produce this afternoon, so we had better get moving. I don't want to miss them." I took our plates and glasses and put them in the dishwasher.

Mom put her new cell phone in her purse and stood. "Grace. We have to talk about this. Nonna is not going to go to a nursing home."

"Mom, here's the plan. The medical team is going to make that decision right in front of all of us. You are not going to be the bad guy on this one. We are going to listen to them tell all of us what Nonna needs and then we will all decide what is in Nonna's best interest, okay?"

"Oh, Lord. I wish Al was going to be there."

"No, you don't. Because he would just bulldoze them and dump the whole thing in your lap and I really think—no, I *know* that this is too big for you to handle. So let's go."

We took separate cars because I fully intended to drive back to Charleston after we had thoroughly investigated Nonna's options and hopefully drawn some conclusions. It didn't go as easily as I had hoped it would.

When we arrived, Nonna's caseworker was standing by her bed with her physical therapist. Her surgeon wasn't available, so these two had to suffice for the moment. The caseworker was holding Nonna's hand and her therapist was rubbing her feet.

"See? Here's my granddaughter and her mother now!" Nonna said.

And her mother? It didn't ring right to my ears. But many things they said to each other didn't sound right to me. Nonna had fallen into a kind of broken English, an indicator of her distress.

"I tell this nice ladies that I no need no more exercise. No more! Today I walked a little bit with her and I'll be fine when I get home. See my strong daughter?" My mom cringed and never looked more like a ninety-six-pound weakling. "She can help me! I no need nobody, no strangers pushing my poor legs up and down. They working just fine. I just need some of those nice pills."

"Hi!" I said. "I'm Grace Russo and this is my mother, Connie."

"Pleased to meet you, Grace," the caseworker said. "We've met your mother. It's nice to see you again, Mrs. Russo."

"Thanks," Mom said.

"Well, how's my grandmother doing?"

"She's doing really well, but she's going to need physical therapy and I'm afraid she doesn't want it."

"That's right," Nonna said, wagging her finger. "I really told them—"

I politely put my finger up to my lips with a polite smile directed at Nonna to politely shut the hell up. Politely.

"So what would happen if she didn't have any physical therapy and we just took her home?"

"Well, that's hard to say, but I don't think that's a good idea," the therapist said.

"You don't?" Mom said. I could see the edges of relief in Mom's jaw muscles.

"Yeah, because no matter how well intentioned the family is, the exercises the patient needs . . . well, they just never happen. I mean, your mother doesn't want to do them now. If you take her home, you can forget about it ever happening."

"What if we took her to therapy? What's that like?"

"Well, here's how therapy usually goes. We're probably going to start with crutches and move up to a walker as quickly as possible."

"Oh, no! I'm not gonna be one of those pity old people with the walker! I no want to be no cripple!" Nonna was getting agitated.

"Mrs. Todero, you won't be! That's the promise of therapy!"

"I'm no gonna do this! Where's my Al?"

Nonna's voice was about two octaves too loud.

"Shh. He's working, Ma," Mom said to her. "He'll be here later."

"We just want to be sure she has her bearings and that she's steady on her feet. Then we do exercises to regain flexibility in the hip and build stamina. The therapist will help you navigate going up and down steps, get in and out of a car, the shower—those kinds of things."

"My daughter will do this for me!"

My mother turned away from her mother's face and looked anxiously at me and then the caseworker.

"Nonna, please let us hear what they have to say, okay?" I said. "Nobody is deciding anything this minute. I promise."

"Gesú Cristo, I think I'm gonna die right here, right now! I saw Nonno last night! He was right where you're standing, Connie! He's coming for me! I know it! Oh! I can't breathe . . . ah! Ah!" She began to hyperventilate.

Nonna was surely going to get a nomination for best actress of the year. The therapist and caseworker rang for the nurse and tried to get her to calm down. When the nurse arrived almost immediately and saw what was happening, she gave Nonna a little shot of something that calmed her in no time. Personally, I think she'd had the syringe prepared from the minute we passed her desk. In fact, she would be well advised to keep one loaded for the duration of Nonna's stay.

We made the smart decision to move our summit to the guest lounge.

"She is really terrified of nursing homes, isn't she?" the caseworker said.

"She thinks that's where old people go to die," Mom said.

"Well, some do," the therapist said, "but I suspect she'll put you in your early grave if you take her home. Unless you're a nurse and a therapist, I don't know how you could possibly begin to handle the care she's going to need. And still, she's not exactly as light as a feather, is she?"

"What are our options?" I said.

"Well, she can be moved to our rehab facility on Lamotte Drive, which is absolutely brand-new, and in ninety days they'll have your grandmother dancing. Or you can take her home and bring in private nurses and health-care aides and bring her to see the physical therapists at the Life Care Center on an outpatient basis with one of those little ambulances to trot her back and forth. Expensive, and for a whole host of reasons, it never really works out as well for the patient. Or you can take her home and try to do this yourself, which would not be the best choice for her sake or yours."

I listened carefully as the caseworker spoke, and the obvious choice was clear to me. Nonna's fear and resistance would have to be dealt with or she and my mother would surely drop dead in short order.

"Mom, taking Nonna home would mean that she becomes the epicenter of your life, twenty-four/seven, and it will ruin your life. Even with the best help coming and going, your house will completely revolve around Nonna. Even more than it does now. Doing it without help would roughly be the equivalent of giving her a Kathy Smith *Walk Fit* video and telling her to have at it because she's not gonna listen to you! So forget it. Forget taking her home. You just can't do that. No way. She's gotta go to rehab!"

Poor Mom. The first of many dreaded moments to come was on her plate. In some ways it would be easier to deal with Nonna's death or, God forbid, an amputation than this decision.

"I don't know," she said. "I just don't know."

"Look, let's talk to Zia Theresa and Dad. Dad can talk sense to Nonna, right?"

"I don't know," she said. "I just hate this."

"Look, Ma, kids don't want to get shots, but if they don't they could die, right? So you drag them to the doctor and hold them down while they get their shots. I mean, what are you gonna do? It's your responsibility to see that they don't get polio and all that stuff. The same deal goes for Nonna, Mom. She may not like it, but this is what's best for her."

"Your daughter's right, Mrs. Russo," the caseworker said.

"Absolutely! I mean, for your mother to have her best chance at maximum mobility and independence, she really needs to be in a rehab facility," the physical therapist said.

Mom burst into tears. It was too much for her. I put my arm around her shoulder and said, "Come on now, Mom. Let's take this one to Big Al. Nonna thinks he's God, right? He thinks he's God, right? So let's let God tell her what she's gonna do."

"You know, Mrs. Russo," the caseworker said, "one thing to consider is that she'll have the support of a whole community of other people going through various kinds of rehabilitation. The company might do her a whole lot of good. And she'll always have her medication on time, a good bath every day, all her meals served to her, and a whole team of people to encourage her and monitor her progress. That would surely be a lot off your shoulders."

"Ten anvils," I said.

"Maybe eleven," Mom said, and finally smiled.

They gave us some brochures and a video of the facility and now there was nothing to do but wait for Dad's opinion and hopefully his help. It didn't look like I was going back to Charleston in time for dinner.

I called Michael. His cell phone rang and rang and finally voice mail kicked in. I left a message, knowing he would completely understand, and as the evening wore on and jet lag got the better of me, my old bedroom started looking pretty good.

By the time Dad got home, Mom had her facts organized to have the big chat with him, and I agreed to help her make the case.

"How's my princess? Come give your old man a kiss!"

I kissed and hugged him, hanging on for a few minutes.

"Wassamadder, baby doll?" he said, his heart the size of Yankee Stadium.

"No joy in Mudville, Daddy. We spent most of the day with Nonna."

"How's she doing, huh? No good?"

"Oh, Daddy. Come on, let's eat. We made lasagna. Where's Nicky?"

"With Marianne. He'll be home later. How's my wife? Over here!" he said, giving Mom a little whack on her butt and opening the oven to take in the irresistible smells of tomatoes, garlic and onions cooking with beef, sausage and cheese. "Smells like a little bit a heaven, right?"

"Oh, Al, we have to talk."

Over dinner and two bottles of homemade red wine from a friend of Dad's in New Jersey, Dad listened. We could see his mood change as he stared at the ceiling after we had recounted all that we had learned.

"*Ah, fongule!* Get Tony and Theresa on the phone, Connie, and you go get on the extension to listen in case I forget to tell them something."

I could feel my eyes begging to slam shut for the night and it was barely eight-thirty. I listened as my dad told my mother's sister and her husband all the grand and gory details.

"It's like this," I heard him say before I nodded off on the sofa. "If she doesn't go to this rehab place and stay there, she ain't never gonna get over this like she should. She won't walk as good and she'll have a lot of pain for the rest of her life. Yeah, yeah. I know. It's a sin. But what are we gonna do? No, next Monday. They want to transfer her next Monday. Sure. No, you don't have to come. I'll let you know."

Dad hung up and sank into his chair that Nonna always sat in and I could hear him sigh again and again. Mom came in from their bedroom and sat on the couch next to me, taking my feet into her lap.

"I feel terrible about this," Mom said.

"We all feel bad," Dad said. "You always will. But we all feel bad."

I didn't say anything then because there'd been no hateful or mean tone in Dad's voice as he said *You always will, you always will* reinforcing Mom's guilt. And suddenly I remembered a curious thing my mother had said earlier. What had she meant when she said that Dad had been *good to marry her*? That she was no prize? I was too sleepy to open that up to discussion and didn't want to provoke my father. It wasn't worth it then. Maybe I would ask her later.

CHAPTER 9

Five-Alarm

I returned to Charleston the next morning, thinking throughout the drive that Big Al had his work cut out for him. I felt sorry for them all. I recognized that part of being the family's patriarch was attending to unpleasant business, such as putting your mother-in-law in a place she thought was the worst insult she'd suffered in her entire life. Nonna was too old and too set in her ways to ever understand why professional rehabilitation was in her own best interest or even how it worked. And even though my father, whom she adored, would be the one to explain why she must go, she would take it out on my mother. Big Al had to be dreading the conversation with Nonna; Mom had to be dreading the inevitable backlash, and Nonna was probably mustering what strength she had to fight back.

It must be a terrible thing to be strong all your life and then in the flip of one second everything changes. Nonna was very old, there was no doubt of that, but she had enjoyed her independence and got around well, despite her arthritis. One wet floor, one careless step, and the entire world as she knew it was gone forever.

I had read somewhere that most people incur eighty percent

of their lifetime's medical bills in the last eighteen months of their life. I wondered if Nonna was in the last eighteen months of her life. If she was, that meant plenty of things were about to change for the whole family, my mother especially. In many ways, Nonna was the anchor of my parents' marriage. A rusty anchor, a crabby anchor—but the anchor. What would they do with themselves when Nonna was gone and Nicky was married—most likely to Marianne—and gone from home, too? Would they fight like cats and dogs? Would they go on a cruise? Would my father take a mistress? Would my mother finally throw out all the wedding favors Nonna had saved—the faded almonds wrapped in net and secured with little silk bows and tiny silk flowers that were too pretty to eat? The Christmas cards with family pictures that went unframed but that fanned out from a contraption that looked like a wire peacock, each feather clip holding a curled and drooping photograph. Would she put away all of Nonna's crocheted creations?

And most bizarre, would Mom inherit Nonna's curse or gift of seeing and talking to the dead? If she did, would Nonna still be able to badger my mother anytime she chose? If that happened, I think Mom might consider plucking out her eyes like Saint Lucy did so that she couldn't see the Roman soldier who wanted to rape her and who, as a result of Lucy's self-gouging, found her less attractive and may or may not have taken a pass on the rape. I certainly didn't want to think about Nonna picking on my mom for all of eternity, but the probability of Nonna's death was real. Not imminent, but real.

It was early in the day, so I decided to go to the office for a while. Things were pretty quiet as it was the end of the week. In the summer, Fridays were days to clean up your desk, surf the Internet looking for interesting new restaurants, spas and shopping in your upcoming destinations, and to return long-unanswered phone calls and e-mail. There was plenty waiting for me.

The group I was taking to Napa Valley was made up of hospitality-industry people. Under twenty people was a manageable group and foodies were right up my alley. True, I wasn't going to have dinner at the Hermitage like Bomze, but I wasn't complaining. As it turned out, the group shrank, and that was a plus from my point of view. Not to Bomze and not to the hotel, but I was still getting over Sardinia, so I was perfectly fine with fewer clients for once.

I loved Northern California and often thought it would be a great place to retire to. It was astoundingly beautiful and the people were shockingly nice. I remembered my first trip to San Francisco and then to the wine country. I had thought that all that perfect landscape and gorgeous weather sort of naturally put people on their best Prozac behavior. And maybe it contributed something to the general attitude there.

The longer I was away from New York, the more I realized how competitive I had been in that life and that acquiring things and more things was not the only measure of success. Not that money was bad, of course. Obviously—obvious to me *now*, that is—getting bundles of it shouldn't be the single fixation of your life. The price of wild ambition was that you missed too many other worthwhile things. But with each return visit to Napa and Sonoma, I felt my pulse slow down and I breathed differently, more deeply. Moving to Charleston had had a similar effect. And New York had given me a lot of ammunition for living because it taught me how to be a warrior and how to take care of myself. In Napa first and then in Charleston, I had learned that I didn't have to do everything gung ho and at warp speed.

We were booked in at the Meadowood, which was right in the countryside surrounding the outskirts of St. Helena. My only regret was that Michael wasn't with me, but this wasn't my vacation, it was a business trip. He loved the area, too, and we had said many times that we would go there together. I made a mental note to plan a long weekend for us.

Meadowood had a fabulous spa, and working with their concierge, I had put together a package for the Monday-through-Thursday excursion that included dinners at all the phenomenal restaurants and wineries we could squash into four days. We were skipping the usual hot-air-balloon rides and concentrating instead on lesser known but highly thought of winemakers like Colgin and Turley. Thus far the folks from Turley could not have been less interested in meeting us, even if we had been traveling with the wine guru Robert Parker himself. But when Ann Colgin realized we were southern, her doors swung wide open.

"I'm originally from Texas, you know," she said.

Well, Texas and South Carolina are different planets, but I wasn't about to make that point. I imagined that when you were as far away from the South as Napa Valley, the southern borders could be blurred by nostalgia.

"It will be like old home week!" I said, and made a note to bring Ann a pound cake from that bakery over on Shem Creek. Yes, I would do that.

So I had that trip just about in hand when I decided to call it a day. I phoned Michael on my cell while walking back to my car. He answered right away.

"Hey, baby! Dinner?"

"Let's go east of the Cooper," I said. "I feel like zooming across the new bridge."

"Why not? We haven't done that in ages. We can stop for a drink on Shem Creek."

"Perfecto! Ciao!"

"I love it when you go to Italy—I get the benefit of a little Berlitz here and there."

"O, ma non rompere!"

"Which means?"

"It means you are my love machine, baby boy."

It meant nothing of the sort.

By six o'clock we were flying over the new Arthur Ravenel Bridge, heading to cocktails and dinner. The sky seemed within reach, bulbous white clouds drifted through the impossible blue of the Carolina sky, and I had never felt better in my life. Dozens of tiny sailboats circled below us in contrast with the enormity of the *Yorktown*, the famous retired aircraft carrier that had a permanent home at Patriots Point, just to our right. Even the most hardened cynic would have had to agree that the world at that moment was a beautiful place.

"Want to go to Zinc?" Michael said.

"I love Zinc, but I was thinking Jackson's Hole," I said.

"Yeah, it's a little more casual and we're not so dressed up."

We pulled into the gravel and oystershell road that ran along Shem Creek and the restaurants that populated its shores. The shrimp boats were tied up along the docks and scores of gulls swirled and swooped, calling out for supper. We got out of the car and climbed to the top of the restaurant and its wildly popular sunset bar.

It was early and there were only a few people there, having a beer or a cocktail, engaging in Thank-God-it's-Friday conversations. I took a seat at the bar a few stools from where the bartender was listening intently to the gal seated in front of him. He excused himself from her and turned his attention to us.

"What can I get you folks?"

Michael looked at me for a clue.

"White wine?" I said. "And maybe some crab dip?"

"Sure thing," the bartender said. "And you?"

"Same," Michael said.

The bartender attempted to put in the order for the crab dip on the computer, but for whatever reason, it wasn't cooperating.

"I'm just gonna run this downstairs," he said, then turned to the woman he had been listening to. "Linda, will you watch the bar?"

"Yeah, sure," Linda said. "I'll make sure these two don't run off with the paper napkins."

"Yeah, we look like a flight risk, right?" I said.

"Nope. Hey," she said, "I'm Linda Jackson."

We introduced ourselves, shook hands, and she nearly crushed our knuckles.

"Oh, sorry!" she said. "I always forget to shake hands like a lady! Are you okay?"

"Sure, no problem, but that's some grip you've got there."

"Yeah, got it from throwing bundles of newspapers, sorry."

We learned that she was married to the bartender and that they owned the place. Most important, I found out she was from New Jersey.

"I knew you weren't from around here," I said. "I'm from Bloomfield!"

"No way!" Her eyes grew large like saucers. "How do you like that?"

"How'd you wind up here?" Michael said, sipping his wine.

"It's a long boring story, but basically I got sick of the weather and my job and I missed my sister who lived here, so I just took the jump. My sister owns the bakery downstairs—she makes banging pound cake, like my daughter says."

"That's your sister? Every pound of fat on my body came from her oven! She's an amazing baker!"

"Yeah, thanks. I'll tell her you said so. She even made our wedding cake." Linda reached into the cooler, pulled out a bottle of wine and refilled our glasses. "It's on me. So how did you guys wind up here?"

"Um, well, Michael's from here, but I moved here to work—I'm in the travel business and . . ."

Brad, the bartender, returned with the crab dip and the conversation continued until the sun finally began its descent. By then the bar had filled with patrons for drinks or dinner or both. Michael seemed especially quiet, but there was a lot of noise and I thought maybe he was just having some trouble hearing. There was no question that the chat between the Jersey girls was at a more fevered pitch than he was used to. Linda and I promised to stay in touch and I even offered to plan a honeymoon for her and Brad if they ever took the time for one.

I decided to drive to Sullivans Island and Michael's mood seemed to improve a little as he changed radio stations looking for one not playing obnoxious ads, until he found Alison and Leo on 102.5, the oldies station, and began to sing "Under the

Boardwalk" so off-key that we were soon both snorting with laughter. Everyone in the South knew all the words—even children.

We got a spot across the street from Station Twenty-two Restaurant and parked. Parking spots on Sullivan's Island were highly coveted and, like the locals say, about as scarce as hen's teeth. Michael took my hand as we walked through the sandy lot, which was filled with potholes, and after a few stumbles, I finally took his arm to avoid certain neck fracture. It was dark and starry, music and laughter spilled out from Poe's Tavern, and we debated eating there or at Station Twenty-two.

"I'm feeling like Aunt Mattie's crab cakes," he said, indicating a preference for Station Twenty-two.

"I could go for fried flounder," I said, agreeing with his choice.

"You have that every single solitary time we come here! Why don't you live a little and get the fried oysters?"

"Nope. Fried flounder. That's it. Fried flounder and hush puppies. And fries." Michael stopped in the middle of Middle Street and stared at me. "Well, at least I know what I want," I said, and squeezed his arm.

We waited at the crowded bar, enjoying a glass of Matanzas Creek Sauvignon Blanc. I was busy people-watching and chatting away with some tourists on the various merits of a home on the developed end of Isle of Palms versus the natural splendor of Sullivan's Island. I heard the rustle of barstools and someone said, "Hey! Watch it!" In my peripheral vision I saw Michael falling. Before I knew what was happening, Michael was on the floor, writhing in a seizure. Someone turned him on his back and called out for Marshall Stith, the owner. Anthony, Marshall's brother and the chief of the fire department who was experienced in first aid, came rushing through the crowd and knelt down by Michael, who was twitching and jerking. I thought my heart was going to leap from my throat and that I was going to drown in a faint so deep I would never wake up. Neither of those things happened. What did happen was that I glimpsed the possibility of what I dreaded most—losing Michael.

"Please stand back," Anthony said.

In a matter of minutes it was over and he turned Michael over on his side. I knelt down beside him and smoothed his hair back from his face.

"It's all right, sweetheart," I said, not knowing what else to say.

"Are you his wife?" Anthony said.

"No, but we are very close," I said, unsure how to describe our relationship.

"Do you know if this was his first seizure, or has he had them before?"

"I can speak," Michael said, and struggled to a sitting position. "I am a doctor. I'm fine."

"Well," Anthony said, "you may think you're fine. But you're not fine. I called EMS and they're gonna take you over to the ER in Mount Pleasant just to get you checked out."

"I think you can cancel—"

Before Michael could finish the sentence I spoke up. "We're going to the emergency room, Michael. Something's not right and we both know it."

They wouldn't let me ride with him in the ambulance, so I followed behind in my car. The ride to the hospital took minutes, but in those few minutes everything in the world ran through my mind. I was consumed by a nauseating fear I had never known. Then, a moment later, I was terrified beyond my wildest imaginings, and then, unable to comprehend and accept that this might be act one of an unfolding tragedy, I told myself that everything would be fine. It had to be. I didn't know how else to console myself.

What if something awful happened? Whom would I call to say that something terrible had happened? Michael was an only child and his mother was all but useless. Were there aunts? Uncles? Cousins? Yes! There was an aunt, his father's sister, who lived in San Diego, and she had children, didn't she? A son in Denver and a daughter in Houston? Was that right? Yes, or close anyway. I would ask him for their names and phone numbers. I would insist that he give them to me. Why hadn't I thought about this before? Because we were too young to consider fatal illness or the need for an organ donor or anything that dramatic.

I ran into the waiting room and then I realized that there was nothing to do but wait. There were other people there, reading magazines, watching television, talking to one another. They all seemed to have someone to comfort them over whatever illness or accident had brought them there in the first place. But I was alone. I was better dressed than all of them, had better jewelry than all of them and probably drove a better car than all of them—but I was alone and they were not. Who could I call? My mother? Bomze?

I was his live-in, not his wife. I had no right to be in the examining room with him. So I got to watch Larry King on CNN, and then, flipping through the stations—because someone left the remote control on a table—I was distracted and then surprised by how many shopping channels there were. None of them had a single thing I wanted. And how many news channels there were. At the moment I didn't give two hoots about what was going on in the world. All I could think was how insignificant it all was in light of what was going on in another room somewhere between Michael and some intern or resident who was unfortunate enough to be on call.

It was getting close to midnight and I was becoming more concerned than anxious. I drank three cups of decaffeinated coffee and read a *Time* magazine from cover to cover. I watched the crowd come and go—obese women with children awake hours beyond their bedtimes; men, still in their work clothes, pacing and going outside every so often to have a cigarette or use their cell phone. A steady stream of humanity came and went and I didn't particularly notice anyone until a well-heeled woman of about my age appeared and sat opposite me. She had a Chanel handbag, sapphire earrings suspended by a wire and

I suspected her suit was either Armani or someone in that universe. She opened her purse and pulled out a worn rosary and began to pray silently. It bothered me. I couldn't have told you why, but the fact that she was praying in public bothered me. I got up and walked outside for a breath of air. When I returned, the rosary had been put away. The woman looked at me and spoke. I could tell she had been crying.

"My father's in there," she said. "We were just coming home from dinner in the city and he collapsed. He's only seventy."

"He'll be all right," I said. I wanted to say, *What the hell are you worried about? My boyfriend—no, the only man I have ever loved besides my father is in there and he might be dying, too! And he's only thirty-five!* But I said nothing.

I went to the desk and inquired about Michael for the fourth time. The staff had just undergone a shift change, so I had a new person to question. She was very nice, but she told me nothing I couldn't surmise on my own except for one small fact.

"If he hasn't come out by now, that usually means they are very backed up in there."

"Oh," I said. "Well, that makes sense. Can I get you some coffee?"

"No, thanks. I'm drinking water. Weight Watchers. You could float away with all the water they want you to drink."

"Right? I do Atkins and it's the same thing. What's normal for wait time on a night like this?"

"Honey, there ain't nothing normal in an emergency room. But the usual wait on a weekend night could be anywhere from two to five hours, depending on what the problem is. Anyway, you said his name was what?"

"Michael Higgins."

"I'll make a call." I stood there while she called the nurses' station inside. "Uh-huh. Uh-huh. Okay, thanks." She hung up and looked at me. "Here's the deal. There was no neurologist here tonight, so they had to call in someone. He should be out soon. You say he had a seizure, right?"

"Yeah. Pretty scary. What if they want to admit him?"

"Not likely. If he's ambulatory, that is. They'll want him to see his primary or they'll refer him."

After another thirty minutes of me feeling like a caged animal looking for something to gnaw, Michael finally appeared.

"Let's get out of here," he said.

"What did the doctor say?"

"The doctor is an idiot."

"Oh. Okay. Fine. But what did he say?" I unlocked the car and opened the passenger door. "This side, gorgeous. I'm driving us home."

"What? Afraid I'll have a seizure while I'm driving?"

"Look, don't get pissy with me. I just sat in there for a billion years waiting for you, you know. No, I never even thought about that, but now that you mention it, you probably should get to the bottom of what's going on here before you drive."

"That's ridiculous. Look, this moron doctor who got out of some medical school in East Jabib about two minutes ago has no idea what's up with me."

"Oh. Okay. Then maybe you might want to go back to the guy who gave you antihistamines and the antibiotic and ask him! But you *have* to find out what's happening to you! This is not a joke, Michael. This might be something really serious or it might not be. But you can't go around having seizures and scaring the crap out of me and you and everybody else!"

"Oh, I'm sorry, Grace. I didn't mean to be impolite by having a seizure."

"Not funny, Michael."

I backed out of the parking space and turned onto Highway 17 South, headed back to Charleston. I turned the radio off and didn't speak to him. Finally, when we were almost over the bridge, he spoke.

"Fine, if it makes you happy, I'll go to the doctor."

I reached over and squeezed his knee. In a glance, I could see him smile with his mouth, but his eyes were worried. I was worried, too.

I opened the windows a little to let the air in. It did very little to relieve the way we felt. But we remained quiet, preferring not to speak because what could we say to each other? Michael was obviously deeply concerned.

I was beyond concerned. I had already imagined all the possibilities of what could be wrong with him. I'd been through his surgeries, his death, his funeral, my mourning, me getting old alone, my family thinking I was stupid to throw away my life like I would do—the whole theater.

Well, I decided as I lay awake that night from the decaffeinated coffee that wasn't quite decaffeinated, I wasn't giving up without a fight. In the same way I was determined to be a rock for my mother, I would be a mountain range for Michael Higgins. I would will him into perfect health.

CHAPTER 10

Rest Assured

All I could think about was how uncertain the world had
become. My grandmother was going to a rehabilitation center
and I knew she was crazy with anger over it. It was more than
surprising that she had actually agreed to go, but when I had
talked to Dad he had the usual Big Al explanation for how he
had finessed the situation.

"I just said, Look, Nonna, I'm taking the entire week off
next week. I am going to personally be there with you every
single day, making sure they know just who you are and that
they treat you right, okay? If there is some reason—and at this
moment I can see no reason at all—but if there is some kind
of reason I can't be with you all day, Connie will be here. And
if Connie can't come—and the only reason for that would be
that she's home cooking for you—then Nicky or Marianne will
be here. And I'm talking about right by your side. Okay? You
have my word on it."

"Wow, Dad. And she calmed down?"

"Hey! In the right hands? Your grandmother is a doll baby.
So how's my little girl?"

"Well, I'm taking a group to Napa next Monday, so that has
me pretty busy, and Michael's not feeling well."

I hadn't meant to tell him about Michael, but the words just slipped out of my mouth.

"Whaddaya mean? What's wrong?"

There was no lying to my father. "He had a seizure last Friday and we spent the evening in the emergency room at a hospital in Mount Pleasant."

"What? A seizure? That's not good, honey, you know that. Don't you? Does this bum have . . . whaddaya call it . . . epilepsy?"

"No! And please don't call him a bum, Daddy."

Silence.

"He doesn't have epilepsy, at least they don't think so. They don't know what it is yet. He's been nauseated and dizzy off and on for a while. At first, they thought it was allergies or a sinus infection."

"Might be inner-ear trouble or something like that along those lines."

"Yeah, maybe. They'll figure it out. Anyway, when I get back from Napa, I'll come down to see you and give you and Mom a day off with Nonna. How long is she gonna be in this place?"

"Six weeks—wait till you see this joint. It's a freaking palace like the Taj Mahal or something . . ."

It wasn't up to me to point out to my father that the freaking Taj Mahal was actually a freaking tomb. I would leave that task to greater minds with more nimble diplomatic skills.

Needless to say, I was working as hard as I could not to worry about Michael. I was sitting in my office surfing the Net, looking for causes of dizziness and seizures and nausea. None of them were good. All of them made me worry. No, obsess. I had to stop or I would be caught weeping at my desk.

I switched back to Google the restaurants in Napa, going over the menus and wine lists at Auberge du Soleil, Martini House and, of course, the famous French Laundry.

The clients on this trip were of various levels of renown and experience, and even though they were hard-core food-ies, not all of them were chefs—some of them owned the restaurants and others ran them. We had four actual chefs and their wives, the owners of the Peninsula Grill and their wives, the sommelier from Cypress with her meaningful other and the publishers of *Charleston* magazine. I had two surprises for our clients—one, Thomas Keller of the French Laundry was going to give them a private demo in the kitchen and let them cook with him for the afternoon; and second, Ann Colgin had arranged for us to visit an olive grower who would discuss the various challenges and the business of olives—whether it was olives, olive oil, soap, body creams or any of the other products made with olive oil—which was exploding all over Northern California. And we would taste olive oil from six different growers who all belonged to the Olive Press, a growers' cooperative. In their rooms they would find a basket of olive products, signed cookbooks from all the restaurants, maps of the area and, last but not least, a special signed bottle of wine from Ann Colgin herself. I was satisfied that it was going to be a fantastic trip.

Over coffee in the morning Michael told me he had an appointment that afternoon with the doctor who had given him the first medications.

"What time are you seeing him?"

"Around four."

"Do you want me to come?"

"Nah. It's no big deal. I'll see you at home."

I was anxious to get home that night and decided to make meat loaf and mashed potatoes, the ultimate comfort meal. If Michael could look at a plate of something that reminded him of a happier day, he might relax a little and divulge more details than if I grilled a steak, nuked a potato and served up a salad from a bag. Ah, that delicious aftertaste of cellophane—that, I could live without. Yes, I was using food as a weapon.

As soon as I could justify leaving the office, I did. Harris Teeter was crowded with people tossing pot roast and chickens, string beans and carrots into their shopping carts. There was always someone with fifty items on the express line for customers with ten items or less. There was always someone writing a check on the cash-only line who couldn't find their driver's license. And unless you made it to the bakery department before six, you might not find the kind of baguette you wanted and you'd be forced to take home a mushy cricket bat that was labeled *bread* but would get you laughed out of New York and New Jersey. That was the frenzied aura of rush-hour grocery shopping and somehow I loved it. It was like a double espresso.

Michael came through the door just as the smells of onions and meat filled the air and I was adding a clump of butter to the whipped potatoes warming in the top of my double boiler.

"Hey!" I said. "Come kiss the cook!"

His face masked something that appeared to be a major piece of bad news.

"My pleasure," he said, and gave me a kiss on the cheek.

He stood back and we looked at each other.

"What?" he said.

"Don't ever give up your day job for a career in poker."

He didn't say anything; he just clenched his jaw. Then he opened the refrigerator and said, "Want a glass of wine?"

"There's an open bottle of Ruffino on the table if you'd like red," I said.

Probably a minute passed before he spoke again, but every second ticked by with all the weight of a tortured lifetime. In that horrible space of dark time, I braced myself for the worst news.

He handed me a goblet and we clinked glasses.

"Here's to modern medicine," he said.

"I'll drink to that, but tell me why we are drinking to the wonders of medicine."

"My ENT friend wants me to see a neurologist and has already set me up for an MRI."

"What does he think? I mean, why an MRI?"

"Because they can get more information from an MRI than

any other kind of test—that is, without surgery or blood work."

"Doesn't that seem like a big place to start? I mean, isn't an MRI a big deal?"

"Well, yes and no. The good thing about it is that it gives the radiologist a three-dimensional picture of your insides. They shoot this differential dye into an IV and it reacts in certain ways to benign bodies and in other ways to things that are more troublesome."

"I won't ask you to explain that, but tell me what you think."

"For the moment I wish my ENT friend could have assured me that this was just seasonal allergies." Michael smiled at me and it was the smile of someone trying to digest shock.

So far I had not flinched. "But he didn't. I mean, he seems sure it's not allergies or a sinus infection or an inner-ear infection. Or something . . ."

"Right. The MRI is to establish a baseline record of my head. It's not intended to scare, as you put it, the crap out of us. So what smells so good?"

"Meat loaf and mashed potatoes. When's the MRI?"

"Tomorrow at four."

"Want me to come with you?"

"Always. Oh, you mean the MRI? Nah. But I do want that meat loaf."

"Nasty boy!"

We had dinner, some of the most phenomenal sex in the history of the world, and somehow lying with my head on his shoulder made everything seem like it was going to be okay. I sort of said a prayer for him and for Nonna and then realized that I had said a prayer for the first time in many years. But like every lousy sinner on the planet, I would admit that I called the Big Guy in the penthouse when I was afraid. And whether I could further admit it or not, it almost always made me feel better.

The next morning we didn't speak of Michael's MRI. We were the kind of denial specialists who would talk about it when it was about one minute to four. I knew that any conversation about it would only increase his anxiety, and what was the point of that? Besides, we didn't know any more today than we did last night. We had to wait for the facts.

All I said was, "Hey, if you need me this afternoon, just give me a call."

He kissed me on my forehead and said, "You worry too much."

Yeah, sure.

The morning was a blur. The afternoon was a blur. Around three I started fidgeting. Bomze breezed into my office with a stack of wine-country books and saw me cleaning out my desk. I almost never cleaned out my desk. If I was missing an earring, I might restack the clutter. But to actually check the two thousand or so Post-its and then copy the information to a permanent home and toss the notes? Only for a photo shoot, never for the sake of cleanliness or organization.

"Grace?"

"Oh, hi, Bomze. What's up?"

"Is there an impending nuclear attack? Are you quitting?"

"Very funny. I just decided to reorganize a little, that's all."

"Yeah, sure." He sat on one of the chairs in front of my desk. "What's going on?"

"Oh, God. You don't want to know."

"Yes, I do or I wouldn't ask."

I looked at him and thought about it for a minute and then decided to tell him because I needed to tell somebody. "Michael's having an MRI in about thirty minutes. That's all. We went out to dinner last Friday and he . . ." That was it. I lost it. Tears began to roll down my cheeks. "Sorry. I just . . . I'm so scared, Bomze. I'm just so scared."

Bomze's face, always animated, became somber.

"Well, you've had a helluva time lately, haven't you? First your grandmother, now this?" He got up and came around my desk to give me a hug. "I know you could file a complaint with the EEOC for this inappropriate behavior, but screw them, you need a hug."

"You're right. I do."

He patted my back as he gave me a hug and I thought it was about the sweetest thing anyone had done for me in a long time. I was always such a rock. I never got upset. I was the wise guy with some sassy remark to suit any occasion—the tough Jersey girl. Now I thought I might dissolve from worry. Then Bomze held me by my shoulders and looked at me so seriously he hardly looked like himself.

"Want to talk about it?"

"No. Yeah. I don't know."

"Start at the beginning, Grace, and let me help you."

I told him everything, and when I was finished he walked to the window and looked down at the street.

"So what do you think?"

"You really love this guy, don't you?" Bomze squinted as he spoke and his words were deliberate.

"Like no other. Ever. He's it for me, Bomze. He's all I want. What do I do?"

Bomze sighed, looked away from me for a moment and then faced me. "I think . . . I think that when you see him tonight, you put on your most fearless face, you throw your shoulders back, and you make him a strong drink. Make one for yourself, too. And then I think you tell him that he shouldn't worry, that he's going to be fine and that you're in this with him. You're a team. It could be something very simple, Grace. Sometimes people have a seizure and it doesn't mean a damn thing."

"Or it might."

"Yes, it might. But if it does, there are so many advances in medicine. Shoot, every time I pick up the paper there's some new discovery about some darn disease."

"Well, there's no point in being pessimistic until there's a reason for it, right?"

"A friend of mine used to say that worriment was like paying the toll twice—wait till you see if there's a toll on the bridge before you start digging around for change."

"That's a popular saying, but it's excellent advice anyway. Thanks, Bomze."

"You're welcome, Principessa. I hate to see you with this concern on your pretty face."

"Thanks, Bomze. I mean it."

We were quiet for a moment and then he said, "Okay, then. Now, are you all set for Napa? I brought you these books to look over, thinking they might give you some other things to talk about. It's a long flight, after all."

"Good idea. Thanks."

The afternoon crawled by at glacier speed. Michael had not called. I suspected the test was taking a while, or maybe they were running late, or who knew? I just kept checking my watch, and when it was five I was out the door and on the way to pick up Chinese food for supper. I had zero desire to cook.

When I walked in Michael was asleep on the sofa and the afternoon news was on. I tiptoed around until he finally woke up.

"Hey!" he said, coming into the kitchen, scratching his stomach. "They gave me something to make me relax and I feel like I could sleep till next week."

"Hey, baby." I kissed his cheek. "How did it go?"

"Stupid. Disgusting. The guy who invented that machine must have a thing for jackhammers."

"What do you mean?"

He poured himself a glass of water. "Well, they tell you it's claustrophobic, but they don't tell you how noisy it is. They give you Valium or something like it, earplugs, an IV to shoot in the dye, and just when you're all cozy on this sliding table, the banging starts. It is so loud you almost can't stand it."

"Humph. I didn't know that either. So what did the technician say? Anything?"

"Are you kidding? They don't tell you jack. The radiologist has to read it and it's like, I dunno, fifteen hundred images?

Anyway, they said I'd know something Monday or Tuesday of next week. They'll call me. What's that? Lo mein?"

"Yeah. Pork. Jeesch. And beef with broccoli. Monday or Tuesday? That's a long time to wait. Want me to fix you a plate?"

"Yeah, I'm starving."

"Of course you're starving. You're a man. Men are always starving."

I smiled at him and he ran his hands through his hair, smiling back. "I'm gonna go wash my face."

We ate and pretended there was nothing to worry about. That weekend we went out for dinner a couple of times and saw a movie and pretended there was nothing to be concerned about. Monday morning I left for Napa as though there wasn't an entire set of steak knives stabbing me in the heart. I knew, and don't ask me how, but I knew that this was the last time I would leave him with our lives still intact.

We are and pretended there was nothing to worry about.
That weekend we went out for dinner a couple of times and
saw a movie and pretended there was nothing to be concerned
about. Monday morning I left for Napa as though there wasn't
an entire set of steak knives stabbing me in the heart. I knew
and don't ask me how, but I knew that this was the last time I

CHAPTER 11

Napa

We arrived in San Francisco, touching down so gently it was as
though the pilots knew they had a bunch of sissies on board.
During the flight, I had chatted up the clients and their spouses.
They were a great group, wise to the ways of the world, all of
them well turned out. In fact, three of the women had the exact
same Burberry cotton quilted jacket lined in the same plaid. I
made a mental note to burn mine.

We took up most of the Business First cabin. Once the flight
attendants saw that we were together, they asked questions
and, deciding we weren't going to be a heavy burden, gave us
more generous servings of wine, help with the crossword puz-
zles and extra cookies.

The driver from Liberty Limousines—a smiling fellow
named Geraldo Sanchez—was there in the baggage claim holding up a sign with Bomze's name on it. Fortunately, everyone
in this highly efficient crowd had carry-on luggage. No one
wanted to keep the grapes waiting.

In the time it took to say Cabernet Sauvignon, we were
headed north toward Napa Valley. Geraldo was polite, conge-
nial and anxious to share with us something of what he knew
about the area.

"I'll tell you a little something about the wine country if you would like to hear . . ."

"Of course!" I said. If Geraldo wanted to be the tour guide for the moment, that was fine with me. After all, he lived in this neck of the woods. I did not. "Would you all like to hear some history?" I asked the group.

"Sure! Please!"

Geraldo cleared his throat, winding up for the pitch. "All right, then. Well, the history of Sonoma and Napa goes way back to the Wappo Indians, who had been here for who knows how long? 2000 B.C.? They named it Napa, which is a Wappo word that means 'land of plenty.' Plenty of scary animals, that is. The archaeologists have found the bones of grizzly bears and panthers from a long time ago. Elk, too.

"Anyway, sometime during 1823, a priest, Padre José Altamira, came out here to Sonoma and built a mission. That didn't last too long because the famous Mexican patriot General Vallejo thought Sonoma would be a good outpost for his government."

"So that's why all these places have Spanish names?" someone said.

"Yes. But California wasn't destined to be part of Mexico. No, not at all. There was an uprising called the Bear Flag Revolt when thirty or so men arrested the general and his men without one bullet! What did they do? They drank wine to mark the surrender!"

"I love it," one of the group, Alan McGregor, said. "They drank wine!" He was a little tanked from the flight, and as if on cue, his wife burst into laughter so enthusiastic and large that I had to open a window.

McGregor was the largest wine and liquor distributor in the Carolinas. He and his wife, Patsy, were slightly loud, to put it kindly. It was not going to be the Alan and Patsy Show. No, no. To send out a warning shot, I gave them a smile that had a little chill around the edges.

Even in the darkened light of the van, Patsy caught my drift and elbowed Alan. They settled down for the moment. Now, on a curious note, you might have thought they would have been the ones to engage my services in the first place, but they weren't. I would have thought that the guy making the most money would have wanted to arrange this trip for the pleasure of his best clients, right? After all, he made his living selling wine and spirits to the restaurants that were owned and supported by the other guests on our trip. Although I had only known them for a few hours, it was abundantly clear that Alan McGregor didn't think he needed to do anything to secure his business with anyone. Like Nonna always says, pride comes before the fall.

It was actually *Charleston* magazine's food editor, Mark Jennings, who had called Bomze Platinum Travel. Mark's idea was to take some of Charleston's leading taste buds and sensitive noses out to California and see what new trends there were and then to write a feature article about it. He and his wife, Julie, had a genuine interest in food and wine. It always amazed me that people like Mark and Julie could remain so thin and fit—all that eating and drinking. If I had their job, I would be as big as a cow.

Geraldo continued talking. "So these priests who came out here decided to raise grapes, for sacramental use, of course." He blessed himself and we smiled at his humor.

"I've never met a member of the Roman clergy who didn't like his cup to runneth over!" McGregor said, and laughed loudly at his own very stupid joke. His dutiful wife cackled, caught my eye again and became subdued. There were little moans from the others.

I could see Geraldo's eyes twinkle with good feelings and he politely waited for a signal to continue again.

"Come on, Geraldo, give us some more," I said.

"Okay. Well, they convinced the Native Americans to help—read: they turned them into slaves—and so they worked in the vineyards and winegrowing began to flourish. But the wine business really took off when this Hungarian named Haraszthy came along. He brought all kinds of varietals from Europe which did very well in Sonoma because we have great dirt. He was the founder of the BV—the Buena Vista, which is the oldest winery out here."

"Hmm, how about that? And I never knew there were Indians out here," I said. "I mean, I just never thought about it. What happened to them?"

"Smallpox," Geraldo said. "Just about wiped them out."

"Whew! I never heard that either!" I said.

"And you know Mount St. Helena used to be loaded with silver—hence the Silverado Trail, and then of course there was the gold rush. Anyway, some of those folks who were unlucky in gold or silver turned to forestry and built sawmills all over Napa Valley. They would ship the timber down to San Francisco on the Napa River. And there was a railroad between Vallejo and Calistoga. They still use it today, but it's for tourists who ride it to have lunch or dinner and roll up and down the valley."

"That's the Napa Valley Wine Train, isn't it?" someone said.

"Yep. Did you folks know that Robert Louis Stevenson took his bride on that train?"

We shook our heads.

"Well, he surely did. This place is what inspired *The Silverado Squatters*."

"Hmm. Humph. Well, how about that?" said George and Leigh Murray, extreme foodies from the Lowcountry and wealthy friends of the rich-as-Croesus Josie and Steven Hughes, who owned several restaurants and legendary cellars.

I leaned against my window to rest for a moment. I was tired and, of course, my personal issues kept crawling to the front of my thoughts. It was an unexpected bonus that Geraldo was so personable. Just as Geri Post had done in Sardinia, it looked like Geraldo would add that extra element of knowledge and wit to our trip to the wine country. I was relieved and delighted at the same time. I loved planning logistics and being in charge. I didn't crave the limelight, nor did I possess the soul of a lost professor who loved to lecture and inform. The perfect trip for me was one that ended without one snag and with the clients finally realizing I had been there in the first place.

I would guess I fancied myself to be something like a director on a film. I set everything up in advance and then watched the action unfold. That's not all there was to it, though. Here's the ugly truth: I most especially loved vicarious living.

I knew all too well who I was and, even more, who I was never going to be. I wasn't rich or powerful, a genius or some great talent. If I hadn't been involved in this particular side of the travel business, I probably would never have known anyone as interesting, gifted, funny, chic or wealthy as most of my clients were. Or as peculiar. Or as grandiose. Or as immature and petulant, selfish and arrogant, pugnacious and demanding . . . Were the very rich any different from the rest of us? You don't have the days left in this lifetime and the next ten for me to tell you how many ways we differ from them.

I loved traveling, eating and drinking like they did, but I also seriously clung to the wide gulf between us. Hell would have been to be born with the supercilious personality possessed by half the wives I met or with an overblown sense of self like half the husbands Bomze Platinum Travel squired around the globe.

But they weren't so bad either. They could be uproariously funny one minute and unlock the secrets of Dubai's politics in the next breath. I enjoyed them for all the unexpected things they were because their great wealth gave me the chance to learn and see things I otherwise never would have glimpsed. But once again, here was the critical difference. Working for Bomze may have produced the keys to the chalet that once was home to the shah of Iran, but these people had actually partied with the shah.

We were almost at the Meadowood and I willed an adrenaline surge. There was plenty of work to do before I could put my head on a pillow that night.

Geraldo and the bell captain quickly unloaded the luggage in the lobby while I checked us all in. Alan and Patsy Mc-Gregor immediately discovered the wine bar by the fireplace and drifted over to it with the others. I separated their luggage by couple, looked at them all once more and assigned their rooms.

"The Jenningses will take a Tree Line Cottage, as will the Adens, the Greenes, and I will, too. The Murrays and the Newtons will share the Hillside Terrace Suite, the McGregors will take the Tree Top Suite, and Josie and Steven Hughes will occupy the Oakview Suite," I said to the desk manager, who ticked the names off on her list.

"Very good, Ms. Russo, and welcome to Meadowood. If there's anything I or my staff can do to make your stay more enjoyable, just let us know."

I took a moment to join the group at the wine bar and told them we would have thirty minutes to change or freshen up before dinner at the Martini House.

"Your luggage will be in your rooms, some small tokens of appreciation from Bomze and the Baroness, and oh! I almost forgot. The Meadowood has a fantastic spa, you know. They have generously donated a Cabernet Crush massage for every-one, which is a body polish and massage done with grape seeds and grape-seed oils. All you have to do is call for a time."

The crowd was atitter over this bit of information and they suddenly couldn't wait to see their rooms.

"I love it!" Patsy McGregor said. "No point in wasting any grapes!"

"Right. Okay, so . . . . There are golf carts outside with at-tendants ready to take you to your rooms whenever you are ready."

I handed each couple their keys and an envelope with my room number and cell number on the front. In the envelope was the itinerary with all the information they needed. I tried calling Michael from my room, but there was no service for my cell phone. Big surprise. We were in the middle of the woods. Rather than pay the premium to use the landline, I decided to wait until we were in St. Helena and try again.

By eight, we were seated around the table and prepared for a feast. The chef appeared from the kitchen and tapped Hampton Greene (the chef from Bailey's in Charleston) on the shoulder.

"Hey, you old dog! Want to go hunting truffles with me next month?" he said.

"Well, look who's here! Only if I get to bring my own pig!" Hampton said, and literally leaped from his seat to shake his friend's hand. "Y'all? This is Todd Humphries, one of the finest chefs in America!"

"Yeah, that's probably true!" Todd and Hampton laughed and knocked each other in the arm. "Are you folks hungry?"

"Are you kidding? This is Grace Russo, our team leader."

"Hi," I said, and gave a little wave from the other side of the table.

"I think she has prearranged a menu for us . . . ." Hampton continued.

"Forget it," Todd said. "I'm cooking for you tonight! Come on, you can help!"

"We used to hunt for truffles in the Hudson Valley years ago when we were just getting started . . . Honey?" Hampton turned to his wife, Darlene. "I'll be back . . . ."

Todd stopped and looked back. "That good-looking woman married you? She must be blind! Let's go."

"Wait! Did you meet Jonathan Aden from Cypress? Jon? Wanna come?"

"No, you big hot dogs have your reunion! I'll take care of the ladies!"

"Hands above the table, okay, Casanova? Darlene?"

"Go!" Darlene said. "We're starving!"

Todd and Hampton disappeared into the kitchen and we were left to shake our heads.

"They're like giggling schoolgirls," Darlene said.

Steven Hughes and Alan McGregor were going over the wine list.

"Personally, I'm glad we came to a place that makes martinis," Alan commented. "I'll take a good vodka over fermented grapes any day."

Steven Hughes turned red. Even his wife, Josie, dropped her jaw. I, along with the others, studied the menu and tried not to make eye contact with Alan or Steven.

"Well, Alan? One of the reasons we came to Napa was for the wine, wasn't it?"

Alan McGregor was a Neanderthal. Steven Hughes was probably his most significant client in the city of Charleston and was considered the area's leading authority on wine. Pairing food and wine on his tasting menus was his rapture. His ecstasy. This guy Alan was a complete slug of the first order, and so far had contributed nothing to building a convivial ambience. In fact, I could see the Hugheses shift in their seats and could read their minds. *How many more days do we have to be with this jerk? How many meals?*

With the two brain cells he had remaining in a corner of his thick skull, it came to McGregor that he had somehow offended Hughes. He reached over and took the wine list from Hughes and said to the sommelier, "Tell you what, pal. Bring us your very best Chardonnay, your very best Pinot Noir and your very best Cabernet Sauvignon. It's on me, okay?"

The sommelier, who had no doubt suffered the Alan McGregors of the world for longer than he cared to remember, said with a smooth smile, "The *very* best, sir?"

I smiled and immediately ate an entire roll. We were about to be served some outstanding bottles and I knew Alan McGregor had just been snookered in the grand style. It always amazed me that even though people got older, they didn't necessarily get any smarter.

Hampton, now in chef's whites, came and went from the kitchen with tray after tray of mouthwatering food: black truffle mousse with porcini tuiles, chilled golden jubilee soup with poached lobster and lemon verbena, pan-roasted wild striped bass with green tomato ravioli, roasted venison with huckleberry coulis—on and on it went. And with the arrival of each dish, we oohed and aahed while Julie Jennings took several digital photographs. We were out of control with food lust. We applauded. We rolled our eyes and we cleaned each plate.

And wine—the wine flowed like a river and it was every bit as delicious as each dish. We were in the deep end of the pool by dessert—two bottles of a 1957 Château d'Yquem and goat-cheese soufflés.

"Mark Jennings, from *Charleston* magazine, would you care to comment?" I said, holding the empty bottle of red wine in his direction like a microphone.

"Yes. Yes, I would. If I were headed for the guillotine, I would like to have my last meal prepared by Todd Humphries and Hampton Greene. And I would like Alan McGregor to buy the wine."

Julie, Mark's wife, said, "That goes double for me. I'm thinking I might have a little nap right here on this lovely banquette!"

When Hampton and Todd returned to the table we gave them such a rousing standing ovation that the entire restaurant stood and clapped as well. Julie took a dozen pictures of them and it was just nuts.

Until the bill for the wine arrived.

Without batting an eye, the sommelier delivered it to Alan McGregor, handing the food bill to me. I thought that if McGregor's eyes bulged another millimeter we would have a medical emergency. He sputtered, turned red, cleared his throat and, with his slightly palsied right hand, slipped his credit card into the leather folder. Every other person at the table knew exactly what had happened. No one acknowledged his distress. Like true Charlestonians, they all spouted their own version of *Alan? Thank you so much! The wine made the meal!*

Priceless.

As the guests gathered up their things I said, "I'm going to just slip outside to make sure Geraldo is there, and I have to make a quick phone call, okay?"

They nodded and continued talking to one another about the meal, asking for directions to the ladies' room, the men's room, a copy of the menu . . .

Geraldo was parked at the corner; when he saw me, he pulled up and opened the door. I dialed Michael. He answered on the first ring.

"Hey!" I said. "How's it going? Any news?"

"Yeah. Not good. They got the radiologist's report today."

"And?"

"There's a mass on the front left of my brain. They want to biopsy it right away."

"What . . ."

My mind was racing a thousand miles an hour. What had he said? A mass? A mass of what? The front left? What did that mean? Was Michael telling me he had a brain tumor? What in the world?

He was talking. I had missed what he said. "Say that again, Michael, I didn't catch it."

"I said, this is not good, Grace."

CHAPTER 12

On the Bluff

If you think that I was about to melt down in front of my clients, you couldn't be more wrong. If Big Al ever taught me anything, it was this—wait until you have all the facts, assess the facts, consider all your options, and then one of two things happen next. One, you go to war with the conviction that you will win. You pull out every trick in your book, you fight with every ounce of strength you have. You never let the enemy sense your fear. And if you don't win, at the very least, you make sure the enemy is severely injured. If there is no chance of victory, none whatsoever, then you get on your knees and try to cut a deal with God. I wasn't about to cut a deal with anybody until I had all the facts. Realizing it would be at least a few days until the facts were known, I opted for self-imposed calm and a huge case of denial.

After all, I was twenty-five hundred miles away and had a pack of hungry and thirsty patrons of Bacchus to contend with. I was a walking zombie, but no one knew it.

The plan for the day was a visit to four wineries and a tasting of their best offerings, lunch and cooking lessons at the French Laundry, and a late dinner at Auberge du Soleil. I looked at my watch. I was waiting for seven o'clock so that it would be midmorning in Charleston and not too early to call Michael. Understandably, we needed to talk.

I got up with the birds because I'd had that same nightmare again—falling, falling—I was going to drown and where was Michael? It was just awful to wake up with my heart pounding.

I was in the Meadowood's restaurant having some organic granola with homemade yogurt—this was Northern California after all—and reading the newspaper. Julie Jennings, the wife of Mark from *Charleston* magazine, came in.

"Good morning!" she said. "Did you rest well?"

"Never better!" I said. *Never worse,* I thought. "And you?"

"You know what? I slept like a rock. Mark and I live out on Isle of Palms and in the morning you hear seagulls and smell the ocean. It has been so long since I've been out here, I had forgotten what it's like to wake up to smelling the forest—it's all kind of loamy and earthy mixed with pine, isn't it? It smells wonderful."

"I hadn't thought about it, but now that you mention it, yeah, it does. It smells like a wood fire. Want to join me?"

"Sure. Mark's still snoozing."

The waiter appeared. "Coffee? Juice?"

"Sure," Julie said.

I held out my mug for a refill. They didn't have enough caffeine in California to make my mind right that morning.

"The granola is outstanding," I said. "I saw some waffles go by a few minutes ago. They looked pretty good, too."

"Well, Mark and I are really happy that the timing of this trip worked out so well. There are so many new trends coming out of this part of the country—even though it started back in the twenties—this whole biodynamic-farming thing just makes so much more sense now than ever."

"What's biodynamic?"

"Well, it goes like this." The waitress handed her a menu, which she didn't even scan. "I'll just have the granola, too.

Thanks." The waitress walked away. "You see, the whole vine-
yard is looked at as one living thing. And biodynamic vineyards are worked in conjunction with the cycles of the moon
and the planetary . . . ." She moved her arms in a large circle.

She yammered on and I nodded as though I understood and
was fascinated by what she was saying.

"So basically they don't need any synthetic fertilizers or any
of those chemicals that pollute the earth. Isn't that genius?"

It was a strain to muster some interest. "Yeah, well, that's the
way the future has to be, right?"

"Oh, yeah, big-time. Or else there just won't be one. Mother
Earth has just about had it with us. Anyway, I think we are
going to have enough material for ten feature pieces from this
trip."

She didn't look like a tree hugger, but apparently she was
something of one.

It was six-fifteen, nine-fifteen at home. Michael was already
at work and I had no cell-phone signal. Within a couple of
hours, it would be time to rally the group onto the bus once
again. Soon they were gathering in the lobby. Geraldo was
there, standing outside by the open door of his minibus.

"Good morning!" he said.

"Good morning!"

"Where's our first stop?"

"Sterling," I said. "May as well start with a big one, right?"

"Very smart, because they are all a crazy house by the afternoon."

It was just before ten when we arrived at the fabulous Sterling
Vineyards in Calistoga. Just as they opened I paid everyone's
entrance fee, including a ride on the tram to the top of the hill
so they could enjoy the view. I followed the group through the
buildings, room to room, watching the videos that chronicled
the history of the winery, its particular process and philosophy, ending on a beautiful terrace that overlooked all of Napa
Valley.

The sweeping panorama was truly a sight to behold. Just as the ocean did with its mighty rushing water, surging and receding, the mountains and the valleys had the power to erase your mind with their majestic silence. For as far as you could see in every direction, there were mountains and trees, rolling valleys of every shade of green, a blue sky so bright, it almost hurt to look at it, and the temperature of the air was perfect, probably between sixty-five and seventy. It was too immense, too gorgeous, too powerful to absorb. I stood in awe and stared just as everyone else did. All of us were absolutely astonished by the sheer size of the sprawl and perfection of the area's natural beauty.

Julie was clicking away with her camera, and when she stopped she came to stand by me at the edge of the terrace.

"Whatcha thinking?" she said.

"I'm thinking . . . I'm thinking that if all this is possible, anything is possible." She looked at me and nodded. Indeed, it was a simple but powerful statement. "I gotta call home."

"Everything okay?" she said.

Normally I would have said, *Oh, yeah, everything's fine,* but everything wasn't fine at all and I felt an overpowering urge to tell someone.

"No, actually, things are really kind of upside down right now. But I'm sure it will work out." I pulled out my cell phone and checked the signal, which was strong.

"You don't look too sure. Want to talk?"

"Oh, no. Not unless the world comes to an end today, then I'd love a pal. But right now I'm just gonna make two phone calls home and check the temperature of the water."

"Just let me know . . ." she said, and walked away.

Nice of her to ask, I thought, and dialed Michael's cell. He answered.

"Hi, sweetheart," I said, trying to sound chipper.

"Hey," he said, "you're up early. How's Napa in the day?"

"Absolutely beautiful. I have to bring you here."

"We'll see. Bring home some wine."

"Okay. Listen, I wanted to ask you something. That test they want you to have?"

"Yeah?"

"When is it?"

"Thursday."

"Do they put you to sleep for it?"

"Well, they give you something because they don't want you jiggling around when they're trying to stick a needle in your brain."

"Jesus, Michael." I shivered all over at just the thought of it.

"Sorry."

"Listen, I'm going with you. I'm coming home. Okay?"

There was a little stretch of silence from his end and then he said, "You don't have to do that."

"I know. But I don't want you to be alone."

"Thanks. I love you, Grace."

"I love you, too."

We hung up. While I had fought off nightmares in my bed last night, I had made the decision that I was going home early. All I had to do was call Bomze to see if he could send a replacement. I was so upset by Michael's news that I didn't care if I got fired. I was going to be with him. Who else did he have?

And who else did I have?

I dialed my mother's cell, but she didn't answer. I dialed the house and she picked up.

"Hi," I said, "are you up? I called your cell."

"Yes, yes! Grace?"

"Yeah, it's me, Ma. Listen, sorry I didn't call yesterday. I was so busy getting everyone organized and all."

"Oh, that's okay. My cellular telephone is in my purse. Anyway, I know you have your own life."

"Right." I loved the way she referred to her cell as a "cellular," but I hated the condescension in her voice. "I just wanted to know how Nonna's move went." Don't want to use the cell? Don't use the cell!

"Humph. How do you think it went? Terrible! She's seeing Nonno every five minutes and screaming at the top of her lungs!"

"Jeesch." She was probably scaring the staff of the rehab place out of their minds.

"Yeah, you said it. Jeesch. But she's in there and your father just went down to see her. He's got huge bouquets of roses for her and the nurses—you know how he is."

"He'll charm the dickens out of everyone."

"Yes, but the problem isn't the facility, it's that Nonna really, and I mean *really,* doesn't want to do all the exercises."

Apparently Mom had taken to calling the nursing and rehabilitation home "the facility."

"Well, Mom, she can be a lunatic if she wants, but those rehab nurses and therapists have dealt with her type in the past. I'm sure of it. So I wouldn't worry too much. Just be glad it's not *you* having to make her do them. Can you imagine?"

"That's the truth. Yeah, it's true."

"So everything's okay?"

"Yeah. You?"

"I'll be home Thursday."

"Your father said Michael isn't feeling well? What's going on?"

Here was my chance. I could tell her and see what she would say. Or I could not tell her and tell myself that she would have had no sympathy if I had told her. I decided that I couldn't be any more upset than I was anyway, so I told her.

"Yeah, they want to biopsy his brain. There's something there that's not good."

There was a long silence and then she said, "Well, he's young. I'm sure it will all work out fine."

Thanks, Mom. Good job in the mother department. Let's not overdo the sympathy and concern. Glad you've got some self-control . . .

I said nothing for a few minutes and then: "Right. Well, I have to go now. I'll call you when I get home, okay? Give Nonna my love."

"Sure thing. Marianne made her fudge."

"Bully for Marianne. Bye."

I was furious. How could she be so cold? If the doctors thought that my father had a brain tumor or something like that, she would have had Frank, Regina, their kids, me, Nicky and the priest all at the house for a vigil with candles, holy water and every statue all lined up on the dining-room table. She would've been reading the sorrowful mysteries of the rosary while we waited for a phone call with the results from the pathologist. Of course, Dad would've been at a sports bar watching a ball game knocking back beer and chomping on super-spicy buffalo wings with extra blue-cheese dip, but hey, that was merely one of the differences between Big Al and Connie. And Connie was completely baffled for a response when it came to any discussion of my relationship with Michael.

Okay, she doesn't want to like him for whatever her crazy reasons are, I thought. I can accept that. But I knew she would give more compassion to a total stranger who told her the same story, someone she met on the checkout line at the Piggly Wiggly, than she just gave to me!

I thought we had made some mother-daughter progress when I had made my most recent trip to Hilton Head. I had come away from that thinking that if I spent just a little more time with her, time directed at her alone, to talk about things she might like to talk about—her childhood, how she and Dad fell in love, the why of Nonna's criticism—that if she could get those things off her chest with someone, we might bond in a new way. But we obviously had not come along as far as I had hoped, because for some weird reason, my mother could only bond with me when I was there with her in the flesh. It had to be hormonal.

All right, I thought. I have to call Bomze and figure out what to tell this group. I dialed his cell-phone number right before noon while the group was in the tasting rooms ordering cases of wine to ship home.

"Hi! Bomze? It's me, Grace."

"Principessa! *Ciao!* How goes the good fight?"

"This group couldn't be nicer or easier, which is why I'm calling, actually."

"Aha! Could you be a little more vague?"

"Bomze, it's Michael."

"What's happened?"

I told him the story and that I wanted to come home early to be with Michael for his terrible biopsy. I asked him if he thought he might like to send a replacement for me, but told him that I really thought the group would be fine on their own. To my surprise, Bomze became irritated with me.

"Grace, this is why our business is different from all the rest. We give them that extra service, that royal treatment . . . all these things give them confidence and they don't have to be concerned about a single detail. This is why we can charge what we charge. I mean, have you let your worries be known among the clients?"

"No! I would never do that! You know that!"

"Okay. Of course you wouldn't. But you can't just walk out of a trip right in the middle of it, Grace. It's not like you and Michael are married, you know."

I got very quiet and thought at that moment that talking to Bomze was very much like talking to Big Al or Connie. Since when had he become so provincial? My mind was racing. Was this to be a showdown? Did I want to quit my job over this? No, I didn't. So I gave him a piece of my mind instead.

"Okay, Bomze, I'll stay and let Michael be put to sleep and have his needle biopsy all alone, since his mother is in a nursing home with advanced Alzheimer's disease and he has no one else to call. Don't worry about it. Sorry I asked."

It was Bomze's turn to be quiet.

"Are you there, Bomze?"

"Yes, I'm just thinking, Grace. You are obviously more concerned about this test than I would be if I were in your place. I mean, it's just a test. It's not, God forbid, surgery. And there is a gal in the Charlotte office who could do your job *easily* as well as you do it. Let me make a phone call and I'll ring you back in a few minutes."

He hung up and I stood there with stinging eyes and a racing pulse. Was Bomze telling me I was no longer his favorite? Had some clients from the Sardinia trip complained that I'd used my grandmother's illness to be late for the boat trip or not been quite as enthusiastic as they thought I should have been because my personal life was getting in the way of my responsibilities? Did Bomze care if I quit? Did he think, I mean really think, I was just being dramatic or unprofessional? And who was this little twit from Charlotte who could replace me just like that?

I made my way back to the bus and waited for our clients to show up. My cool was in charge. I even concentrated on making sure my jaw wasn't tight. I didn't want anyone to see the slightest hint of anything on my face.

Josie and Steven Hughes boarded the bus.

"Hi! That was fabulous!" Josie said. "We got a great Cab reserve and a delicious Pinot!"

"Great," I said, and sounded like I meant it.

Mark and Julie Jennings showed up next, followed by the rest. I was counting heads when my cell rang. It was Bomze.

"Excuse me for a minute," I said, and climbed down from the bus. "Hello?"

"Grace? Marilyn Lambert can't come. She's in England on a bicycle tour with a group of insurance executives—biking with gourmet Druid cuisine and ritual thrown in or some such itinerary. I don't have anyone else I like as well."

"Oh, well, then, I'll stay."

"Look, I've been thinking. Your trip ends Thursday, right? So come home Wednesday night. Just tell them you have a family emergency. One day won't kill anyone."

"Look, Bomze, thanks. Don't worry. We have a fantastic driver and I'll just get him to take up the slack for one day."

"Give him a couple hundred dollars and expense it. Or if

he doesn't feel comfortable leading them around for whatever reason, the concierge might have a thought on this."

"Thanks, I owe you one."

"No, you owe me your blood."

I could hear him smiling through the phone and I relaxed. I got back on the bus and it was clear to the clients that I was much happier than I had been in the morning.

"Haul freight to Yountville, Geraldo! Thomas Keller and Ann Colgin are waiting!"

"And the oysters of my dreams!" said Hampton Greene.

We rolled down the road for the short trip until Geraldo pulled up alongside the French Laundry and I wondered for a moment if this was the right place. It seemed so modest considering its grand reputation. It was just a gentrified farmhouse. But with each step through the courtyard, the place began to cast its spell. Each shrub and tree was perfectly manicured. The enormous old door felt like it could've been plucked from Normandy two hundred years ago. Peeking inside, I saw that the low-ceilinged rooms were small but furnished on the scale of the shorter people of another century.

A kind of reverence came over the group as though we were entering a church. In a way we were, because on both coasts Thomas Keller's kitchen was considered the high altar of contemporary haute cuisine. And all we wanted to do was find our spot as we prepared for the biggest thrill of the trip.

Ann Colgin was there to welcome us, standing alongside one of the assistant chefs, a smart-looking fellow of about thirty whose embroidered jacket sported the nickname of Bob.

"Hey! Thomas is out back, but he'll be back in a moment. He's cutting herbs," Ann Colgin said to me, and extended her hand.

How could anyone that successful in the wine-and-food business be so young? "What a thrill this is for all of us!" I said. It was.

For the next three hours Thomas Keller; Craig Diehl, another member of the group; Hampton Greene; Mark Jennings; and Ann Colgin were lost in a nonstop conversation about the various amounts of galangal to use in curries versus which wine to serve with mussels when they are prepared with mint and Thai chilies. There was a protracted conversation about the ratio of cloves to coriander seeds in preparing brine for pickling oysters (it was about fifty-fifty, taking mass into consideration) and whether or not it was possible to overuse a chinois (your sauce could never be too clean). The rest of us were the happy recipients of some of the most outrageously innovative, stunningly delicious food we had ever tasted.

If you came to Thomas Keller's table as a bologna-on-white-bread-with-mayonnaise kind of patron, you would never know what hit you, except that it was—yes indeedy—remarkable but probably too much work and too complicated to try to re-create at home. For the rest of us who appreciated a great meal on occasion, we knew we had just been given the ultimate American culinary experience.

"I didn't even know oysters could taste like that," I said as the group members climbed on the bus, tired and sleepy.

"Me either. And I've been eating oysters all my life!" Mark Jennings said. "Custards in eggshells? Foie gras with cherries? Fabulous!"

"And that artichoke barigoule? I could eat a whole lot of that before I got tired of it," Leigh Murray said. Her husband, George, nodded.

"Pretty shocking," I said, my mind spinning from the magic of it all.

The bus was quiet as we made our way back to Meadowood. The group had taken a vote. They wanted a nap. They wanted room service for dinner. Their decision was fine with me.

I tried to sleep. The air was cool and fragrant and the sun was well on the other side of the hill. But no matter what I visualized or how I positioned myself, sleep wouldn't come. Finally, I got up and walked outside on my small porch that overlooked the sloping woods. The landscape was decorated with the light of broken shadows formed by the shapes of the leaves from the branches above. Somewhere in the near distance, water trickled with a steady rhythm. Every now and then, leaves would rustle as some small creature scurried across the forest floor. Birds sang out to one another as the afternoon began to wind down for them, too.

I thought about nothing for a while. I just stared at the woods—the colors, the textures, the sounds. But after a few minutes it was difficult not to think about the vast and obvious orchestration of all of nature and how it existed in harmony with thousands of layers of the natural world's complexity. Even if I had earned advanced degrees in environmental studies, I would never, even then, grasp it all. Did anyone? To my sudden comprehension, its probability of being accidental or a matter of mere natural selection was nil.

CHAPTER 13

Cure-all

Michael was in the midst of his procedure Thursday morning. Calling the brain biopsy his "procedure" was roughly the equivalent of referring to Nonna's nursing home and rehab center as "the facility." I sat in the waiting room. I paced up and down the hall. And then I went looking for my fourth cup of coffee of the day. The wadded tissues in my hand were beginning to dissolve into wet lint. And finally, minute by hour, the afternoon arrived.

I told myself that I should take a meditative approach and imagine that all would be fine in a matter of just a few hours. The doctor who did the "procedure" would appear and tell me that although they didn't have results yet, everything appeared normal to him and he wasn't concerned. He would tell me to take Michael home and give him Tylenol, and that as soon as the pathology report was back, he would call us. But, he would say, he was almost a thousand percent certain that there was nothing to worry about. He would say, *Seriously, Grace, I make my living doing this and usually I can tell just from the look of the fluid whether or not there's a big problem. This looked completely normal to me.*

I would take Michael home and make him a bowl of fettuccine, his favorite, with just some butter and shaved Parmesan and maybe a Coca-Cola over cracked ice with a straw. Maybe I would run over to Simmons Seafood in Mount Pleasant and bring home a key lime pie. Michael loved key lime pie.

That's what I wanted to happen more than anything in the world.

Hours passed. I asked about Michael. They told me he was in a recovery area sleeping off the anesthesia. Okay. That made sense to me. Sometimes people were very sensitive to any kind of sedative and slept for hours. Fine, I thought, I'll wait.

And at last Michael was there, seeming as normal as could be. I choked back tears of relief and hurried him to a seat.

"I'll get the car. Don't move. How do you feel?"

"It was the best nap I've had in years," he said, and gave me a lopsided smile.

I kissed his cheek. "I'll be right back." That smile of his was so heartwarming and reassuring of the just-restored normalcy in our life that I actually stopped worrying then. Why should I fret? Any passerby could see that we were young and in love. An ideal couple. Anyone could see we were fine.

At home I made him that bowl of fettuccine, that Coke over ice, and he draped himself all over the sofa to watch an old movie.

"So how was it?"

"I don't remember a thing. Good drugs."

We looked at each other. Every fear, every possible horror, sprinted to the front of my mind and I pushed them back just as quickly as they arrived.

"Quit stressing," he said. "It won't change the outcome one iota."

"Mind reading is an invasion of privacy," I said. "So listen, gorgeous, I need to talk to you about Nonna."

I told him the whole story and he said, "Did Marianne's fudge have nuts in it? I love nuts in fudge."

"Screw you."

"Make Nonna some cookies and take them to her. Oatmeal raisin and chocolate chip. Those tollhouse cookies are pretty darn good, too."

"Why should I make cookies for her? She already weighs a thousand pounds. That's half her problem. I feel really sorry for her physical therapist. Besides, I hate to bake. You know that."

"Oh, quit whining. Make them low-fat."

"I could just make them smaller."

"Yeah, then you might leave some of them here for a certain somebody else to eat."

"I'll be back in an hour," I said, and picked up my purse.

"What's for dinner?" he said, clicking through channels.

If he was asking about dinner and asking me to make cookies, he had to be feeling pretty optimistic.

"Don't know—I'll shop for inspiration," I said. "Gotta run. Simmons closes at six."

I raced over to Simmons Seafood to buy Michael a pie and wound up with flounder fillets, half a pound of shrimp and half a pound of lump crabmeat. And, of course, a pie. My man was having a crabmeat cocktail and a piece of stuffed flounder for dinner and that was that. Then I stopped by Harris Teeter and bought all the other things I needed to make cookies, the rest of dinner and other boring items I needed for the house.

And my anxiety returned. What if something terrible was wrong with Michael? What if this was one of the last dinners I would make for him? What if he died? I couldn't inherit anything from him. There wasn't anything to inherit. Minor detail. We weren't married. It wouldn't be legal. Who would feel any sympathy for me? How would I pick up the pieces and go on? What would I do? Where would I start?

My little inner voice—the one I usually wanted to strangle because it was constantly reminding me to exercise and not to eat refined sugar, to use moisturizer and write my thank-you notes immediately, to hand-wash panty hose and to floss every day—that little voice was clearing its throat for a speech. Oh fine, I thought, let's have it.

People don't have a brain biopsy for no reason. Something is wrong and you had better steel yourself.

I decided to call Frank and Regina on my cell while I drove home. I was losing my mind and I needed help.

Regina answered the phone.

"Frank's chaperoning Tony's swim-team cookout," she said. "What's going on?"

I ran through the big parts about my trip to Napa, Nonna's predictable belligerence and finally got around to Michael and his "procedure." That was when my voice started cracking.

"Jesus," Regina said. "Listen to me. I don't know all that much about brain tumors, okay? But I don't blame you for being upset. You must be scared out of your mind. But I didn't marry a philosophy professor for nothing, okay? Here's what your brother would say and I would agree with him . . ."

"What?"

"He would say, go home, have a nice dinner, drink some wine, and if Michael's head isn't killing him, have sex. Take an OTC sleeping pill tonight, take Nonna some cookies tomorrow morning and keep yourself very busy until you have the report. And look, half the time these things turn out to be nothing. Right?"

"I know. You're right. That's what I'll do."

"You want me to tell your brother to call you?"

"Nah," I said. "Tell him I'll call him after I see Nonna. Give him a kiss for me, okay?"

"You got it," Regina said. "And, Grace?"

"Yeah?"

"I'll say my special novena for you guys."

"Thanks," I said.

My face turned red and my eyes burned with the threat of tears because Regina thought she needed to pray for me. But I also realized that when most people offered prayers on your behalf, they thought there was a real reason why they should. And Regina thought it was time to pull out her big-gun novena.

I just hated the belief that saying certain prayers with the right emphasis or number of repetitions would result in some nebulous God's mercy. If there was a God out there—and lately I had come to think that there was *something* of a plan to the world—prayer couldn't hurt. But I would never accept that you had to use exact change to get his phone to ring. To me, that was what rosaries were and what novenas were—prescriptions that promised a higher possibility of heavenly contact to those insiders who knew exactly how to administer the medicine. I recognized then that I had grown from a juvenile, genuflecting, bead-pushing, novena-saying, Friday Fish Fry staunch believer into a lonely, cynical agnostic. A lonely, cynical agnostic. So in my time of need, I turned to what I trusted—the wisdom and love of my brother and sister-in-law.

Regina's advice was right and that was why I loved her so much. Basically she told me to chill, live in the moment, eat cookies, drink some wine and whatever was going to happen would happen anyway. You couldn't rush it or prevent it. The truth would arrive not on my schedule but in its own time. My hands began to tremble. I knew the truth was going to be more than I could bear alone. I began to cry. What would I tell Michael when he saw my puffy eyes?

I would tell him the truth. At some point, Michael and I needed to have a serious discussion about his health. I mean, what if he got into an accident and died? Did he want to be an organ donor? Where would he want to be buried? Or did he want to be cremated and spread the ashes . . . where? And how could I claim to be so in love with someone about whom I knew so little beyond the day-to-day mechanics of our concentric orbits? It made me see how far we had yet to go.

When I got home, Michael was upstairs, sound asleep. All I had to do was glance at his face and I could see that he had been crying, too. His nose was a red knob of betrayal. The deep sighs that came from him began somewhere in the bottom of his own well of terror and my heart sank a little lower.

There was no point in waking him up for dinner and no point in me rushing to prepare it. I kissed him lightly and went downstairs.

The fish was so fresh I decided he could have it Friday or Saturday night in case I stayed over with my parents. I made the stuffing, seasoned the fish, assembled it and covered the small baking pan with plastic wrap. I wrote out the instructions on how to bake it and taped them to the top. The crabmeat cocktail was in a champagne saucer on lettuce with a fresh wedge of lemon, also hermetically sealed against whatever lurked in my refrigerator that might possibly overpower its delicate flavor. Then I made dozens of cookies until midnight, stopping now and then to cry a little and blow my nose.

I went to bed with my head swirling in clouds of brown sugar and butter, curled up next to Michael's back, more grateful and desperate for his love than I had ever been. The last thought I remember was wondering how I could feel so at peace that night when there was every reason for panic.

In the morning, Michael was snoring but in a quiet way that was rhythmic and lovely. I slipped out of bed, showered and dressed. I made coffee and took him a mug. He was still snoozing, but he had turned over to my side of the bed and was holding my pillows in the crook of his arm. I put the coffee down on his bedside table and pulled the sheets quietly up and over his shoulder.

As discreetly as I could, I was digging around in the closet for my sandals when I heard him mumble in a croaking voice, "What time is it?"

"It's only just eight. How do you feel?"

"Fine. I think. Yeah, I'm fine."

"There's coffee there."

"Thanks." He sat up on one elbow and reached for the mug. "You going down to Hilton Head?"

"Yeah. I'll be back by six, but if I stay over there's dinner in the fridge."

"No cookies?"

"There are plenty of cookies, little boy . . . What? Wait! Michael!"

Michael hooked my thigh and pulled me back onto the bed. Then he climbed on top of me and held the sides of my face with his hands.

"Tell your old man I'm gonna live forever and he's not." He had the biggest smirk on his face I had ever seen.

"I'll tell him."

"And tell him . . . tell him to be nice to Connie."

"Okay."

"And don't drive like a lunatic. Only one of us can have a trauma at a time."

"Fine. Whatever." Michael was staring at me like he was trying to tell me something else with his eyes. "What?"

"Nothing. I love you. That's all."

"I love you, too. Now get off of me before you start something I don't have time for or I'll never get there and back in one day!"

"Say, 'Michael Higgins is the best-looking hunk of burning love in the world and I am his personal property.'"

I started to giggle. "Michael Higgins is the best-looking—"

That was as far as I got. I didn't get to Hilton Head until noon.

"Ma?" Mom's car was in the driveway, so I figured she was home. "Ma?"

"I'm in here! Nonna's room. Where were you? I thought you were coming earlier."

I went down the hall to my grandmother's part of the house and there was my mother, up on a ladder, shuffling through the shoe boxes on the top shelves of Nonna's closet.

"The traffic was terrible," I lied. "What are you doing?"

"What does it look like I'm doing? I'm looking for things Nonna wants—her pictures of Nonno, her number three crochet hook, her holy card of Saint Drugo or somebody, the patron saint of broken bones."

"Says her. Sounds illegal."

"Yeah, well, it's easier to just do what she wants, you know?"

"You would know that better than anybody. Come down. I'll get up there."

"Fine, I'll look for her baby blue bed jacket with the tissue pocket. And her navy terrycloth slippers with the wavy-ridged rubber bottoms. And her . . . Grace? Can I tell you something?" Mom climbed down and gave me a hug. "Your grandmother is finally seriously driving me crazy."

"So? This is news? What's going on?"

Mom sighed and shook her head. "Okay. First, it was that she couldn't sleep. She said it was like being in a fishbowl. People came and went like it was Macy's whenever they wanted to. She has no privacy, she says."

"Well, she's probably not wrong about that."

"No, I'm sure she's not, but, hello? She's in a hospital, even though it's not exactly a hospital . . ."

"Don't worry. It's not exactly a nursing home either."

"Thank you! Okay, then she doesn't like the sheets. She says they smell like bleach. In fact, she tells everyone who will listen that they smell like bleach."

"So you took her sheets down there and now you're running a laundry service?"

"You got it! And I don't even mind that so much. I mean, it's nicer to have your own sheets and quilt. And towels. I have no argument with that. But then it's the food."

"She hates the food?"

"What do you think? She says she's starving to death. That she's lost twenty pounds."

"Has she? I mean, that wouldn't be a bad thing, would it?"

My mother made the sign of the cross and said, "God forgive me, Grace. Maybe she's lost weight, but I can't see it."

I came down from the ladder with a box of old photographs and holy cards. I spread everything on the bed. "But she's got you bringing her all her meals? You're catering?"

"Italian bread with Fontina cheese and Nutella or honey and fresh fruit for breakfast with orange juice and coffee with half-and-half . . ."

"She won't even drink their orange juice?"

"It has pulp and she hates pulp. And too much acid. You know that. Lunch? She's gotta have soup with some kind of macaroni, with more bread or focaccia and a brownie or a cookie."

"I get the picture. Jeez. Will she eat on their dishes at least?"

Mom looked at me and I knew the answer to that.

"God, Mom. It's a little much, don't you think?"

"Wait, you don't know the whole story. So then she can't sleep, right? So she's up at all hours watching what's going on with everybody and their coming and going and all that. And the cleaning girl comes in to wash the floors in the hall and then Nonna asks her to wash her floor. Well, she sees her dilute the cleaning solution. This girl doesn't wash in the corners. She doesn't wipe down the baseboards and, of course, the smell of the solution makes her stomach hurt worse than the orange juice."

I started laughing and I couldn't stop. My poor mother, who was on the verge of tears, plopped herself on the bed next to me and began to laugh, too. Her voice was so rusty, so uncalibrated, that I knew she hadn't thought anything was amusing in a very long time.

"Don't tell me she made you wash her floor!"

"Augh! There I was, on my hands and knees, under her bed scrubbing her floor, and in comes Miss Marianne and her fancy-schmantzy mother all dressed up in St. John, straight from the gift shop with a teddy bear and balloons."

"Did you just about die?" Clearly Connie's affection for my probable future sister-in-law had diminished.

"Yeah, but . . . oh, my God, you're gonna love this, she tells them to 'shut uppa you mout,' for God's sake—her words, I swear—because she's watching *General Hospital*!"

"Did Marianne see you down there on the floor?"

"I don't know because they got very insulted and stomped right out! They were only there two seconds."

"Oh, my God. I love it. Go, Nonna! She's a pisser, boy, isn't she?"

Mom and I were lying side by side while Mom continued to recount her story to the ceiling. "Wait! You haven't heard the best. She called 911."

"What? Why?"

"She said she wanted to go home and they wouldn't let her, so she called the police."

"Please don't tell me this. What did the hospital-slash-rehab-slash-not-a-nursing-home-but-a-facility do?"

"They put ten milligrams of Xanax in her pill cup and told her it was an anti-inflammatory."

"They should've done that from day one."

"Right?"

"So what does Dad say about you doing all this?"

"Al? Oh, honey!" Mom slapped my thigh, sat up and looked at me. "Honey? He thinks it's great preparation for when I have to take care of him!"

I groaned, rolled over and buried my face in Nonna's decorative sham that was only for show.

"And now it's time to take her dinner down to the facility."

"Let's poison her."

Mom laughed so hard I thought she might fall off the bed. "Bad girl! Bad, bad girl!" She spanked my backside about five times, but all her little slaps were in good humor.

"Come on! It's a good idea! We could take the cookies I made and brush them with rat poison!"

My poor mother! She looked worn out, too.

We packed the cardboard box with disposable plastic containers filled with each course, a setting of flatware, a bottle of Pellegrino that was actually filled with seltzer, a place mat and clean dish towel and a glass.

"I keep a salt-and-pepper shaker down there," she said.

"Good call."

"And they have a microwave I can use."

"God forbid dinner's not quite the right temperature."

"Fresh! Get in the car."

"I'm blocking you, so let's take my car." Backing out of the driveway, I noticed that the walkway was finished. "The walkway looks good, Ma."

"Don't get me started . . ."

At "the facility" we walked down the hall to Nonna's room fully prepared to meet the dragon. We passed the nurses' station and Nurse Divine was there.

"Hi," I said. "How's it going?" I knew at a glance that Nonna had infuriated her more than once. As I looked over at her she rolled her eyes and then winked at me.

"My secret weapon is in your grandmother's room," she said.

Imagine our surprise when we found a handsome older man in the zone of Nonna's age standing at the foot of her bed. His left arm was in a sling and they were having a lively and pleasant conversation.

"Come in! Come in!" Nonna said as if she were the ambassador of goodwill for the entire state of South Carolina. "Come meet my new friend, George Zabrowski!"

She introduced us and then he spoke.

"I was just saying to Mrs. Todero that as soon as she's really up to walking, I would be so honored to have her as my canasta partner over at the senior center. There's a whole group of us and we have a game going every afternoon."

"Isn't that a wonderful idea?" Nonna said.

I began unpacking the dinner and watched the dynamic between Nonna and Mr. Zabrowski as this visit unfolded. Nonna was flirting with him!

"I brought your bed jacket, Mom," my mother said.

"Oh, you can take that home," Nonna said. "I am making some big progress. That thing's for old people!"

"And your slippers, too . . ."

"Who cares about slippers? I'm going to be needing some good sneakers, I think."

"That's the spirit, Mrs. Todero," George Zabrowski said, and swung his good arm through the air in a salute of sorts.

"And maybe a velvet running suit—navy blue or burgundy?" Nonna said.

"Ah! Velvet! My late wife, Maria? She loved velvet. It's so soft to the touch, like a fabric made for royalty," he said, looking a little sad.

"But aren't you Polish? Your wife, she was . . . ?"

"She was from Italy," he said. "And a very devout Catholic."

"Ahhhhh!" Nonna said.

"I think we can go, Ma," I said in a whisper. "It's not like she even knows we're here."

We stepped out into the hall with the plastic containers to warm them in the microwave.

"What's going on? Grace? What's going on?"

"What's going on is that Nonna just began her rehab, Ma. And she's hot for George."

My mother's face had the strangest expression. It was as though an enormous magnet from the ether appeared and pulled the weight of the world from her entire body. The weight rose into the air like a flotilla of helium balloons, each one popping with delightful musical sounds, and all of Mom's troubles with Nonna were never to be seen again.

"My God!" my mother said under her breath.

"What?"

"Wouldn't it be wonderful?"

"Wouldn't what be wonderful?"

"If he could get her up and moving!" Mom put the container in the microwave, closed the door, set the time and temperature and hit the start button.

"He probably will. Watch them start dating."

The sounds of the microwave's fan whirred while we considered the possibilities of Nonna in a *romantic* relationship.

"Not happening," Mom said.

"Why not?"

"She'd never betray Nonno."

"Nonno's dead."

"That's what you think. Doesn't she talk to him every day since he went?"

"So she says. Listen, knowing her, if she thinks she can swing getting something going with old Mr. Zabrowski in there, she'll announce that Nonno came to her and said it was a good idea."

The microwave's alarm rang. It was time to feed the beast.

"I don't know," Mom said. "We'll see."

Nonna thanked us profusely and basically told us we could leave and go home whenever we felt like it.

"No need to stick around here!" she said brightly. "My friend can help me if I need anything."

"Are you sure, Mom?"

She ignored my mother. "Isn't my granddaughter beautiful? Her name is Maria Graziana—it means—"

"Mary Grace! Hail Mary! Full of grace!" George said. "What a beautiful name for a beautiful young woman!"

He was quite the charmer.

"Now go on home, Connie, and feed your family! I'll see you tomorrow."

We drove home, both of us in a little bitty state of geriatric-romance shock.

"I've never even considered my mother being with another man," Mom said.

"Whatever 'being with' at that age would possibly mean."

Mom reached over and lightly slapped my arm.

"Bad!" she said. "You certainly do have a smart mouth today!"

"Nah, not really. I'm just trying to make you laugh, that's all."

"It is pretty funny, though, isn't it? Wait till I tell your father."

"Yeah. But listen, Ma, what's not funny is Nonna making you her slave and Dad thinking it's okay to run you ragged. That is not okay."

She was quiet for a minute and then the sighing began. For the rest of the ride neither of us spoke. We pulled into the driveway and she got out.

"Your father's home. And Nicky's here. Can you stay? I could use the help tonight."

My cell phone started binging that I had a message. "Sure," I said. I had not heard it ring, but there was probably no signal in "the facility."

I looked at the number of the missed call. It was Michael. Mom was already on the way inside and I dialed him back.

"Michael? Hey. It's me. What's going on?"

"It's cancer, Grace. I have cancer in my brain."

I could feel everything drain out of me and I thought I was going to faint. "No. That can't be, Michael. It's *got* to be a mistake."

"It's no mistake. My buddy Larry has a friend in the lab and he found out and called me. He's coming over. We're gonna drink tequila until we puke."

"We'll go see another doctor, Michael. There's this guy at Duke. I know about him—"

"Hey, I just wanted to tell you. That's all. There will be plenty of time to get second opinions and all that. And it's caught early and, well, it sucks, right?"

Michael went on for a few minutes and then he asked me when I was coming home.

"Oh, God. Mom asked me to stay tonight, Michael. She's really exhausted. But I can drive back after dinner. In fact, I will—"

"No, I don't want you on that two-lane road in the dark. And you don't need to see me get as knee-walking drunk as I intend to be. So come home in the morning. I love you, Grace."

"Oh, Michael! I love you so much! Please! Don't worry too much. Whatever this is, we will just get rid of it, Michael. I swear we will." I started to cry and struggled for him not to hear me.

"It's okay, baby." He choked up, too, and I knew we were rushing to hang up to avoid a complete meltdown. "I'll see you tomorrow and we will plan a battle, okay? Don't forget to tell Big Al what I told you, okay?"

"Okay."

We hung up and I thought, Well, now I know for sure what I already knew on some gut level. I was going to lose Michael. And I was going to lose him alone because no one else cared. I felt a rush of panic and heartbreak coming up from my heart like a freight train and I had to hold it back. I had to.

It was time to go on the stage of my parents' life and so I blew my nose. I couldn't let them know. I put on a little lip gloss. I wouldn't discuss it that night. I would keep it to myself until I knew what we were really dealing with. How big and gnarly was this enemy? It might be ridiculous for me to go into a full-scale panic and wail all over my parents. That's right, I told myself, get a grip.

I went in through the garage. I could hear Marianne's voice before I saw her, and I don't have to tell you that I was in no mood for her. Or Nicky. I decided it would be a quiet night for Grace. I would let them talk about their stupid insignificant lives and I would just help Mom get dinner on the table, do the dishes, sweep the floor and go to my old room and sob into my pillows all night.

I took a deep breath.

"Hi, Daddy!" I said, and hoped I sounded like the entire future of my world hadn't just crashed.

"Princess! Come give your old man a kiss!"

I hugged him, and without thinking, I hung on to him for a split second longer than usual. But Big Al's radar was on cue. It was enough for him to hold me away from him and examine my face. But before he could say, "Is everything okay?" and before I could respond, "Sure, everything's fine," Marianne opened up her mouth and threw me just the hunk of bait I was looking for.

"Grace? Your brother said that I should have a BMW like yours and I just told him that I wasn't all that materialistic, and—"

"Shut up, Marianne, just shut up, okay?" I said in what I thought was a pretty calm voice given all the circumstances.

"What?" she said, and puffed up like a blowfish. "Nicky, she said—"

"Apologize. You had better apologize, Grace," Nicky said.

"Or what, Nicky? You're gonna do . . . what? Put me on restriction?"

"Marianne is going to be your sister-in-law, Grace. I just proposed to her tonight."

I had a couple of options then. I could have been cold to her or I could have tried to regain my composure and be gracious. For my mother's sake, and only for her sake, I chose the latter.

"No kidding? Well!" I let out a rush of air with a *whew*! "Congratulations!" But there was no ring. Until there was a ring, I didn't have to be so nice.

Everyone began to talk at once. I should have noticed the champagne glasses on the table, but I had not. We got through dinner and I drank all the wine I could get my father to pour in my glass. When he quit pouring I helped myself. I listened to Marianne go on and on about the dream wedding she had planned, and I thought it was best to ignore her as much as possible or else she would have to die by my hand. *Yes, they buried her in her wedding dress! It was such a sin! Yes, the sister-in-law is in jail . . .*

Jail? Whoa. Back up the bus. No, jail wasn't in my plans, so I decided to let her live for another day or two. We were all doing fine on the surface until I saw her waiting for me outside the powder room after dessert and coffee had been offered and passed up by everyone in favor of more champagne.

"Gwaciee?"

Ah, crap, I thought, was she going to use that baby voice on me, too? No way.

"What May-wee-annie?" I was definitely under the waves.

"You didn't apologize to me, you know."

I was suddenly very sober. I got up close to her and looked

her in the eyes as coldly as I could. I said, "Let me tell you something, you stupid phony bitch. You want to be happy in this family? You stay out of my face, okay? And never, I mean never, take advantage of my mother. Is that clear?"

A few minutes later she returned to the kitchen and said, "Did Grace tell y'all what happened?"

"No," my mother said. "What happened?"

Marianne the consummate liar had arrived to collect her trophy. "Well, Grace has agreed to be my maid of honor! Isn't that just wonderful? Isn't that just marvelous? I finally have a real sister!"

CHAPTER 14

Everyone's Opinion

There was no road longer or more depressing than the one that separated me from Michael that Sunday morning as I drove back to Charleston. I needed to talk to someone, and so as soon as I could get a clear signal, I called Frank and Regina. They weren't home and didn't answer their cells either. I left messages. They were probably at church. I waited. I started crying, then wailing, and finally I pulled myself together again. I was exhausted and hungover. I couldn't bear the thought of losing Michael and I knew just enough about brain tumors to know that very often they snatched away life. I was terrified.

I called home and Michael answered.

"'Lo?"

He sounded like he was answering the telephone from under the covers, in a cave a thousand miles away. I was obviously the first call of his day.

"Whoa! You don't sound so good."

In an odd way, I was delighted he had gone overboard the previous night. On a selfish note, it meant there might be less shock and anger from him to deal with. And I was glad he had a male friend for the things men would say to each other that they wouldn't really want to say to a woman in this kind of dire situation. On the other hand, I was jealous and remorseful that I had missed a single thing.

"Uh . . ."

"Hungover?"

"Yeah, uh . . ."

"How about if you go back to sleep and I'll just see you in about an hour and a half?"

"'Kay."

Click. Michael Higgins had left the cellular service area and returned to the fog of dreams.

I made a mental note to pick up fresh bagels, cream cheese and smoked salmon. Although a greasy burger might have been the ticket for his stomach, depending on how hungover he was and how queasy he felt. My cell phone rang and it startled me. It was Frank.

"Where are you?" he said.

"Driving back to Charleston from the Russo Show."

"So? What's going on? I have to call them today at some point."

"Well, let's see. Our stupid brother got engaged to that stupid girl and somehow she railroaded me into being the maid of honor."

"No way. Man. That's rough duty."

"You said it. So brace up for a family wedding. Nonna has met a man at 'the facility,' which is how we refer to the not-a-nursing-home where she appears to believe she is incarcerated. He's Polish, but not to worry, his dead wife was an Italian Catholic and he wants to take Nonna to his canasta club. And needless to say, Nonna is wearing out Mom with catering and laundry services, which Al thinks is all fine. The good news is that this Polish guy, George, I think that's his name, might actually get Nonna out of bed and moving again."

"Well, if she would cooperate with the physical therapist, she would get out of there a heck of a lot sooner."

"Exactly."

"Any news on Michael?"

I knew he was going to ask. Even though I had called Frank earlier to discuss this very topic, all at once I didn't want to talk about it. I think I was being so talkative to divert his attention because Michael's illness was the kind of thing that if I talked about it, it became real. I was still in the denial business even though it was, yes, it was time, time to face the truth.

"You there?" he said.

"Yeah. It's not good. The pathologist called him and it's cancer."

"Oh, God. Regina told me they did a biopsy. What kind of cancer is it and what's the prognosis?"

"We don't know anything yet, Frank. Just that the fluid had cancer cells."

"Oh, no. I'm so sorry, kid."

"Thanks. This guy in the lab is a friend of Michael's friend and he called him as soon as they did the pathology. Needless to say, I'm beyond panicked."

"Imagine how Michael feels."

"Yeah. I can only imagine. To tell you the truth, I am more than a little nervous about how Michael feels."

"What do you mean?"

"Well, what if he gets really sick? Really depressed? Really angry? I don't know what might happen, Frank."

"Take it one day at a time. They'll probably want to operate and do some follow-up treatments, Grace. You're going to have your hands full for a while."

"Yeah, well, before anybody operates on anybody, I want Michael to look into the brain-cancer center at Duke. It's supposed to be incredible. I mean, we should at least get a second opinion, right?"

"Absolutely. How old is Michael?"

"Thirty-five."

"Look, I know you're deeply troubled by this because you really love this guy. So even if it is the Big C, he's young, Grace. They'll be aggressive in the treatment." Frank was quiet for a moment and I knew he was struggling to find the words for what he was going to say. "Grace, think about it. Even if the news is catastrophic, he's not going anywhere tomorrow. Checking out from an illness takes a while. Sometimes years."

"Oh, great! That makes me feel a lot better, Frank. You mean we can still go to the movies next week? Thanks a whole lot."

"Grace? I know you are upset. If this was happening to Regina, I would be completely freaking out. But the fact is, this is Michael's cancer in Michael's brain, and thank God it's not in yours, right?"

"Well, of course. I know that."

"Yeah, but at the same time his illness is happening to you, too, right? I mean, you're not sick, but you are afraid you might lose the only guy you have ever really loved, correct?"

"Yes, the dog in the fight is mine. Frank? You don't know Michael, but he is the most wonderful, thoughtful, generous, brilliant man I have ever met in my life. When he looks at me, I feel like the most beautiful creature on earth. When he comes into a room my whole body quivers. He's smart like you, Frank. He loves learning and he loves giving. This is the most horrible and unfair thing that could happen to a guy like him. It's evil. What am I going to do? How do I stop brain cancer?"

"Let me think." He was quiet for a moment. "Okay," he began. "Here's a plan. Tell yourself you're going off to war together. Just imagine this was happening to you and take care of him exactly like you would want to be cared for. Fight with him against the enemy. Be his best advocate. God knows, he's going to need someone with strength to navigate the medical system, never mind medical insurance."

"Well, if there's one blessing in this, it's that we both have incredible health-care plans."

"Then be thankful for small favors. If you want, I can send his pathology to my friend over at Mount Sinai in the city. I can see who Regina knows; all the doctors love her."

"I'll let you know, Frank. Thanks."

"Listen to your old philosopher brother, Frank Russo. Disasters can bring out the worst in people or they can bring out the noblest and most heroic part of them. Be vigilant about yourself, Grace, so you can be proud later on."

"Wow. You are sure right about that. Thanks."

"Well, you're my sister and my only sibling I can relate to."

"Same goes for me, Frank."

"And I really love you, kid."

"I love you, too, Frank."

We talked a little more, and after we said good-bye I thought for a moment about Frank and Regina. They were rock-solid dependable. Frank was a great friend. An excellent friend. He knew me through and through, and before I could even say anything, he knew exactly where the greatest weaknesses in my resolve were and how to shore them up. He knew there was a cowardly part of me that at some point might consider running away.

But it wasn't the day for me to bail out on Michael. And to be honest, I couldn't foresee a day when I would. That was one more significant fact about really loving someone; when you really did, you stayed.

I came into the house with four grocery bags, my duffel bag, a ton of mail, the newspaper and my purse. The downstairs was a disaster. The sink was filled with glasses and dishes with the residue of take-out Mexican food stuck to the plates and flatware. The microwave door was wide open and it looked like nachos with Cheez Whiz had exploded in there. The garbage can was overflowing with wet paper towels that smelled like stale beer, and sure enough, empty Corona bottles were all over the counter, along with little containers of salsa, bags of chips, the remains of a couple of dried-up limes and a paring knife. There wasn't a seat cushion left on the sofa and DVDs were scattered all over the coffee table. The main culprit, an empty bottle of Jose Cuervo Gold, was on the floor next to the side chair, its cap missing in action. It must have been some night.

I could hear the shower running. I dumped the groceries on the dining-room table and started cleaning up. By the time

Michael came out of the bathroom, the dishwasher was running and all the garbage was outside in the big cans. I threw the cushions back on the sofa and wiped down the counters twice.

"Grace? That you, hon?"

"No, it's Merry Maids! There are six people down here doing cleanup!"

"Sorry! Sorry!"

Michael came bounding down the steps in his khaki shorts and no shirt. He was still pink from the steam and no man on this earth ever looked so appealing. He put his arms around me and we hugged hard.

"It's okay," I said. "Just sorry I missed the party."

"Don't be. It was ugly."

"Uh, yeah. Next time you want to get that trashed, go to his house."

"Are you kidding? Larry's married. His wife would kill him."

"Oh, well, that explains it, then."

"I'm kidding. Did you bring bagels? I'm starving."

If this was a man near his death, he sure didn't seem like it to me. I decided I was going to take my cue from him. If Michael felt like being active, I would put on my running shoes. If he wanted to be quiet, I would curl up with a book. Right now he wanted to spend the day on the beach.

"Let's do it," I said.

I packed the car with beach chairs and towels, a small cooler of cold water bottles, a bag of Cheetos and a tote bag of seaside accoutrements. We drove over to Sullivan's Island and parked near the lighthouse.

I put the top up, unfolded the reflector over the dashboard and locked the car while Michael unloaded the trunk.

"It's going to be a barbecue grill in there when we come back," I said.

"So we can have swordfish for supper."

I smiled at his easy mood, and knowing in the back of my

mind that there were probably going to be some rough days ahead, I was determined to enjoy the ones that weren't painted black.

We tromped over the dunes and chose a place to settle that was about halfway between the dunes and the water, close to the little waves that washed the sand as the tide went out. We had our chairs in place and shared the bottle of suntan lotion, greasing up each other's back.

"Wanna swim?" I said.

"Yeah. Let's cool off and then we can sit and read or whatever."

Holding hands, we waded up to our thighs in the surf, pausing and turning to face each other when waves rolled over us. Every now and then one would crash over our heads and we would shriek our surprise and then settle down again until the next one came along. Eventually we sank into the water, letting it cover our shoulders, and I was thinking how marvelous something as simple as a dip in the ocean could be. It was so pleasing to feel my skin cool down and to feel buoyant. I didn't even mind the salt.

"What are you thinking about?" he said.

"I'm just thinking that this whole ocean is here and it's free. Isn't that kind of wonderful?"

"Yep. I've been giving a lot of thought to what's wonderful and what makes life worth living. And you know what?"

"What?"

"I'm thinking we should put some sperm in the sperm bank. There's this nasty possibility that my treatments might leave me sterile. I mean, I know I said I didn't want kids because of what happened to my brother and all. But I think we should have that option. So what do you think?"

"I say definitely—do it. We don't have to have kids this week. It would be stupid not to have the option. We could change our minds next year."

"Okay. Good."

I was floating on my back looking at the sky, pretending that my life was without problems when in fact it was in the worst turmoil ever. And if you took my state of mind and multiplied it by ten or a million, that was Michael's.

"There's a lot that makes life worth living, Michael."

"You don't have to tell me that. Let's go dry off for a while."

We swam back to shore and then walked back to our spot, shaking the salt water out of our hair and the despondency from our shadows that stretched long across the sand. There was no pretending. We were drawing lines, the agreement of our lives. Was I in or out? Was he fighting or not? Was I with him in what he would eventually decide he wanted? Was he in charge of himself? Was I going to try to impose myself on issues that weren't really mine?

Just how in the hell were we going to deal with brain cancer? Could somebody have given me a clue?

I towel-dried my hair for a moment and then dropped into my chair after moving it and Michael's a few feet farther toward the water's edge. I ran a comb through my salty tangles, put my sunglasses on and thanked everything that I'd had the presence of mind to choose very dark lenses. My panic was well withdrawn from view and I could pose in my chair as someone merely interested in disguising the girth of her thighs with a particular positioning of her body.

Michael said, "Do you want a bottle of water?"

I said, "More than a puppy for Christmas."

The plastic cracked on its opening and I drank like someone in danger of dehydration. He settled down into his chair with his own bottle of water and I almost relaxed.

We were quiet, but the wall of thought we were raising was built of barracudas. When two people are in a moment like that, they both know exactly where the other one is, and so the responsibility shifts back and forth. Every sentence is fraught with other meanings.

"Are you comfortable?" I said. *Are you in pain?*

"Yeah. It's one gorgeous day, isn't it?" *It could be one of my last.*

"Every day should be so gorgeous." *I hope we have years left.*

"Every day *is* so gorgeous." *I never realized how much my life means to me.*

"Yes," I said, and disobedient tears slid down my cheeks. "The ocean makes my nose get stuffed up." *My heart is breaking.*

"Mine, too," he said, and I looked over in a swift and careful moment to observe his few tears and sighs as they betrayed him as well. *I don't want to die.*

We were quiet for a long time. A long time. The tide crept out and we moved closer to the water's edge every so often, clearing our throats and taking deep, noisy sniffs.

"Beach-head," I said, explaining my sinus condition.

"Me, too," he said.

"It's okay," I said, and stretched my hand toward him. He took it, grasping it with a familiarity I had never known with anyone else. Across the wet packed sand I could see the shadow of our joined hands and wished I had a camera at that moment. I wanted that picture—long and lean across our fireplace—just that position of our hands locked together in light for always. It was a silhouette of us and it ripped my heart in two.

I looked over at Michael and at that moment something changed. I didn't know what exactly, but there was a shift of energy, determination and knowledge of another outcome that had nothing to do with what would be predicted by the odds. Even the light on the simple beach of Sullivan's Island changed from yellow to blue. Don't ask me how or why. It just did.

We were determined steel beams. We had decided we would both survive his illness intact, but neither of us knew how. It was that simple and I didn't even know why. Michael didn't either. It was something else but something formidable. We were consumed by this powerful force that was so good and all-powerful in its nature we didn't even have a word for it.

Michael in his chair and me in mine, holding hands, immersed, covered up, buried in the deepest love we could imagine. He had brain cancer. We said no, we won't have this kill him; it just can't be. This thing can't have him! It just can't. He has work to do, cures and treatments to discover and a world of his own fascination to change. This disease has no place in the body of Michael Higgins—it has to go. Sorry, but it has to go. It just can't stay. It just can't.

It cannot stay.

It cannot be.

I began an internal dialogue with Michael's cancer.

Have we met? I'm sorry, I'm Al Russo's daughter, Big Al's princess. My name is Maria Graziana—Big Al's girl—and Maria Graziana Russo wants to let you big bummer from hell know that you had better just go. Just go and don't look back. That's right. Start moving. Yeah, you. Go. Our love is way stronger than your lousy whining cancer cells.

wanted to delay chemotherapy for as long as six months to a

CHAPTER 15

Stand By

"So when's your next trip?" Michael said.

"A week from Tuesday. Taking a bunch of guys and their wives to Vegas."

"On the same trip? Isn't Vegas where you are supposed to go to fool around?"

"Yeah, but this trip was booked as a family vacation. They're bringing kids, nannies—the whole family. Grandmothers, too!"

"Play the slots for me—I'm feeling lucky."

"Yeah, right. You've got a string of idiots telling you that you have a very ugly brain cancer and you feel lucky? How crazy are you?"

That was how we had come to talk of Michael's disease—as something we would only have to suffer for the short term. Michael was going to be fine. It was Wednesday and we were on the way to see our third neuro-oncologist. They all said pretty much the same thing. Michael has a malignant glioblastoma that is almost always fatal. The problem with this particular kind of brain cancer, they said, with their somber faces and starched white jackets, was that the tumors were like hot peanut butter spread on English muffins—they sank into your nooks and crannies. So you operated and removed what you could, but because the tumors left roots, they grew back. And you could only operate on a brain so many times before it turned into a cauliflower.

Well, that was an unacceptable response. I mean, it wasn't that we didn't recognize that Michael's future was in jeopardy; we just wanted to massage the odds to be in our favor as much as we could.

We were looking for the neurological team we believed would be the most aggressive in surgery and afterward with the radiation and chemo. The other two doctors we had seen wanted to delay chemotherapy for as long as six months to a year, or longer, because they thought radiation and surgery would probably be enough. They only wanted to administer chemotherapy if the tumor recurred.

But Dr. Christian Papenburg, lately of the Duke brain-cancer center, the chief neuro-oncologist there, relocated to Charleston for the climate and to bring the MUSC team of brain-tumor experts up to speed. And to save Michael Higgins.

"The most infuriating part of this is that in five years, stem cells will probably cure this," he said to us from across his massive desk.

"I don't have five years to wait around," Michael said.

"No, you don't," Dr. Papenburg agreed.

I reached over, took Michael's hand and squeezed it, and to my surprise, his hand was pouring perspiration.

"So what's next?"

"My team has gone over your MRI and the pathology. Surgery is first, followed by radiation and then chemotherapy. If that doesn't wipe it out, there are a few new therapies we can try. There are some fast-track drugs out there we can get our hands on."

"What's a fast-track drug?" I asked, thinking, *Let's talk about this.*

"One that they are rushing for FDA approval. Fortunately,

Michael, you're young and in good health. My personal recommendation to the radiologist will be to be extremely aggressive."

"What are my odds of survival?"

"Odds?" Dr. Papenburg got up from his chair, came around to the front of his desk and stood very near us. "Look, your odds may be slightly better than most for a couple of reasons. Your age and health, as I said. And our diligence."

"That's it?"

"Michael, I'm sure you've done your homework on this. The biggest problem won't be removing the tumor. It's the regrowth. But we are going to watch you very carefully. I hope you enjoyed your MRI experience because you're going to have them every sixty days for the next three years."

"How long will all of this take?" I said. "I mean from surgery to the end of chemotherapy?"

Dr. Papenburg looked at me and smiled. "Because of his youth? We can probably have the whole treatment over with by the end of October, middle of November."

"And then we watch and wait?" Michael said.

"Yes. We watch your brain for the slightest changes and pray there are none."

I was still uncertain about the nature of glioblastomas and why they were so much worse than other brain tumors, so I asked Dr. Papenburg.

"The cancer cells in glioblastoma are hypoxic, which means they have low oxygen content."

"Meaning?"

"Radiation and chemotherapy just work better with higher oxygen levels. But there are some drugs in trial now that appear to enhance oxygen delivery to hypoxic cells. We'll see."

"When do you want to do the surgery?" Michael said. "Is after lunch good for you?"

Papenburg smiled. "I have you penciled in for Friday morning. Is that good for you?"

"I'll miss *Jerry Springer*," Michael said.

"I'll TiVo it," I said.

"My nurse will give you all the particulars," the doctor said, and returned to the other side of his desk to buzz her on the intercom.

We all looked at one another, knowing that moment might well mark the date of the end's beginning. But neither Michael nor I was ready to surrender to anything.

I left Michael to the reams of paperwork that had to be done and walked out into the morning air. God! The day was gorgeous! The sky was the shocking blue of robins' eggs and the huge downy clouds seemed to roll and slide. In fact, all around me was such great beauty that I felt encouraged.

But I was foolishly numb to what Michael and I were facing. The terror I had felt over the weekend had vanished and in its place was an exquisite bubble in which I now moved from one day to the next. We had a plan. We had engaged the best doctors we could find. Those doctors were very on top of their medicine and knew what was available in clinical trials. There wasn't anything more we could ask for. And I didn't know what else to do.

The Las Vegas trip was almost a week away and Michael would be back on his feet by then. I'd be home by Saturday. Radiation couldn't begin for two weeks. It would all work in my tidy schedule. Yes, it would all work.

Las Vegas. All that glitz and glam would certainly be a good diversion for me. We were staying at the Ritz-Carlton, which was my all-time personal favorite. There would be shopping, a Cirque du Soleil production, shows and, of course, gambling. I had no use for gambling. It wasn't that I had anything against it. I just didn't believe in it. I didn't believe in it because I never had enough spare cash to consider it. But if people wanted to go throw money away, it was a free country. So I was thinking about all this as I drove back to the office and almost slammed right into Bomze in the parking lot on George Street.

"Hey!" he said, and then he saw it was me who'd almost taken the back fender off his Lexus as I came screaming across the lot to grab a space. "Grace! Wait!"

I parked, got out and locked my car. "Sorry, Bomze! I didn't see you."

"Come with me to the Haven, little girl. I'll buy you a cup of coffee."

"I'm yours for a Philly cheesesteak and a diet soda."

"No Charlestonian says 'diet soda.' You may say Diet Coke or Pepsi, but the generic term of *soda* immediately identifies you as a, pardon me, Yank."

"Wha'evah, yo." I gave him my best Jersey accent.

Bomze chuckled. "So where were you all morning? Bob Ellis Shoes?"

I hesitated because he had sort of growled at me when I was in Napa, and then I decided to tell him. When I was finished with the bulk of the story and had wiped up the last bit of ketchup with the last soggy french fry, I noticed he hadn't touched his burger.

"Bomze? You're staring at me like I have salad hanging from my teeth. What's the matter?"

"Well, first, Miss N.J., I think I just heard you choke back tears at least five times in the last fifteen minutes. I didn't think anyone north of Baltimore had tear ducts. Secondly, I had no idea Michael's situation was so serious. You wouldn't even know this talented young man except for the extreme kindness and generosity of your Bomze and his Baroness. So we accept some modicum of responsibility in all of this." Bomze wiped his lips and sat back. "When did you say Michael was having his surgery?"

"Friday morning."

Bomze drummed his fingers on the table. "Okay, here's how you are going to earn your keep until the end of January."

"What are you talking about?"

"First of all, you're not going to Lost Vegans. Sprout eating and slot playing indeed. That group is not our style anyway. I'll send somebody else."

"Bomze, I can handle this. I have everything figured out."

"Hush. Bomze's wheels are turning . . . Okay! Yes! Here's

what you are going to do. I gave a trip for twelve to Mexico City next January to St. Mary's Church on Hassell Street. I don't know what possessed me, but the priest there is from Poland and that's almost the same thing as Romania. Well, he and the Baroness were cocktailing at a birthday party for the bishop, who was planning this fund-raiser for St. Mary's, and he needed a raffle prize. Well, you know me! The next thing you know I'm saying, 'Sure! Why not?'"

"Oh, Bomze!"

"So, listen to me, my little cannoli, your mission is to research the living doodle out of Mexico City and figure out how this isn't going to cost me a dime, okay? Find some charming B and B where they can stay, and just . . . you know what to do!"

"Make it fabulous but make it cheap."

"Cheaper than cheap. And meanwhile, I don't want to see your face at the office until after New Year's Day. Got it? Take care of Michael and figure out how you're gonna save me twenty thousand dollars, okay?"

All at once it registered that Bomze was really giving me almost five months off with one little trip to plan and full pay. I burst into tears and covered my face with my hands. Bomze reached across the table and touched my arm while he pulled out a handkerchief from his pocket. He shook it out, offered it to me and sat back.

"Use it," he said. "Don't worry about it. Throw it away. I have hundreds of them. The Baroness has an aunt in Budapest who loves to monogram and embroider."

I blotted my eyes and then opened the handkerchief and blew my nose like a tugboat captain.

Bomze smiled. "Grace? If you save me money on this little trip, I'd like to send you and Michael to Cancún for a few days at the end of the trip. My treat."

"Thanks, Bomze."

"It's the least I can do. I am very fond of Michael. So is the

Baroness. You have a rocky road ahead of you. You know that, don't you?"

"Yes."

"The rockiest."

"Yes, I know."

"Call me if you want to talk or you want another doctor or anything . . ."

"Thanks. Michael's doctor, this neuro-oncologist, ran the Duke brain center for like ten years. They practice the same medicine as Sloan-Kettering or anywhere. Maybe even more cutting-edge. His colleagues here and elsewhere have already reviewed Michael's biopsy and MRI. They all say if they don't operate, Michael will surely die. If they operate, give him crazy radical radiation and superdoses of chemo, they might be able to get it all. Meanwhile, somebody might figure out a stem-cell solution to this or something. We just have to keep Michael alive and healthy long enough. And there are already some new treatments that look pretty promising . . . What?"

"Oh, Grace. You poor baby."

"Yeah, poor me. But poor Michael."

"True. But poor you, too. Let's get out of here." Bomze paid the check and we stepped out from the coffee shop into the brilliant light of the afternoon.

"Wow," he said.

"Wow, what?"

"Oh, I guess it's just hard to understand how the world can be so beautiful and tragic at the same time."

"I had the same thought about an hour ago, Bomze. But maybe this won't be a tragedy. Please be optimistic for me and for Michael." I smiled at him, put my arms out to give him a hug and he hugged me like mad.

"I'll pray for Michael and for you, too," he said.

On another day at another time I might have said, *Prayer is a waste of your good breath,* but recently, with everyone offering to pray, I just said, "Thanks. I didn't know you were religious."

Bomze looked up and down the street, perhaps to see if the devil himself was lurking around. "In times of trouble? I'm on my knees like everybody else!"

"Well, yeah. You never know. Prayer might help."

At least it would make Bomze feel better.

Michael was admitted to the hospital on Thursday afternoon. He had a semiprivate room, and thankfully, the other bed was empty. I brought him dinner and hung out with him for a while, and around nine that night he decided it was time for me to go home.

"There's no point in hanging around, baby. You go and get some rest. By ten o'clock tomorrow this whole thing will be behind us. I'll be fine."

"Are you sure?"

"Grace? I have full confidence in Papenburg and his guys. Really. I don't want you roaming the streets late at night. Now go. What if some lunatic grabs you?"

Naturally, he grabbed me and threw me down on his bed.

"Who's the lunatic now?" I said, and over the next few minutes there was some heavy-duty hooking-up in play.

We rolled around those hospital linens like sweaty wrestlers, knowing perfectly well we were misbehaving but not caring about decorum one bit. And P.S., if the sheets smelled like bleach, I didn't notice.

The door opened and there stood a forbidding-looking, gasping nurse holding a tray with a pill cup. We looked like two kids on lovers' lane busted in the bright beam of a patrolman's flashlight. My shirt was unbuttoned, Michael had his hand inside of my dislocated bra, and I had my hand inside the front of his pajama bottom.

"Ahem," she said. "Visiting hours are over? Sorry y'all."

It was just a little bit awkward.

"Sorry," Michael said, and stood up in front of me to give me a chance to adjust things. But Michael was standing, facing the nurse, and the awkward moment was now hers. It was a romance-novel revelation of the "equipment" and its potential.

The nurse averted her eyes and cleared her throat. "I think I'll just step out and, you know, give you kids a moment to, you know, cool *down*, um, I mean *off*. I mean, I'll be back in a minute, okay?"

"She called me a kid! I love that," Michael said when the door whooshed to a close. "Here, take my watch and my wallet."

I took them and thought about him having no belongings to distinguish him from any other patient. Except for his plastic patient's bracelet. I kissed him on his forehead and said, "I'll be here bright and early."

When I put my key in the lock, the house phone was ringing. I hurried in to grab it.

"Grace?"

"Oh, hi, Mom," I said. "What's up?"

"Nonna. She wants Juicy Couture velvet exercise clothes. Can you imagine such a thing? Doesn't Saks carry that line?"

Nonna wanted Juicy Couture sweats? "Yeah, but not in *her* size."

"Well, she's got her heart set on Juicy Couture. I just can't see my mother with juicy plastered across her backside. But you know how she is, now that she has George in her life . . ."

Mom went on and on. I thought my head was going to explode from listening to her stupid ramble about what, once again, Nonna wanted her to do. At some point I put the phone down to grab a bottle of wine from the refrigerator. By the time I found the corkscrew and a glass and picked the phone up again, she knew what I had done and was annoyed.

"Grace? If you don't want to talk to me, you could just say you're busy or something. You don't have to insult me by—"

For the third or fourth time in the last forty-eight hours, I started crying again.

"Grace? What in the world? Darling . . ."

"You know what? You and Daddy and Nonna and Nicky and that stupid Marianne . . . you think you're the only people in the world. You have no idea what goes on in my life."

"We do not think that!"

"Yes, you do. It's like every time I come down there I'm a bit player in some kind of reality show that's real to everyone else, but when I walk out of there it's into some kind of a fake life or something . . ."

"I do not!"

"Mom? Yes, you do." I didn't know how to say it as this whole conversation wasn't rehearsed, so I just blurted it out. "No one, you included, has ever recognized my relationship with Michael. You don't know him, but he is brilliant and talented and—" I really broke down then and I couldn't help it. I sobbed and sobbed. I had finally fallen in love and I had fallen so hard it was shocking. It was such an improbability that I would be in love that even my own family never gave it a second thought, except to criticize and second-guess it. How could I explain how I felt to my mother, who seemed oblivious to everything except the shackles she wore? And the possibility that I might lose Michael was leading me to utter hopelessness. I was exhausted from the seesaw of up one minute—making a plan, going through the paces—and down the next—putting him in a hospital, considering the odds.

"Grace? Grace?"

I could barely speak. I took several sips of the wine I had poured and tried to compose myself. I knew I sounded horribly desperate and miserable. I couldn't help that either. "He's dying, Mom. He's dying. He's the only man I ever loved and I'm going to lose him. You all don't understand how much this is completely tearing me apart." My voice was a whisper then. "I feel like I'm dying, too. I am."

"Grace, baby, I am so sorry. What's the matter with him? What can I do?"

"Nobody can do anything. He's having surgery tomorrow morning. I checked him into MUSC today. Mom, he has a brain tumor and the survival odds are about zero. He's got about a year, even with radiation and chemo."

"Oh, dear heavenly Mother! Grace! He's so young!"

"And you know? I keep trying to bolster his spirits and give him hope and be strong for him, but like tonight I had to ask him for his aunt's phone number and his cousin's, too . . . I don't even know his next of kin . . . I don't know his next of kin. All I know is that I'm not it!"

"Oh, honey, this is no time to worry about being married. It really isn't."

I refilled my glass and thought about that for a moment and then I said, "Look, Mom. That's not even the point. There's just a lot about me that isn't working as little Gracie Russo anymore. That's just how it is, Mom."

"I know, honey. I see that."

"I'm tired of having to leave Michael every holiday. I run down there to try to help you with Nonna and to please everyone and then what? Does anyone appreciate the fact that I am leaving Michael out because his ancestors are from Ireland? No, they do not."

"Grace? I don't want to fight with you about that. You obviously have a lot on your mind and I would be upset, too, if I were in your shoes. Listen, honey, we have a prayer group at church that prays continuously for the sick. I would be happy to add Michael's name—"

"What is all this bull about prayer? Why is everyone offering to pray for Michael? Do you really think it would make a difference? I mean, it's so stupid! It's just naive! Why don't we fund stem-cell research and let them find a cure for all these horrible diseases?"

"First of all, prayer is not bull, Grace. And second, the Holy Father says—"

I hung up.

I had reached a new personal low. I had hung up on my mother. To my surprise and relief, she didn't call back.

After the worst night of almost no sleep and that same horrible nightmare torturing me when I did sleep, I went down to the hospital before it was even daylight. I looked in Michael's room and he was sound asleep. I knew they would be getting him up soon. He already had an IV and I suspected they had given him some pre-op sedative. Sure enough, minutes later the door swung open and a nurse and two orderlies came in with a gurney to move him.

"Good morning, Dr. Higgins," the nurse said. "Are you ready to take a ride?"

I stood up as Michael stirred with the transfer from bed to gurney. I leaned over and gave him a kiss on his forehead.

"I'll be right here, baby," I said. "I'll wait. Love you."

He nodded and opened his eyes for a second. Then he smiled at me. I was so glad I was there. Even though I knew he probably wouldn't remember seeing me, I was just glad that I had arrived in time. The nurse directed me to the waiting area and said that as soon as Michael was in recovery his doctor would come to tell me how he had fared during his surgery. I was so overtired and the waiting area was already crowded, so there was no place to curl up. Nonetheless, I must have nodded off because a while later, I felt someone shaking my shoulder. I looked up into the face of my mother.

"I brought you a carton of orange juice with low acid and no pulp," she said. "And a sausage biscuit."

"Thanks," I said. I opened the Burger King bag and pulled all the food out. "What are you doing here?" Obviously, she was there to be with me, but I was surprised to see her.

"What do you think I'm doing here? I came to be with my daughter in her hour of need. That's what I'm doing here."

I looked at her face, and even though we had extremely different politics and views on most everything, I thought that her coming was just about the sweetest thing she had done for me in many years.

"Thanks, Mom. I mean it."

"You're welcome. Now tell me everything the doctors have told you."

It all came pouring out, the illness, the prognosis, Bomze's gift of the time off to help him plan the little trip to Mexico, but most of all, I told her about our general terror. Mom listened with intense focus, occasionally shaking her head and taking my hand in hers. Her eyes were misty and I thought she might break down and cry, too. In the end, she put her arms around me and hugged me. She rubbed my back in circles and suddenly I remembered that she used to do that when I was a little girl and came running to her crying over one thing or another.

"So he has to have chemotherapy and radiation?"

"Yeah."

"Oh, dear."

"Well, it sucks because it will probably be worse to deal with than the operation."

"He might lose his hair."

"It'll grow back."

"And it might make him sterile, Grace, you know that, don't you?"

"Yeah. We talked about it. He's frozen some sperm so that if we ever change our minds about children and marriage and all that, there will be something saved."

My mother lifted her chin and she inhaled profoundly with surprise. "Frozen sperm? You're not talking about . . . I mean, you aren't considering artificial insemination, are you?"

"Yeah, I am. Why? Is the Church opposed to *that,* too?" I could feel my anger rise.

"You *know* they are. It's unnatural."

"Look, Mom, if you wanted to come to Charleston to make me feel better, this isn't making me feel better at all! Should I never have children because a bunch of old men in dresses have some hypothetical problem with a science they don't even understand?"

"The Holy Father says—"

"Who *cares* what he says? Thousands of people have children with help from a lab. It's not a sin! What is the *matter* with you? It's like you don't have your own mind—you just do what everyone tells you to do and—"

With that, my mother stood up from the sofa and said, "I'm

leaving, Grace. I hope Michael comes through his surgery fine and that your science can heal him of something no one has ever survived. If I were you? At this point I'd try to find my faith and beg God for mercy."

My face was buried in my hands and I didn't even look up when I said, "Just go, Mom. Just go." But when I did look up, she was way down the hall, walking out on me.

There went my mother, I thought, who spent her life parroting her mother, her husband and her pope. What a miserable way to be, I thought. It was worse than being Victorian. It was worse than anything because it kept us from being what we should have been to each other.

I wept and wept, for my mother, for myself and then for Michael's mother. What was the universal demon that kept too many of us apart from the one woman we needed most? How could I ever hope to be a good mother with the lukewarm mother I had? I knew I had a smart mouth. I knew I wasn't the perfect daughter. But why in the world couldn't she bend just long enough to listen? Why couldn't she walk me through an issue without a ceremony? Oh, I was so wrung out. I wished Regina had been with me. It was the longest day I had ever lived.

Finally, after waiting for what seemed like eons, I went to the nurses' station. I was told Michael had just been returned to his room and was resting comfortably. The surgeon never came to reassure me and tell me what he had found, but the nurse said that Michael had done very well.

"He's young," she said.

"Yes," I said. Too young to die.

After I was convinced he was stable, I went home for a while. When I opened the refrigerator door there were four Mason jars of my mother's homemade chicken soup and four jars of her marinara sauce. On my table was her most loved chocolate coconut cake in her ancient Tupperware cake carrier. She had used the extra key to bring food to me. It was what she knew how to do. Bring food. She couldn't put herself in my shoes. She couldn't consider my feelings about the Church and prayer and Ireland and all the complete nonsense I tolerated from them. But she had left her bed very early that morning to arrive when she did and she had probably been cooking long into the night. I was so confused and so upset, I didn't care.

I sank into one of our dining chairs, opened the cake carrier and put my guilty finger into the icing. It was just as delicious as it always was.

I wanted to call Regina and get some sympathy, but I was too tired to dial the phone and I didn't have the energy required to relive it all. Besides, I would have had to hear Regina tell me that I didn't accept advice or criticism well. She would say, *What do you expect from your mother? To go back on what she's believed all these years? It's how she's wired, Grace. If she agrees with you then her whole paradigm is screwed up.*

Oh, Connie? Why? Why are you so rigid? Especially today of all days? She hopes my science can take care of this?

And had my father called? No. My stupid brother Nicky? No. His twit? Thankfully, no.

I ate some more icing, but with less relish. I felt extremely bad about losing my temper with Mom, but it would be a while before I called her to apologize. She was just wrong. They were all just wrong.

CHAPTER 16

Let's Not Fight

It was October when I finally called Mom to apologize. We had spoken many times during the weeks. But I was so busy with Michael and taking him back and forth to the radiation oncologist and she was so busy with Nonna that we had somehow never gotten around to the apology part of the apology. I just wanted the air officially cleared.

"I always told you children, there are enough people out in the world to fight with. You don't need to fight with your family."

"You're right, Ma, you're right."

"I know this is a very stressful time for you. I asked around and I know pretty much what you are facing. Worse than that, I know what Michael is facing and therefore what you are facing—"

"Just imagine if it was Dad."

"I can't."

"I love Michael like you love Dad."

There was silence and then a tiny voice from my mom said, "We have to have a moment together, you and I. We have to have a moment to talk. And when I tell you what I . . . I will tell you, Grace, what I have never told anyone. And when I tell you these things, maybe I will seem like someone who makes more sense to you, not like someone who is a doormat."

"Okay. Anyway, I'm sorry, Mom. I really am." What was she talking about?

"Let's not speak of it ever again. I know how you love me because I know how I love you. And if you tell me you love Michael with so much passion, you have to know that a mother's love is that passion times fifty or more times a number that doesn't even have a number. I can forgive you almost anything, Grace."

"Jesus, Mom. Let's not be so dramatic, okay? I mean . . ."

To my surprise, she ignored that, but she was quiet for a moment and then she said, "May I just point something out?"

"Sure . . ."

"For someone who claims not to believe in God or the Church, you sure do bring up their names an awful lot, Grace. I mean that in the nicest possible way, sweetheart . . ."

"Right."

"Anyway, we are all praying for Michael, Grace, whether or not you believe in the power of prayer."

"It's not that I believe in prayer or that I don't, Mom. It's just not about that at all."

"Okay. What's it about?"

"I don't know. I just don't think God gets involved, because if there was a God who listened to your prayers and could change the outcome of things, we never would have had concentration camps or terrible hurricanes or any number of all the horrible diseases. I think prayer is a coping mechanism. It makes people feel better to think there's a God on their side."

"Grace, Grace, Grace. When did you get so cynical? Did you ever stop to think how much *worse* diseases and catastrophes and wars could be *without* prayer?"

"Well, I guess everything is point of view, right? Anyway, Michael is tolerating the radiation and chemo extremely well. Although he's lost his hair and a little weight. He's back at work, part-time. His youth is certainly helping, and the fact that he was in excellent shape when this whole party got started."

"So his doctors are satisfied with his progress?"

"Yeah. You would think that brain surgery would have you locked up in intensive care for months. But it is a superfast recovery, at least to get back on your feet anyway."

"He's not complaining? No headaches?"

"Nope. He feels better now than he did before the surgery. And he's asking for another chocolate coconut cake."

I could hear the pleasure in Mom's voice. "Tell him I'll bring him one the next time I come to Charleston."

"I will. So? How's Nonna?"

"How's Nonna? Hoo, boy! Well, she's using a walker, but she's getting around better than ever. The good news is that she spends almost every day over at the senior center playing canasta and crocheting. She's with this fellow George constantly. The bad news is that I have to cook everything. She's given up cooking for love. And she's on the South Beach Diet."

"Please! Seriously?"

"I'm telling you the truth! At least she's happy. She's losing weight like nobody's business and she thinks she's in love. I caught them kissing. That was pretty embarrassing, let me tell you."

"Ew! I think there's a little bit of vomit in my throat."

"Right? Mine, too. She says she saw Nonno and he was happy for her to have a gentleman friend. Anyway, that's the story with Nonna."

"Gross. Well, I'd love to come down and see y'all, but I'm taking care of Michael, his mother—to the extent that anyone can—and I'm still working on that trip to Mexico for January."

Mom knew that Bomze had given me time to be with Michael and to plan a Mexican trip. But she didn't know I was taking a group of devoted Marian Catholics to see the shrine of Our Lady of Guadalupe. If she and Nonna knew that, they would have been on the plane with me. That was the last thing I needed.

With that I realized that I almost forgot I had to be at St. Mary's rectory at three o'clock. It was two-thirty and I didn't want to be late for my first appointment with a freaking priest.

"How is Michael's poor mother?"

"Pitiful. Honest to God, Mom . . . I mean, *honestly*. Alzheimer's has got to be the most unfair illness there is. I mean, really. You live your whole life as a dignified woman and in your final years you're reduced to this mindless, skeletal shadow of who you used to be. I've been out in Summerville with Michael like three times this month, because Michael's still not driving and it's terrible. Man, if that was you, I'd cry my eyes out. I really would."

"Thank heavens we don't have that in our family."

"I think if I found out I had it, I'd drink the Kool-Aid. Seriously."

"Don't say that! Suicide is a very serious—"

"I'm kidding, Mom!"

"Oh. Okay then, give Michael our best."

"I will, Mom. Thanks."

Well! *That* was a change in the parental attitude. We had arrived at a place of pleasantries. Not bad. I'd take it.

We hung up and I scooped up all my papers and rushed over to St. Mary's Church. If I had been a good Catholic, St. Mary's is where I would have been attending Mass on Sundays. I wasn't.

I rang the polished brass doorbell, and in a few minutes, a housekeeper answered.

"Hi! I'm Grace Russo from Bomze Platinum Travel. I have an appointment with Father John at three."

"Please come in," she said. I followed her into a room that looked like an office and a library. "I'll tell him you're here."

She left, closing the tall doors behind her. The ceilings of the first floor of the rectory had to be twenty feet high, with crown moldings trimmed in a Greek key motif. The walls were lined with bookcases filled with old leather volumes of every description. And the oversize oak desk looked to be at least a hundred years old. There was a framed picture on a side table of a Franciscan priest with Pope John Paul II and another of the same priest with Desmond Tutu.

"I was a much younger man then."

I turned to face the priest of the photographs and found the kindest face I thought I had ever seen. In fact, it was startling. I had expected him to be larger and more ecclesiastical and threatening or something. But he was wearing simple black cotton trousers, a short-sleeved black shirt and, of course, a small Roman collar.

"Please, let's sit down. Martha is bringing us some iced tea." Rather than sit behind his desk, he sat opposite me in one of two chairs in front of his desk. "Well, it's nice to finally meet the face behind the voice."

"Thank you, Father. It's nice to meet you, too." I handed him my business card. "What a beautiful rectory this is, and I know St. Mary's is supposed to be beautiful, too."

I saw him knit his eyebrows and glance at my card. I could almost hear what he thought. *What? Russo? She's Italian and not a Catholic?*

"Well, we'll have to see that you get a tour, Ms. Russo."

"Please, call me Grace."

"All right, it's Grace, then."

"So about our trip. Here's what we have so far. And I guess I should tell you this first. Since this is a donated trip, it's not exactly going to be luxurious. Your group can pay for upgrades where they are available. But we're talking about basic rooms, traveling by nice tour buses, not limos, meals that are the same for everyone in nice restaurants but not five-star—"

"Ms. Russo, the parishioners who won this trip are very normal folks and not the kind of people who would demand anything. Mostly they are seniors and they haven't stopped talking about seeing Our Lady of Ocotlán and the shrine of Our Lady of Guadalupe. This is a huge event for them and we are very grateful to Mr. Bomze for his generosity."

"Thank you. I'll let him know. Anyway, I was thinking about adding in a tour of the Museum of Anthropology. It's loaded with pre-Columbian art and artifacts. Fascinating place."

"That sounds wonderful," he said.

"Yes, and there's an old convent I think they might enjoy in Coyoacán, right outside of Mexico City in San Ángel . . ." I went on and on about all the interesting spots I had put together in the itinerary and he listened carefully.

"My goodness! I can't believe you have devoted so much time to this trip and it's a gift!"

"Well, I'm working from home right now and—"

"Oh? Oh, of course, times have changed so much. With the Internet and so forth, an office is hardly necessary anymore, is it?"

"Well, actually, I am sort of helping my boyfriend recuperate from brain surgery, and he doesn't feel up to driving yet, so I get to be nurse and chauffeur."

"I'm sorry to hear it. That has to be a strain on you, a little bit anyway? Is his prognosis good? Can St. Mary's offer you a free stab at divine intervention?"

He smiled as he said it, but he had no idea he had touched such a raw nerve. He could not have known how physically and mentally exhausted I was, or maybe it showed on my face.

"Father John, may I ask you a question without seeming like a complete philistine?"

"Of course! You wouldn't believe the questions I take."

"Okay. Here it is. Do you think—I mean, do you believe prayer really matters? I mean, do you think it makes a difference?"

He sat back in his chair and looked at me for what seemed like a few very long minutes, but I'm sure it was just seconds. First, there was a little sadness in his eyes and then the pastor in him saw an opportunity to save an errant soul. He leaned forward with his hands on his knees.

"Grace? You have asked a question that has been pondered by all the great minds for thousands of years. Saint Augustine, Francis of Assisi, Flannery O'Connor . . . The Church's answer is yes, it makes an enormous difference. But if you're asking me, John the *man,* what I think, I would have to admit that deliverance as a result of petition seems to be a little bit of a hit-and-miss affair."

"Right? It is, isn't it?"

"Yes, but you have to remember what the essence of prayer is supposed to be. It's not just about begging God to give us what we want. Prayer is supposed to be conversation with God. If it's true that God has a plan for each of us, and I believe He does or I wouldn't be sitting here—"

"Seriously? You believe there's a plan for me, Grace Russo, on God's hard drive?"

"Yes, I do."

"Really?"

"Yes, and that plan may be for us to experience many things. Didn't He so 'love the world that He sent His only Son'? And why? To have the human experience. The closer we are to God and the more we talk to Him . . . and, well, would you listen to me? I'm proselytizing like some television evangelist. I've taken up way too much of your time. This can be a discussion for another day, Grace. I like to talk about the nature of faith and why some people have it and others don't."

He stood and I did, too.

"I might like to listen, Father. I really might enjoy that."

"Well, if you're a good listener, I'll reward you with a tour of the church and show you the painting of Saint Peter. It was done by Caesare Porta in the early nineteenth century . . . and the poor devil has six toes on his right foot!" He opened the office door and motioned for me to follow him out.

"I love it! Why does he have six toes?"

"No one knows. Maybe it's to show that only God is perfect, or maybe Saint Peter really had six toes on his right foot? But you have to remember something."

"What's that?"

"Just because it walks like a duck doesn't mean it's a duck.

Every chink isn't a sign of something; sometimes it's just a chink."

I smiled at him, having no clue what his duck/chink joke meant. He wasn't pompous and he wasn't seeping theology from his every pore. He would be fun to travel with, I thought. Maybe interesting, too.

"Right! Well, here's the itinerary and I'd like it if you could just give it a glance and be sure it's not too rigorous for any of the people coming. And if you could let me know about food allergies and so forth—there's a form in there for each of them to fill out for medications, emergency contacts and all that stuff . . ."

"My goodness, you are so thorough!" He opened the front door and waited for me to pass through. "And don't worry about Michael. I'll say a Mass for him."

"Thank you, Father. I'll talk to you soon."

I was walking back to my carriage house and I had a paralyzing thought. I had never spoken Michael's name. Had I?

CHAPTER 17

Father Knows Best

It was November and the holiday season was heralded in retail outlets across the land. In all the grocery stores, smiling cardboard turkeys sporting Pilgrim hats swung from the ceiling of every aisle. Boxes of Christmas candies and the ingredients for fruitcakes and cookies appeared overnight in beautiful displays. Store employees wore Santa caps and sat at prominently placed tables taking orders for spiral-cut honey-baked hams and other specialty items while chatting with customers about how many people would be around their table that year.

Michael would not be at my family's house for Thanksgiving, but I would. We didn't bring it up to each other because what was the point?

We had done some grocery shopping and we were feeling pretty good as we pushed a cart through the throng of holiday shoppers at Lowe's, intending to buy only a bag of mulch for the survival of our tiny winter garden and to restock our supply of lightbulbs. Needless to say, many other things found their way into our hands.

"Look at this cordless drill," he said. "It's like only thirty bucks! Boy, I could use this!"

"Put it back so Santa can surprise you!" I took it from his hands and replaced it on the shelf. "Of course, depending on how good you were this year?"

"Are you kidding? *This year*? This year I was a saint."

"Yeah, you sort of were," I said, and smiled at him.

He leaned over and kissed me on the cheek. "So were you."

"Don't give me unrealistic expectations of some fantastic gifts from you, Dr. Big Shot," I said. "I'm thinking about a big shiny Rolex."

"Yeah, right. Don't let me forget to go to Barnes & Noble."

"With diamonds. What, so you can buy me an Itty Bitty Book Light, you Don Juan, you?"

"No, so I can pick up the load of books on tape for my mom's nursing home."

"Oh."

"And large-print paperbacks. They're getting rid of a bunch of old stock and it's cheaper to donate it than it is to return it, I guess."

"You are so good to do that. Really, Michael."

"Hey, old people need love, too, right?"

"Like my genius brother says, duh."

"Besides, it gives me a chance to sit with my mother for a while."

Sit with his mother and do what? I knew he was getting depressed just thinking about the futility of it all.

We walked down some more aisles looking at bathroom fixtures and new screen doors and came to a forest of artificial trees, decorated and lit. I felt a rush of childish hope and wonder. Even fake Christmas trees always had that effect on me. And I hoped that maybe it would cheer him a little, too. "Michael? Why don't we put up a Christmas tree now."

"It's not Thanksgiving yet. You can't have a tree until after Thanksgiving."

"Says who? Let's make the season last."

He looked at me and, shaking his head, he said, "You got lights somewhere at home?"

"Are you serious? I'm Italian. I got bubblers, blinkers, multi-colored and little white ones."

He picked up a box that held a six-foot tree and crammed it in our cart. "Then I say let's go home, turn on the air-conditioning and light a fire."

"I've got some old Perry Como somewhere we can play and I can make us some hot chocolate."

"Skip the hot chocolate. Let's have a bowl of pasta and a bottle of something red."

"Perfecto!"

I could hardly believe it, but Connie and Big Al almost invited Michael to Thanksgiving dinner. I say *almost* because that's the kind of invitation it was.

Mom said, "So? What's Michael doing for Thanksgiving?"

"He's going out to the nursing home to be with his mother."

"Santa Maria, *Madre Dio*! How is the poor woman?"

"It's beyond bad. We're talking bleak here. She can't swallow, so she can't eat. It's ice chips and morphine. She's bedridden, can't speak, can't register anything—I mean, how much worse could it be?"

"Still. It's gonna break his heart to lose his mother."

"If you asked Michael, he would tell you that he lost her a long time ago. He says he's just caring for her body out of respect. But I know Michael's heart. He's hoping for just one more glimmer of recognition, something, anything. It's just very sad."

"Well, Grace, maybe we can send him a plate of food. Do you think he might like that?"

"I'm sure he would love that, Mom. Thanks."

I started to laugh to myself. He wasn't asked to come to the table with the family, but a plate piled high with turkey and stuffing could be wrapped up to go. Would the Little Match Boy out there in the snow like something to eat? It was a step, but a pathetically comical one.

I had convinced myself that something had changed for the

better between my mother and me, and then I wasn't sure for a while. But when she almost invited Michael to dinner, I was positive of it. I wasn't her peer, but I was no longer just her daughter. Or maybe she simply respected the fact that I had stayed close to Michael during his illness.

It was extremely unfortunate timing that during the weeks of Michael's recovery, his mother began a terrible downhill slide. I thought his mother's illness was too much for him. He needed optimum conditions to fight his own disease, and his mother's decline was dangerous to his own health. All that stress and the accompanying anger and frustration of not being able to change a single thing. I mean, I didn't want to sound cynical, but she wasn't my mother and Michael was my everything.

I said I would stay with him for dinner but he said no, it didn't matter, that his mother was in such poor shape. He was determined to spend the day at her side, just talking to her. I thought it wasn't such a great idea because I didn't think he needed to get hit in the head—no pun intended—with the fact that his mother was on the way to the next world, assuming there was one, which Nonna assured us there was as she continued her dialogue with Nonno, who was encouraging her from beyond the veil to keep playing canasta with George Zabrowski.

Mr. Zabrowski was coming to dinner, too. The world was coming to dinner—Frank, Regina and the kids, Nicky, Marianne and her mother, me, Mom, Dad, Nonna—we would be a baker's dozen and an indoor traffic jam. And I had decided on my own without any consultation from my live-in doctor that I was going to make him a little Thanksgiving dinner on Wednesday night.

What was the holiday update from Hilton Head? Maybe because Nonna had stopped cooking and maybe because they all thought there was more room in the yard than in the house—which was true by a long shot—Big Al had a sudden interest in cooking a turkey on a spit on the grill. And he wanted oysters. Lots of them. He didn't just want oysters on the half shell, he wanted them steamed and in chowder and in the turkey's stuffing, and did my dad need a little boost? Ew. Nasty! Mom didn't ask. She simply ordered a bushel of oysters from Bluffton, which were the world's most perfect examples of the juicy little bivalves.

The Thanksgiving plans were well under way and we all wondered if this was the day Nicky would cough up the diamond Marianne was expecting—like Garfield and a giant hairball. Well, the others wondered—I dreaded the thought. I could see it all now.

We would gather around the Thanksgiving table, and before the antipasto, the zuppa 'scarole, the manigot, the inevitable oohs and ahhs over Big Al's bird from the grill, there would be flashes of blinding light from her big-ass tacky diamond with the oval one-carat baguettes raised high in the platinum princess setting, resulting in permanent cornea damage for the whole family except for Nicky and Marianne, who would wear sunglasses to the table. And a manicure—Marianne would have had tips applied and Frenched . . .

The thought of Marianne coming into my family depressed me, but not as much as having to be in her company for extended periods of time. As soon as she got pregnant, Nicky would run around on her with a cocktail waitress from the strip joints out at the border, running his cheap honey over to the Squat 'n Gobble in Bluffton for fried chicken and sweet tea only to be discovered in a teary screaming scene. Then Nicky would start fooling around with the newly crowned Miss Striped Bass, whom he would fall for in Manning during the weeklong festival. They would soon be spotted at the Chat 'n Chew in Turbeville, having pancakes and coffee discussing why there was a ban on alcohol in the town. There would be no end to Marianne's histrionics and no end to Nicky's deceit, and in ten years they would have five daughters, all of whom would be clones of Marianne. The rest of my life would be filled with Mariannes in various stages of hormonal development at every family gathering, whining, bickering and all of them speaking in a baby voice. Nonna would be crocheting them baby blankets and then blankets for their Barbies, Mom would be teaching them to bake cakes, and Big Al would put a thousand miles on his Cadillac taking Nicky out for a moment of peace over a beer in the original titty bars out at the state border that started the problem in the first place.

The future that Marianne wanted so desperately to realize was the one that always gave me a panic attack. But not as much as it used to. As you know, just to be sure, *just in case* Michael and I were wrong about marriage and families, zillions of hearty little swimmers were waiting in the deep freeze for us to have a change of heart. Needless to say, I never discussed this with my mother again. I didn't feel like having another argument with my catechism-beating mother over artificial insemination while the rest of the family drooled over Marianne and her ring.

Before I left for Hilton Head, I had a brief meeting with Father John to pick up all the forms and to answer any questions he might have about our Mexico trip.

His smiling housekeeper let me in and I waited for him in his study. There was a small fire in the fireplace; even though it wasn't that cold outside, it had been raining. The warmth of burning wood took the chill out of the room. I stood waiting, looking at the flickers of the red-and-gold flames, and thought how nice it was to be in that room. Father John's desk stood directly opposite the large doors. As you entered the room, on your right was a well-worn sofa and two chairs with reading lamps. And on your left, the street side, was a large table with eight chairs, probably used for meetings more than dining. It was very old-world and very familiar to me—probably from all those ancient movies with David Niven and Loretta Young.

I wondered for a moment what it must have been like to lead a life that was consecrated to anything, much less God. It must have been a tremendous comfort to have a rule book to follow that led to the pearly gates on your death. That kind of confidence and assurance had eluded me in my life, up to that point anyway. But I didn't have any illusions or expectations that I ever would have it. I was just glad that Michael appeared to be doing as well as he was.

"You seem deep in thought, Grace," Father John said.

I almost jumped out of my skin. "I didn't hear you coming!" I said, and laughed at my own clumsiness as I bumped into a wing-back chair. "How are you, Father John?"

"I'm fine. Fine. I have lots of responses for you. Let's sit down, shall we?"

"Sure, thanks." He handed me a folder and I glanced inside.

"A couple of the older people were a little concerned about spicy food and about the water. I assume that they have some gastrointestinal issues or something, but I was thinking that in the restaurant area—"

"Don't worry, Father. I always make sure every restaurant can provide something very bland, like broiled chicken and rice for the delicate stomachs, and we only drink bottled water. And I travel with a kit of emergency items, like over-the-counter tummy meds."

"Good, fine! That's great. One other thing that may be of interest to you . . ."

"Sure, what's that?"

"I taped an EWTN special on Our Lady of Guadalupe for you. You know, brush up on the story and all that?"

"Sure, but, I mean, you know religion's not my thing, really, but sure. Why not?"

"Ah. That's right. Well, here it is anyway."

"Thanks."

"Sure. Now tell me, how is Michael doing?"

"Well, you'd never know to look at him that they said he had incurable brain cancer. He's doing just great. He just got back an MRI and there's no sign of regrowth."

"May I ask what kind of brain cancer?"

"Sure. He had a really nasty one—glioblastoma, stage four."

I saw Father John's jaw twitch, which told me he was trying

to figure out what to say, knowing this was a deadly situation.

"And what is the next step?"

"He gets another MRI soon and they watch him very carefully for the next two years."

"And I assume he's happy with his doctors?"

"Well, Michael is actually a doctor at the medical university, so he knows who to go to, but yes, he's pleased with them. Very much so. At least, so far!" I chuckled a little. "Gallows humor."

"Right, good one! Well, let's hope he stays healthy and lives to be an old man with grandchildren bouncing on his knee."

That remark gave me pause, and thinking I had nothing to lose, I said, "Father, can I ask you a question?"

"Fire away."

"What is the Church's position on in vitro fertilization or artificial insemination?"

"How much time do you have?"

He smiled warmly and it appeared that he might give me some ammunition I could use if I had to take on the Russos and the Vatican over the coming holiday.

"Well, first, there's the greater issue. Would you like some coffee?"

"Sure, that would be great."

He rang for his housekeeper and asked her to make a fresh pot and to see if maybe there wasn't a cookie or two to be found.

"This time of day I always need a little something to keep me going. I have the rosary society tonight and I need my energy!"

I nodded and he continued.

"We're talking about a married couple that wants a child and their inability, for whatever reason, to conceive a child. Am I correct?"

"Yes. Let's assume they are Catholic, too."

"Okay. Well, a child conceived in marriage is a gift from God, not a piece of property like a new car. The Church also teaches that husbands and wives have the right to give themselves to each other, and that in and by that marital act, they may receive the gift of a new life."

"That's pretty archaic, don't you think?"

"No, why?"

"Because modern medicine can give families children."

Father John had a good chuckle. The coffee arrived with a plate of Pepperidge Farm Milanos.

The coffee looked murderous, so I said, "A little milk, please? Thanks," I said to his housekeeper, who poured for both of us and then left the room.

"Grace, this is a complicated matter and the answer you would get today would very much depend on whom you asked and what the details were of the case. Each couple has their own unique set of complicated issues. I guess my question to you is this. Of all the many things you could ask a priest, why ask this particular question?"

"Good question, and I guess you have me on the ropes, a little bit anyway." I saw that the words I spoke seemed to be more thoughtful when I was in Father John's company. I didn't want to play *gotcha!* with this man. I wanted to have an intelligent discussion about the ethics of living and the Church's position on the mix of faith and science. Besides, I had a sneaking suspicion that he could beat me at *gotcha!* any day of the week.

"Well?" he said, and took a cookie.

"How much time do you have?" I asked, and smiled at him.

"Until seven-thirty tonight and then the rest of my life."

"Well, here it is, then."

I told him about my family and how I had grown up in an Italian Catholic parish in Bloomfield, New Jersey. We talked about Nonna and how she claimed to see Nonno all the time, how they drove me crazy and decorated my room from Catholic.com.

He laughed. "She really might see her dead husband. Who knows?"

"Well, she does manage to make extremely reliable predictions after one of his visitations. And she says she inherited this ability from her mother, and that when she dies, my mother will get the curse, and when she goes, guess who's next?"

He cleared his throat with no small amount of skepticism. "Then, Grace, it is conceivable that during my lifetime you will inherit this blessing or curse of second sight."

"Maybe, but I think it's a bunch of bull."

"You'll let me know?"

"Yeah, we'll stay in touch. Anyway, then there's my father . . ."

We talked about Big Al and the way he discounted my mother's opinions and made her feel like a servant and how I had always suspected that he ran around on her because he was such a horrible flirt. That was one reason why I wasn't so excited about marriage. Then I told him that my parents didn't even want to know Michael.

"Why not?"

"Because he's Irish?"

He threw his cupped hands up and fanned them toward his shoulders as if to say, *Come on, we both know there's more.*

"Okay, but if I come clean with you, I don't want any judgmental, you know, attitude from your side of the cookie dish, okay?" That was about as delicately as I had ever said anything to anyone and I was rather proud of myself. I took two cookies as a reward and he smiled as if he already knew my thoughts.

"We live together."

His elbows were on the arms of the chairs, his fingers looped together, he was leaning slightly forward, and he was waiting for the rest.

"He's not exactly a practicing Catholic and *in his career he does embryonic stem-cell research.*" The second part of that revelation sped out at about eighty miles an hour.

Father John burst out laughing and clapped his hands, which was pretty much the same reaction I'd had from my brother Frank.

"Whoo-hoo!" he said. "You're a pip, Grace!"

"A pip. Thanks. Thanks a lot." I laughed, too.

"More?"

"Yeah, one last thing . . ." I told him about the frozen sperm and his face became more solemn.

"Listen, Grace, here's the thing. At the end of life on this earth, we are all accountable to God. In many situations, we have to make decisions based on our conscience and don't have the opportunity or even the thought to run haywire and consult a member of the clergy before we act. A clear conscience is of utmost importance. The trick is not to rationalize your decisions knowing they displease God."

"I agree with that. And I think our ability to rationalize anything is pretty scary."

"Exactly!" he said, and pointed a knowing finger at me. "Let's tackle just a couple of these issues. Stem-cell research? Science will find a way to make stem cells without cloning. I follow this field because I have a great interest in it."

"Me, too. Well, sort of. Michael's mother is in the final stages of Alzheimer's and I think Michael would've given everything he has to be a part of a team that could've cured it or got closer to a cure. Or even just, I don't know, improved the quality of the last days of her life."

"Alzheimer's is a cruel customer," he said. "But back to alternative ways of conceiving children . . . I think the Church's major area of concern has always been that children are *begotten not made*. Is it right to *make* children in a laboratory setting just because we can? Well, all the great thinkers of the Church have examined this question and have sanctioned two procedures. But the methods of those therapies are so close to the ones you asked about that I think it almost becomes moral and ethical nitpicking to say that one is fine and the other is not. Does this make sense to you?"

This time I was the one on the edge of my seat. "You have no idea how much sense you make. I can't believe I'm going to say this, but I agree with every word you said. Listen, are you available for Thanksgiving?"

"Oh, thank you, but I—"

"No! Of course you have plans! But I was just thinking how much I would love to have this conversation at my parents' table with you at my side."

"Don't you think your parents would be a little shocked if you brought home a priest?"

"Yeah, just a little. Ha!" I stood to go. "Thank you for the chat, the cookies and the coffee. And the tape. I hope you have a wonderful Thanksgiving, Father."

He walked me to the door. "Happy Thanksgiving to you and Michael, Grace, and to your family also. I'll say a prayer for Michael's mother, too."

"Thanks, Father. Prayer can't hurt and it might do some good. Who knows?"

"I have the feeling that *you will,* Grace. You will."

Oh, whatever, I thought, and in the next instant had second thoughts about my cynicism. I shouldn't discount Father John's prayers. I had been pleasantly surprised to hear that the Church had grappled with the issues. I always thought they just said no to everything. But the current conclusion on conception wasn't the only point. The weighing of the morality and ethics was just as important. Father John only barely represented the Church I had grown up in. The Church I had known was the one that *Nonna* had known. Who died and made her the pope? Maybe I didn't know the Church at all. Maybe Michael didn't either.

I walked home in the late-afternoon drizzle, stopping at Harris Teeter for a turkey breast and the other things I needed to make our small Thanksgiving-eve dinner. The dark side of me had a fleeting thought that Michael was being a martyr to insist on spending the day with his mother. But just that morning Michael said he thought he had worn me out from all his illness and he wanted me to go enjoy the holiday with my family. I had not seen them in some time.

"Seriously, Grace. I think a couple of days with them would do you a lot of good. I'm just going to go out to Summerville and see what I can do for my mother."

"But I really don't mind telling my family I can't come for Thursday. I can drive over on Saturday and spend the night."

"That's not right. Look, your brother and his whole family are coming, and if they can, so can you. What do you think I would give to have some other relatives around here? A lot. Go! You'll enjoy it!"

I said, "*Enjoy* being with that whole crazy crew?"

"Sorry," he said with a sly smile.

"I'm not sure anyone ever really enjoys family holidays."

"Sorry," he said again, and chuckled.

"Sure, you laugh. Go ahead. Look, *you* tolerate the crazies—Nonna. *You* try to keep the egomaniacs on the other side of the room—that would be Nicky and Marianne. You seek out the ones you really want to talk to—and that's Frank and Regina. But *enjoy*?"

"No, huh?"

"Are you serious? At Connie and Big Al's table? It's kind of like climbing Mount Everest. You're glad you survived it, but you would never recommend it to a friend."

"I'm sure. By the way," Michael said, "Larry volunteered to shuttle me back and forth to Summerville so we don't have to worry about me driving alone."

"Good, sweetheart, but you know Papenburg said that there's no real medical reason you can't drive."

"I'll start driving again, Grace," he said. "I just want to feel ready and I'm not ready yet."

"Well then, don't. I don't think anybody should drive who doesn't feel comfortable behind the wheel. Don't worry about it."

I was going to Hilton Head to please Michael and making this early Thanksgiving dinner to please myself.

That afternoon, when Michael arrived at home, the turkey was in the oven and almost done. Between the gravy and the roasting meat, the creamy corn pudding I had made and the lingering aroma of onions and celery, the house smelled wonderful. One whiff and he was immediately in a good mood.

The table was set with little pumpkins and gourds and fall-colored candles. The cloth was deep red, the napkins were rust, and the plates were gold. A little trip to Williams-Sonoma and I had a molded glass turkey to hold my cranberry sauce and seasoned focaccia croutons for the stuffing. The house, the table—it looked terrific and smelled like heaven, even if I said so myself.

"Hey! My woman!" Michael said. "Look what I brought us."

He gave me a sloppy, noisy kiss, a grope here and there and handed me a shopping bag.

"Somebody's in a good mood. Thanks! What's this?" I unwrapped two hand-carved painted wooden Pilgrims and a little turkey. "Michael! They're precious!" I put them on the table and suddenly it was Thanksgiving.

"And look what else I got," he said, and held up another bag.

"Dom Pérignon? Wow! What are we celebrating? Did you win the lottery?"

"Wise guy. I'll tell you in a minute," he said, and took the bottle to the sink to pop the cork. I handed him two champagne glasses; he filled them and handed one to me. He raised his and said, "To us, Grace! I was thinking today. You do so much to make my life happier and better in every single way. I just wanted to say thank you. And that I love you. And—and this is *the* big *and*—this is the last holiday we are spending apart from each other. Oh, and one more thing."

"What's that?"

"Happy Thanksgiving, I'm alive."

"Happy Thanksgiving, sweetheart. I agree! Big Al and Connie will just have to deal."

I filled a plate for Michael and he devoured it. I could see him eyeballing the turkey and everything else on the stove.

"A little more?"

"Sure. Just a little. So tell me some more about this priest you met."

"Well, it's just that he's a very cool guy. He isn't a priest like the ones I knew growing up—the ones who truly started the Goth movement. I mean, maybe they were cool, too, but they didn't seem like it to me. Anything's possible. You want gravy?"

"Drown me with it. A cool priest? So this guy is getting excommunicated when?"

"Very funny. Listen, between us, I made the fatal mistake of mentioning to my mom that we froze sperm in case of an emergency and she went a little off-the-wall, as expected, because—"

"Oh, great."

"No, listen to me. This priest, Father John, had no problem with it."

"Yeah, as long as they stay in the freezer."

"Not so."

"Look, Grace, we've talked about children and marriage before, but I think I should tell you that I'm still not ready for that kind of commitment."

A million thoughts ran through my head.

"Who's asking for a commitment?"

"I love you and you know that."

"And I love you, too. Anyway, Father John says he's not against stem-cell research because he says he thinks that scientists will figure out how to make stem cells without making anything that could ever become an embryo. Did I say that right?"

"Yeah, oddly enough." Michael smirked and shook his head. "How does he know about that?"

"I told you. He's a smart man."

"Well, he reads the paper anyway. Actually, there's a whole deal in Boston going on right now where they remove the genes from an adult cell, then add the altered cell to an egg. That can't grow into an embryo, but it can grow stem cells."

"Aha! Whatever that means that you said."

"No cloned embryo, no ethical problem? Getting the eggs is the problem at this point. But they'll figure that out pretty soon."

"The sooner the better."

"You can say that again."

Naturally I was thinking that I would love to see them figure it out before Michael's cancer decided to come back and try again to kill him.

"Well, why don't you go pack and take a shower and I'll do the dishes," he said.

"You are the perfect man," I said. "Is there any more champagne?"

"You can have mine," he said.

"Thanks. I'll just take a sip." I got up to clear our plates and he grabbed my skirt.

"What's on your mind, Mr. Wonderful?"

"Dessert."

"I bought a pumpkin pie?"

"Hate pumpkin."

So he didn't do the dishes right away. Anyone have a problem with that? No.

CHAPTER 18

Gobble It Up

"I left a lemon tea cake and a loaf of pumpkin bread on the counter for you to take to the nurses at the nursing home," I said. "I'll call you later."

From the hinterland of our sheets and blankets came this response: "Okay. Thanks. Love you. Be careful."

All the way to Hilton Head I thought about Michael and how relieved I was that his treatments were in our past and not our future. Maybe he really was well. The chemotherapy had worn him to a frazzle, but he was rapidly becoming himself again. The color of his complexion was better, his appetite was normal, and his general, um, stamina was in check. Maybe they really had been able to remove the whole tumor and kill off any leftover cancer cells. God, I hoped so. More than anything.

If it were possible to heal a terminally ill person based on the strength of sheer will, between my stubbornness and Michael's submission to the hell days of science and medicine that he had been through, he would never even suffer a hangnail for the rest of his days.

I was on the outskirts of the island before I knew it, but then I had been doing a lot of daydreaming. It was so funny to be in an almost tropical environment for Thanksgiving. There were palmettos galore on either side of the highway, and as soon as I crossed the bridge onto the island, egrets and great blue herons were everywhere. The marsh grass was turning brown, and if I hadn't known better, I would have said it was a field of mink. It was beautiful but still foreign. But it was home now because my parents and grandmother were there and it was where we all got together. It would never feel as familiar as Bloomfield, but that said something about the power of childhood to leave its imprint on you forever.

I remembered Thanksgivings in New Jersey when the weather was cold and I was so little I couldn't fill my own plate. Nicky and I had existed in our own world of turkeys made from tracings of the outlines of our hands, colored in with crayons and taped on Mom's walls, and after dinner we fought over the wishbone. At Christmas we covered her living-room windows with angels, reindeer and Santas created with artificial snow, sprayed through stencils. We made paper chains for the tree and potholders for gifts and stole bits of fruitcake soaked in rum and pretended to be drunk. But then I hit puberty, Nicky became a jerk, Frank went to college, and those days were gone forever. And now here we were, years later, still trying to breathe life back into our childhood by getting together and practicing our family's rituals.

Those thoughts led me to Father John. He had not been judgmental in the least about my life and he had not tried to convert me. No matter how I tried to poke holes in the things he said—not aggressively, out loud, of course, but politely in my mind—I could find no fault with his words.

The Catholic Church of my youth had been one of guilt and self-denial, but perhaps that was because Nonna, who lived across the street, had so heavily nuanced every Sunday and every religious event with old-world customs and the ancient beliefs of her own childhood. I was very little, but I could remember Nonna and Nonno telling my mother and then me and my brothers what to do.

"Did you get your ashes? It's Ash Wednesday, you know."

"Ashes? Seriously?" my mother would say, horrifying her parents.

"Some example you set! Come on, take your kids, get in the car, and I'll take you down to the church."

"I don't want ashes on my forehead. I just washed my hair," I would complain.

"Come on, Grace," my mother would say.

"I'll take you to Holstens for ice cream after," Nonno would say. "That's a good girl."

Well, for a trip to Holstens Brookdale Confections, you could smear ashes all over my face.

And my mother? She objected but in the end did what she was told. They said get in the car, she got in the car. My mother would never have objected to Nonna's insistence that our whole family observe every saint's feast day in Christendom.

During Lent, we attended daily Mass and fasted in between meals. The adults refrained from drinking alcohol and the children gave up candy. We kept Christ in Christmas with an Advent wreath, had a molded plastic crèche with about fifty pieces or so, and we never put the baby Jesus in the manger until Christmas morning. Naturally there was always a fight about who got to do it. And Nicky, a natural-born pain in the neck, always put the sheep on the roof and just generally vandalized the Nativity's sacred mysteries.

We sang our hearts out in the church's children's choir and participated in the Christmas pageant. One year when Nicky was about eight, he was a wise man and that caused no end of snickering and rib-poking while he walked up the aisle in a fake beard and long robes. He carried an empty tissue box wrapped in gold foil with colored glass gems glued all over it. Help me. Frank and I died laughing, and seeing us with tears running down our faces, Nicky began to giggle.

That's just how it was. Nonna and Nonno had dinner with us almost every night. We said grace before every meal and Nonna always heard our prayers at night, correcting us if we made mistakes or left out a dead relative or a saint she thought deserved mention.

All those things, those rituals and observances, were inextricably woven into our lives. We passed our days always mindful of the Church's liturgical calendar. It had seemed perfectly normal when we were kids, but later on Frank and I began to choke on the excessiveness of it all. Nicky, of course, went through all the motions, never allowing a cloud of doubt to mess up his pretty head.

Our obsessive Catholicism had probably driven Frank to study philosophy and me to reject any organized religious faith. Regina had reeled Frank back into the Church's good graces, but there was no one to do the same for me. The brand of Catholicism my family practiced was so easy to walk away from and twice as difficult to reclaim. It was just too much from either end.

I pulled into my parents' driveway and Frank's car was there. I sighed and realized that I sighed with the same resolution as my mother did when there was a challenge ahead and a job to be done. But for all my anxiety about so many different things, I was always slightly giddy with excitement to be home.

I went in through the front door—it was Thanksgiving, remember? No garage entrance for me that day. Even though I had never lived in that house, I honored all the customs.

The living room was blockaded with two long folding tables and every chair we owned. The tables were draped to the floor in big pieces of olive green velvet, and thrown over them were some kind of Indian bedspreads laid on the bias. Mom had bought centerpieces of mums and some kind of berries and had stuffed them in glass pumpkins. There was a beautiful bentwood cornucopia on top of the entertainment center filled with silk flowers. Last year's Christmas cards with photographs had finally been put away, but the old wedding favors were just pushed to the side. What did I expect?

"Hi!" I said. "Happy Thanksgiving!"

"Oh! Aunt Grace! You're home! Happy Thanksgiving to

you, too!" my niece, Lisa, said. "Hey, you guys! Aunt Grace is home!"

"I'll be right back." I went to throw my weekend bag in my room.

Little Lisa's heavy black eyeliner and colloquial "you guys" marked her as someone from north of suspicion, just as I did when I said "soda." I giggled because I had never divided the country in those terms until that very second and I realized how ridiculous it was. If she had said "y'all," it would have seemed equally ridiculous, mangled by a New Jersey accent.

"Grace? Grace?"

It was my mother calling me. I envisioned her winding her way through our eccentric cast of characters just to see my face as though I had been gone for years. She burst into my room, hugged me and then sighed with a vehemence that revealed her obvious exhaustion.

"You're home safe and now the holiday can begin!"

"Ma! You sound like I've been living in Mozambique! And look at you; the sun's still high and you're already dragging. You gotta let me help you, okay?"

"Are you kidding? I even bought you your own apron! My feet are throbbing."

I made the rounds of hellos and inquiries. *Hi, Nonna. How are you feeling? How much weight have you lost?* She actually did look a little thinner. Her boyfriend was to arrive at three, she claimed to have lost twenty-three pounds, and she was finishing a new crocheted cover for Mom's tissue box.

"Nice, Nonna! An Indian-corn motif!"

"Yeah, I thought it was classier than the Pilgrims from last year."

"It's very nice. Really."

What could one say?

"Nonno told me he liked it last night."

"And what does he say about your friend George?"

"That he might be cheating in his canasta game—I should watch him very closely."

"Yeah. Keep a close eye on him!"

I ruffled the hair of my two nephews, who moaned at the interruption of their Xbox game, and in the kitchen I gave Regina a hug.

"Hey, you!" she said, and hugged me back.

"Hey, yourself! You losing weight, too?" She looked thinner.

"Yeah, right. I'm gaining a pound a day. It's the tunic."

"Sure. Where are the men?"

"Hurry outside and say hello to your father and your brothers and then get yourself back in here! I'll tell you it's a good thing I have that extra oven in the garage!"

"Ma? On Thanksgiving you could use three stoves and ovens," I said, taking a huge shrimp from a platter and loading it with cocktail sauce.

"Don't you dare pick at my food!" Mom slapped my hand. "Go, go!"

Outside, Dad was at the grill drinking beer with Nicky and Frank and basting his turkey. We all hugged and kissed.

"We've been out here since eight o'clock this morning! It's a twenty-eight-pounder," he said. "I told that guy up at the Piggly Wiggly I wanted the biggest goddamn turkey he could find! This little pipsqueak tries to tell me that I should cook two fourteen-pounders and I says to him, Whaddaya saying? It don't look right to have two turkeys! There's people starving out there!"

"You're absolutely right, Dad," Nicky said, his nose nearly in the crease of my father's butt.

"It's very impressive," I said. "Reminds me of that movie . . . what's that old movie where they cook that kid's pet turkey? And everybody cries at the table?" They looked at me like I had lost my mind. "Well, I would think that turkeys make lousy pets anyway. I'm going inside."

I settled into the kitchen with Mom and Regina. The entire house was swollen with sounds and mouthwatering smells as my mom, Regina and I worked on dinner.

"So where are Marianne and her mother?" I said.

"Late," my mother said.

"Probably stuffing her bra," Regina said to me under her breath. "Right?"

"What was that? She's bringing a pecan pie," Mom said.

"Nothing. I hate pecan pie for Thanksgiving," I said. "That's for Christmas. She never heard of pumpkin pie?"

"And she's only bringing one," Mom said.

"My *gavones* will eat the whole thing," Regina said. "Watch. Just watch."

"You got it!" I said, and continued my nightmare of Annoying Episodes with Marianne. "Watch. Nicky won't get a slice of her freaking pie because my darling nephews will scarf it and she'll make a whole scene. Uck. I can't stand her. Sorry."

"Well, let's just try to be nice to her, dear," Mom said.

"Only for you, Ma. Only for you."

The doorbell rang. It was George Zabrowski arriving like an aging Uncle Fester. He had a corsage for Nonna, cut flowers for my mother and the biggest box of Russell Stover chocolates I had ever seen. Old George wore a nice tweed sport coat and a tie, his remaining hair was wet-combed, and when he got closer to shake my hand, he smelled like he'd forgotten he had put on cologne the first time.

"So here's the wonderful and beautiful granddaughter I haven't seen since the day I met your Nonna," he said.

Okay, I take back that little dig about him and his cologne.

"Yep! That's me!" I blushed because don't you know this old coot took my hand and kissed it? I adored him. Right then and there I fell in love with an old Polish geezer. Well, how do you like that?

I looked over to Regina as he kissed her hand, too. By the time he got to Mom, she was holding this Miss America bouquet of flowers to her bosom and grinning like a young girl as he kissed her hand and then held it, telling her how honored he was to spend such an important day with our family.

I wanted to say, *Wait, you'll see what a pack of jackals we are,* but before I could make a smart remark, my mother spoke.

"Oh, no, George, the honor is ours to have you! Would you like a shrimp?"

Well, it went on like that, with George eating the forbidden shrimp and flattering everyone until he depleted his repertoire of superlatives to heap on females. Normally I would have gagged, but all I could think was how great it was that Nonna had this sweet old guy who came into her life with a trunk filled with courtly mannerisms. He was perfect for her. Even if he was full of it.

At ten minutes to four, ten minutes before we were to sit down, Marianne and her mother arrived.

Marianne, nearly breathless with her specialness, brought her pie into the kitchen and placed it on the counter like she'd taught Martha Stewart how to bake. "Hey! How y'all doing?" Naturally, the pie was in a ceramic pie container with a fake cherry pie for a cover.

"She's gonna waste my poor son's last dime," Mom whispered, bending down to me as I pulled a casserole out of the oven.

I stood up and had a look at her. Of course she was wearing a tight cotton turtleneck covered in tiny turkeys dressed like Pilgrims. And had a fresh French manicure.

"Hi, Marianne," I said, wondering if she realized her entire ensemble was a size too small. "Where's your mom?"

"Oh! I didn't see you there, Grace! How's my maid of honor? Happy Thanksgiving, y'all! Mama's in the living room."

"Same to you," Regina said. "Your bad boy is outside hydrating with mine."

Marianne had no clue what *hydrating* meant. I was sure of it.

"Tell Al to bring in the bird," Mom said. "Everyone is starving."

We cleared the center island and put three bottles of Chianti and two bottles of Pellegrino on the table. The Pellegrino was a special request from Nonna for the sake of her romance so we wouldn't look like a band of Gypsies, drinking water from the tap.

The turkey was given an exalted position on the end of the island on an enormous cutting board, right by the outlet, so Dad could use his electric knife to carve. All the other dishes of food were lined up like soldiers on warming trays with serving utensils by their sides. We all found our way to the table except for little Lisa.

"That turkey could be a toddler," I said to Regina.

"That's a little sick," she said with a laugh. "Lisa! Come on! We're gonna say grace! Teenagers," she said. "Did you notice that eye makeup?"

"Who cares?" I said. "It washes off."

Well, here came trouble out of the guest room and swishing into the living room, where we were all gathered around the table. Lisa had changed into the kind of lace-trimmed silky camisole that is popular with young girls and a very short skirt that was destined to give Big Al, and possibly Frank, agita like they never had in their lives. Her bra straps, from the bra she had yet to need, were showing. Big Al hadn't seen her yet, but Frank's eyes were bulging.

"In the name of the Father . . ." Big Al began.

Frank shot Regina a death ray. Regina looked back at him as if to say, _Who knew?_

"And of the Son . . ."

Any minute now, I thought. But we got through Dad's special grace for the holiday. Just as Mom and I got up to get the platters of antipasto, Big Al went off like a Scud missile.

"Holy Mother! What the hell? Regina! Cover your daughter!"

"Pop! What?" Lisa said with the expected defiance.

"Oh, God," Regina said.

"What?" Lisa said again.

"You come to my table in your underwear? Where's your respect? Answer me that?" He turned to Regina. "You let your daughter dress like a *putana*? Whaddaya, nuts? You want—"

"Calm down, Al," my mother said, in a low voice everyone heard. "We have guests!"

"Maybe you had better go put on a sweater, sweetie," Regina said.

"No!"

"You're not sitting at my table half-naked!" Dad shouted.

"What's the problem?" Nonna said.

"Your great-granddaughter is not dressed decent!" Dad said.

"Stand up, honey," Nonna said. "Stand up."

Lisa, more angry than humiliated, stood. Nonna gave her the once-over. And then here came Marianne's two cents.

"Well, it *is* a little skimpy, hon. I think I might wear a jacket if I were—"

"Stay out of this," I hissed.

"Watch it, Grace . . ." Nicky said.

"You watch it, too!" I said back to him.

"I think she looks adorable!" Nonna said. "Now, sit! Let's eat!"

My father had been trumped by Nonna and shrugged his shoulders. But it didn't matter to Lisa that she'd quickly been exonerated by the queen of Naples. Lisa had been demoralized and singled out for a public reprimand. Therefore, she was entitled to stew in her self-righteous indignation, and dammit, she was going to stew and sulk for the remainder of the meal.

"Don't mind Pop; he can be a poop," I whispered to her between the tortellini in brodo, the oysters on the half shell and three more bottles of Asti Spumante that Dad had set aside for the day.

That made her smile and she said, "No duh."

Peace was restored.

When it was time to carve the turkey, we all got up and went back to the kitchen. One by one, the plates were piled high with meat, stuffing, gravy, cranberry sauce, string beans with garlic and bread crumbs, whipped sweet potatoes, mashed potatoes, breaded cauliflower and asparagus. And just in case we overlooked a food group, there was a platter of pickles, olives and celery and dishes of relishes.

"Boy, if I didn't have to get up for more food, I wouldn't get any exercise at all," Regina said.

"Reg, I like my women to look like women," Frank said in his most manly voice, and slapped her on the backside.

"Hey!" she said, pretending to be annoyed. Then she stood on her tiptoes and kissed him on the cheek. They looked at each other the same way Michael and I looked at each other and I missed Michael then.

Suddenly I realized that Nonna was with a Polish man. How come it was permissible for her to have a Polish boyfriend and my Irish one wasn't worthy? Then I remembered, it was because of Michael that I led a godless existence. Right. *Have another glass of wine, Grace.* I could say I had made friends with a priest and then see how that went over with the ruling party. As soon as we all sat down again, I did.

"Guess what, Dad? I met a priest."

"Where? At Mass?"

"No. At his rectory."

"What were you doing in a rectory?"

You see, this is the problem with alcohol. I had intended to keep the details of my trip to Mexico under wraps until the last possible moment. But once you poured more than two glasses of wine for me, I would tell you anything you wanted to know. I might even make some stuff up. It wasn't my finest personal quality and I knew it. But I wasn't going to lie to my family at Thanksgiving. That was just too tacky.

"Well, here's the story."

I told my father all about the trip and how excited all the old people were about it. Then I told him—not that he cared, but I made him listen anyway—that Bomze had given me some time off to care for Michael, and in return I was to figure out how I was going to get the trip organized for as little money as possible.

"So how's it going?"

"Michael?"

"No. The pilgrimage."

"Well, I got the airfare all donated, but I can't find hotel rooms yet."

"Old people shouldn't have to stay in some dump," Dad said.

"What's that?" Nonna said.

"I said, old people making a trip to see the Blessed Mother in Mexico City should stay in a nice place that's safe and, you know, nice."

"*You're* going to see Our Lady of Guadalupe?" Nonna said as she blessed herself. "Madonna!"

Then Big Al turned to me. "How many senior citizens are we talking about here?"

"I think the number is fourteen."

"Make it fifteen—take your nonna—and I'll take care of all the hotel rooms. Got it?"

"Are you serious?"

"Yeah, I'm serious. I'll make the check out to St. Mary's as a donation and they can pay the hotel. That way I get a tax credit. Or . . . wait a minute. I got a buddy who's building a new hotel and he's got a couple of places in Mexico City. You don't worry, Grace. Your old man's gonna handle it."

"Daddy, you're so wonderful. Thank you."

"Hey! No big deal. Just tell Bomze Big Al saved him a lot of *'shcarole*! Now tell me some more about this priest."

I rambled on and on about Father John and slipped in a few comments about Michael, which no one acknowledged except Frank and Regina, who winked at me to imply that we would talk later. Finally, it was time to clear the plates and bring in the platter of finocchio. I could eat raw fennel dipped in peppered olive oil until it came out of my ears. Most days, but not that Thanksgiving. Picture this. We were thirteen people, all of us overfed, ten of us overserved and three kids ready to launch into a sugar frenzy, when two of them weren't trying to sneak a glass of wine and one of them wasn't looking for an opening in the action so that he could run outside and snitch a cigarette.

The finocchio had arrived and was disappearing with dwindling enthusiasm, and we had yet to rise from the table for coffee, dessert and anisette. Marianne's mother—I couldn't remember her name for beans and didn't care either—was talking to my mother. Nonna was completely smitten with George and who could blame her? And I had Michael on my mind. I couldn't help but wonder if he was suffering through the day. Maybe he was talking to the nurses or had his mother propped up in bed trying to talk to her. I felt so guilty about being with my family—such as they were—when he had only me and a couple of relatives scattered to the winds. Guilt stuck again as I realized I was always thinking my family was a caricature of some sitcom when in truth they were reasonably loving and generous to a fault.

"We've got pies to eat," my mother said. Everyone groaned and no one moved. "Okay, should we have dessert later?"

"Let's begin the impossible dream," I said.

"What's that?" Regina said.

"A clean kitchen—what else? Otherwise . . ."

"We'll die right here at the table," she said with a laugh.

It was Mom, Regina and me who began clearing the table.

"Come on, Lisa," Regina said. "You're old enough to wear makeup on the holidays? You're old enough to use a dishcloth. Let's go."

Then you-know-who piped up. "I can help tooooo."

What? And wreck that fifty-dollar manicure?

"That's okay," I said. "You can serve your pie later."

"Nicky?"

Some whispers were exchanged between the lovebirds, which I ignored, and then Nicky came into the kitchen, where I was rinsing plates and loading the dishwasher. Regina was in charge of plastic wrap and Mom was putting aside those dishes and things that were to be hand-washed later.

"Come on, Grace," he said. "Cut her some slack. She wants to be a part of things, you know?"

"I understand, but not this part."

"You're a real bitch sometimes, you know that?"

I smiled, thinking it was something of a compliment. "Hello? She's company, okay? Company doesn't do the dishes. What's the matter with you?"

"Oh. You're right. Sorry about calling you—"

"Get out of the kitchen, Nicky. You want them to call you a sissy?"

Nicky slinked out and back to Marianne's side. I saw them get up and go toward his bedroom. Scandal. You didn't go into a bedroom with a member of the opposite sex unless you were married. Never mind it was the twenty-first century outside the front door. If Dad saw them, he would start yelling, but I looked out the window to see Dad gathering up all the dirty utensils from his grill. He and Frank were deep in discussion about something. If Nonna had seen them, she would do the same as Dad, but I looked back to see her focused full throttle on whatever it was George was saying. And then the screaming started.

"Yes! Yes!"

Marianne came running down the hall waving her left hand and stopped to show the ring to her mother. Jane maybe? Janine? Eventually, I imagined, I would remember her name. They came into the kitchen and showed it to my mom first. The ring sparkled like a disco ball from the eighties and even my heart fluttered for her. After all, this was the moment of her engagement and that is a pivotal moment in any girl's life.

"Oh! Let's see!" my mother said. "Oh! Marianne! Welcome to the family!" My mother gave her a big hug.

"Let's see," I said. "Oh, Marianne. It is a beauty. Congratulations!"

Actually, it wasn't beautiful. On inspection, it was puny. If I was going to marry someone like Nicky, he would have to give me something the size of that sapphire Gloria Stewart threw off the back of the boat in *Titanic*. Seriously. Poor Marianne. She now had Nicky *and* a dinky ring. I rewarded her with a dish towel.

"You can dry," I said. "But you'd better go show it to Dad first."

"Ooookay!"

"Can I be in the wedding? Oh! It's gorgeous!" Lisa said. "Can I?"

"Of course!" Marianne said.

She scooted out the sliding door and I shot Regina a look. She snickered and so did I.

"Poor Marianne," I said.

"Poor Marianne," she agreed. "She should know what we know."

"No, she should never know what we know. About Nicky, about life or—"

"About raising kids!" Regina said. "Look."

She pointed to the grill area, where Frank, Dad, Marianne and now Nicky, all of them animated, were giving one another congratulatory handshakes and hugs while to the side stood Tony, Regina and Frank's oldest, chugging a Budweiser as fast as he could.

"He is so totally busted," Regina said, and went outside to deal with him.

Lisa stood next to me as we watched Regina slapping Tony all around the sides of his head while he ducked and tried to escape. Frank grabbed him by the back of his shirt and held Regina back. It looked to me like Dad was now getting involved.

"Nothing like a little drama to make the holidays bright," I said.

"It's his third," Lisa said. "I only had one. But don't tell Mom, okay?"

"No aunt ever betrayed her niece while she scrubbed the pots." I handed her a scouring pad.

"I'm going to change my top," she said. "I don't want to ruin it."

I could have said, *You should have done it hours ago.* I could have said, *You have to remember where you are, you're with your grandparents and your great-grandmother. This is their house* . . . but I didn't say anything more than "Okay, go ahead." I just reminded myself once again that I should make some effort to be a better aunt. Maybe I would take her for a couple of weeks the following summer and try to talk some sense into her head before she turned into a screaming slut.

It was getting late. We finally served dessert and coffee and cleared all the dishes away. Dad, Frank and Nicky were putting away the folding tables and moving all the chairs back to where they belonged. Marianne, her mother, George and Nonna were looking at some old photographs of Nonna's from Italy. The kids had all been excused. Mom and I were drying the last of the glasses. My cell phone rang. It was Michael.

"Hey, sweetheart," I said, "how did your day go? We're still drying dishes."

"I'm still here with my mom, Grace. She's not doing so well."

"What do you mean? Do you need me to come?"

"No. But thanks. I've been sitting here all day and just reading to her. They say that even though she's unconscious, she can still hear me. I'm going to go home and get some sleep. I think I'll come back tomorrow and just be with her. Oh God, Grace, I just hate this."

"I'm so sorry, Michael. Is there anything I can do?"

"No, I just wanted to tell you that I love you and that this stinks, I guess."

"It sure does. I'm so sorry, Michael. Look. I can be there in two hours."

"No, sweetheart. I don't want you on the road. It's dark and that highway is too dangerous."

"Yeah, and we swallowed a lot of grapes around here. Still, you say the word and I'll be there, Michael."

"I know that, baby. It's okay. I just can't believe that's my mother in that bed. It's just so incredibly sad. I could just—" His voice cracked with emotion.

"Hang on, sweetheart. I love you and we'll get through this together."

We hung up and I looked at my mom.

"What's wrong?" she said.

"I'm going home tomorrow morning," I said. "Something tells me Michael's mother is at the end."

I didn't have to wait that long to find out. I had the same nightmare again—I was going over a bridge in a car with Michael, he disappears, the car disappears, and I begin to fall. I was lying in bed in a sweat, trying to relax, and my cell phone rang. It was five-thirty. It was Michael and he was in shock and huge gulping sobs nearly disguised his voice. His mother had passed away.

"I wasn't even there," he said. "I missed her death! I feel so terrible, Grace! I wanted to be there!"

"Hush, baby, it's all right," I said. "I'll be home as fast as I can."

Back in Charleston, Michael made all the arrangements. His aunt couldn't come, but she sent beautiful flowers. So did his cousins and many friends from work. Frank and Regina sent flowers, too. Michael's mother was cremated and her ashes were to be buried in St. Lawrence's Cemetery, in the same place that held the remains of his father and his brother.

It was a beautiful and chilly Monday morning. The sky was clear and a brilliant blue. We were to meet the minister at McAlister's Funeral Home and accompany Michael's mother's remains. I sat in the limo with Michael. We rode the short distance in silence until Michael spoke.

"You know, it's funny. I knew she was going to die. There were even a few moments that I wished she would—it was just so terrible to see her that way. But when she finally did die, I think I was completely surprised by it. Isn't that weird?"

"Not really. I can't imagine what the day will be like when I bury my parents. It has to be so profound."

"It is. *Profound* is the word for it." He was quiet for a moment and then he reached into his pocket and put something in my hand. "I almost forgot. This is for you. It was my mother's and I want you to have it. She wore it every day from the time she was a girl."

It was a little gold cross on a thin gold chain. It was very simple and very beautiful. I put it on immediately.

"Oh, Michael! This is so lovely. Thank you. It's a treasure."

"She would have loved you, Grace. She really would have loved you."

He held my hand tightly for the rest of the way, and although he was looking out of the window, I knew he was crying. We finally arrived and our procession pulled in the entrance. We made our way down the bumpy road, passing live-oak trees, draped in torn sheets of Spanish moss. There was no doubt the trees had been planted hundreds of years before.

His family's plot was surrounded by a low wrought-iron fence with an opening, and the headstones faced the Cooper River. I could think of no site that would have been more fitting and beautiful for Michael's loved ones. Michael and I stood together by the graves of his grandparents and great-grandparents, and some of the headstones were so ancient, you could barely make out the names or dates. Larry and a few of Michael's other friends were there and the minister from his mother's nursing home led a short service and said some prayers.

The group was small, but everyone there meant something special to Michael or his family in some way. When the minister was finished we sat in the folding chairs the funeral home had provided. I felt a tap on my shoulder. It was my parents.

"Sorry for your loss, son," my father said, and shook Michael's hand. "You shouldn't have to bury your mother without people to help you get through the . . . the . . ."

"Thank you, sir," Michael said.

My mother, who had been known to weep openly in the drugstore from reading greeting cards, welled up and cried quietly. Seeing her cry made me burst into tears. She put her arm around my shoulder and leaned toward Michael.

"I feel so terrible, Michael. I just, you know, wish we were meeting under other circumstances."

"So do I," Michael said, and smiled for the first time since I had come home.

"I want you to come for Christmas," my mother said.

"Yeah," Dad said, "we talked it over on the way here. My wife and I. We want you to come down with Grace. You'll spend Christmas with all the Russos. There are worse places to be, right?"

"Oh, Daddy . . ." If I didn't get a grip on myself, I was going to lose it.

"Thank you, sir. I'd like that very much."

I squeezed Michael's hand and thought, at last, my parents were finally beginning to understand. Big Al, the mighty oak, had decided to bend with the wind.

CHAPTER 19

Christmas

"He said it's as clean as a whistle!" Michael was referring to the MRI he'd had earlier in the week.

"No sign of anything suspicious? *Nothing?*"

"Nothing, nada, zilch, *zero.*"

"Oh, Michael! This is the very best possible news. Now we can have ourselves one absolutely fabulous Christmas! Want to meet me at Saks?"

His news gave me chills all over my body. I was so relieved I felt like I could fly. I knew that when I hit my bed that night, I would have the first sound and restful sleep I'd had since we began to think that Michael might be ill.

I had never told Michael about the nights I spent tortured by nightmares. The same horrible dream. Over and over—the same terrible scene would play out, night after night.

But the days weren't much better. When I tried to work, I had these continuing visions of Michael in a casket, pale and cold to the touch, and me, all alone in the funeral home. I would be undone by it. On television or in a magazine I would see an ad that showed old people walking the beach, holding hands, happy that they had done careful financial planning. Thinking that might never be Michael and me, I would feel the tears sliding down my face. I never told Michael or anyone about these terrors because it seemed like recounting my horrible imaginings would only make them worse. All these weeks, I had been holding my breath for his test results.

The news of a clean MRI was of colossal proportions; the alternative would have meant sure disaster. For the first time since his diagnosis, we had real hope. And just by the way, if I never had to make chicken soup again, it would be just fine with me.

Michael found me at the men's fragrance counter at Saks. I had just chosen aftershave for Frank, Nicky and even for young Tony, which I thought he might consider a compliment.

"Come see what I picked out for Big Al," I said.

"I didn't know Saks sold muzzles."

"Oh, God, you are so bad!"

"Get him a karaoke machine."

"Stop!"

I had chosen a beautiful lamb's-wool cardigan for my father and leather slippers I knew he liked because I had seen them in a catalog my mother was browsing through. She had pointed them out and said, "See if you can find them cheaper in Charleston. He never buys anything for himself except golf shirts. He must have a hundred golf shirts." But that's how my father was. He would pay for a block of hotel rooms for people he'd never met so he could thrill Nonna with a trip to a shrine, and then he would go around without slippers. Actually, that's how both my parents were. They spent their money on things that were important to them, leaving the rest of us to wonder.

Michael and I were walking down King Street, window-shopping and musing about who might like to have this set of bar glasses or that wallet.

I was quiet for a while and he said, "What are you so deep in thought about?"

"Christmas makes me sentimental, that's all."

"Come on. Tell me."

"It's just that this has been an amazing year, don't you think?"

"Yeah, it has. Losing my mother was the worst thing ever, next to my brain cancer, of course."

"Absolutely. Losing your mother *was* tragic, but at least she's not suffering anymore."

"Yeah. God, I miss her. When I was a kid, every Christmas she would decorate the house like something out of a magazine. She and my father would have these huge parties and my father would make eggnog. He had an old recipe that was his father's and it went back to his father and who knows?"

"Was it, like, fabulous?"

"You've never had homemade eggnog?"

"Are you kidding? The closest we ever got to homemade was when Welsh Farms started putting it in bottles. We thought a glass bottle made it, you know, real."

Michael laughed and said, "My dee-ah! You have been deprived! I will make eggnog this year and your little heart will sing 'Dixie'!"

"Better yet, make it for my whole family. I *really* wanna hear them singing 'Dixie'!"

"I'll do it!"

I saw Michael look up at the sky and a wistful expression came over his face.

"She's in a better place, Michael."

"Let me guess. You think she's in heaven with my father?"

"Maybe. I would *like to think* something wonderful happens for you when you die, especially after suffering a long, terrible illness. Or after a long and worthy life. Wouldn't you?"

"Of course I would. It's just that intellectually I know the afterlife is a bullshit concept. Emotionally? I love the idea. Love it."

We were standing in front of Berlin's clothing store on the corner of King and Broad. And I don't know what made me say this, but the words just tumbled out of my mouth like someone else had put them there. I said, "Well, let me ask you this, okay? If stage-four glioblastoma kills every single person who is diagnosed with it, why were you spared? Maybe there *is* a God out there."

"Or maybe we just got the right team of doctors? I mean, who knows?"

"Perhaps. But you have to wonder, Michael. If you're spared and hardly anyone else ever survives, doesn't that give you some kind of responsibility to do something really spectacular? I mean, Michael, a lot of people would say it's a miracle."

"Grace, I don't want to cast a pall . . ."

"A pall?"

"Yeah. A pall."

"Who the hell says *pall*?"

"Old people and me. It's like a shroud. Anyway, I don't want to be depressing or ruin the holidays, but the truth is, I've only been clean for a short time."

He was right. It wasn't such a long time. But I was having no part of anything pessimistic.

"But clean is still clean, Michael."

"Let's be realistic, Grace. If we pass a year and nothing grows back, *then* we can go crazy celebrating."

I looked him deeply in the eyes. "You're not leaving me, Michael Higgins. Ever."

"That's a deal. I don't want to go anywhere. And by the way, Miss Grace Russo, I happen to think the work I do *is* rather spectacular."

"Sorry. That didn't come out right," I said.

"I know. I have to go back to the la-borrrr-a-tory, Nurse Frankenstinkel, and save the human race. Give me your bags. I'll throw them in the trunk and bring them home later."

"Thanks, baby." I giggled, gave him a kiss on his cheek and watched him walk away.

There was no doubt that Michael Higgins was in possession of the best-looking rear view in Charleston, if not the entire state of South Carolina.

I continued to shop, trying to find one really fabulous gift for each person on my list that was within my budget. I was saving the biggest chunk for Michael. I found an antique wristwatch at Crogan's that was so beautiful and symbolic. After all, our life was about time and how much we had, wasn't it?

The wrapped presents continued to pile up on the floor next to the sofa and then under the sofa and in the coat closet until finally I was all done.

It was just a few days before Christmas Eve. Michael and I were having dinner in a booth in the bar at Peninsula Grill. I loved to eat there so I could watch everyone who came and went. By their mannerisms, you could tell who had been there before, who the regulars were, who the tourists were and who was there to celebrate a birthday or some landmark occasion. And it was the kind of place where you might just stop in for a drink and then be on your way. Between Cypress and Peninsula Grill, there was some of the best people-watching in the city. And it was decorated for the holidays with fresh garlands and flowers everywhere, which I loved.

"So we have to make a decision about something," I said.

"What?"

"My mother wants us to come Christmas Eve. Every year she makes this huge dinner with seven kinds of fish and then they all go to midnight Mass. She *says* she doesn't care if we don't go to church with them, but *I know better.*"

"Want a bite?" Michael filled his spoon with onion soup and fed it to me.

"Mmm."

"Why not eight kinds of fish?"

"Tradition. Why else?"

"Well? What do you want to do?"

"I don't know. Another option is that we could go there early on Christmas morning and spend the day or the night or stay until New Years'. Frank and Regina are coming with their kids and you'll like them. I'm sure of that."

"I'm sure I will. Look. Here's what I think. I think we go Christmas Eve and stay until you can't stand it anymore."

"What about Mass?"

"We'll go to Mass, Grace."

"Are you serious?"

"Sure. Look, if my friend dropped dead and they had a service at the Baptist church, wouldn't I go even though I'm not a Baptist? You go out of respect."

"Yeah, but this is different."

"No, it's not. Look. It's one hour out of a long family holiday. We'll do what the family's doing and that's it. No big deal."

"What about Communion?"

"You want to see lightning strike the church and set it on fire?" He laughed. "You just sit back and let the others pass. That's all."

"Maybe if we put a fifty in the collection basket, they won't say anything."

"I'll make it two fifties and pass them under Big Al's nose."

"Okay," I said, "okay."

I wasn't sure how to prepare Michael for the realities of the Russo household. I knew the tree would be too big for the living room, but it would smell heavenly. I knew every end table would hold tons of biscotti, plates of dried figs and nuts, and the candy dish would be loaded with torrone and candied almonds. The panettone—which was our version of fruitcake—would be so deadly dry it would be like eating Styrofoam. Dad would be sitting at the kitchen counter with Frank, both of them dipping chunks of it in wine. There would be struffoli in a sticky sprinkled mound on my mother's Spode Christmas china platter right in the middle of the kitchen counter. The miniature crèche set would have replaced the cornucopia on top of the entertainment center and Nonna would have covered every piece of upholstered furniture with red-and-green afghans. And all day, every day, Frank Sinatra, Al Martino and Jerry Vale would be singing Christmas carols—ones that were popular during World War II—on their stereo when *Holiday Inn* or *It's a Wonderful Life* weren't running on the DVD player.

I told Michael all these things as we made the drive to Hilton Head and he laughed and laughed.

"It sounds like the Hollywood version of the ideal American family at Christmas."

"You don't understand."

"What?"

"I'm just telling you, that's all."

"You're more nervous than I am! Relax! I love you!"

"It's that house on the right." Michael shot me a look and I could feel my cheeks getting hot. "Yes, the one with the multicolored blinking lights, which are on at ten o'clock in the morning . . ."

"And Santa and the reindeer on the roof . . ."

"And the life-size Nativity scene in the yard . . ."

"Without the baby Jesus . . ."

"Because it isn't Christmas morning."

"And the candy canes lining the walkway . . ."

"Yep. This is the house. Okay. We're home."

We went in through the front door—it was Christmas Eve, after all—and the scene was basically a repeat of Thanksgiving, right down to the Xbox, except, of course, for the decorations. And Michael. Michael Higgins was in my parents' house with every one of my immediate family except for my aunt and uncle and their kids from up north. I was excited and I was very nervous.

"Hello, sweetheart!" my mother said, coming toward me, wiping her hands on a dish towel. She hugged me and then, to my relief, she hugged Michael. "Welcome, welcome! And Merry Christmas!"

"Merry Christmas! Where should we put Michael's stuff, Mom?"

Michael already knew we weren't sleeping together. I wouldn't have considered it in my wildest dreams. Michael had said he'd be uncomfortable about it, too.

"He'll sleep in Nicky's room with him. You'll have to share a bathroom, Michael. I'm sorry the accommodations aren't more glamorous."

"It's fine, Mrs. Russo. I lived in a dorm not so many years ago."

"Then you'll be right at home here," she said, and then added, "I'm so glad you're here, Michael."

"Me, too, Mrs. Russo. Thanks for having me."

"Call me Mrs. R. You make me feel like I'm a thousand years old!"

I could see Mom staring at Michael's blue eyes and slipping through them the same way I had so many times. They were like water at the perfect temperature and they called you as though a swim in them would make you feel better about everything in your life. Maybe more important, he had this way of looking at you and making you feel like you were young and beautiful even if you weren't. And without being bold or brash, he made you think that you were desirable. I had seen Michael's charm at work again and again. He was never out of line, but he loved women and it showed.

We put our things away and I introduced Michael to everyone. Frank took an immediate liking to him, and the next thing I knew all the males were in the backyard playing two-hand touch football and drinking beer. Michael was giving Tony and Paulie throwing lessons. Even through the glass doors I could see that he had taken a shine to them.

Mom was draining spinach to stuff the flounder that was laid out on waxed paper. Marianne had yet to arrive and compromise my mood. But Regina was there arranging antipasto platters. Nonna was still using a walker, but she had it parked by the kitchen counter. She was perched on a barstool, chopping green and black olives to mix in with the baccala salad.

"He's cute!" Nonna said. "He's Irish, huh? He could pass for Milanese."

"How's he doing, Grace?" Regina said. "I mean, this is his first Christmas without his mother, so that's gotta be tough going for him."

"You know, he hasn't said much about it except that he misses her. It's really nice that you invited him, Ma. Otherwise it would have been a lousy Christmas for us."

"Is that oven hot yet?" Regina said. "I want to throw in another batch of cookies before we start frying."

"We're glad to have him, Grace. This business of your father only wanting you to marry an Italian is so stupid. Anyway, I told him, Grace loves Michael? Then we love Michael."

"It's not stupid!" Nonna said. "Don't tell me the way I've lived all of my life is stupid!"

Nonna must have been feeling better because she was on my mother's case again. Although I could see her wince in pain every time she got up or sat again.

"I'm not saying that, Mom, and you know it," Mom said in what I thought was a rather bold way. But then she blew it by saying, "I meant no offense."

"Abbastanza!" Nonna said. "After all, we are all aware that Mr. Zabrowski is of Polish origins."

"Yeah, but you're not having his children, Ma," Mom said, and giggled.

"Is he coming for dinner?" I said.

"Yes," Nonna said, "and he's coming to Mass with us, too."

"Are you and Michael coming to Mass, Grace?" Mom asked.

There it was; the first shot of the holiday had been fired over the bow. But I was ready. "Of course!" I said. "I even brought a dress with me. By the way, the tree looks good, Ma."

And the tree did look good. There was a noticeable absence of the usual ornaments, and little gold and red bows were tied to the tops of probably one hundred strategically placed red glass balls. Then the best half of Mom's old ornaments were interspersed among them. Careful placement made the chipped and faded junk from our childhood seem like heirlooms. And all the Christmas cards that were usually taped around the doorway to the dining room were attached to a gold wire garland of round paper clips and draped.

Regina rolled her eyes and nodded to me.

242   *Dorothea Benton Frank*

"Marianne and Nicky decorated everything this year. Well, he got Santa up on the roof. She did the tree," Mom said. "Don't you think she did a nice job?"

"Yeah. We should rent them out to the neighbors."

"Hey! That's a sweet little cross you have on there, missy," Regina said.

"It was Michael's mother's."

"What? Let me see!" Nonna said.

"Let me see!" Mom said. "Oh, my! How nice!"

By six o'clock, we were ready to serve dinner. Marianne and her mother (Jeanette? Janine?) had arrived and George Zabrowski was pouring wine with my dad.

The meal was a rerun of Thanksgiving except for the menu and the decorations. This time the folding tables were draped in the same green velvet, but the overlays were ivory to match the background of Mom's Christmas china. There were red flowers and red candles, and despite the fact that Marianne had commandeered the decorating of *my family's* Christmas tree, everything else was living up to our expectations. Even Lisa arrived at the table modestly dressed in a red cotton sweater and a tartan plaid skirt.

Dad said grace and made a toast and the meal began, but the conversation got off to a slow start.

"So, how ya doing, Michael?" Dad said.

"Fine, sir, thanks."

"Good. How ya doing, George?"

"Fine, and you?" George Zabrowski said.

"Fine. Good."

Mr. Zabrowski cleared his throat and said, "When I was a young boy in Warsaw, Christmas Eve dinner was very much like this. We had a seafood dinner—only seafood. No meat. This is wonderful."

"Oh, yeah?" Dad said. "So, Tony? How's school?"

"Good."

It was clear that unless somebody jumped into the conversation and opened it up, dinner would be remembered as a Pap smear/colonoscopy/root canal. But then along came my future sister-in-law.

"Does anybody want to hear about the wedding plans?"

Her eyes were so filled with excitement that as much as I wanted to say, *No. No one cares,* I couldn't bring myself to do it.

"Sure," Regina said. Regina was always a sport.

So through the baccala salad, the fried calamari, the spaghetti with clams, the shrimp scampi, the stuffed flounder, the fried baccala and finally the lobster tails, we listened to Marianne talk on and on about herself.

"And y'all? The bridesmaids' dresses are going to be so lovely. They really are ones you can wear again, and I was thinking that if everyone wore the same nail polish . . ."

"Blah, blah, blah," I whispered to Regina in the kitchen as we changed the plates for the next course. "Jeesch! Can't somebody tell her to just shut up!"

"She sure does like the sound of her own voice," Regina whispered back.

"Honestly! Right? Where'd she get that southern accent from? I thought she was from Ohio or Indiana or something?"

"Nothing worse than a convert. You know that. Come on. Let's keep moving here."

We knew that even old Connie had finally had enough of Marianne's continuing wind when she said, "What's Santa going to bring you this year, Paulie?"

"I don't know. Probably not a pony, huh?"

Marianne turned scarlet at being ever so politely issued a gag order by her future mother-in-law. She helped to clear the next course and cornered me in the kitchen.

"Let me ask you something, Grace, and I want the honest truth."

"Sure. Is there any other kind?"

She sucked her teeth and said, "Does everybody in this family just plain old hate me? What did I ever do to y'all to deserve this?"

"This what?"

"There I am talking about the most important day in my whole life and your mother asks that fat little Paulie, who somebody *should* really put on a diet, what he's getting from Santa! I was right in the middle of a sentence!"

"No, you weren't. You were right in the middle of monopolizing my mother's Christmas Eve dinner, Marianne. You should have realized that when people started falling asleep in the clam sauce." I said it all nicely and with humor for two reasons. One, it was Christmas Eve, and two, I really didn't want to fight with her. I didn't mind giving her a jab, but I didn't want the holiday to be remembered as our personal slugfest.

Regina, however, had other plans. She had overheard everything.

"Whose kid you calling fat, huh?"

"Well, he shouldn't weigh so—"

Regina stuck her index finger almost *in* Marianne's flaring nostrils and said, "Lemme tell you this. When you have your own kids you'll understand. But you never say a word about mine. Do I make myself clear?"

"Crystal," she said.

"Never!"

"Fine!"

"Merry Christmas," I whispered to Marianne as I passed her with a stack of plates.

Sorry. I couldn't help it.

Finally, the meal was done, the dishes were done, the tables were put away, and six empty bottles of some special Mezza Corona Pinot Grigio Big Al bought in Savannah rested in the recycling bin. Mom, Dad, Nonna and George, and Marianne's mother (Justine?) were sitting down for a break in the living room while everyone else did the dishes. Marianne and Nicky dried plates and glasses. Tony and Lisa scrubbed pots under Michael's supervision. Frank and Regina swept the floor and Paulie helped me wrap up leftovers and deliver espresso to the elders.

"You know, some people triple their risk of a heart attack after eating huge meals like this," Regina said.

"Nice," Frank said. "Now she tells us."

"No! Frank! You know it's true!"

"Happy Holidays, Regina!" Nicky said.

"Well, look, if you don't have a heart attack in three hours, you probably won't," Regina said.

"I'll set the alarm clock," I said. "What time is midnight Mass?"

"Midnight, duh," Nicky said.

Everyone laughed. "No, you dumb-ass. I meant, is there a choir performance before it or anything like a parking problem?"

"I'll find out," Regina said.

It turned out that we had to leave by eleven if we wanted to sit together, and indeed there was choral music beforehand. Somehow we managed to arrive on time.

I had not been to midnight Mass in years, always managing somehow to dodge it. To be there with my entire family was, surprisingly, very emotional. Nonna went up the aisle first, my father at the ready to catch her if she stumbled. She moved carefully with her walker, every step deliberate. She was so frail and I worried that this might be her last Christmas with us. Then my mother followed with George at her side. Frank and Regina pushed their kids ahead of themselves. The rest of us trickled in behind them. Dad and Nonna waited at the end of the pew, telling each of us where to sit. They had decided that two half pews were more to their liking than one long row of Russo and Company. So we filed in, genuflecting and making the sign of the cross—Paulie's the most exaggerated, causing snickers, and Marianne's the most fervent, resulting in more eye-rolling.

"She makes me want to puke," I whispered to Michael.

"Hush! You're in church!" he whispered in mock horror, smiling in agreement.

There had to be over one thousand people at that Mass, and to be honest, that amount of humanity gathered under one roof to worship had an unmistakable effect on me. I think it would have startled the biggest cynic in the world. It wasn't just the thunder of group prayer. Call me crazy if you want, but when a prayer ended, there was something that lingered in the silence that followed, like an echo. I don't know if it was a radiation of emotion or if it was my ears simply readjusting to the acoustics. Something was going on that I had never noticed during all the years I had attended Mass with my family.

It was a little creepy at first. But eventually I became interested in the phenomenon as I watched my father pray. The sincerity with which he mouthed the words and the effort my whole family made to say the prayers in sync with one another, and indeed with everyone gathered, fascinated me. In one moment I felt like we were participating in something tribal, and when a prayer abruptly ended, I was released from the power of a thousand drums only to be swept up again the next time the congregation prayed as a whole. At some point I would ask Father John what he thought.

After Mass we were standing around outside the church saying hello and wishing everyone a Merry Christmas. The air was damp and cool. Dad went with Frank to get the cars. I turned to Michael.

"So Merry Christmas, sweetheart. How did you like Mass?"

"Merry Christmas! Um, Mass was quite a workout, to be perfectly honest. I'm tired."

"Yeah. Me, too." I wondered if he had the same reasons I did. "It's been a long day anyway."

"So what's next on the Russo agenda?"

"Sleep, I hope."

No such luck. Regina and Frank sent their children to bed after they kissed everyone good night. Nonna said good night to George and he kissed her on the cheek. Marianne and her mother (Janelle?) came in, said good night and left almost immediately.

"I'm embarrassed to say this," Frank said, coming back through the kitchen with Regina, "but I'm starving."

"You want cake?" my mother said.

"No, I was actually thinking about a sandwich. We got any salami in here? It's after twelve, right?"

Plastic containers tumbled to the floor when he opened the door.

"Get out of your mother's refrigerator," Regina said, picking the containers up and scooting him aside.

"Yeah, you could die in a landslide," I said. "I could eat half of something. You hungry, Michael?"

"Are you kidding?" he said. "I'm always hungry."

"I know there's potato salad in here and some cold cuts. I saw them earlier. And some provolone . . ."

Regina kept digging around and tossing me various items. A platter of sandwiches were thrown together in a flash by the experienced hands of my sister-in-law, and I put plates and napkins on the table. Dad placed an open bottle of red wine on the table, and my mother excused herself for the night, after helping Nonna to her room.

"Too late for coffee," Dad said, and handed everyone a glass. "To Christmas!"

"To Christmas!" everyone said, and began eating.

"So? How you doing, Michael? You feeling okay?" Dad's face got serious then.

"Yeah. Thanks." Michael smiled at my father and my father remained somber.

"This whole family got on their knees and prayed for you, you know."

"Yes, sir. And I appreciate it, too. Thank you . . . all of you."

"Do you pray?" Dad said in a Big Al moment. It seemed like the room inhaled.

"Well, I went to church with you tonight, didn't I?"

Then it seemed that the room exhaled.

But Dad didn't like Michael's answer and I wasn't particularly thrilled by it either. Michael had skirted the issue by answering with a question, leaving my father and everyone to think whatever they wanted to think. I realized it would not be the only time that my family would question Michael about what he held sacred, if anything. Because they were in the beginning stages of admitting Michael into the family bosom, they wanted to understand the full measure of his character. I also knew Michael well enough to know that he did not believe the dawn of Christmas was the time to engage in that particular discussion. It would have been ill-mannered, especially as a guest.

Dad and Michael looked at each other and finally my father spoke.

"We'll talk."

CHAPTER 20

Round Table

Sometimes what is unsaid has more power than spoken words. Late in the day, as I passed through the rooms of my parents' house, every face seemed peaceful and content. The quiet spoke volumes about making the effort to come together for every holiday, because over time we developed a renewed solidarity. Yes, Nicky was a pain in the neck, but he was *our* pain in the neck. Frank and Regina carried the heaviest load because they lived so far away, but they never complained about the travel. Sure, they would joke about seeing interstate highway every time they closed their eyes, but the truth was that they wanted their children to know who they were and that they were a part of a larger fabric. For me, I only had to drive down from Charleston, but the fact that my parents had finally made a move toward accepting Michael was very gratifying. It had been a wonderful Christmas. The house smelled good, looked as good as it ever had, and the excellent spirits were almost a palpable thing.

By late in the evening, Dad, Mom, Nonna and George brought Christmas to a close, nestled into sofas and chairs, watching one more holiday special on the television. Lisa, Tony and Paulie were assumed to be happy with their haul because there was no bickering from their quarter. Marianne and Nicky left for her mother's (Jerry Anne?) house to watch old home movies of Marianne's dance recitals.

What a day it had been! The Russo Machine of Holiday Cheer completed the annual task of Santa, swinging into action from the first ray of daylight. When all the presents had been opened, we cleared away enough debris to fill a Dumpster and then, without a hiccup, we produced yet another meal of epic proportions. It seemed like we washed thousands of dishes. Just when normal human beings would have surrendered to a stupor of exhaustion, we did not.

Michael, Frank, Regina and I were in the kitchen, believe it or not, eating pie and still talking. With our words and what appeared to be insatiable appetites, we tried to slow time, to stretch the perfect day just a little longer.

Michael was engaged in conversation with my brother.

"I love your kids, Frank, especially that Tony. He reminds me of myself when I was his age."

"Thanks. He's a handful, though."

"A handful? *That's* being generous. Wait! I forgot to smack him this morning!" Regina said.

"Why would you do that? What did he do?" Michael said.

"He didn't do anything! But when you have a kid like him, you smack him . . ."

Frank chimed in. "In the head anyway. Even on Christmas."

"It's a family joke," I said.

Michael grinned and Regina said, "Well, I'll smack him twice tomorrow. It gets his day going."

"Ah, I see," Michael said. "Well, this has been an amazing two days for me, I must say."

"Why is that?" Nonna said, thumping into the room with her walker.

Regina got up. "Here, Nonna. Sit."

"No! You sit! I can stand up and eat a piece of pie."

"Yeah, right," Frank said. "Headline: 'Grandmother on Walker Expires While Eating Pie as Healthy Grandchildren Do Nothing.' Please sit, Nonna. Join us for a few minutes."

"Well, all right, I could go any minute, you know," she said. "It could be our last conversation."

"You're going no place, Nonna," I said, and turned to Michael. "She says that all the time."

Michael nodded and I shrugged.

"I've seen that silly movie ten times anyway. Did I show you? It's a little loose because I got so skinny. But I can take a link out." She held out her wrist so we could see, for the tenth time, the inexpensive but lovely wristwatch George had given her. "He gave me cologne, too!"

"Beautiful!" I said, and showed her the wristwatch Michael had given me, for at least the third time. Nonna's clothes were actually hanging on her frame. Somewhat.

"Oh! How beautiful!"

"Thanks. Did I show you this?" Michael said, and for at least the third or fourth time showed her the one I had given to him.

"Oh! So extravagant! But does it signify something you want to share with her grandmother? I am still the matriarch of the clan, after all. At least for the moment."

"We know, Nonna," Regina said. "You could go any minute."

"It means she is the most important woman in my life," Michael said.

"I don't care *what* they say about you, Michael. *I* think you're wonderful. And if a certain someone named their baby girl Francesca, she might inherit this watch someday."

Nonna's remarks were so crazy that no one knew what to say. Michael cleared his throat and got up to get a glass of water. Regina, Frank and I just looked at one another. I figured Michael was mortified. But maybe he was amused. Frankly, I couldn't tell.

"Oh! Come on! We're not getting married tomorrow, folks," I said, hoping to show that we weren't offended. "Let's just relax on that, okay?"

"Should I return my gift? Ha. There's a salad bowl already gift wrapped in my hall closet."

"I could use a salad bowl . . ." I said, and Michael reached over to pinch me.

"I think the holiday has gone very well!" Regina said. "My kids are crazy about you, Michael."

"Put my plate in the sink, please, sweetheart," Nonna said to me.

She was an old fox. Nonna knew exactly what she had said. *Get married. Have a baby. Name her after me.* I thought, How about *no?*

"Sure," I said. "Should I cut a piece for George?"

"That would be very nice. Frank? Help me here, please."

Frank helped Nonna gain her bearings on her walker and I stayed by her side as she inched along. I handed the pie to George, who'd followed Nonna into the kitchen, and helped Nonna get comfortable on the sofa.

"Well, you can all rant and rave, but I'm not going to Mexico," she said.

"What are you saying? Of course you're going," Dad said.

"Oh, come on, Nonna!" I said, secretly relieved like you cannot imagine.

"No, no. I'm too old. Grace will bring me a statue and a holy card and that will be plenty for me. And take my rosary to be blessed."

"This is terrible! Al already paid for your room, Ma!" my mother said.

I said, "I can get him a credit."

"No, listen to me. I have thought on this for weeks. If I could get around like other people, I might go. But this walker is impossible. I ache everywhere in the mornings . . . It has become out of the question."

When I came back into the kitchen, they all looked up at me and shook their heads.

"She's not going to Mexico and that's it."

"I don't blame her," Regina said.

"I think it's a sin," I said. "It would've been the biggest thrill of her life."

"Grace?" Frank said. "How did you think you were going to get Nonna all around Mexico City with a walker anyway?"

"Well, Mexico City would probably have been easier than the suburbs."

"If she took a nurse with her, she could go anywhere," Regina said, smiling.

"You want to go to Mexico as Nonna's personal aide?" I said. "You're kidding, right?"

"Only halfway. I have always wanted to go to Mexico. But I couldn't go now even if I was just part of the group."

"Work? Kids?" Michael said.

"You got it. Ah, Meh-hee-ko! So romantic and mysterious! That whole story of Our Lady of Guadalupe? That's by far the most interesting one the Church has. For my money, anyway."

"What? They got the Blessed Mother growing out of tortillas now?" I said, thinking I was pretty witty.

"Shut your pagan mouth," Regina said, teasing. "No, don't you remember the story from Sunday school?"

"I must've missed that Sunday," I said.

"They had Mary growing out of a bialy or a bagel in Brooklyn a couple of years back. Remember?" Frank said.

"And appearing on the side of some bank building in Florida," Michael added. "But once they washed the windows, that was it for her. Or something like that . . ."

"Stop! You're all a bunch of heathens!" Regina said. "Seriously!"

"Okay, okay," I said. "I have a tape, but I haven't watched it. Give us the Cliff Notes version of the myth."

"It's no myth," Regina said.

"Yeah, okay. We're all ears," Frank said.

"Well, it was 1531 or around there, but anyway it was December and cold in the mountains. This poor Indian fellow, Juan Diego, is passing by on his way to Mass. He hears this music and these voices singing and looks around to see the Blessed Mother standing there."

"How did he know it was her?" I said.

"Because she *said* so! Jeesch!" Regina said, with no small amount of exasperation in her voice. "She tells him to go see the bishop and to tell him to build a sanctuary in that spot."

"I love these stories. It's always some poor wretched schnookel who gets fingered for immortality," I said.

"Yeah, a schnookel with an unmentioned history of mental illness," Michael said.

Regina stopped and tightened her jaw. We had insulted her with our sacrilegious jokes that honestly meant no harm.

"Okay. Whatever," Regina said. "Make fun."

"I'm sorry," I said, and tried not to snicker. "Really. Come on, Regina."

"No, you listen to me," Regina said. She was seriously annoyed. "All of you. There are things in this world that happen that can't be explained—bad things, miracles . . ."

"Do you seriously believe in miracles? Really?" Michael said.

"I see them all the time," she said.

"Like what?" I said.

"Preemies," she said. "Good example."

"Premature babies?" Michael said.

"Yeah. You get this baby who weighs less than a tuna sandwich, right? He's in an incubator. His mother is there stroking him with her fingertips and telling him how much he means to her and how much she loves him. She's praying and he starts growing like a weed. Meanwhile the baby next door in another incubator with the same issues and no mother or nurse cooing to him is getting sicker and sicker. You don't think that's a miracle?"

"I think that's very hard to quantify and document," Michael said.

Regina stared at Michael, a little surprised by his skepticism, and then turned to Frank. "What do you think?"

"I don't know, babe," he said. "I mean, I don't want to sound like I'm waffling here, but I think you're telling the truth and Michael's right, too. That said, if I was very ill, I would much prefer to have my name going around a prayer group than not. You know, hedge your bets?"

"Well, that's the whole problem with the world in a nutshell. Nobody believes in anything anymore."

"I believe in good medicine," Michael said. "And a positive attitude can be a great asset."

Regina leaned across the table toward Michael and said in a low voice, "What about God, Michael?"

"Come on, Regina," Frank said. "Let it go."

"I'm not asking because I care what Michael believes," she said. "That's his business. I'm asking because I think it's interesting. I just like to hear different theories on what people think the deal is, that's all."

Michael leaned back and took a long look at each one of us.

"You don't have to answer that, Michael," I said. "Does anyone want anything from the fridge?"

"It's okay," Michael said.

"No, I'm good. Thanks," Frank said. "Michael, don't let my wife paint you into a corner."

"No, listen, it's fine. Look, Regina, here's what I think. I think faith is a gift that gives a lot of people answers and hope and all sorts of good things. But do I believe there's a God up there or out there that is counting the number of hairs on my head? No, I don't. And I don't think it matters because if there was tangible proof of the existence of God, we would have heard about it by now. Don't you think?"

"A lot of people might argue that that's what the Bible is, Michael," Regina said. "And Jesus . . . you know? That stuff?"

"Touché. But answer this. If there *is* a God, then *why* is there so much suffering among innocent people all over the world? Why wouldn't God put a stop to it?"

"Well," Frank said, obviously growing a little weary of the question and of the day, "people bring suffering on themselves and always have."

I decided it was time to come to Michael's defense. "Not certain diseases or birth defects or any number of things that can happen . . ."

"So who put the image of the Blessed Mother on Juan Diego's poncho that should have disintegrated five hundred years ago and didn't?" Regina said.

Michael turned beet red. He didn't want to tell Regina he thought her religion was baloney and he didn't want to say he believed in something he didn't just for the sake of my family. So he simply said, "I don't know."

"Okay!" Frank said. "It's bedtime! Let's take this up another day! Come on, Regina." He stood up and pulled Regina to her feet. "Let's pack it in."

"Oh, God, I'm sorry, Michael. I didn't mean to hammer you," she said.

"No problem," he said. "Look, it's not that I don't *wish* there was a God out there who knew the number of hairs on my head, but it's just not something I spend a lot of time trying to understand. I have put years and years into trying to ease human suffering through science and research. And I try to be a decent human being by making my contribution to that science and research. If there's a God out there, I think He would forgive me for not recognizing Him if I have lived a good life."

"Well, I sure hope so, for your sake," she said.

"Regina!" Frank said.

"Sorry, I'm pooped," she said. "We'll see you guys in the morning."

Michael and I were left in the kitchen to wipe up the crumbs and turn out the lights around the house. Everyone else had turned in or gone home.

"Your sister-in-law is pretty adamant, isn't she?"

I brushed the crumbs from the table into my hand, threw them in the sink and ran water to flush them away. "I don't know what got into her tonight. She's usually a pussycat."

"No, she's nice enough, and it's not even that I disagree with her. Hand me a towel and I'll dry." I threw him a towel and he picked up a plate. "I mean, she sure holds the popular opinion on religion and so forth. I guess what I'm trying to say is that it would be nice to believe in something with that kind of *conviction*."

"Yeah, Regina really has her faith ducks in a row."

"You think Frank does, too?"

"Who knows? I think it's like he said—he's hedging his bets."

"So are you going to this shrine in Mexico?"

"Like I have a choice? Of course I'm going. I'm taking a bunch of Catholics on a pilgrimage, for God's sake."

"Better you than me," Michael said with a laugh, and slapped my butt with his wet towel.

"Ow! Come here, you!"

"What?"

I put my arms around his waist and pulled him close to me. "I just want to say thanks for being here with my crazy family and all that. You know? Thanks."

At the door to my bedroom, he kissed me good night again and stood there grinning.

"What's so funny?" I said.

"The world. The whole world is hilarious. Merry Christmas, Grace."

"Merry Christmas to you, too. What time is it?"

We both looked at our new wristwatches and then smiled at each other.

"Nice watch," I said, tapping the crystal on his. "Is it new?"

"Yeah. So is yours. Nice, I mean."

"Yeah."

Suddenly our lame humor faded away and we were faced

with each other's thoughts. We had celebrated a religious holiday we weren't sure we believed in, in a house filled with people who were absolutely certain. We weren't bad people; we were just hypocrites, measly, uncommitted-to-much-of-anything weasels who wished on some level that our philosophical differences with the others could be more easily resolved.

We limped through the remainder of the holidays without another confrontation. Michael and I resumed our lives in Charleston as though we had never spent a Christmas without my family. I thought that things were really good between all of us and I had thanked my mother a thousand times for inviting Michael for Christmas and New Year's. She was unusually sweet about our visit, telling me that she understood how I felt and that she could see why Michael was so important to me.

January was moving slowly, but then Michael's headaches returned. He didn't say so, but I knew it. His eyes became dark and he was completely distracted. For me, it became a time of waiting, and the silence between Michael and me grew, deepening with each day.

There were only hours remaining before I left for Mexico. Michael was to join me in Cancún at the end of the week as we had planned. I organized his clothes for him and was looking for his sandals. The phone rang. It was Dr. Papenburg.

"Michael's not here. Can I give him a message?"

"No. Um, HIPAA laws, you know. Just ask him to call me, okay?"

"Oh. Sure. Has he been in to see you?"

"Ms. Russo, you know I can't discuss that with you." Then his voice went from officious to kind. "Listen, I just think it's best if I could get Michael in here to see him and talk to him."

"Well, we're going to Mexico together—that is, I'm leaving tomorrow and he's coming down Sunday. Can this wait?"

He hesitated and then I heard him sigh. "Sure. You two have a good vacation and tell him I called. And to call me when he comes back. Okay?"

"Okay. Sure."

He didn't have to say *the word*. Once again, it was the *unspoken* that told me everything. I had no intention of telling Michael anything. I knew his cancer had returned. The phone rang again and it was my mother. My heart was pounding so fast I thought I might faint, and now I had to speak to my mother and pretend everything was all right? It was not possible because she heard the panic in my voice.

"What's happened?" she said. "Do you need me to come?"

"No. It won't change anything. Oh, Mom! I knew the minute I heard Dr. Papenburg's voice that Michael had had another MRI and that something was wrong. I mean, I knew he was having headaches. I could see it! He wasn't eating. He's been nauseated. The whole evil thing is coming back! Mom! Michael's going to die! He's going to die!"

"Grace! No! Stop it! You have to get control of yourself! You're not helping Michael or yourself if you're hysterical!"

"You wouldn't be hysterical?"

"Of course I would, but I'll tell you . . . I'll tell you . . . pray for him, Grace."

"*You* pray for Michael, Mom! *You pray!* I can't pray to a God I don't believe in. He would laugh at me! Oh, what am I saying?"

I began to sob and I could hear my mother breathing heavily on the other end of the phone.

"Grace. Listen to me. You're going to Mexico tomorrow. And you're going to see one of the biggest miracles in the history of the Catholic Church. This story of Our Lady of Guadalupe is no joke. Go over to St. Mary's and ask this priest friend of yours to tell you about it. Do it, Grace. Go right now."

"I don't know . . ."

"Well, call him, Grace. Call him."

"Okay, okay."

"Oh, Grace. I'm so sorry, honey . . ."

That was all I could bear. I disconnected my mother and

cried for an hour. I wasn't calling Father John. I would've felt ridiculous. I knew him, but I didn't know him well enough to confide something so horrible. He wasn't my pastor; he was my client. I knew Father John would make me feel better, but that wasn't what I wanted. It wasn't about me. I wanted Michael's brain cancer to be gone forever. I wanted it to disappear.

CHAPTER 21

Mexico City

It had not been easy to leave Michael and it had been even more difficult to keep the secret from him that Papenburg had called. Surely he could see that I knew his cancer had returned because I was so acutely aware of his agony. But there was no reason to lay it all out then. He would've said that he wasn't going to meet me in Cancún. Knowing what I knew, he would've canceled the last vacation we would ever have together. I would have said that I agreed with him, that I understood why he didn't feel like flying thousands of miles to go to a beach when what he really wanted was to figure out how fast they could put his cancer into remission again and to get busy doing that. But he didn't say anything and I didn't either.

When I left the house, Michael and I hung on to each other. We were being brave for each other and we both knew he was doomed.

"I'll call you as soon as I get there," I said.

"Okay, good. And I'll see you in a few days. Have a safe trip."

"Yeah, and you behave yourself, Mr. Higgins."

That was about all we said and I left with heaviness in my heart like I had never known.

My group boarded the plane, settled in their seats and the flight took off without a hitch. There was nothing better or more desirable than an uneventful takeoff except for an uneventful landing. As soon as we were at thirty thousand feet and the seat-belt light went off, I got up to check on everyone. They were a sweet group of seniors who were very excited to be headed to Mexico City. I told them I had my grandmother's rosary with me to be blessed and they agreed on the importance of it, encouraging me to buy one for every member of the family. Why not?

The dinner on the plane was chicken with rice and vegetables. I made sure everyone had what they wanted and was surprised to see almost all of them order double cocktails or double wine. Maybe the trip wouldn't be so dull after all.

I decided to order some vino myself and drank it with my meal. Once I had any time to think, my thoughts turned back to Michael and what would become of him and of me. Then I thought about traveling with all these nice people who viewed this little jaunt as a pilgrimage. I was certainly an unlikely character to lead such a thing.

I remembered that in Sardinia I'd had that odd experience at the church, watching all the women praying the rosary, and then running outside, ill and fainting, waking up to a shake of my arm. What had happened to me? And then there was the weird business of being overwhelmed at midnight Mass by the vibration of all those people praying together.

Was Mary waiting for me in Mexico City? I laughed to myself then, remembering. If you were really in trouble, I'd been told as a child, she was able to intercede on your behalf with her Son, whom we all believed was anything but a number two guy. There had been many occasions when I had begged Mary for something to happen—a teacher to be ill on the day of a test I had forgotten to study for, or for someone to ask me to a homecoming dance. Mary had always pulled through, although she didn't seem to be willing to render my enemies pockmarked by horrific acne. I laughed to myself remembering the depth of my youthful devotion. It seemed so ridiculous to me now.

Somewhere along the line I had surely fallen off the boat. There was a rule to be followed for almost every act of living and a penalty if the rules were broken. Ugh, the list was too long and dreary. What was I supposed to do?

Catholicism was inconvenient when you reveled in indulging yourself in the glittering world of material desire. The older I became, the less attractive religion became. I mean, I loved the ideas of Buddhism, and believed in not harming the earth, yourself or anyone else. And I was totally on board about the importance of compassion, with the possible exception of Marianne and a few others. But I wasn't about to throw away my shoe collections and go join an ashram. And I doubted if I would ever see the Buddha that dwelled within Marianne.

It wasn't like I could go out and join the Episcopal Church or some other Protestant denomination. Talk about awkward moments? Me receiving Communion in a Protestant church— that's awkward. Being a Catholic progeny of Connie and Al was like being Brazilian. You couldn't wake up one day and decide to be Swedish. You were a Catholic—good, bad, cafeteria style or indifferent—and that was it. I was somewhere in between lax and indifferent, but I didn't believe for a minute that such a position would send me to hell. Okay, I fretted about it sometimes in the middle of the night, but I wasn't possessed by it.

I looked up to see Father John. The seat next to me was empty. He must have heard my thoughts in the air and come around to issue a penance.

"Do you mind if I join you for a few minutes?" he said.

"No, of course not," I said. I gathered the magazines in the empty spot and pushed them under the seat in front of me. I thought, Great, I'm trapped now.

"You appear to be concentrating on something serious. I thought I'd come over and see if I could help."

I patted his arm. "Oh, thanks, Father. I don't think there's anything anyone can do."

"Well, I don't mean to pry, of course . . ."

"Oh, gosh, no, it's not that. You're not the prying kind. I'm just sitting here thinking about life in general. And about what a lousy Catholic I am."

"Why are you a lousy Catholic?"

"Well, I don't go to Mass, I haven't been to confession in years, I don't think birth control is wrong, and I'm pro-choice."

"Hmm. That doesn't make you a lousy Catholic, Grace."

"It doesn't?"

"It doesn't nominate you for sainthood, but it doesn't mean you can't reconcile your differences with the Church."

"Well, how about this? I'm not opposed to gay marriage, but I am wildly opposed to the pedophiles within the clergy . . ."

"Grace." Father John took a deep breath and then chuckled. "Oh, Grace. Anyone with a brain is opposed to pedophiles. It's horrible! But the Church is deeply committed to an entire cleanup of the clergy."

"It's about time. Sorry, but it is."

Father John shrugged. "I completely agree with you."

"Okay, but what about all the other issues?"

"Look, the worst thing you can do is practice situational ethics. That is, it's wrong to engage in something that's strictly forbidden by the Church because it suits you to do so. But let's take the issues one at a time."

"Okay, but look, Father, I don't want you to feel obliged to slug this out with me. I mean, you're on vacation!"

"Yes, but the rest of our group is in a perfect state of grace."

"How do you know that?"

"They're asleep. Every last one of them."

I stood up enough to glance over them, and sure enough, they all had their eyes closed.

"Amazing," I said.

"Look, we can sum this all up in the same way we did when we discussed various ways to conceive a child. Churches have an obligation to provide us with their very best thought on how to live a righteous life, right?"

"Yeah, but Rome's a little stringent for some of us."

"Just hear me out . . ."

"Sorry."

"Hundreds of dedicated people, men *and* women, come together all the time and try to tackle all the issues you mentioned and others. They think them through and have plenty of discussion. Loads of it! Their conclusions are based on what they believe would be the most pleasing to God. Then they advise us on how to approach things like birth control and attendance of Mass."

"And?"

"And they issue guidelines."

"Which only a saint can follow to the letter."

"That's exactly right! Look, the last time we discussed your family, I seem to recall that you implied their devotion seemed a little, well, too much for you. Is that right?"

"You have no idea." I felt a pang of guilt. "Look, what do I know? They mean well. They really do. It's just that they think there's a novena or a saint's intervention to solve every situation in the book and I don't."

"For example . . . your boyfriend, Michael? How's he doing, by the way? He was sick, right?"

"Yeah, he's very ill."

"Oh, I'm sorry. Isn't he supposed to join you at the end of the week?"

"Yes. We're going to spend a few days in Cancún . . . worse, he doesn't know he's as sick as he is. I do. Wait! This is a perfect example! Here you go! If we were on the ground and life was different for me, I would go to church and pray and then I would feel better about everything. But because I can't swallow all the canon law of the Church, I can't go there and feel welcome. That's not right. Is it?"

"No, it's not right and it's also not true."

"What do you mean?"

"You are welcome in my church anytime. In fact, you are welcome in *any* church at any time. I am sure of that much. But at some point, you have to commit." His face was very kindly, in fact, so loving I was inclined to agree with his assessment that I used God *only as necessary,* like nasal spray.

"You mean, like have a relationship?"

"Yeah, something like that." Father John straightened himself in the seat and said, "Grace, if you want me to be your good shepherd and bring you back into the fold, you're going to have to buy me a scotch."

We burst out laughing. "Done!" I waved at the flight attendant, got her attention and ordered two scotches and a minibottle of Pinot Grigio for me. "Will save souls for booze?"

"Something like that. Now, where were we?"

For the next hour or so, Father John and I hashed it out. On some issues he agreed there was some latitude, and on others, he wasn't budging. Finally, after agreeing to continue to pray for Michael, he returned to his seat, leaving me with enough to think about for the next fifty years.

That was his single goal—to make me think. How was I living my life, where was I going with it, and what kind of a woman did I want to become? Most important, did I want God to have a role in my life, and if so, how much of one?

There was time enough to give the revival of my spiritual life serious reflection. There was no imminent reason to decide anything at that moment or even that week or month. It was only important for me to have an open mind and a reasonably clear conscience. And to think.

Late in the afternoon, we landed in Mexico City, got our luggage and made our way to the hotel. Mexico City was a maze of ancient buildings and modern architecture. Everywhere you looked there was an interesting alley or side street filled with people, street vendors and the smells of food. Our driver, Miguel, barely spoke English, but it was better than my Spanish. He only needed to know where to take us, and somehow we managed to converse. The burning question was about where to have dinner and Miguel suggested a place in the north end of the city, near the famous Basilica of Our Lady of Guadalupe. It was a charming and lively area and it would give our group a chance to get familiar with the neighborhood, since they intended to spend the bulk of the weekend there. I'd been given the name of a place near our hotel, but Miguel's suggestion was infinitely more appealing. We agreed to meet in the lobby at six.

The first thing I did was call my father to thank him.

"Dad?"

"Yeah, sweetheart? How's my girl?"

"Dad! The rooms are beautiful! I can't thank you enough."

"Well, that's good, baby. That's good. Hey, I got something to tell you that ain't such great news."

"What?" My heart dropped. "Is it Nonna? Is she okay?"

"Who? Nonna? Oh, no, she's fine. It's Marianne. She and your brother got in a little car accident and she broke off her front teeth. I tell them all the time to buckle their seat belts. But she *had* to sit next to him on the console of the truck, and that's what happens. His truck hit a pothole, she hit the rear-view mirror, and *pow!* Broke 'em right in half. It's a sin, I'll tell you! A sin."

"God, Daddy, that's awful!"

"Yep. And your brother got a black eye to boot."

"How?"

"When she bounced back, she creamed him with her elbow. A real shiner he's got!"

"Oh, Dad! That's just terrible! Well, listen, give them my best."

Okay, you know I couldn't wait to hang up so I could laugh my guts out, which was not a very auspicious beginning for the leader of a religious pilgrimage. When we did say good-bye, I stretched out across my bed and thought about divine justice. I thought about Marianne freaking out, rushing to the emergency room and then to a cosmetic dentist or someone who took care of disasters like that. Marianne was probably in bed, in a lavender negligee with mint trim, living on Valium, painkillers and Tazo chai. Nicky was probably wearing sunglasses indoors and falling over furniture. It was too much fun to consider all the possibilities. I would have to call Mom and get the complete details of their pain and suffering. Oh, so big deal—I'd gladly do a little time in purgatory for the pleasure of a good cat session. If the rest of the trip would lift my spirits so well, I might consider staying in Mexico forever.

At about five-fifteen, I went down to the lobby to wait for the group in the Bar Caviar and ordered a glass of wine. No one was there yet. I sent an e-mail from my BlackBerry to Bomze to let him know we had arrived safely.

There were still faint streams of daylight pouring in through the large glass windows and I thought for a moment that back in New Jersey it was probably snowing like mad and black as pitch. I got a little homesick for the smells of wood fires burning, the feeling of freezing fingers in January and how the lights of New York twinkled and seemed like billions of diamonds. I remembered being very little and riding up to the top of Eagle Rock Reservation with my parents to look at the Empire State Building and how Dad lifted me up and pointed it out to me in the distance. Maybe if we could get Michael to survive another round of his treatments, I would take us there and show him the old neighborhood where I grew up. I was weary from the trip and weariness seemed to open the door to nostalgia.

"Are we the only two here so far?"

I looked around to see Father John smiling and signaling for the bartender.

"Looks like it. How's your room?"

"Just fine. In fact, much nicer than I expected. I have a view of the Chapultepec Castle. You'll have to thank your father for me one more time. And Mr. Bomze."

"What will it be, Father?" the bartender said.

"Oh, white wine would be fine."

"Put it on my tab," I said.

"Oh, Grace, you can't keep doing that!"

"I'm buying time off in the flames," I said with a smile.

"Well, a glass of white wine is good for five days, but a great single malt? A year. Easy, a year." His eyes twinkled with merriment. "Uh, Grace, I hope I didn't bombard you with a lot of lecturing on the trip here."

"Oh, no, Father, not at all. Actually, you happen to be the first and only priest I have ever talked to about what's up at the Vatican since I made my confirmation. It's been a while. I mean, your attitude isn't really that far away from what I think anyway. The right-to-choose thing is a tough one for you, I know, but—"

"Aha! Let me ask you this, Grace. If you conceived Michael's child right now and you weren't married, and you knew what it would do to your parents, could you abort that child?"

"Of course not! But let me ask you this. If I was a thirteen-year-old child with Down syndrome and the father of that child was a raving-lunatic, HIV-positive homicidal escapee from a maximum-security prison who beat the tar out of me, completely violated and traumatized me and left me for dead, does God want me to have that child?"

"Good grief!"

"I wanted a worst-case scenario."

"Wow! You sure got one!" He took a deep breath and a big sip. "Look. I think the family would be shattered over the violence. I would listen to them and try to comfort them as much as I could."

It was a very good answer. His role was not to perform the abortion himself. His role was to counsel, advise, ask for forgiveness on their behalf and to listen. I had not asked him if abortion was all right in that situation. I had asked him where the Church stood and what he thought.

"It would be a terrible decision to have to make," I said.

"Yes, it would."

"We are saved by the gang!" I motioned to the bartender for the check and quickly signed it to my room. "Let's go."

Dinner was delicious and Miguel had been right on the

money about the festive atmosphere. After we paid the bill, we walked around the plaza. People were everywhere and live mariachi and salsa music spilled out of the various restaurants and bars in the area. There was one fellow with a plump, bright yellow bird in a cage and for a mere five pesos, the bird would pick a fortune for you from a basket of small folded papers. In the square, there were Indians in full costumes of feathered headdresses, breastplates and leggings who danced nonstop. And there was a priest of some unknown faith with a pack of boa constrictors encouraging people to touch them.

"Snake handler! Holy cow! I thought they were all in the backwoods of Appalachia or something!" I said.

"Apparently not," Father John said, and chuckled.

As I stood by the door of the bus with Father John, helping each of our travelers up the few steps, I glanced back at the basilica.

"I wish it was open," I said, hardly believing my own words. "I can't wait to see the image on Juan Diego's poncho or serape or whatever you call it."

"*Tilma*. You'd better watch yourself," he said.

"Why?"

He smiled and looked into my eyes. "For several reasons. One, the image of Our Lady of Guadalupe is the most profound proof of Mary's reality in the world. Second, her mission is to save lives and to convert millions."

"What do you mean, save lives? You mean souls, don't you?"

"Both. She's pregnant in the image. So you figure it out."

He waited for me to board the bus, but I was having a little trouble closing my jaw and moving along.

Of course the group was very tired and anxious to turn in early. So while we rode back to our hotel I gave them the plans for the morning. My hands shook as I held the itinerary and tried to read it over to make sure I hadn't left anything out.

"Beginning at eight o'clock tomorrow, we have a complimentary continental breakfast available in the Café Royal, overlooking the Paseo de la Reforma. If you want anything more, it will be added to your bill, as will any other expenses you incur in the hotel gift shop, the bar or the minibar in your rooms. At ten sharp, we board the bus for Tlaxcala to visit the shrine of Our Lady of Ocotlán . . ."

I went on with my announcements, watching Father John from the corner of my eye. He was thoroughly amused because he knew that in his pragmatic way, without spouting any dogma or judgments, he had knocked at least one leg out from under the riser of doubt that held my soapbox so high in my clever world of skepticism.

Although it was only nine-thirty when we arrived back at our hotel, our body clocks read after midnight. We all squashed ourselves into one elevator, and when Father John got out, he turned to me.

"You'll have to decide for yourself, Grace. Good night, everyone."

"I wonder what he meant by that?" someone said.

"We can talk about it tomorrow," I said. "Here's my floor. See you in the morning!"

I closed my hotel door behind me and leaned against it, my mind in a bit of a swirl. It should come as no surprise that I wasn't exactly poised for conversion. I would freely admit that all the conversations I'd had with Father John were stimulating, but they only resulted in a brief visit to my positions on things. It was interesting to be in a place believed to pulsate with some unique spiritual significance. But I wasn't on the diving board for full-time anything.

I would have said that perhaps my issues with Rome and my family were not the same as my issues with the existence of God. I just couldn't figure out *what* God was. Yes, I sneaked in the occasional prayer on the off chance that somebody, some higher power, might actually be listening and forgive me for this or help me with that. If help came through, I was grateful, but you would probably never catch me in a church in Sardinia spending my last dollar to light a candle in thanksgiving.

Mostly I just went on with life and didn't think about all this sin and redemption business too much. Now suddenly I found my flippant agnostic self on a trip with a dozen devout grandparents without a single complaint and the coolest priest I had ever met. If Rome found out about Father John, they'd probably kick him out.

I got ready for bed with the next day's journey running through my head and reminded myself to be respectful of the beliefs of the others. I would keep the skepticism well hidden and let my group enjoy the day. I decided it would be more gratifying to help old people visit a shrine than to cart a gaggle of women with too much money to a designer shopping area. But they all paid the bills and they were all basically nice, so I shouldn't judge anyone too harshly. Besides, I liked to shop myself. Who was I kidding?

The next morning was bright and my group was just bubbling with excitement as they boarded the bus. Father John spoke to everyone as we crossed the mountains.

"I thought I would tell you a little about Our Lady of Ocotlán and the shrine of San Miguel del Milagro. *Milagro* is the Spanish word for 'miracle' and today we will visit the site of two very important miracles. In the spring of 1541, this poor native Indian, Juan Diego Bernardino, was going to get water from the Zahuapan River. The people of Tlaxcala were dying from smallpox—in fact, nine out of ten of them—and they believed the water of that river could cure their illness. So who does he run in to? A beautiful lady, who directed him to a ravine at the bottom of the hill . . ."

"The Blessed Mother?" one of the older ladies said.

"Who else?" Father John laughed and threw his hands in the air. "Anyway, sure enough, there's a spring there and she tells Juan Diego to tell everyone to drink the water and they will be restored to perfect health. She also asked him to tell the Franciscans that they would find an image of her in the area."

Father John went on to say that everyone who drank the water was cured instantly. And, of course, Juan Diego delivered the message to the friars and naturally they didn't believe him.

"The Franciscans don't trust anyone! Especially their household help!" Father John said, and laughed.

Priestly humor would never cut it on Leno, I thought.

"Anyway, they didn't want the villagers to see them, so the friars sneaked out that night with Juan Diego and followed him to the ravine in the woods, and what did they find?"

No one knew, so Father John continued.

"There was one oak tree, completely ablaze from top to bottom. No other oaks, just this one tree. They marked the tree and went home to scratch their heads. The next day, a crowd followed them as they made their way back. The marked tree had shrunk but had not burned to cinders as you might expect. Juan Diego chopped it down, and inside the trunk was a statue of the Blessed Mother!"

"Get out of town!" I said. I couldn't help it. It just slipped out.

Father John laughed at me. "Miss Russo? For your further edification, you should know that *ocoti-ocote* means 'oak' and *tlatla-arder* means 'to burn,' so Ocotlán means 'the oak that burned.'"

"No way!" I said.

"Yes," said Father John.

"There's a statue of Mary *in* the tree? Come *on*!"

"Yes! In the tree! Inside the trunk of the tree." He stared at me. I said nothing. "A full-blown statue of Mary."

"Is this the same Juan Diego of Guadalupe? If it is, he sure did get around."

"Different Juan Diego," Father John said, and laughed so hard I thought he might strain something.

The whole group laughed now, delighted by my impudence. What was so funny? Did they think that this statue was undeniable, miraculous proof of Mary's visit to this poor Indian? I was in for a ride to Religion Shock City?

"Grace? You had better brace yourself because you are in the Land of Milagro!"

"Father's right!" someone said.

"You'll see," someone else said.

Consumed with resistance and belligerence, I stared out the window until we got there, and what can I tell you? If it wasn't the Land of Miracles, it certainly was bizarre. I was told that the statue perspired and that its complexion changed from pale to deep rose. On occasion her expression changed, it was claimed. I thought it was all crazy. Then I saw the statue myself. Every hair on my body stood on end and I shivered. It was unlike anything I had ever seen.

Later on I was most certainly in some kind of a daze. Against my better judgment, I bought two bottles to fill with water from the spring and put them in my tote bag, thinking I would give one to Nonna. Then I bought two medals, two rosaries and six holy cards. Then I had the local priest bless Nonna's rosary. I took pictures of everyone in front of the basilica for good measure and they took one of me with Father John. I took a deep breath. Something very weird was in the air. The only way to describe the feeling was that I felt safe and peaceful and less like a doubting Thomas than ever. I wasn't sure of anything, but I liked the atmosphere very much.

When we arrived back at the hotel, the surprise of my life was waiting in the lobby. Michael. I ran up to him and threw my arms around him.

"Hey! What are you doing here now?"

"Some fancy travel agent you are! My ticket was for today and there were no other flights until next week without a huge penalty, so I came today."

"Wait, what are you saying? That your ticket was made out for today? No, it wasn't. I did it myself. I'm sure of it." I was certain beyond a doubt that I had booked it correctly because this was one mistake I had *never* made. How could this be . . .

Father John walked up to us and said, "Is this the famous Michael?"

"Yes, it is!" I was grinning from ear to ear and holding his arm.

They exchanged greetings and I noticed that Michael's luggage was on the floor next to the chair where he had been sitting.

"You didn't check in?"

"Um, they wouldn't give me a key to your room without you being here to okay it. I wasn't expected for a few more days and it changes the rate and—"

"Give me your passport and driver's license," I said. "I'll take care of that right now." I looked at Father John and back at Michael. Their faces were sheepish and I could read their minds. None of us wanted to start a scandal in a place where you could feel the breath of sinners and saints on the back of your neck. "I'll see if they have a room for you. I'm sure they will."

Father John covered his mouth with his hand to hide his amusement and Michael blushed, staring up at the high ceiling.

"Come on, Michael. I'll buy you a Coke while Grace works this out. Something tells me there won't be a problem."

"Why? Is the hotel not all that busy?"

"No, Michael, because there are no coincidences."

"I'll be right back," I said, and picked up Michael's suitcase. "I'll meet you in the bar."

Sure enough, there was a room available for Michael, and the reception manager gave him the group rate, for which I was grateful. I left his bag with the bell captain to deliver to Michael's *separate* room and found him and Father John in the bar. They were talking a mile a minute about medical research and I devoured most of the peanuts in the bowl in front of us.

We had an early dinner with the group, and back in the bar later on, Michael and I had time to talk. He was exhausted; I could see it all over his face. It had been a long flight; I knew that. He was drinking a scotch on the rocks and I was sipping a glass of wine.

"So how are you feeling, babe?"

"Like crap," he said. "My head's killing me. I find that when I get overtired, I get headaches. And I ate way too much. But

I'm glad to see you. How's the trip going? Where did y'all go today?"

"Wait till I tell you *this* freaking story," I said.

I gave Michael the full report on Our Lady of Ocotlán. He was incredulous.

"So what do you think?"

"Well, I'm not sure."

Michael suppressed a large burp and said, "Where's the men's room?"

"Over there? You feel sick?"

He rolled his eyes, stood up and hurried away.

His cancer was definitely back. I was sure of it. I started getting upset and felt my eyes fill with tears. In the last six months I had turned into a fountain. I reached into my tote bag for a tissue and my hand hit the bottle of water from the shrine. I pulled it out and looked at it. It was just a plastic bottle in the shape of the Virgin Mary filled with allegedly miraculous curative waters. I thought about it for a moment and said to myself, Well, if it can cure a village of Indians with smallpox, one lousy case of cancer shouldn't be too much to ask for. I unscrewed the crown from the top of her head and poured a small amount into Michael's scotch, quickly replacing it in my bag. A few minutes later Michael reappeared looking pale and weak.

"Montezuma's revenge?" I said.

"Yeah. Big-time. I'm gonna turn in. You got my key?"

If he left now, he wouldn't drink the water. I had to get him to sit and take another sip. My mind raced.

I said, "Baby, sit for a minute, then I'll come and tuck you in."

"Nah, I'm really off-kilter here, Grace," he said.

I remembered I had some Lomotil in my bag and I said, "I have something I can give you for it. Sit for a second."

"Okay."

I dug around and produced the pill. "Take it with your drink. The booze will help kill the germs." *Come on, Mary.* I said it in my head and knew it wasn't the most correct way to ask the

Mother of God for anything. It sounded more like I was urging an athlete across a goal line. Whatever. So I was a little rusty in the religious-petition-and-prayer department.

"I'll just chew it," he said. But when he did it was so bitter that he reached for his scotch to wash it down.

"I feel better already," Michael said.

"Good," I said, thinking he was saying that so I wouldn't worry about him all night.

I walked him to his room, pulled down his covers, kissed him on the cheek and said good night.

"Get some sleep," I said. "Tomorrow's a big day."

"You, too, sweetheart. Thanks for the pill. My stomach is completely settled."

"Good."

I smiled at him and he smiled back, using his whole face, including his eyes. You could see his affection spill out from them and I thought he must be the most wonderful man who had ever lived.

CHAPTER 22

Something About Mary

In the morning, Michael decided to sleep late and skip the tour to the National Museum of Anthropology, saying perhaps he would go on his own later in the day. It was a long trip from Charleston to Mexico and he was understandably tired.

"No, I'm not sick or anything. I'm just not feeling like a museum this morning. You go and have fun. Call my cell when you're, like, half an hour away and we can figure out where I can join you."

"Okay. Love you."

The museum wasn't the first stop on our agenda. There were so many sights to see in Mexico City and the surrounding area that we could have stayed for a year and still never have seen them all. So we took a group vote and decided on a few. First Miguel took us up to the top of the Latin American Tower to take in the panoramic views of the city. From there we could see the Zócalo, an enormous square in the heart of the city. Every inch the tourists, we took pictures—panoramas, digitals and even the old-fashioned kind on film.

"El Plaza de la Constitución. Capital de la Aztec Empire," Miguel said to the group.

"It's *mucho grande!*" I said in miserable Spanish, indicating its enormous size with my arms.

Miguel laughed and said, "*Si! Primo?* Tiananmen. *Secondo?* Red Square. Y El Zócalo is numero tres! In all the world!"

"How do you like that?" I said. I did not know that.

"*Y la bandera?*"

"Bandera?" I said, and looked at Father John. "What's a *bandera*? A scarf?"

By that time Miguel was waving his handkerchief.

"Oh! The flag! I think that's *bandiera* in Italian? Jeesch, I should know this stuff."

"Yes, Grace. We were counting on you to translate," Father John said.

"Then you got a big problemo," I said.

"Problemo?" Miguel said.

"No, no! Everything is *bueno*," I said. "*Alora, la bandiera?*" Okay, so I'd use the three words I knew in Italian and see where it got me.

Miguel began, "Okay. The emblem? Historia de la Aztec. *La verde?* Independence. *Y blanco?* Purity?"

"*Si!* Purity *es blanco*," I said, and looked at Father John with a smug little smile.

"Your Spanish is very much improved," he said with a wry little smile of his own.

At this point Miguel was laughing, thoroughly amused by the way Father John and I were giving each other a hard time but enjoying what Miguel was telling us.

"*Y la roja? España* and *los hermanos* who fight?"

"*Gracias*, Miguel," I said, and he turned away to take a picture of two couples with the city in the background. *And thank God your flag doesn't have eleven colors. We could be here all day.*

"So, what do you think about El Zócalo?" Father John said as we made our way back to the bus.

"Well," I said, "it's nice to know that somebody has a bigger flag than Al Russo!"

Miguel struggled through the crowded streets with our little bus and pulled up near El Zócalo. We all climbed out.

"All right, everyone!" I said, gathering our crowd together. "Over there you have the National Palace, which has some of the most amazing murals, painted by the famous atheist and Marxist Juan Diego—"

"Um, Grace? Excuse me?" Father John said. Everyone turned to him. "He had a deathbed conversion. He went down a Catholic."

"Another one! Gee whiz. Okay! And over there is the Metropolitan Cathedral, which is slowly sinking because of the sand under it, which became soft due to twenty million people sucking the water out of it. In fact, a lot of historic buildings in Mexico City are sinking. So why don't we meet back here in one hour? Is that long enough?"

Everyone said an hour was fine and went their own way, leaving Father John and Miguel with me.

"With bus, with bus," Miguel said, to mean that he had to watch his bus.

"Okay, *yo comprendo*," I said, in tourist Spanish, unsure of pronoun and tense.

"So?" Father John said. "Diego Rivera first and then the church?"

"Why not?"

The outside of the National Palace reminded me a lot of the Louvre. It was a long building of several stories. Imposing but not particularly beautiful. From the patio courtyard, the architecture of the arched balconies reminded me of the barracks at the Citadel in Charleston when viewed from inside their quadrangles. Except that the National Palace had a fountain. And, it was massive.

"Holy smoke," I said. "Look at this."

We were at the stairwell that took you to the first floor and the walls were completely covered in Rivera's work. The murals were crowded with people playing out every single significant event in Mexican history. And they were gorgeous.

"Cortés in full regalia, Aztecs in loincloths . . . they're all here."

"It's breathtaking," Father John said, his voice reduced to a whisper of amazement.

"He was a wild guy, you know."

"Yes, I know, but an interesting character, too. He was actually partially responsible for convincing the government to give Trotsky asylum here."

"I read that somewhere. We're going over to Trotsky's house after lunch."

"Good! I'm anxious to see it."

We wandered through the rooms where the president used to live and where government officials met, and finally emerged into the sunshine.

"It's impossible to think about the art of Mexico without Rivera, isn't it?"

"Yes, I agree," Father John said.

"Hey, Father?" He looked over to me. "Why do you think he had a conversion on his deathbed?"

"I would like to think it was because he came to terms with his life and realized that God was real. But I suspect he didn't want to spend eternity in foul company and he knew he was dying. Besides, he was actually born on the feast day of Our Lady of Guadalupe. December eighth. Did you know that?"

"That's completely creepy," I said, and rubbed the chill bumps from my arms.

"A lot of people have deathbed conversions, including Oscar Wilde."

"Oscar Wilde? Wait a minute! Don't tell me he was born on the same day!"

Father John had a major belly laugh then, wiped his eyes and looked at me. "You are so funny, Grace! Oh Lord! I haven't laughed that hard in ages! Come on or we'll be late."

The Metropolitan was the first cathedral built in North and South America. It was classic Baroque in style, but for me, the most outstanding feature was that it had eighteen bells in two enormous neoclassical towers that had been added centuries after the cathedral was dedicated. When they rang, I would bet you a dollar that you heard them all over the city. Just like the Colosseum in Rome had provided the marble for St. Peter's, Cortés had this massive church built from the stones of demolished Aztec temples. Recycling had arrived in Mexico early.

"It's imposing, to be sure, but it looks like any other European cathedral, if you ask me."

Father John just shook his head.

We had a brief lunch of beans, rice and shredded chicken at a little cantina on the square simply because the restaurant smelled so good. And then we were off to Trotsky's house.

We got on the bus and I began to give our group the lowdown on how Trotsky wound up in Mexico.

"They say the house is haunted and a lot of people have had some pretty funny things show up on their film when they take pictures of his study."

"Do you think it's haunted, Grace?" one of our group said.

"I don't know, but if this guy could organize the Russian Revolution, he might be able to haunt a house!"

We spent less than an hour there, roaming the gardens and pausing at the site of Trotsky's ashes.

"How did he die?" Father John asked.

"A friend of his from the KGB stopped by for a drink and stabbed him in the head with an ice pick. Turns out that guy was actually better friends with Stalin."

"You can say that again!" an older man said. "That's a pretty violent exit!"

We pushed on to the National Museum of Anthropology and History. The museum was an architectural wonder. Its roof was supported by a single pillar. We wandered through the exhibition halls, following the instructions of the audio guides, stopping of course to gape at the Aztec Calendar Stone. The galleries were filled with so many Mayan and Aztec artifacts that after a while they all started to look the same to me. My ADHD was kicking in. I paid attention for as long as I could stand it, but ancient artifacts just weren't my favorite and I started getting antsy. Too bad this trip didn't have a budget for my Sardinia buddy Geri Post. She would have been in heaven.

"I think some of our group are showing signs of fatigue, Grace," Father John said.

"Including the leader," I said. "Let's get out of here."

We polled the group and they admitted they were bleary-eyed and ready for a siesta. I pulled out my cell phone to call Miguel. Then I called Michael to let him know we were on our way back.

While we were standing around outside waiting for Miguel I turned to Father John.

"May I tell you a secret?"

"I'll give it the seal of confession," he said with a grin.

"Good grief." I rolled my eyes. "Last night, I laced Michael's scotch with the water from the shrine of Our Lady of Ocotlán."

"What?"

"Look, he's dizzy, nauseated, he has headaches . . . he's got every sign of this horrible brain tumor again."

Father John put his hand on my arm. "Let's think positive, Grace. You know what they say. God works in mysterious ways."

"What do you mean?"

"Just that. Look, I had a wonderful chat with him yesterday. I think God has a purpose for him and it's not a premature obituary. And I have a little plan for your Michael, too."

"You do? What?"

"You'll see."

Back at the hotel the group dispersed, agreeing to meet up again at six. That evening we had tickets to a performance of the Mexican Folkloric Ballet at the Palace of Fine Arts and a quick dinner beforehand at a nearby cantina chosen by Miguel, who admitted to me in private that it was owned by his brother-in-law. But I was accustomed to that sort of nepotism. Of course he only recommended family and friends for various jobs and destinations! In a city of twenty million people, you had to look after your own.

Michael was waiting in the lobby when he spotted me with Father John.

"Hey! Why are y'all back so early?"

"Well, the average age of this group is about seventy-five, and even though they're in good shape, they get tired, you know? It's normal," I said. "How are you feeling?"

"Like a new man," he said. "I slept like a pile of bricks."

"I think they are all going to have a nap," Father John said, "but if you two are up for it, I have someone I'd love for you to meet."

Michael and I looked at each other and then back at Father John.

"Who do you know in Mexico City?" I said.

He ignored my question. "Michael, I have a friend over at the Basilica of Our Lady of Guadalupe who was on the National Catholic Ethics Board. He taught at Duke and still holds a chair. He was involved in that MIT study. Brilliant guy. I think you two would find each other fascinating. Want to go? We'll be back here in an hour and a half."

I looked at my watch.

"It's only two-thirty," I said. "Sure. Why not? Let's go."

Miguel took us there and we walked across the sprawling plaza to the entrance. The basilica was enormous. Father John told the admissions people who he was and that he was there to see Monsignor James Mirenda. Mirenda must have been some big holy deal because this gal jumped up, made a quick phone call and then led us through the cathedral to a small bank of offices the average tourist never would have noticed.

On the way we must have passed ten thousand people—young, old, infirm with various maladies, but also many who seemed blissfully happy. I saw faces wrenched in pain and others beaming through tears, as though they had just been delivered of some terrible suffering.

"Look at all these people!" I said to Michael and Father John. "What's up with them?"

Father John stopped dead in his tracks and looked at me. He sighed so hard it startled me. Had I said something so wrong?

"Grace Russo," he said, and managed one of his smiles that for the first time I was sure was forced, "you are one piece of work. I'm going to put you in my friend's chair and let him introduce you to a whole new world."

The admissions attendant opened the door and led us into Mirenda's office. The monsignor stood to greet his old friend and finally us. He seemed like a regular fellow and I wasn't afraid of being lectured in the least. You see, now that I had a priest for sort of a buddy, the whole army of them didn't scare me anymore.

"Please sit down. May I offer you something to drink? Coffee? Tea?"

"Anything cold would be great," I said.

The monsignor went to his closet, which held a small refrigerator, and returned to his desk with bottles of water and Cokes.

"Help yourself," he said. "This time of day I like a Coke. Wakes me up."

"Me, too. These two are my latest challenge," Father John said with his trademark benevolent smile, opening a bottle of water and passing it to me. "Her in particular."

"What is that supposed to mean?" I said, feeling my nerve ends tingle and my shields start to rise.

"Now, now," Father John said. "Just hear my friend out. I'll even make you a little bet."

"What?"

"If you don't think your life is changed forever in the next thirty minutes, you will never have to listen to me about anything ever again. If it is changed—and I mean a profound change that causes you to question many things—then I expect you to act on that with your excellent mind."

I didn't know what he meant but I knew I was about to find out.

Monsignor Mirenda turned his focus to Michael.

"Father John tells me you're a scientist, Michael."

"Yes, I am. I work at the Medical University of South Carolina."

"Well, they have certainly made great strides in research. But you have to watch out with this stem-cell business. It's a very slippery slope."

"It's one hot tamale," Michael said.

I thought that had to be the corniest joke he had ever made. But then I realized it was a ploy to dodge further discussion.

"Father John thought that both of you might find the science of Our Lady of Guadalupe to be interesting."

"Well, you know the story, don't you?" Father John said.

"Not really," I said. "I went to Catholic schools, but I don't remember if they covered saints and miracles. They talked more about social issues like prejudice and the environment. My grandmother is sort of the family resource for that stuff, but she's more focused on Italian martyrs."

"And you, Michael?"

"All-boys private school."

"Well," Mirenda said, "I don't want to bore you with a long-winded talk but the miracle is important. You saw all the people out there, right?"

We nodded.

"We have thousands of visitors every day. In the summer months, I couldn't begin to tell you the numbers. It's shocking, even to me, and I used to be stationed at the Vatican. Anyway, Mexico, as you know, has a long and rich history that pre-dates Cortés and Montezuma; but let's begin with them. When Cortés arrived here in 1519, Montezuma was the Aztec emperor in charge. He ruled all the various tribes and each year sacrificed anywhere up to twenty thousand Indians to appease his pagan gods."

"Not nice," I said.

"To say the least," Mirenda said, and cracked a little smile. "Anyway, Cortés and his army were Spaniards and therefore Christians. Basically, they went to war and whipped Montezuma's army. The priests were the next to arrive and continued the business of converting the Indians to Christianity. These were dark days, as I'm sure you know."

"Very," Michael said.

I could see Michael shifting in his chair and knew he was thinking that he couldn't wait to get out of there.

"Then, by 1531, after much fighting over Mexico City itself, Cortés was firmly rooted in the Mexican government, which was now loyal to Spain, and the Catholic faith was taking hold of the natives. Okay, enough boring history, unless you want more?"

Monsignor Mirenda looked at us and then laughed.

"You two look like you're waiting to have your fingernails pulled out!"

"Sorry," I said, and elbowed Michael.

"Sorry," he said.

"Cut to the chase, Jimmy," Father John said, laughing, too. "These two have plans for dinner with a group of tourists from my parish!"

"Oh, all right!" Monsignor Mirenda said. "I know! Why don't we take a walk and go see the image and I'll tell you about it on the way."

"That sounds good," Michael said.

As we made our way through the church, Father John and Monsignor Mirenda told the story, one throwing in details the other had skipped. It seemed that a fellow named Juan Diego, a reasonably wealthy and educated member of the Chichimecca tribe, not a poor Aztec Indian as previously thought, had recently converted to Catholicism. He was on his way to Mass on December 9 in 1531. It was cold and he was walking the fourteen miles, which apparently was common among the people.

"If I had to walk fourteen miles to church, I'd never get there," I said.

"Yes, well, it would be a challenge for a modern woman," Father John said, shaking his head.

"Well, anyway, he's crossing a hill and hears music and a woman's voice calling him. Of course we know it was Mary, the Mother of God."

I winced a little and shot Michael a glance. It was odd to us to hear someone refer to Mary as the Mother of God. I mean, we had both grown up believing she was, but we didn't just throw her name around in conversation.

Monsignor Mirenda continued.

"She said, 'I am a merciful Mother to you and to all your fellow peoples on this earth who love me and invoke my help. I listen to their lamentations and solace all their sorrows and their sufferings.'"

I wondered if I prayed to her to ask Jesus to help Michael, she would hear me, and then I decided there was no reason that she would hear the prayers of a half-baked, sarcastic, cynical, *fallen-away* Catholic like me.

"She told him to go see the bishop and ask him to build a church in that spot. Not sure what was happening, he said, 'You know, you should probably get someone more important to do that for you.' But she said, 'No, I want you to do it.' So he goes and, after some difficulty, gets in to see the bishop. The bishop says something to the effect of 'Why should I believe you? Bring me a sign.' The very next day, on his way to Mass, Juan Diego sees her again. She says, 'The bishop wants a sign? Go and gather those roses.' Now remember, it is December and there is snow on the ground. But when Juan Diego looks around, there are roses everywhere, including a Castilian variety that had yet to be introduced into Mexican horticulture."

I was beginning to get interested in the story at that point. "No kidding?"

"No kidding," Father John said. "Wait, it gets better."

"So Juan Diego goes back to the bishop's office, and after some more difficulty, he gets in again. He drops the roses on the floor before the bishop and the bishop nearly faints in surprise because on Juan Diego's *tilma*—which is the garment we are about to see—is the image of Our Lady."

I shivered and so did Michael.

"And you believe this to be . . . it's actually real? I mean, this is true?" Michael said.

"I know it for a fact," Father John said. "Here's where the science comes in. Come this way. We're going to take you on the altar."

There were literally thousands of people on the people movers below the sanctuary floor that slowly passed the image. I felt a little bad that they, who were so devout, were not in our place.

Father John and Monsignor Mirenda genuflected as they came to the main altar. Bumbling around a little, Michael and I did the same. We were about ten feet away and I looked up to where the original image hung on the wall behind the altar. For a split second, her eyes looked alive. I don't know how else to say it except that if you had told me she was alive on that wall and in that garment, I would've said yes, she is.

Monsignor Mirenda was whispering now.

"The image is a codex," he said.

"What's a codex?" I said.

"It's a story in pictures that many illiterate Indians of the day would have understood. And then there are attributes that were not understood until centuries later. For example, the stars in her mantle are in the exact position of the celestial sky over Mexico City on December ninth, 1531."

"You've had that authenticated?" Michael said.

Father John shook his head, looked at his friend the monsignor and then back to Michael. He was a little irritated for the first time since I had met him. "What do *you* think? You are standing in front of a self-portrait of the Mother of God. Think about it, Michael, and you, too, Grace."

Monsignor Mirenda said, "This garment has been put to more rigorous tests than the Shroud of Turin and Veronica's Veil. Listen to this, Michael. Both eyes hold the reflection of

Juan Diego. He is present in the pupils. Not only is he visible, but the reflections are accompanied by Purkinje-Sanson reflections."

I had no idea what that meant, but Michael, in a quivering voice I might add, told me it had to do with how the eye reflects images—first on the cornea, then on the back of the lens and then on the front surface. Both of us were extremely unnerved. What was happening? Our tremors and sputtering didn't stop Monsignor Mirenda or Father John from whispering away like naughty schoolchildren.

"Needless to say, the Church has allowed ophthalmologists and all sorts of experts on various subjects from around the world to examine the image at different times, and every single time it is judged to be miraculous—the gold, the colors, the symbolism, the eyes . . . Of course, the *tilma* itself should have disintegrated five hundred years ago, but there it is."

We were speechless. And finally Michael spoke.

"Can we go back to the stars again?" he asked.

"Of course," Monsignor Mirenda replied.

"When did they figure out they were correct?"

"In the eighties. Computer technology."

"Do you mean to say that no one suspected anything before that?"

"Maybe. I don't know. But this priest . . . What was his name, John?"

"Sánchez, I think. A Mexican priest. He studied it for decades. Listen, folks, we could go on and on about this forever. I just thought you might like to meet my friend and see the *tilma*. When we come here with the group, we'll never get this close. It's really amazing, isn't it?"

"Wait!" I said. "Do we have to leave this minute?"

"No, of course not," Monsignor Mirenda said.

You have to understand that we stood there staring at the image of Mary, transfixed and perfectly still. I could not have known what was happening on my right or my left as my eyes were glued to the *tilma*.

"Michael? What do you think?"

"I don't know," he said, grabbing my arm. "I'm feeling very weird. I think I might need to sit down. My legs feel like rubber."

"Of course," Father John said. "Come sit here."

My adrenaline surged with alarm as we led a shaky Michael over to the area where the choir sang, and Michael slumped into a chair.

"Michael! Are you all right?" I felt his head. He was perspiring like crazy, but he was cool to the touch. He was breathing heavily, but I felt his pulse and it seemed normal to me. "What happened? Talk to me."

"Oh, my God," Michael said.

"Do you need a doctor?" Monsignor Mirenda said. "Water?"

"No, no. I'm okay." Michael leaned over and put his head between his knees.

"Do you feel faint?" I said.

Michael sat up slowly and looked at all of us. "No, I'm fine. I think I'm fine. I just felt this . . . I don't know how to describe it . . . like an electrical charge run through my whole body. Seriously. It was a little like being electrocuted. But I feel perfectly fine now. There was a loud buzzing in my ears . . . it was crazy. I've never felt anything like it."

I saw Father John whisper to Monsignor Mirenda and the monsignor nodded in agreement.

"What's the big secret?" I said.

"Michael has just received a spontaneous healing. I'd bet my reputation on it," Father John said.

"Yes," Monsignor Mirenda said. "I agree. I saw one at Medjugorje once. It was exactly as you describe."

"Oh, please," Michael said. "Come on. I'm absolutely fine. There's nothing wrong with me."

"Michael?" I said. "I have something to tell you and I guess now is as good a time as any." He looked at me, not knowing what I was about to say. "Papenburg called. He wants to see you when we get home. You've been to see him, haven't you?"

"Yes," he said. "Sorry I didn't tell you. I did see him and had another MRI."

"We can talk about complete disclosure another time," Father John said. "Why don't we get Michael some fresh air?"

"Wait," I said. "Please? Give us a minute."

Father John and Monsignor Mirenda stepped away and began babbling to each other. I looked back at Michael.

"Oh, Michael! Oh! I just . . ." I put my head in his lap and he stroked my hair. For what seemed like the billionth time, we began to sob almost uncontrollably. Michael pulled me to my feet, and after we found some tissues and blew our noses, we walked back to the center of the altar and looked up. There was Mary, smiling as sweetly as you would imagine. Her head was dipped to one side in what seemed to be a modest gesture of piety.

"Grace?"

"Yes, sweetheart?"

"Grace, something just happened that I'm not sure I understand at all."

"I know. How could this be? But if it's true, then . . ."

"If it's true, we have a really heavy responsibility."

"If it's true, then it changes everything, doesn't it?"

"Yes, everything. Oh, my God . . ."

When we all got outside, squinting in the light, Michael turned to Father John.

He said, "Look, Father John, I mean this in the nicest possible way. I don't believe in all this miracle stuff. I just don't."

"Well, Michael, just because *you* don't believe in the power of God does *not* mean that God's power doesn't exist."

"That's true," Michael said. "And I feel very different."

"Something happened in there. Something happened to you," Monsignor Mirenda said. "I saw it with my own eyes."

"Yes, it did," he said.

"So what do you think it was, Michael?" I asked.

"I don't know," Michael said. "You really think I'm healed, don't you?"

"Your doctor can answer that, Michael, but here's what I think. If you are indeed completely healed, I'm wondering how much longer do you think the Lord will seek you out if you don't respond?"

The rest of our visit to Mexico City was spent in a state of wonder. From the moment we returned to the hotel and met the group for dinner, the story traveled like wildfire. We were still in shock and unsure of how to answer the many questions.

"What did it feel like?"

Michael retold the story.

"How do you feel?"

"Perfect. I feel like I am in the most perfect health I have ever known."

"What kind of tumor did you have?"

"My sweet Michael was basically a dead duck," I said.

"Little Miss Sensitive strikes again!" Michael said with a laugh. "Listen, all I can tell you is, I thought I was going to die and now I think I'm going to live. I feel perfectly healthy. Obviously, I have to confirm that with my doctors and I will as soon—"

"As we have our little trip to Cancún," I said in all innocence.

Everyone stopped and looked at me like I had lost my mind.

"No!" they all said at once. And the chorus got into gear.

"You can't go to Cancún!"

"You've got to go straight back to Charleston! Get an MRI tomorrow!"

"Call us! Holy Mother!"

Michael and I looked at each other. More than anything, we wanted to believe his cancer had vanished. What if it really had?

We called Papenburg and left a message with his service to arrange another MRI as soon as possible and let him think Michael was a nut job. I already knew that the doctor was going to tell Michael he needed more radiation. But how stunning would it be to compare a new MRI to the most recent one Papenburg had called about and see that the cancer had disappeared? If it had.

That night, after dinner, the show and a lot of tequila, Michael got philosophical.

"Why would Mary single me out to save? In the eyes of the Church, I am a fornicating sinner who does stem-cell research and completely unworthy for any recognition, much less this. That is, if it's true that I am okay."

"Well, maybe in Mary's eyes you aren't. Maybe she sees you going on to do great things. Maybe she wants you to live for another reason. I don't know. I just know I hope it's all true."

"*You* want it to be true? How do you think I feel?"

"I think you feel perfect."

Dr. Christian Papenburg was a practical man. He dutifully returned Michael's call and listened to what Michael had to say. He became intrigued and then very curious.

"I've heard of this sort of thing, but I've never been a witness to it myself."

"Well, let's hope those two priests are correct."

"Like an electrical shock to the body, you say?"

"Yes. It was like nothing else I have ever felt."

"Well, when can you be here? Let's get to the bottom of this immediately."

The next day, we left our fingernails in the tarmac of the airport in Mexico City. We dreaded knowing the truth as much as we couldn't wait to find out. The flight was long, but to us time had stopped. It could've been an hour or it could've taken a day. But the next thing I knew we were falling into our bed and we were scheduled to see Papenburg the next morning.

I waited in the outer office while Michael went through the MRI and finally it was over. Papenburg's radiologist had agreed to read it right then. We went out for coffee to help Michael shake off the sedative he had been given for the procedure. I was holding my breath, but my sleepy Michael was guardedly confident. He wasn't making a lot of sense to me as he spoke and I wrote it off to the drugs.

"This is going to change us, Grace. You'll see. Everything is going to change."

"Yes, sweetheart. I know it will."

"Our whole world is going to change."

"Of course it will. Now drink up!"

I patted the back of his hand and said a prayer. (Yes, I said a prayer!) I just asked God if it was okay if I came back to the Church if Michael was healed. And then I asked God what we should do with our lives if Michael was healed. In fact, I had a lot of questions.

When we returned to Papenburg's office at four that afternoon, we were ushered straight inside by a smiling nurse.

"I've never seen anything like it in my entire career," Papenburg said, grinning from ear to ear, which did a lot to put us immediately at ease and in a mood of anticipatory celebration. "I made the radiologist go over it three times."

"What?" we said.

"It's gone."

"Gone?"

"Gone. As in *G-O-N-E*."

"Oh, my God," Michael said in a quiet voice. We fell into each other's arms and began to weep tears of joy. Tears of thanks. Tears of humility.

"Precisely," Papenburg said, choking on his own tears, "because there is no earthly explanation."

CHAPTER 23

Revelations

We left Papenburg's office on a natural high that was so high it was almost frightening.

"I'm never using a curse word again!" I said as I got in the car and slammed the door.

"Me either!"

"And I'm never talking shit about that bitch Marianne again!"

"Um, you just cursed."

"Right! I take it back!"

"And, Grace?"

"What?"

"We're going back to church."

"The Catholic Church?"

"You got it. You and me. We're going to get ourselves back into church every Sunday and we're gonna start a foundation to raise money to send really sick kids to Mexico City. Or Lourdes or Fatima or wherever they want to go when there's no hope left."

"Michael, spontaneous cures happen to Protestants, too. A foundation's good. But maybe you want to consider the Catholic membership thing a little more."

"I know that. But, nope. My miracle happened in a Catholic church and that's what we're doing. And the foundation's going to have a Web site where we can collect stories about other people's miracles because they can give sick kids hope."

"Michael! You're serious?" I looked at him and he shot me a glance. "You *are* serious! Do you know what this means?"

"Yep!"

"It means we have to go to confession! It means we can't . . . we shouldn't . . . I mean, just how far down this straight and narrow path do you intend to pull me?"

"I don't know. We gotta talk about all that stuff. Call Father John's cell right now!"

"He doesn't have a cell! But he got back late last night. I'll call the rectory."

I left a message for him and was certain he would call as soon as he could.

Then Michael and I started laughing and realized we were deliriously happy. We actually had a future before us and we moved in to a kind of euphoria. We were as happy as the day we realized we were in love—no, happier. When it came to changing your mood, there was nothing like thinking it was all over and then getting another chance.

As soon as we got home, I called my parents. They were so overwhelmed by the news, they burst into tears.

"*God Almighty! Thank you!* I've got the heebie-jeebies here," Dad said. "I'm so happy for you, son!"

"Thanks, Mr. Russo! We are understandably thrilled out of our minds!"

"So are we!" Mom said. "I'm going to church tomorrow to offer a thanksgiving Mass for you, Michael."

"Thanks, Mrs. R!"

"And I'm going to make you a chocolate coconut cake tonight!"

"Thanks, Mrs. R!"

Dad went on to say he would save his best whiskey for Michael so they could share a drink and go over the story again, just the two of them, man-to-man. By the time we hung up with them, we were both ready to sleep for twelve hours.

Then my cell phone rang. It was Father John.

"Father? You will not believe what I am going to tell you."

"Yes, I will. I can hear it in your voice! Congratulations! I am absolutely thrilled for both of you, but obviously, especially for Michael. It's a stunning miracle."

"How can we thank you?"

"I'm not the one you two should thank, Miss Grace, and I think you know what I am talking about."

"I do, Father, and we should discuss this. Michael says he thinks we should get back in the Church. You know, go to confession and the whole nine yards."

"Grace, my door is always open. But hear your confession? Let me know in advance so I can pack lunch! Ha!"

"Oh, brother," I said, and groaned. "Here, Michael wants to talk to you, too."

"Good. That's good. But why don't you both come by this weekend? Say Sunday morning at eleven?"

"You mean, come to Mass?"

"Yeah, something like that. We can have coffee afterward, if you'd like."

"That sounds great. Here's Michael."

It was not meant to be because when I picked up the house phone, I heard the broken dial-tone signal that meant there was a message. It was from Nonna. I called her back.

This time she whispered. "You're coming for your father's birthday dinner, aren't you? And you're bringing Michael, aren't you?"

"When is it?"

"I'm cooking! I haven't cooked since I fell on your mother's wet floor."

"Well, wonderful. You're the world's greatest cook, Nonna." I thought that she would blame my mother for all of eternity.

"Thank you. We're celebrating it this Saturday night. I need you to get the roast beef for me from that nice Italian butcher down there—what's his name?"

"The Real New York Butcher, Nonna. He's Bill. You want me to bring bread?"

"Two loaves, and if he's got fresh moot-za-rell . . ."

I made a list of what she wanted. Michael had stepped outside to talk to Father John on the cell and came back inside after he hung up.

"Call him back, hon. Tell him we're going to be in Hilton Head. It's Big Al's birthday party that they're having a week early. Ask him for a rain check."

"Okay."

"I'm gonna wash my face."

"Go ahead."

I went upstairs to the bathroom and rubbed a cold washcloth all over my face. It felt so good. Then I looked at myself in the mirror and thought, *Girl? What have you got now? You got your smart sassy self an obligation to the Blessed Mother herself. How are you going to handle that?*

"I'll get help. I'll ask Father John what to do," I said to my reflection.

"He said, No problem. Give your family my best. Family comes first. And could he give you a letter to take to your father to thank him again for the hotel rooms?"

"Of course."

I was becoming a delivery service.

The phone rang an hour later. It was Father John again.

"Everyone has been calling me and calling me. Even the bishop. Needless to say, they all want to talk to Michael. Maybe we could arrange something with his doctor to have a little dinner? I didn't think of it until after we hung up."

"I think Michael would enjoy that. Hold on. I'll get him."

I called Frank and Regina next.

"I heard! Connie and Big Al called," Regina said. "Hang on, I gotta turn down the television." I could hear her yelling in the background. *"Don't eat that, Paulie! It's for your dinner!"* She picked the phone up again. "Hang on. I'm gonna take this in my bedroom, where I can hear myself think." I waited a few more minutes. She picked up her extension, put her hand over it and yelled back to her kids to hang up the other phone. Finally, there was a click and she said, "Where were we?"

"Kids making you crazy?"

"You have no idea. Now give me every single solitary little detail. I am so thrilled for you and Michael, you just don't know. And your brother, too. He's been like, 'You don't know, this is the only time I ever saw my kid sister in love, and if he dies she's gonna be devastated! Oh, my God! Now he's cured! I can't believe it!'" She related all this information in a singsong voice that reminded me of gossiping in my high-school locker room about who said what to whom. "You two must be flipping out!"

"Completely. I mean, you have to understand that Michael didn't ask for a miracle. He just got it. Sort of like catching the flu."

"What are you saying? You mean, you knew he had this recurrence and he suspected it and neither one of you were on your freaking knees in the church?"

"Yep. Them's the facts, ma'am. We were standing there like a couple of gringos and *kaboom!*"

"Well, I hope like hell you're on them now!"

"I have a kneeler reserved at St. Mary's."

"Good idea, kiddo. You want a lightning bolt to come out of the blue and fry your behinds?"

"What can I tell you? I mean, it's the most fantastic thing that has ever happened. Although, I must say, we both recognize that there's a responsibility that comes along with a gift like this."

"You're right."

"Michael wants to set up a foundation . . . ."

I told her the plan and she said, "That is a truly excellent idea. Truly excellent."

And before I went to bed, despite the hour, I called Bomze.

"No, I'm not sleeping yet. Is everything all right?"

"Better than all right, Bomze." I told him the entire story and he gasped and gasped. Then he laughed and called out for his wife. "Darling! Do we have any champagne on ice?"

"Anyway, Bomze, you're the guy who got this train in motion and there is no possible way we could ever thank you enough or repay you."

"That's true! Oh! Grace! We are thrilled. Just thrilled. Tell Michael I have a lawyer who will set up his foundation pro bono."

"Bomze? You are one in ten million. Thanks."

I could have just been happy that Michael was going to live. But every night after Papenburg gave us the good news, I would lie in bed, think about it and try in my heart to understand what the heavens expected from a woman like me.

Finally, I came to the conclusion that Michael was right. We needed to make it right with God.

Saturday morning Michael and I were in the car with the letter from Father John, eight pounds of roast beef, two loaves of bread, two balls of fresh mozzarella and a pair of summer pajamas wrapped up for my father's gift. Michael was bringing him a book.

"Dale Brown actually signed it for him. It's a first edition, of course, but do you think he'll like it?"

"Are you kidding? He adores military thrillers!"

For the rest of the drive, it seemed like all we talked about was Michael's miraculous cure and, most important, how to handle it.

Michael was right again. Our world had changed forever.

When we arrived at my parents' house, we went in through the front door. After all, it wasn't a national holiday, but I was with Michael. He was company. Only family used the garage.

Mom came to the door, took one look at Michael, burst out crying and hid her face in her hands.

"I'm sorry. I'm so happy for you, Michael. I'm just so happy."

"Come on now, Mrs. R! Let me give you a hug."

"Hi, Mom."

Michael took my mom in his arms and hugged her for a few minutes until she stopped gushing and regained her composure.

"I feel better now," she said, and then sniffed. "Put Michael's things in Frank's room, Grace. Come, Michael, let me get you some coffee. Is that the roast beef? Here, I can take that. Did you eat breakfast? Or do you want a sandwich? It's almost noon . . ."

"Hello?"

Michael Higgins, the Irish baby butcher from hell, had achieved sainthood with the Russos, during his lifetime.

I giggled, shook my head and took Michael's bag to Frank's room, stopping for a moment to scan the relics of my brother's childhood. There were *Star Wars* posters on the wall and all of his favorite books on the shelves. There were soccer trophies, debate-team trophies and something of which our brother Nicky could only dream: a state-champion trophy for the chess club at Rutgers. There was a picture of Frank from each graduation and a picture of him with Nonno taken on an Easter Sunday when he was maybe three years old. I picked it up. Frank was sitting on Nonno's knee and next to them was our dog, Butchie. Frank's little chubby hands held an Easter basket filled with candy and a stuffed duck. He was perfectly adorable.

Our mother was such a romantic. Frank was married with nearly grown children and yet my mother had moved his room from New Jersey to here intact, just as she had moved mine. Home was home and she wanted us to know it was always waiting. And I did know that, although I knew I would never live there and Frank wouldn't either. Nicky might. Nicky and that dimwit of his might inherit it someday when Connie and Al went to . . . went to, well? Heaven. If admission to heaven was based on lifelong devotion and other things like generosity, they would surely be rushed right inside.

I dropped my bag in my room, dug out Father John's letter, the Mexican rosaries, holy water, statue and holy cards and joined Michael and my mother in the kitchen. Nonna was there stirring her gravy and pasta hung from everywhere.

"Hey, Nonna. How are you? It's good to see you."

"*Ciao, bella.* Come and give me a kiss. I'm so tired I could lie down and die. I've been cooking for three days and I've been talking to your miracle man."

"Great! He sure is that." I kissed Nonna's cheek and slipped her rosary into the pocket of her apron. I said to Mom, "Where's Dad and Nicky?"

"What did you bring your poor old mother? Nothing? They'll be back soon. They went to the car wash. And to get gas."

"Nope," I said. "This is a letter for Dad. And I brought a statue for the house and a rosary for you, too. And put this water on any aches and pains, Nonna. It might help." Then I handed all the things I was holding to my mom.

She unwrapped the tissue from around the statue and sat it on the counter.

"Is it blessed?"

"Of *course* it's blessed," I said. "What do you think? That I'd bring you some hunk of carved wood with no soul? After what we've been through?"

Mom actually giggled. "You know, Michael, my mother and I are just itching to hear everything that happened to you, but if you tell us now, you'll have to tell it all over again when Al and Nicky get here. So give us the short version because I can't stand the wait."

Michael was eating an overstuffed ham sandwich and drinking coffee. He wiped his mouth and sat back in his chair.

"It was incredible, Mrs. R. Grace and I were taken down to the altar by this priest friend of Grace's who she was traveling with . . ."

"The one from St. Mary's?" Mom said.

How many priests did I know?

"Yeah, that's the one. Can I have a sandwich, too?" I said.

"Sure, help yourself. The ham's in the hydrator and the bread's in the bread box. Now continue, Michael."

You may surmise that Mom wasn't making me a sandwich. Usually she and Nonna commandeered the entire kitchen. "Aren't you afraid I might cut myself with the knife?"

They were all seated at the table now and completely ignored me except to say, "Shush!"

I put the cutting board on the counter, got what I wanted from the refrigerator and started making something to eat.

"So anyway, Father John and his friend, another priest named Father Mirenda—"

"Monsignor," I said, and slathered the bread with mustard.

"Right," Michael said. "They were explaining the story of Juan Diego to us and the whole drama of life in the sixteenth century with Montezuma and Cortés, and suddenly I felt this jolt of like, I don't know, an electrical current? It just went all through me and my ears were buzzing like crazy and then it was over. The whole thing only lasted less than a minute. Then I felt like I was going to faint. So they all made me sit down for a few minutes, and when I stood up, I felt fine. Perfect, in fact."

"But you knew something was wrong again before you went to Mexico, right?"

"Oh, yeah, I knew my cancer was growing back. I had every symptom. That's why I had been back to my doctor and had another MRI. But I hadn't told Grace because I didn't have the results."

"But the doctor had called the house for Michael and his voice was very grim," I said as I cut my sandwich in half. "I knew *exactly* what he wasn't telling me."

"So when you got home from Mexico, you went back to the doctor and had another MRI?" Mom said.

"Yep," Michael said, "but I knew I was cured. I just knew it."

"Gesù Cristo! *Miracolo!*" Nonna said, making the sign of the cross. "Praise God!"

I giggled and sat down next to them with my sandwich and a napkin.

"Use a plate, sweetheart!" Mom said. "So then what?"

I ignored her and took a bite. Then she reached over and took the other half.

"I'm starving," she said.

"Well, the MRI before Mexico showed regrowth of the glioblastoma and the new MRI showed nothing, as though I'd never had anything. New brain. New, improved brain."

"Unbelievable," Mom said. "Just unbelievable! Do you understand what this means? Do you realize that there are hardly any miracles ever in the world? And you, Michael, must be an extraordinary human being to have been chosen by the Blessed Mother to be given such a gift. And we, too, are blessed to know you, to have you in our house, at our table. Has anyone notified the Vatican?"

"I'll send them an e-mail," I said.

"Don't be so sassy, Grace. This is dead serious." Mom went on and on.

Nonna had tears running down the miniature gutters in her ancient lined face and she was unusually quiet. Probably for the first time in her entire life, she was speechless.

We heard some rattling around and looked up to see Big Al walking in through the garage, of course. When he got to the kitchen, he immediately grabbed Michael in a massive bear hug.

"Come here, you!" he boomed. "You know, Michael, if you were wearing a ring, I think I would have to kiss it!"

He was serious. Had Michael's stock gone up or what?

"Where's Nicky?"

"He went to get Marianne."

Great. I couldn't wait to see her.

"Let me look at you, Michael," Dad said. "Your color is good! You look very good!"

When my dad gave a diagnosis, nobody had to run for the thesaurus.

"Let's you and me have a drink," Dad said.

"Sure," Michael said. "I'm not driving home until tomorrow."

I knew my family was going to be thrilled that Michael had been given a miraculous cure, but I'd never seen them so excited. I mean, Nonna was speechless and Big Al practically bowed to Michael. These two small events were unprecedented. And Mom? Well, she was almost apoplectic. With the way they were acting, anyone would've thought the pope had just stopped by for a cappuccino.

How was my Michael coping with all this? His male ego was in check and he seemed more at ease than I would have thought. Adulation from my family was a nice change from the scorn he had known. He seemed to be very flattered by Mom's opinion that he was a chosen person. Like Moses. I was hanging with Moses now.

Wisecracks aside, Michael was highly focused on what they were saying. I wondered what he was thinking and decided he was fascinated that they were reading the event only in a religious context. Michael was having the same thoughts I was. This wasn't science.

"Okay, guys, that's enough for now. We're here to celebrate Dad's birthday, remember?" I said.

"Yes, Grace is right, Mrs. R, let me help you set the table," Michael said.

Nonna got up and went over to the stove to continue cooking, and still she didn't say one word.

"Nonna," I said, "what time is George coming?"

"Che? Che cosa?" Nonna said, not seeming to understand what I asked.

"George, Nonna, George—when is he coming over?"

"Oh, later," Nonna said, and never looked up.

Everyone's behavior was odd.

Nicky arrived with Marianne through the garage door. Marianne was wearing a pearl choker and a lavender sweater set with a gray pleated skirt. I looked down at my torn-up jeans and striped cotton men's shirt and decided I would always be an Oscar to her Felix. I could not have cared less.

After a lot of hellos and *ohmagawdmichaels!* we launched into the cocktail hour. Every time Marianne tried to bring up her wedding plans with anyone, her intended victim would feign an audio processing disorder and turn their attention right back to Michael. Even George, who brought a party-size bottle of Chivas Regal for Dad's big day, and who under other circumstances would've listened politely to Marianne until she wore herself out. But not on that day. Michael's cure was headline news, and because we were so naive, Michael and I had not even considered the deeply spiritual impact it would have on others. Everyone felt like they had been given a peek at heaven simply to be so close to someone who had been blessed by a bona fide miracle.

At dinner, George questioned Michael about every aspect of his illness, his experience in Mexico and the two MRIs. George was so moved that his hands shook. He turned to Nonna and spoke.

"If God is this good, this compassionate, then surely we have nothing to fear."

"I've never been afraid of God," Nonna said in a weary voice. "I worried my children might not come home at night or that I might lose a child in a war. But worry about God? No, I can tell you that God doesn't want us to suffer. He doesn't want us to ever feel alone."

And then the *Thing That Could Not Be Contained* spoke.

"So, Michael?" Marianne asked. "Does all this mean that you're going to go to church now and become a decent Christian again?"

Michael could have said anything to her and the whole table would have overlooked it. The sudden silence of the room was deafening. She was beyond a tactless idiot. Michael had been through so much and neither of us had any idea that a cure could be as tiring as an illness. He had been talking since our arrival, which was unusual for him. I could see he was completely exhausted from being the center of attention. But Michael, ever the gentleman, leaned back in his chair and cleared his throat.

"Marianne? I don't know how to answer that question."

"A simple yes or no would be fine," she said, and giggled.

I thought, *A slap across your face would be fine.*

"Well, maybe for you but not for me. You see, I am still trying to figure it all out. I mean, why me? Apparently there is a reason for me to be kept alive. I don't think that the power that healed me is arbitrary and without some kind of rationale. But yes, I am going to start attending church and we will see where that leads us."

Michael had used too many big words for Marianne and it was plain to see that she was trying to figure out what he just said. I couldn't control myself.

"Marianne? He means that his healing wasn't an accident and it happened for a reason."

"I knew that!" she said, and repositioned herself for a big sulk.

"Of course you did. Well, Michael? You do think God healed you, don't you?" Mom asked.

They were putting Michael on the spit. I wanted to crawl out of the room and go live in Nairobi or somewhere.

"To be honest, Mrs. R, I can't come to any other conclusion. And you know enough about me to know I tried."

"More potatoes, anyone?" I said, and stood up. I did not have to call a mover.

"Sure," Michael said. "The mashed potatoes are the best I have ever had, Mrs. R."

"I made them, not Connie," Nonna said. "The secret is to heat the milk and melt the butter, Grace. You, too, Marianne."

I gave Michael seconds of everything and turned to Dad. "More?"

Of course he wanted more. That dinner was his favorite and he was going to eat as much as he could. So was Michael, and even George said he thought he might like another plate of food.

By the time we served cake and decaffeinated coffee and Dad had opened his presents, everyone was nearly dozing off in their chairs. Dad loved his pajamas and book. Mom had bought him a new pair of golf shoes and a branding iron with his initials for the grill. Marianne bought him a framed picture of herself with Nicky. Naturally. And Nonna gave him the complete recordings of Frank Sinatra.

Nonna stood.

"I'm going to say good night," she said. "My hip is a little sore and I spent too much time on my feet." She walked around to my father's place, kissed him on both cheeks and said, "You're a wonderful man, Al. Happy birthday." Then she kissed each of us good night. When she got to Michael, she said, "Say a little prayer for me now and then, okay?"

"Sure thing," Michael said.

George, knowing this was his signal to pull the rip cord, got up and left the room with her, wishing Dad a great year and thanking Mom for dinner. Nicky, recognizing an opportunity when he saw one, said he was going to take Marianne home. She objected, saying she wanted to help with the cleanup, but Mom stepped in.

"No, sweetheart. Next time. It's getting late."

With a flamboyant hug and kiss for everyone, Marianne reluctantly bid the deeply saddened crowd adieu.

"Parting is such obnoxious sorrow," I said when they were gone.

"Here, I'll get all the flatware," Mom said. "That was a great dinner, don't you think?"

"Michael and I can handle it, Mom. You go get a bath if you want."

"Well, you know what? All right!" she said, and led my dad from the room.

"Hey, Grace? Michael?" Dad said. "Having both of you guys here really and truly made my day. Thanks for everything."

"No problem, Dad. Happy Birthday. Love you!"

He blew us kisses and left with Mom.

I said, "You know, even two years ago, they would've been up with us until the crack of dawn. They're slowing down." I got up and started gathering plates and glasses.

"Oh, I don't know," Michael said. "I mean, you are a better judge than I am, but I think birthdays and holidays put stress on people—stress to make them larger than any other old regular day of the week, you know?"

"Yeah, all those expectations, right? You scrape and I'll rinse."

"No problem. Are we saving the potatoes?"

"Are you kidding? You never heard of potato gnocchi? There's a container in that cabinet. Know what?"

"What?"

"I never thought I'd be standing around doing dishes with you in my mother's kitchen. I could scrub pots all night long."

"Yeah, it's pretty sweet. I love you, you know."

"As you should. If I hadn't dragged you to Mexico, this whole thing might not have happened and we'd still be in the soup."

"You're terrible to remind me," he said, "but that does bring us to another point. Give me a sponge and I'll wipe the counters."

"Here. And the point is?"

"That you're right. Do I think this would've happened here? Like in this kitchen? Maybe, but no. No, I don't think it would have."

"Why not?"

"Well, obviously it could've happened here. But it didn't and I think that's because it was like a double whammy."

"You mean like if it happened in the steam room, you might have thought the steam cured you?"

"Yeah. That just about sums up my faith until it happened. But it happened in a church, right? Therefore, even I can deduce that it is of a miraculous nature. Yes?"

"Well, I have to say that I agree with you."

"And what do we do about everything? Our lifestyle?"

"I've given that some deep thought, Michael, and I think the answer is that we need Father John to help us figure it out."

"Definitely. I think he's a great guy. There has to be a way back into the good graces of the Church without us being hypocrites, don't you think?"

"I say, let's find out what our options are and then we can decide. I'm still on the fence about a lot of things."

"Whew! Am I glad to hear you say that because there's nothing worse than a fanatic who goes around spouting chapter and verse. I can't deal."

"Me either."

"But I'd like to go someplace and feel okay about it—especially after this. Basically, God fingered me. Shouldn't I be able to say thanks in a church without feeling like the son of Satan for not attending church for all these years?"

"I'd say yes. You should. But let's let Father John help us kick our way through all that."

I looked up at the kitchen doorway and there was Mom, standing there in her bathrobe, pale and clearly in some kind of trouble.

"Mom! What's wrong?" Something terrible had happened. I could feel it in every one of my bones.

"I just . . . I just saw Nonna."

"Yeah, so?" I was confused because their bedrooms were at opposite ends of the house and I thought Nonna had gone off to bed a long time ago.

"Her feet . . . her . . . She wasn't touching the floor." Mom was shaking from head to toe.

"Oh, God!" I screamed, threw down my towel and ran to Nonna's bedroom. Michael had his arm around Mom and they were right behind me. When I got there I stopped at the door. "I'll look, if you want me to, Mom."

Mom nodded and said, "You can if you want to, but I know she's gone. I just know it."

"Well, somebody needs to see for sure," I said. I opened the door and went in, standing by Nonna's bedside. There wasn't a bit of life in the room besides me. Nonna was lying in her bed, on her back, with her rosary in her hands. She looked like she was sleeping, but she was dead and gone. "Call Dad."

The next few hours were as you might expect. We called EMS and the paramedics were on the way. Nicky came crawling in, half in the bag. He was very surprised to see us all awake and walking around the house.

"What happened?"

"It's Nonna, Nicky," I said. "She's gone."

"What? You mean she's . . . she's dead?" he said. "Oh, my God!"

I gave him a hug and he choked up. Then I choked up.

"She went to bed, was saying the rosary and either fell asleep and had a heart attack or she had a heart attack and just went."

"I'd like to think she died in her sleep," Dad said.

"I would, too," I said.

"Wow. This is terrible! Oh, my God! I can't believe it," Nicky said. Then he returned to himself as he said in almost a whisper, "We got anything to eat?"

"Kitchen's closed, Nicky. It's like two in the morning. If you want anything, help yourself and clean up behind yourself, too," I said, thinking he was probably stoned. But then, I wasn't sure because Nicky could always eat no matter what time it was.

"You want a sandwich, Ma?" Nicky said. "You doing okay? You all right?"

Mom was sitting on a kitchen barstool with her hands folded on the counter, staring into space.

"No," she said.

Dad came over to Mom and said, "You know, I got that letter she gave to open on her death. I should get it, huh? While we're waiting for EMS?"

"Yeah," Mom said. She sounded like a zombie.

Dad returned in a few minutes and sat down at the counter next to Mom. There he was in his bathrobe and slippers, and as he put on his reading glasses he sighed, expelling his sadness over the sorrowful job he had to do. Mom was in no shape to take over and so Dad just assumed he was the one who would direct everything.

Dear Al,

When you read this I will be gone to heaven to be with Nonno. If I go during the middle of the night, don't call Theresa and Tony until morning. It won't change anything. They need their rest as they are on their feet all day.

These are my final wishes for my funeral. Since Nonno is buried in New Jersey and you and Connie are here, we have a little bit of a dilemma. I want to be with him and I want to be with you. So the best solution is, after a requiem Mass, have my body cremated. I know, I know! I always said never, but that's the only way. Give half my ashes to Theresa. She can keep them in the bakery or at home for a while, but eventually I would like them buried next to Nonno. You and Connie keep the other half. I don't care what you do with them, just don't stick them in the bottom of a closet. I'm claustrophobic as it is . . .

"It sounds just like her," Al said.

"Well, she wrote it, didn't she?" Mom said.

On any other occasion Dad would've said, *Hey! Watch your mouth with your husband!* But at that moment he was so upset that he just agreed with her.

"No viewing, she says. Well, that's good because they *skeeve* me anyway. Just a Mass and a get-together back at the house. She wants the Twenty-third Psalm read and she wants the organist to play 'Ave Maria.' Okay, that's fine. For pallbearers, she wants Tony, Nicky, Frank, Paulie, Tony Junior and Michael

Higgins!" Dad looked up. "Hey! She wants you to be a pall-bearer, Michael! How do you like that?"

"It's an unexpected honor," Michael said.

"Right, but nice. Okay, she says to look in the freezer in the garage. There's three trays of lasagna with Bolognese for the gathering after the Mass . . ."

"Oh, my God! How weird is that?" Nicky said. We all looked at him. "I mean, how did she know she was going to die now? Man! That like spooks the crap out of me!"

He was such a moron it was almost intolerable. "Maybe she would've used it for something else and then replaced it?" I suggested. "What do you think?"

"Oh, yeah. Maybe."

"Okay, I know what we gotta do," Dad said.

Dad called the funeral home Nonna wanted, and when EMS arrived, Dad went into Nonna's room with the paramedics and took Nonna's rosary from her hands. He brought it to me.

"Here," he said. "She would've wanted you to have it."

"Thanks," I said, and started feeling weepy again. I didn't think I had any tears left.

While they were taking Nonna's body away Mom refused to look.

"I just can't look at my mother like that," she said.

"I don't blame you. Mom? I know you're not going to be able to sleep very well," I said. "Can I give you something? Warm milk?"

"No. I'm just going to lie down and hope sleep comes. Who's going to tell George?"

"I will," Dad said. "Come on, Connie. Let's go rest."

"My mother is dead," Mom said, and began to sob.

"Come on, sweetheart, there now," Dad said. "I'll rub your back."

She put her head on his shoulder and they left the room, breaking my heart.

Nonna's funeral Mass was arranged for Tuesday, so Michael

and I stayed in Hilton Head. My mother gathered her strength and appeared to be getting a handle on her loss. She was, after all, a practical woman.

"You all right, Ma?" I must have asked her that every thirty minutes between Sunday morning and Tuesday night.

"I have to be all right," she said. "Every time I sleep, there's my dead mother giving me more instructions. How would you handle it?"

"With wine. A lot of wine. Or maybe medication. Ma! Tell her to give you a break!"

"She didn't listen to me when she was alive. What makes you think she'll hear me now?"

"Are you sure you're not just dreaming all of this?"

"Well, here's one way to find out. Ask Michael what he did with the wine buckets his father bought his mother. Nonna claims Michael's mother came to her and said to tell Michael a few things."

"Oh, brother! What?"

"To use the wine buckets from Tiffany and fill them with flowers, that she had prayed hard for his miracle and is thrilled it was given to him, and something else . . . . oh, well, never mind."

"What? Come on! That's the worst thing to say. *Hey! Oh! Never mind.* Come on."

"That Michael is meant to do great things."

I was sure my mother was lying. "Yeah, sure, Mom. Come on. What did she say?"

"Something about him making a good confession, and you, too."

I stared at her. In the past, I would've flown into a rage. Now, instead, I started laughing. Having a hotline to Nonna on the Other Side was going to be interesting.

"Well, I know you won't believe this unless I can produce sworn affidavits, but Michael and I are going into counseling with Father John. You know, to see what we can do about the future of our immortal souls. I promised to call him this week."

"Oh! Grace! That's wonderful, sweetheart. You know there are a lot of reasons to be in a church besides the benefits of Mass."

"Like what, Miss Connie with the Eyes That Pass Through the Veil?"

Mom laughed at that. "For community, Grace. It gives you a place where you belong."

"I know where I belong, Mom. With Michael and with my family."

We shared a long-overdue hug and sighed. Nothing was more consoling or comforting than my mom's arms.

Nonna's funeral service was lovely, and to my surprise a lot of people were there—parishioners who had known her, people from "the facility" and, of course, George, who sat with our family. Nonna's obituary had asked that donations be made to the church in lieu of flowers, but flowers came from Bomze and other friends anyway.

Afterward, Mom and I served lasagna, salad and garlic bread as Nonna had asked. For once, Marianne didn't say anything stupid. That in itself was another miracle.

Michael was wonderful. The following day, he suggested that he and I go to the airport to drop off Uncle Tony and Aunt Theresa.

On the way back I said, "So, Michael?"

"Yeah?"

"Take this exit. Um, by any chance do you have a pair of wine buckets that belonged to your parents? From Tiffany?"

"Yeah. How did you know?"

"You don't want to know. Here. Turn right here."

"What are you talking about?"

"I'll tell you later."

Frank and Regina were leaving in the morning, and so were

we. Once again, we were up late at night with them, this time toasting Nonna with a nightcap.

"Nonna was a good egg," Frank said. "She made a helluva Bolognese. To Nonna!"

"To Nonna!" we all said.

"Michael, with all that's happened, we haven't had a chance to congratulate you on your clean bill of health," Frank said.

"Thanks, Frank. It's incredible, isn't it?"

"Amazing! Regina and I were ecstatic when we heard," said Frank.

"Oh, Michael, we prayed for you, and our prayers—all our prayers—were answered," Regina said.

"Thanks!" Michael said. "*Now* I realize what prayer really means."

"I knew your heathen brain would come around," Regina said. "Just kidding, okay? Listen, seriously, we both just want you guys to know how happy we really are for you. Miracles don't happen every day."

"No, they sure don't. I called Monsignor Mirenda, the priest I met in Mexico, a couple of days ago and we had a great discussion. This guy spent a lot of years at the Vatican and he's no dummy. So we got into this business of miracles and you know what he said?"

"I'd love to know," Frank said.

"He said that when you start digging into the mystical part of the Church and all the apparitions and miracles, you realize that science fiction has bubkes."

"How come you don't ever hear about it?" Regina said.

"Because miracles are extremely difficult to authenticate. The process the Church has is unbelievably complicated. They're bigger skeptics than we are. All I know is that I'm cured, and boy, am I glad about that!"

"Absolutely! You know, Michael, Frank and I had some choice words on the way home after Christmas. Thank God the kids fell asleep. Frank thought I was rude to you."

"What? When?" Michael said.

"See?" I said. "He's so thick-skinned he didn't even notice."

"Well, I certainly didn't mean to be rude. Anyway, I just want you to know that we love you."

"Thanks, Regina," Michael said. "I love you, too." He shot Frank a glance. "In a platonic way, of course."

"Of course," Frank said, and smiled.

"Oh, and we want to be included in your audience with the pope when you have one." Regina laughed.

"Well, the next time we get together, we'll all be dripping in lavender and mint," I said.

"Oh, please. When is the wedding?" Regina said.

"Memorial Day weekend. Help me."

"I'm going to hit the sack," Frank said, "and dream about the happy couple. Come on, Regina."

Michael and I turned off all the lights, said good night, and I went to my room. As I waited for sleep to come I thought about Michael and me and my family once again. Against all odds, we had found our way into Connie and Al's hearts as a couple, never mind occupying separate bedrooms. And against all odds, Michael had been given a second chance at life, by a God he had long refused to acknowledge until he'd exhausted all other explanations.

But both of these things were drastically changing our point of view on everything with each passing day. I couldn't even begin to imagine how things would play themselves out. It didn't matter. I was convinced there was a higher hand at work that would see to the plan and all the details. Convinced. Wind was invisible, but you could see the effects of it. You couldn't see love, but the power of it was everywhere in plain sight. For the first time in months, I was going to rest easy. Much more important, for the first time in years, my conscience was on the mend. I reached over in the dark to flip the button on my alarm clock so that I'd wake up early enough to say good-bye to Regina, Frank and their children. My hand brushed something else. It was Nonna's rosary, which I'd left there. I gathered it up in the palm of my hand and held it close to my chest. Suddenly I remembered one of the last things Nonna had said. *Worry about God? No, I can tell you that God doesn't want us to suffer. He doesn't want us to ever feel alone.* For no particular reason and for every reason in the world, I finally believed it was true.

CHAPTER 24

Joy (Not the Perfume)

May finally rolled around and FedEx delivered the box that held my dreaded bridesmaid's gown. I decided to wait until Michael was home to try it on. No matter how I had worked on the tailoring, I knew it was going to look ridiculous. It did.

Michael waited downstairs in the living room while I descended the stairs, swishing and rustling taffeta, net and silk.

I looked at Michael's face and his eyes grew as large as they could. "Well! I must say, um, yes. That is some, um, big dress, Grace."

"It makes noise. I don't like to wear clothes that make noise."

"Like new corduroy pants?"

"Exactly. There are going to be eight of these noise machines rolling up the aisle. They'll drown out the organist."

"I doubt it."

"Do I look like an idiot? Tell me the truth." I put on the broad-brimmed dyed-to-match hat with the tulle veil and trailing bow so he could get the full effect.

"No, no." And then he burst out laughing and so did I. "Of course you don't . . ."

"The hat's nice, too, right? Now you know why I hate her guts?"

"Because she has all the taste of a milkmaid from the Alps? Or what's her name from *Gone with the Wind*? Melanie! You look like Melanie!"

"Shut up! I have to spend a whole night in this hemorrhaging tulle! I feel like a Civil War reenactor."

"May I have this dance, Miss Hyacinth?"

"My name is Iris, you big jerk!"

There was nothing to be done about it. I was going to have to wear the disaster and the only comfort was that there would be seven other girls in the same dress, all looking equally idiotic, making noise like cows charging through a cornfield.

"I hate her."

The best thing about the wedding weekend was the rehearsal dinner of steaks from Big Al's grill. Dad was in his glory as he and Nicky supervised the cooking of the meat. The weather cooperated and we were able to eat on the terrace. Mom rented round tables and draped them to the floor in lavender-and-mint plaid linen. Her centerpieces were etched hurricanes with pale green candles surrounded by off-white roses, tucked in ivy all around the bottom in a shallow bath. This was my mother's major foray into Hilton Head society and she was hell-bent and determined that it would all be perfect. It was.

It turned out that Marianne's mother, whose actual name was Janine, came from a family that manufactured housepaint. They were loaded. I could tell by the wristwatches of the out-of-towners, always a dead giveaway. And haircuts. They were very nice and not horrified by my family at all. Or else they were just very polite. The whole gang of them came to my parents' house for the rehearsal dinner, after I got to pretend that I was marrying my brother Frank during the rehearsal.

Sometimes in May you could have legions of mosquitoes and no-see-ums, but Dad had prepared for the worst with not one but two machines that attracted bugs and then sucked them into a bag.

"You see this pellet, Michael? It smells like sweat. Give it a whiff."

What could Michael do? He whiffed. "Whoa! I'll bet that works, too."

"Hmm. Appetizing!" I threw in from the sidelines.

"Ninety percent of the bugs are gone. Just like that!" Dad snapped his fingers. "Well, actually, you have to get this contraption going about six weeks before your party to be sure it's working. But it really does the job."

Dad was surely right about the importance of debugging the yard. There was nothing worse than a yard filled with hungry mosquitoes when you were trying to have an outdoor party.

Mom had hired some help to pass hors d'oeuvres and they were very professional and attractive. And she even hired a bartender.

"With seventy people you have to have help," she said. "I'm just not willing to kill myself anymore."

"Mom? Most people have help when they have a party this big. Otherwise, you can't be with your guests."

"You're right, Grace."

"You guys really went for the whole enchilada on this one, didn't you?"

"Well, we don't have a family wedding every day."

Marianne actually looked beautiful. She wore an exquisite pale green linen sundress similar to something Jackie Kennedy might have owned. And she was nicely tanned, courtesy of a tanning salon somewhere on the island.

I didn't want to hate her. I wanted to be a good sister-in-law. After all, she was going to marry my little brother and try to make him happy. To that end, I even bought her a gift from Crogan's in Charleston—a beautiful gold bracelet. It was just a simple bangle, but I thought it looked like something she might like.

"You can exchange it if you would like to," I said. "I mean, I want you to have something you want to wear, you know?"

"Oh! I would never do that, Grace! I think it's beautiful and

I can't believe you did something so sweet for me! Thank you so, so much!"

There were actual human tears in her eyes. She couldn't fake that, right?

So I said, "You're welcome," and I gave the simpleton a hug.

Saturday morning finally dawned and I got up early to start coffee for everyone. Frank and Regina were in Nonna's old room; the air mattresses got one more inflation for the kids, who took the floor in the den; Aunt Theresa and Uncle Tony were in Frank's old room; and Michael was bunking with Nicky.

When I saw the kitchen I said a prayer of thanks to the caterer from the night before. The room was spotless. I set up the coffeemaker and took the breakfast breads out of the refrigerator to warm them.

"What are you doing up so early?" Nicky said, coming into the room.

"What are *you* doing up?"

"You kidding? I'm a nervous wreck! I've been puking all night."

"Well, that's nice. What's up?"

"I'm getting married! I'm really doing it and I don't know if it's such a hot idea after all."

"Oh, come on, Nicky. It's going to be wonderful. Marianne loves you to pieces. She's going to be a great wife. You want a piece of toast?"

"Yeah, maybe."

He sat at the counter on a barstool and rested his forehead on the heels of his hands. I felt sorry for him. I popped a piece of bread in the toaster and got out the peanut butter.

"What you need is a peanut-butter-and-banana sandwich with a Coke. Hangover food. Good for the stomach."

"Okay."

I made the sandwich, poured his drink and put it all in front of him.

"Now. Tell your big sister what's worrying you. Spill it."

"I don't know. I'm just an asshole."

"Well, Nicky? That's not news."

"Oh, thanks a lot."

"Come on, be serious. What's bothering you?"

"What if I get bored? What if I want to, you know, pick up some hot little girl and screw her brains out?"

"Ah! Fidelity issues?"

"Yeah. I worry about that."

"Well, Nicky, I think it goes like this. You're gonna do what you want to do. Just remember that you have to live with it and that if Marianne found out she'd kill herself and you'd have to live with that. I'm not sure screwing around is worth the price."

"That's what Dad says."

"See? I knew it! I always thought Dad stepped out on Mom from time to time."

"What? Dad? Are you crazy? Mom's the one who screwed around. Not Dad. Why do you think Nonna was always riding her ass?"

"What the hell are you saying?" My ears started ringing and I had to sit down. "What did you just say?"

"You didn't know that?"

"Um, no!"

"Yeah, back in Jersey when Mom was a teenager, she had some hottie from the gas station she was tooling."

"How about if you don't say *Mom* and *tooling* in the same sentence, okay?"

"Whatever. Yeah, and he wasn't the only one. After they got married, there was another guy who used to wash their windows or something and that piece of crap was like thirtysomething and Mom was like twenty-five."

"Holy cow!"

"That's why Nonna found Dad for Mom and made her—I mean she strongly encouraged her, to marry him and settle down. Dad was a dishwasher and then a bartender at the Knights of Columbus and Nonna used to go to dances there with Nonno. Nonna knew Dad for years before she brought

Mom there to meet him. And after they got married and all that shit went down, that's why Nonna and Nonno were always in our house every day! Then Nonno died and Nonna moved in with us! But yeah. That's what happened. I thought you knew all this?"

"No! Wait, come to think of it, I had some conversation with Mom a while ago about passion and so forth. She was trying to make me understand that she knew how I felt about Michael."

"This was before they canonized him?"

I laughed then and said, "Yeah. It was way before. So *that's* why Nonna was always giving her hell. She didn't trust her!"

"Nonna didn't trust Mom to buy toilet paper."

"Boy, that's the truth, isn't it? Poor Mom! She's been a mouse all these years because of something stupid she did when she was young? That's ridiculous."

"Exactly! And I don't know, Grace. You know me. I like a pretty girl and all that, and what if Mom's genes kick in and I want to, you know . . . see what something else might be like?"

My head was still swimming from the notion that my mother had a wild youth and had gone on to actually commit adultery. But I thought about it and said, "Look, Nicky. You love Marianne, don't you?"

"Oh, sure! I love her with all my heart."

"Then you marry her, okay? You don't stand a woman up on her wedding day. That's grounds for murder. You're just nervous. And you should be. This is a big step in your life. And she really loves you—why, I have no idea—"

"Hey!"

"A little joke, brother. Anyway, you two are perfect for each other."

"Do you really think so?"

"Yeah, I really do. Go get a shower. You don't want to stink up the church."

Nicky drained the rest of his glass and came around the counter to give me a hug.

"Thanks, Grace. You're the greatest sister a guy could have. I love ya."

"I love you, too. Now get lost. Brush your teeth. Your breath smells like a sewer."

Nicky left and I stood there wondering just how guilty and insecure Nonna had made my mother feel all those years. And that there was something perverse in the way Dad let Nonna get away with it—that Mom just took it—and that Dad did nothing about it, perpetuated it. Families were crazy and they all had their secrets. Someday, but not that one, there was a conversation about all this with my mother that had to happen. I had to let her know she had overpaid for her sins and to let it go.

I poured myself a second cup of coffee, threw all the bread in the oven to warm and walked out to the backyard. There was no sign that so many people had been there last night. There wasn't a toothpick to be found.

My stupid little brother was marrying stupid Marianne in a few hours. Time to get the show on the road.

Back inside, I set up glasses and a pitcher of orange juice on the counter and mugs, cream and sugar, napkins and whatever else I could remember Mom would want to put out for everyone to help themselves to breakfast.

When I saw Lisa in her bridesmaid's dress and she saw me in mine, we shrieked.

"You're wearing my dress!" I said. "Take it off!"

"No, you're wearing mine! You change!"

Lisa was bubbling over with excitement. She looked like she had grown at least two inches in the last few months. "Know what, Aunt Grace? I can't believe I'm going to be in a wedding. This is the first time I've ever done this!"

Her clean-scrubbed face was just beaming.

"Come on," I said. "I'm gonna do your makeup."

"Really? Mom said—"

"Don't worry about it! Just a little for pictures. Listen to me. By the time you're my age, you'll have enough bridesmaid's dresses to give every girl you know something to wear on Halloween."

I gave her a thin foundation, a little blush and mascara and a swipe of rosy-colored lip gloss. She looked beautiful. And she looked eighteen. Regina was going to kill me.

"If your mother says anything, tell her your grandma said you looked beautiful."

Lisa looked at her face in the mirror. "Wow, you covered up my zits."

"Yeah, and your childhood. Maybe we should wash it all off."

"No way. I'm almost fourteen, Aunt Grace."

"I keep forgetting, honey. You're right. Now let's go or we'll be late."

When we arrived at the church, we gathered in a large meeting room that had been transformed into a dressing room for the occasion. Marianne was just slipping her gown over her head and her mother was helping her straighten out her skirt. She looked like a dream bride from a magazine. She really did. Her shoulder-length hair had been put up in a smooth French twist. Her makeup was flawless and the only jewelry she wore was pearl studs and, of course, her engagement ring.

"Holy cow, Marianne! You look so beautiful I think I might start crying!"

I couldn't help it. The compliment just flew out of my mouth. There were years to come for me to rectify that.

The wedding ceremony was so traditional it made me grind my teeth. We went up the aisle, one by one, fueled by the music of Handel performed by a chamber-music quartet and the smiles of two hundred guests. The flowers on the altar were gorgeous. There were Nicky and Frank, standing up there, and I'm telling you the truth, Nicky looked like a movie star. No lie. I winked at him and he winked back. As I stepped into position the organ music rose and began the Wedding March. Marianne appeared at the back of the church on the arm of her uncle and everyone stood.

Marianne had a demure smile, but when she saw Nicky her bottom lip began to quiver. And wouldn't you know it? The devil made her trip on her skirt, she dropped her bouquet and nearly fell on her face, but her uncle caught her by her arm and steadied her on her feet. He bent down, picked up the flowers and bowed dramatically as he offered them to her. The congregation oohed and aahed at his chivalry. As Marianne tried to compose her wits, the giggle monster arrived and possessed her like a demon. To the sheer horror of the guests and wedding party, poor Marianne giggled like an uncontrollable hyena the rest of the way to her mortified waiting groom.

"Do you want a glass of water?" I whispered.

She shook her head and continued tittering.

"Marianne?"

She glanced in my direction and I saw that she was shaking all over, one step away from virtual crash-and-burn. She needed to snap out of it.

"Marianne? We know you're nervous, but this has to cease or I'm going to slap you," I whispered as quietly as possible. I knew if I made her angry, she would refocus and regain control. It worked.

Marianne turned red, immediately stopped laughing and everyone sighed in relief.

"In the name of the Father . . ."

Their priest began the nuptial Mass, and inside of an hour it was all over.

The reception was under a tent at the country club and the East Coast Party Band was in full swing by the time we arrived after taking a thousand pictures. Michael and I were to be seated with George, Regina and Frank, their kids, and Marianne's first cousin and his wife from Akron.

We walked across the parking lot holding hands and found our table.

"You did great, Lisa," I said. "I was very proud of you."

"The family would like to thank you for not slapping the bride across the face," Regina said.

"It was close, let me tell you," I said.

"Yeah, what did you say to her, Aunt Grace?"

"Nothing, baby," I said. "I don't remember."

"Must've been curse words," little Paulie said.

"Aunt Grace *never* curses," I said.

All the children giggled.

"May I have this dance, Miss, um, Bo-Peep?" Michael said.

"Great idea," I said.

It was a slow dance and we moved across the crowded dance floor.

"You looked really spectacular at the altar, sweetheart," Michael said.

"Yeah, me and all the other Bo-Peeps," I said. "But thanks."

"Well, you did what you had to do. You're a good woman. So what *did* you say to Marianne?"

"I told her you thought she was a horse's ass."

"You did not."

"Right. I told her you had given Nicky a list of twenty-five guys and their phone numbers who said Marianne slept with them and that she liked kinky sex. Really kinky."

He held me back and looked at my face. "No way! You didn't!"

"You'll never know, will you?"

He began spinning me around and around and we laughed and laughed. We were so happy then, like never before.

"It just keeps getting better, Grace, doesn't it?"

"Yep."

I looked in his eyes and he looked in mine. We were eternal, filled with the incredible joy only love brings. I wanted the song to last forever, to be held in his arms forever, and in those few minutes I knew I could truly trust that we shared the same depth of feeling and commitment. How sappy is that? Well, I know it's sappy, but it was really true.

Later, after the bride and groom's first dance and the mother of the bride and groom danced with the father and uncle and ultimately with the married couple, after the seafood Newburg and the roasted capon, after an ocean of champagne had been consumed from the bridal fountain with the ice sculpture of two doves that cost an extra five hundred dollars, Big Al got up and took the microphone to make a toast.

Ping! Ping! Ping!

Forks tapped the sides of goblets and everyone got quiet.

"Good evening, everyone. I'm Al Russo, the father of the groom, and I'd like to say a few words. First, I'd like to thank everyone for being here with us on this very important day—the joining of two families, and there's nothing more important than family. Am I right?"

Everyone clapped wildly.

"I want to take a minute here to remember those who are no longer with us. Francesca Todero, my wonderful mother-in-law, went home to heaven this year. But if she could've been here, Nicky and Marianne, she would've said this was the most beautiful wedding she had ever seen. Somehow, I think she's with us anyway. So, Nonna? Here's to you!

"And Frank? And Regina? Frank, my oldest son, and his lovely wife, Regina, put thousands of miles on their car driving back and forth to New Jersey to be with the family here. Anytime we ask them to bring us real cannolis? They get in the car."

Everyone laughed.

"Anyway, I want all of them, especially Lisa, who was a bridesmaid today, to know how proud I am of them."

"Is he going to thank each person under the tent?" Lisa said to no one in particular.

"Shut your mouth," Regina said.

Dad continued.

"Nicky? My youngest son. I'm so proud of you today. And every day. Thank God you had the good sense to marry Marianne and bring her into our family. I'm expecting lots of grandchildren, and soon!"

Marianne groaned and Nicky made a lot of "yeah, let's go get 'em!" gestures that were identical to the ones he made at the television when the Giants were playing. Everyone laughed again.

"It's only my daughter, Grace, who's holding out on me. She's got this fellow, Michael, who we all love . . ."

I wanted the floor to open and let me be swallowed alive.

"Aw, God, Daddy?" I said under my breath, but don't you know that somehow Dad heard it.

"I love it when my little girl calls me Daddy! But I want to know if her Michael would care to comment?"

Everyone started whooping and hollering. The crowd was well lubricated by that point.

Michael stood up. "Mr. Russo? Everything is okay. We'll talk later."

"Good save," Frank said.

"And one final toast to Janine, Marianne's beautiful mother. We are so proud to welcome you into our family and all of your family, too! I always wanted to go to Ohio . . ."

The crowd groaned and Big Al recouped the moment.

"Wait! Wait! Okay! I got a little carried away with the Ohio part! I admit it. Look, I would love to see where our lovely Marianne grew up, so I'll just leave it at that." There was some applause and some more groaning. "Anyway," Dad said as he raised his glass, "congratulations to the families and to the bride and groom! *Saa-loot!*"

"*Salute!*" the guests said, almost in unison.

The band started playing again, another slow song, and I thought it would be nice to dance with my dad.

I made my way to him and said, "So, Big Al, care to dance with a southern-belle impersonator dressed in enough lavender to scare off a pack of vicious carpetbaggers?"

He looked at me and laughed. "It would be a pleasure," he said.

He led me out to the dance floor with his hand on the edge of my elbow and we began a waltz.

"That was a great toast," I said.

"Thanks," he said. "You think so?"

"Yeah. It was really good, Dad."

"Good. So? How are you and Michael doing? With the Church, I mean."

"Good," I said. "We went to confession and now we go to Communion at Mass on Sundays."

"But you're still living in sin!"

"Yeah, but we go to confession once a week—"

"You're using it as a—"

I put my finger to his lips to make him stop. "Don't worry, Daddy. It's all going to work out fine. We even had dinner with the bishop!"

Just then Michael tapped him on the shoulder.

"May I have a word with you?"

"Sure," Dad said.

They stepped away for a moment and I stood there in the middle of the dance floor like a mannequin. Then I saw Dad shake Michael's hand and then Dad grabbed him in a huge embrace and I knew they had cut the deal. Next Dad reached in his jacket and gave Michael an envelope and Michael took it and slipped it in his jacket.

Michael, smiling like he just won the Powerball lottery for a jillion dollars, came to me and we began to dance.

"So what did my dad give you?"

"A check for the foundation."

"No kidding? Well, that's very nice."

"Yep. Five thousand dollars. He's a wonderful man, Grace. You should be very proud of him."

"I am. I am. Really. So? What else did you say to my dad?"

"Oh, nothing. I told him about some new paving material I read about."

"But he hugged you to death!"

"He was very grateful."

"You're such a liar."

"Grace? This is your brother's day. Not ours."

"But ours is coming?"

"Can you keep a secret?"

. He reached into his pocket and pulled out a piece of string. Then he looped it around the fourth finger on my left hand.

"What are you doing?"

"Just checking."

He smiled at me and I kissed his cheek—nice Italian girls don't get down, hook up and make out with their boyfriends in public. No, we don't. I put my head on his shoulder and let the whole world, except for the two of us, drift away. Nothing else mattered. What else is there to say?

EPILOGUE

Another Message from Michael

Isn't it just classic that I got to have a few words in the beginning and now here I am again at the end? I'm laughing about this actually, because is there an end? I sure hope not. And when was the beginning? Who remembers?

Listen, I don't want to keep you longer than you intended to stay, but there are a few loose threads here, somebody has to be the cleanup guy, and I guess that's me. I wanted Grace to tell you the story because she has this phenomenal heart, sense of humor, and coming from her it is just a whole lot more engaging than the clinical report you would get from me. We are just wired differently and that difference is a very good thing.

First, but not necessarily most important, Grace finally told me about the Tiffany silver. That just about took off or added ten years of/to my life. Hopefully, added. She could not have made that up. No one knew. No one. Not because it was a big secret but because the silver was relatively unimportant to me. But there it was. Another piece of evidence of life after death. Trivial as it may seem to some, it was not to me. Or Grace. It

meant that my mother was someplace and had not really evap-
orated. I cannot tell you what a relief that was to have something, even something so seemingly insignificant, to cling to in
the moments I missed her. And I missed my mother a lot. All
the time, in fact. I missed who she had been, and just as much,
I missed who she was never able to become. But the message
was that she had been a part of the cheering squad or whatever
for my cure, and true or not, I wanted to believe it.

Oh, there are a lot of things we could talk about now—the
Church, our commitment to it, our relationship, the whole
crazy business about Mrs. R and her sidesteps in life . . . here's
the thing. It's important, so important, to know when you have
something worth fighting for. One by one, let's go.

The Russos? Okay, they are pretty dramatic and to be sure
they are about as opposite as they can be from the way I grew
up. But you know what? I love their whole shtick. A holiday
with them is an endorphin frenzy. You never have to guess
where you stand, they are fiercely loyal to one another, and
when they love somebody or something, they love with a zeal
I have never before experienced. Now that I'm familiar with
that passion, I think that to take on any other approach to life
would leave me feeling cheated.

The Church? Well, we're still working on that and I think
the bottom line is that when you become the kind of person
who can be a good Catholic, it's easier to be one. Oh, I hear
your chuckles and I don't blame you for them. That's okay.
Really, it is. But if anyone can help us figure it out, it's our
two Men in Black, who are now my daily e-mail buddies. They
keep telling me to watch myself on the stem-cell thing, which
I will do because an end cannot always justify reckless means.
I think they just want to be in the loop. Fine by me. We are all
on the same side of the fence because we would all love to see
an end to needless human suffering. Probably them more than
me on some days—but that's just a guess.

Anyway, all this other stuff? We can talk again. Grace and
me? You want to know what's up with us? Maria Graziana.

What a gal. She is full of grace and love and beans . . . don't worry about Grace and me. We are dancing on stars or under them anyway. If you think that's, I don't know, sappy, then you've never been in love like us and you've never been to Mexico City. If you go, let me know. I know a place you should see. And take my advice, drink the water. It might save you from yourself. It just might save you from yourself.

ACKNOWLEDGMENTS

It takes the thoughts and hands of many generous, talented people to recognize the possibilities of that first tiny idea for a new story and shape it into a full-length novel. I'd like to thank the following friends for their support and input: first and foremost, Marjory Heath Wentworth, South Carolina poet laureate, whose beautiful words give considerable loft and a more soulful explanation to mine. The real-life Eric Bomze, who drove me all over Sardinia in the blazing heat to find just the right chapel for a supernatural meltdown—thank you for your patience and precious nuggets of information about the island. To Fred and Claire Eckert for your love and support in my foggy moments. To Michele and Rosario Barbalace of Montclair, New Jersey, for your help and humor with my miserable Italian. To George and Audrey DeLange for the very helpful information and spectacular photographs of Mexico City to be found on their Web site at *www.delange.org*. And to Randall Sullivan, author of *The Miracle Detective*, should our paths ever cross, dinner is on me. Thank you for your amazing work.

To my New Jersey writer friends: Pamela Redmond Satran, Deborah Davis, Debra Galant, Benilde Little—your talent is awesome, your friendship is priceless—and love to all the members of MEWS. To my South Carolina writer friends: Josephine Humphreys, Anne Rivers Siddons, Sue Monk Kidd, Cassandra King, Nathalie DuPree, Jack Bass, Barbara Hagerty, Robert Rosen, Mary Alice Monroe, William Baldwin, Robert Jordan, Roger Pinckney, and yes, to the great man himself, the cantankerous but totally loveable Pat Conroy, without whom I never would've found the courage to write a second book. To the out-of-state belles, Rhonda Rich, Kathy Trocheck (Mary Kay Andrews), and Patti Callahan Henry—love y'all madly! In fact, knowing all of you is the greatest reward of a writing life. Okay, that's a little bull—having a home on Sullivan's Island is the best part and we all know it. But having you all over for gumbo is an unbelievable thrill. Seriously.

That house never would have become a reality without the faith and support of my agent, Gail Fortune. Gail, huge thanks for reading this book and all the others a thousand times and for all your generous support that arrives whenever I need it! And to John Talbot—glad to know you! You two are some team!

To my new fantastic editor at William Morrow, Carrie Feron—whew! Made the deadline! And could not have done it without you—thank you a thousand times! And to Tessa Woodward, Adrienne DiPietro, Pam Spengler Jaffee, Debbie Stier, Virginia Stanley, Lisa Gallagher, Michael Morrison, Brian McSharry, and all the fabulous sales team, especially Carla Parker and Michael Morris, and the artistic visionary who gave this book its gorgeous cover, Mumtaz Mustafa—I am thrilled to be in your company and look forward to many years together!

To Debbie Zammit, we did it again! Hooray! Thanks, girl, and I love you to death! And to Ann Del Mastro, Mary Allen, George Zur, and Kevin Sherry—thanks for keeping us all alive, fed, solvent, and the computers running during this process!

Of course to the booksellers—especially Patti Morrison from Barnes & Noble in Mount Pleasant, South Carolina, Tom Warner and Vicki Crafton of Litchfield Books in Pawleys Island, Jennifer McCurry of Waldenbooks in Charleston, Andy and Carrie Graves of Happy Bookseller in Columbia, Frazer Dobson and Sally Brewster at Park Road Books in Charlotte, and booksellers everywhere—huge thanks and love for your support.

And a special thanks to my cousin, Charles "Comar" Blanchard, Jr. He not only makes South Carolina a wonderful part of my family's life, but we love him to pieces!

Obviously, I owe the largest debt to my husband, Peter, and our two children, Victoria and William. Victoria and William? I am so proud of y'all and I love you both so much. Of everything in my life, having you was the smartest decision Daddy and I ever made.

If Peter Frank wasn't so understanding, sympathetic, brilliant, generous, and forgiving about dinners, the house, and why I get so stressed out, I couldn't write at all. I love it at the end of the day when he sticks his gorgeous head in my office and says, "Can I get you a glass of wine, sugar plum?" Is he kidding? But who wouldn't adore a man who after all these years still calls you "sugar plum" and offers you a glass of wine? Seriously, Peter, thank you for being all you are and you know how much I love you.

So that's about it. If I left anyone out, please forgive me. I know my acknowledgments are always a short story on their own, but my momma always said it was extremely important to remember to thank people when they do something wonderful for you. I hope she would approve.